1

SHACKLETONS

— of —

CHAPEL ST

LORNA HUNTING

Published by Goldcrest Books International Ltd
www.goldcrestbooks.com
publish@goldcrestbooks.com

ISBN: 978-1-0369-0769-3

This book is dedicated to Jim who describes himself as my "driver", but who knows he means much more to me than that.

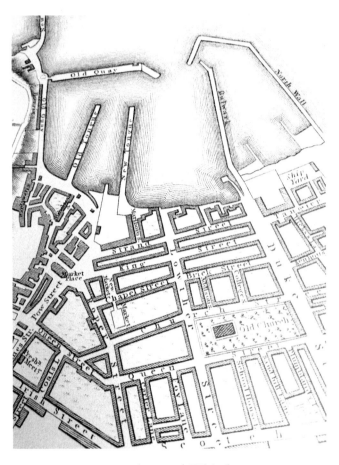

Map of central Whitehaven

CHAPTER ONE

Thursday October 17th, 1861
Whitehaven, Cumberland

'Can't a man have his breakfast in peace?' asked Fergus.

'Be careful, you sound just like your father,' said Becky, laughing, as another loud knock sounded at the door.

The Louisa Line's bookkeeper, Dicken, was standing on their doorstep, sporting a wide grin. Huge drops of water were falling from his cap.

'What brings you here in this rain?' Fergus asked, motioning him inside. 'I'm going to Cockermouth this morning.'

Dicken took a step forward. 'I know, and since you won't be calling at the warehouse, I thought I ought to tell you we've post. Letters, a deluge, dropped off at Brocklebanks' Liverpool offices by their clipper and delivered to us no more than ten minutes since. They're from Cape Town.'

The words Cape Town caused Fergus's stomach to turn over and his throat to contract. He swallowed twice. No news had been good news, but now, all the ruinous scenarios he'd imagined over the past two months and more leapt to the forefront of his mind. Did letters from Cape Town indicate the SS Ketton had arrived there safely? Or perhaps she'd limped into port. What about the crew? What of the state of the ship? Questions, demanding immediate answers, were scurrying around his brain.

'The courier said to tell you it was Captain Fletcher, recently back from Shanghai, who carried the post.'

'He's a Whitehaven man, known to me. Return to the warehouse, I'll be there shortly.'

With Dicken departed, Fergus, his appetite stifled by the news, ignored the remnants of his late breakfast.

He called through to Becky, 'There's post from Cape Town. I'm cancelling Cockermouth, I can go tomorrow.'

'News at last, thank goodness.' She hurried into the hall and picked up an umbrella. 'Take this, you'll need it.'

Fergus shook his head, shunning her offer. 'I'll run down, but not before you've had your goodbye kiss. I'll not hurry over that, not even for post from Cape Town.' He leaned forward and gave her a loving, generous kiss on the lips then dashed out into the street.

Becky was right, he did have need of an umbrella; it was raining quite hard, but he didn't have time to bother about that. All he could think of was what news the post had brought and how it was going to affect his financial affairs.

He was met at the Chapel Street warehouse by Dicken, waving a sheaf of papers. It was all Fergus could do to refrain from rudely snatching them from his hand. On July 18th the SS Ketton had left Glasgow bound for Mauritius, laden with machinery for the sugar plantations. That was two and a half months ago and since then they had heard nothing, apart from a short note saying the ship had arrived in Madeira without mishap.

Sitting at his desk under Dicken's watchful eye, Fergus sorted through the material. There were three bundles. The first, he saw straightaway, contained an official copy of the ship's log along with some invoices and receipts, which he put to one side. The second bundle held letters from the ship's master, Bill McRae, to Fergus, along with the senior crew members' personal letters for their families. The third bundle consisted of sealed letters, notes and drawings, all of which were addressed to different people, yet all seemingly written by the same hand. These would be from crewmen who could neither read nor write, who had paid someone literate amongst the crew to scribe for them. Besides the *Ketton*, Fergus ran two other ships as part of the Louisa Line – the *Sophie Alice* and the *Eleanor Bell*. He had once heard the cook on the latter describe the writing of letters for others at sea as 'a nice little earner'.

Fergus wanted to know everything at once. He started with the ship's log because it would tell him all he needed of the voyage – the technical details of position, weather, and incidents, both good and eventful, although the human aspect would be lacking. He began reading, all the while conscious of Dicken watching him with rarely blinking owl's eyes. Fergus couldn't blame him; as a company employee, the information contained within the correspondence related to his livelihood and well-being, too.

'Return to your work, Dicken,' Fergus said, 'and allow me to peruse the documents. I will advise you of the news in good time.'

Dicken returned reluctantly to his desk and with an almost inaudible 'humph' he straightened his shoulders and opened one of the office ledgers. The back cover slipped from his grasp and landed with a dull thud on the sloping desktop as if it too was in a huff.

With the scratching of Dicken's pen prickling his ears, Fergus returned his attention to the log.

After leaving Madeira, the ship had encountered fair weather, but steering a little way to the southwest had met contrary winds for several weeks. These had brought 'thick weather and rain'. Keeping to the recognised route, under sail she'd turned southeast some way off the coast of Africa, en route for Cape Town as being a combination steamer she needed coal. All this had been expected, but as he read on, Fergus's heart sank. He gave what he thought was an inward sigh, but it was enough for Dicken to stop his scratching and ask if something was amiss.

'She's in for repairs in Cape Town.' Fergus scanned the paper.

Dicken pulled a face. 'Is it serious?'

'It's not yet clear. Allow me to finish.' He put down the log notes and rifled through the second bundle of letters, selecting the one addressed to him from Bill. He began reading while Dicken picked up his pen, dipped it, and resumed his scratching.

'*Cape Town, September 17th 1861 (Tuesday)*'

A month since the letter had been written. Hopefully Fergus was about to learn that the repairs had been taken care of swiftly and at no great cost.

'*Dear Fergus, my good sir,*

You will have seen from the log we made good progress to Cape Town. The crew are pulling together well and apart from a few misdemeanours and the usual grumblings they have caused little trouble. The facilities here are somewhat undeveloped and although a start has been made, there is, as yet, no working harbour.'

Fergus read a little more and then in a loud, sharp voice told Dicken, 'She's suffered a collision, causing damage to the hull.'

Dicken, forever judging anything connected with the Louisa Line from a financial perspective, replied, 'That'll cost us time and money.'

'Captain McRae has been unable to give a firm estimate, but anticipates any delay to be of two weeks minimum.'

'Do you think it could be worse than they think?'

'How can I know? It's certainly made me anxious, and I shall remain so until all is back on a firm footing and she's docked and coaled in Port Louis, in Mauritius.'

He returned to McRae's letter.

'*I am collating witness reports with invoices for insurance purposes, which I shall include with my next communication before we leave. The second mate, unbalanced by the suddenness of the collision, received a sharp blow to the head from which he is recovering, and several of the crew suffered bruising to their limbs, but it could have been much worse. We were caught in an unexpected swell emboldened by an unseasonal westerly wind. This, with the lack of proper harbour facilities, which causes continual chaos in the approach to Cape Town, brought about our ill fortune. I have spoken with several captains who witnessed the accident, and they all agree with me as the harbour master recorded: "It was an unfortunate accident occasioned by the swell and the unavoidable pandemonium due to the lack of a completed harbour and dock." I am given to believe that such collisions are regular occurrences. In my opinion, this is a most unsatisfactory state of affairs and I have expressed these views to the authorities.'*

The remainder of the letter described Cape Town in some detail, providing Fergus with the image of an industrious, if somewhat disorganised, nascent port – a crossroads of diverse goods, minds, languages and cultures. He asked himself whether he was in any way envious of Bill's experiences and concluded, having been married less than a year, that he would rather be in Whitehaven with his wife, Becky, than looking out on a slipway in Cape Town. However, were Becky by his side on that slipway, then that would be a different matter indeed. Perhaps, depending on their parents or, dare he hope, their children, he might be able to convince her to take a long voyage one day.

Bill brought his letter to a close with –

'I shall use this unexpected delay to glean up-to-date information from experienced traders regarding goods and prices, which hopefully will prove useful preparation for our arrival in Mauritius. There is much talk of the need for cotton in England and I am advised we can make fine profits. I will forward this information to you before we set sail for the last leg of our outward voyage. There is also the opportunity to clean and check parts of the hull.

Yours truly, and wishing you good health and spirits, sir,

Bill.'

Fergus passed the copy of the ship's log to Dicken for his perusal and to file.

'We'll sort the letters,' he said. 'Then you must put a notice outside stating we have crew letters to be collected.'

'Won't you be advising the families directly or delivering to their addresses?'

'I'll deliver the senior officers' post myself. As for the rest of the crew, you'll see, word will pass through the town so quickly, I'll wager within half an hour of the notice going out there'll be a long queue outside.'

'In this weather?'

'I doubt the heavy rain will deter them.'

'In that case I'd best sort the letters into alphabetical order and get ready for the rush.' While Fergus put on his still-damp topcoat, Dicken picked up the pile of family letters, glanced through the first few and frowned. 'This is no good,' he said. 'Some don't have surnames, and there's one with "Tall John's wife" and another with "Cadger Jack's brother". And two saying "Mary" and nothing else.'

'Handing out the post can be difficult. Those letters and notes are private. Do the best you can. I think you'll find relatives know the crew's working nicknames. I'll leave you to it. I'm away to Brocklebanks' offices to see if they have further information about Captain Fletcher's whereabouts. I'd like to talk with him sooner rather than later.'

'Won't he be in Liverpool, at their main office?'

'He'll have docked there, but many of Brocklebanks' clipper captains hail from these parts.

The anxiety Fergus had initially felt on learning that post had arrived from Cape Town had multiplied threefold. Bill and he hadn't discussed bringing back cotton. Fergus was starkly aware that everything was completely out of his control. By now, Bill would hopefully be in Mauritius and would know if their enterprise was going to be a success or not. With his ship thousands of miles away, there was nothing Fergus could do except wait for further news and pray. He had handed control of the voyage to Bill with complete confidence, but that didn't satisfy the nervous knot taking up residence in his stomach. He had everything to lose.

It was a lowering thought to feel himself as vulnerable to debt as his men, but the thought of the home he'd staked on this venture reminded him of his crew. As he was leaving, he turned back and said to Dicken, 'I forgot to mention creditors. They sometimes arrive seeking news of our men and demanding payment from their wages.

Turn them away. Their grievances are with the individuals concerned, not with us or their families.'

With the officers' post in a small leather satchel, Fergus called first at the engineer's house, then made his way to Church Street to Bill's wife, Mary. Seeing him at the door with post in his hands, she beamed and invited him in.

The McRaes' infant son, William, was sitting in the middle of the floor, sucking on a dolly peg surrounded by brightly coloured building blocks. He saw Fergus and his face crumpled. Fergus bent down to ruffle the boy's hair then, seeing his expression, thought twice about it. Instead, he said, 'You're growing into a fine chap, young man.' The boy continued to eye him suspiciously.

'He's a bit grumpy today. It's his teeth making him dribbly, so I've given him a peg to suck on. I understand it's early for such goings-on.'

Mary spoke with pride, as if early teething were a sign of advanced intellectual development. Fergus was all at sea where babies were concerned, but perhaps that might change in the near future. He hoped so.

Mary poured some runny honey from a clear jar into a small blue-and-white striped jug. She took the peg from William, who immediately let out a distressed howl, his eyes filling with tears. He clenched his tiny fists and began waving them in the air.

'Don't fret, little one, you'll have more in a moment,' Mary said. Dipping the peg in the honey, she told Fergus, 'This will buy us a few minutes' peace, although he's as fast as the devil himself at sucking the sweetness off.'

With William settled, Fergus handed over Bill's letter

then gave her a brief résumé of the *Ketton's* log. He could see, by the way she turned the letter over in her hands, she was anxious to read it. He stood and his thoughts were confirmed when she did not seek to delay him.

As Mary was seeing him out, she asked after Becky.

'She's in good spirits, thank you.'

'Still helping her ma out at the Indian King?'

'Only in an emergency. Dolly thinks it better Becky keeps her own house now she's married, rather than working behind the bar.'

'No longer doing the Friday evening shippers' wage payout then?'

Fergus shook his head. 'People began asking her mother when she was going to give that up. The impression we got was that they thought Becky was taking a job she didn't need and depriving someone who could do with the wages from having it.'

'Oh, my goodness. It must have been a hard blow giving that up. She's been doing it for years and knows all the crews.'

'She's taken it badly, she misses the pub, but when she thought about it, it seemed best for her to step down.'

'I'll call round after choir practice tomorrow afternoon and share the latest news from Bill with her.'

'She'll be delighted to see you, of that I'm sure.'

As Fergus walked away clutching the post, he wondered if he could delay reporting to the Louisa Line investors until he'd heard from Bill again. He would make an exception for Nicholas Fincham, who had alerted them to the potential profitability of carrying machine parts to

Mauritius. Having spent years at sea, the doctor would not be alarmed by the incident. Personally, Fergus had not anticipated such a hold-up. Regarding the remaining investors, it would make for a much easier meeting if he was able to state the *Ketton* had pulled into Cape Town for minor repairs and then proceeded to Mauritius, rather than the latest news that she was still sitting halfway up a slipway. In fact, probably better not to mention the repairs at all if he could get away with it, but that would be dishonest – and besides, they were a canny group.

CHAPTER TWO

Becky consulted several new recipes before deciding on a tried-and-tested almond-and-raisin cake. She was excited to learn Mary was planning to call, not least because preparing for her visitor gave her something constructive to fill her morning. As she laid the tea-table, she hummed one of her father's favourite folk songs. Her ma had suggested that, since Fergus could well afford a maid, Becky should take advantage of it. And Fergus's mother, Elizabeth, had been at pains to persuade her for some months, saying it was unseemly for her not to have a maid now she was a Shackleton. But Becky had not given in to their insistence.

As soon as she saw Mary's smiling face peeking out from beneath a new bonnet, Becky's spirits lifted. She guided her guest into the sitting room and bade her sit on the sofa, close to a small octagonal table upon which the freshly baked cake held centre stage. She returned to the kitchen and placed the still shiny wedding-present kettle on the range's hot plate.

With the tea made, they settled down to chat.

'You must tell me all the news from Bill,' said Becky.

It was as if verbal floodgates had been wrenched apart. While Becky poured the tea and offered the cake, Mary launched into a vivid account of the *Ketton's* voyage. This included the unexpected death of one of the pigs, which had eaten First Mate Sven's favourite cap and suffered the consequences, and their subsequent arrival and collision in Cape Town. It was so detailed an account, Becky thought Bill's letter must have run to ten pages or more, written on both sides. She knew he had the neatest of writing.

After almost an hour, several cups of tea and a generous slice of cake for each of them, when Mary paused to draw an extra-deep breath, Becky took the opportunity to say, 'You must miss Bill terribly.'

A momentary look of sadness passed over her face and Becky regretted making the remark. The wife of a sea captain with a young bairn couldn't help but miss her husband. And worry. There would be the constant worry.

'Oh, but I do miss him. All the time. The only consolation is, judging by his letter, he misses me as much as I miss him. But I've plenty to occupy myself, with our wee bairn and the choir. Singing is a great solace to me.'

Mary declined another cup of tea.

'You must bring William with you another time,' Becky said. 'Or perhaps I can mind him for you next choir practice.'

'I'm afraid the novelty of having a grandson is still fresh with Ma. She'd go into a right gruff if she thought I were side-lining her.'

'Perhaps when the novelty wears off, then.'

'I'm sure it will, and when it does, "dinna fret tha'sen", as Nan used to say, because I'll be calling, bonnet in hand, asking you to mind him for me. Although by then there could be another on the way, if Bill returns safely.'

In reality, Becky was in two minds about looking after "our wee bairn". He was at an adorable stage and was beginning to take a real interest in his surroundings. He also knew Becky and would voluntarily raise his arms to be picked up and cuddled. However, he also served to remind her that after five months of marriage, there was still no prospect of a bairn of her own to fuss over. Shortly after they wed, she and Fergus had become legal guardians to a young orphan lad, but Rory was now approaching twelve, and as apprentice cook on the *Eleanor Bell* he was often at sea.

Becky consoled herself, albeit somewhat unsuccessfully, with an acknowledgement of the privileged freedom she enjoyed being childless, whilst occasionally facing the unthinkable – that she might be barren.

Mary was looking at her with a kindly, encouraging expression on her face. 'You seem a little distracted today,' she said. 'Is something amiss? Is there bad news from Cape Town that's not been shared with me?'

Becky was tempted to keep her emotions to herself, but Mary was her best friend and she knew she could trust her with her private feelings. 'No, it's nothing like that.' She gave a small sigh. 'If truth be known, I feel now I'm married I don't have a purpose in life.' She placed her teacup on the table. 'There I've said it. There's plenty to do, but it's all rather routine.'

Mary shuffled to the edge of the sofa and put her hand on Becky's. 'I'll admit, I've been wondering how you fill your time now Rory's at sea and you're not needed at the Indian King anymore.'

'It's difficult, but it's as you say. I'm not needed rather than not wanted, because my place is here now in my married home. Ma says she misses me and she's always happy to see me, and she drops round when she can, but she's a busy woman. We've lost the spontaneous chats we used to have as we worked alongside each other. I miss those and all the laughter that went with them.'

Mary pressed Becky's fingers. 'It must seem quiet here after the hustle and bustle of the Indian King.'

'Please don't say it will all change when I have a bairn, even though I know it will. I mean, what if I can't have children? I need something more in my life. I'm used to working.'

'I'm sure you'll conceive in time. But what sort of something in your life?'

'I don't want to be like my mother-in-law Elizabeth, deciding menus and running my fingers along ledges, checking for dust.'

Mary's eyebrows rose. 'Do you mean you want to work? A real job for wages?'

'Not such as would interfere with giving Fergus the support and the home he deserves.'

'Why don't you put your mind to more sewing? It's the sort of thing women in our position do. After all, you and your ma made your wedding dress, and in record time too.'

'What kind of sewing? Needlework?'

'Any kind. Embroidery, tapestries, clothes, quilts, that sort of thing. We could do it together.'

They talked for another few minutes and then Mary cast a glance at her bonnet.

'I'll leave you with thoughts on sewing,' she said. 'I've to collect William.'

As soon as the door closed behind her, Becky rushed upstairs. In the bedroom she lifted the lid of a large oak chest, taking care not to shake the lock mechanism, which was loose. Three linenfold carved panels decorated the front, with the year 1691 engraved in the top of the central one. Dr Fincham had given them the chest as a wedding present and did not know its provenance. It had a comforting ecclesiastical air to it, so Becky thought it must have come from a church. The doctor had called it a blanket chest, but Becky used it for storing all her sewing paraphernalia.

Lifting the pieces of cloth out of the chest and laying them on their bed took half an hour. When she'd finished, their bed-cover had disappeared under a sea of cottons, muslins, blanket strips, linens and balls of wool. Becky ran her hands lightly over a piece of blue-striped linen ticking cloth, an old friend she was happy to see again.

In one of the chest's corners, carefully wrapped and hidden from view, and protected from dirt and dust in sailcloth, were the remnants from making her wedding dress. There were also some silks, laces and ribbons sent from Dublin by Fergus's agent, Padraig Conran, as a wedding present. A smaller package, as carefully wrapped, contained offcuts of a purple linen-silk mix Fergus had given her before they were married.

Becky stepped back to survey her treasures. Then, sighing to herself, she began returning the materials to the chest, all the while pondering whether sewing was going to be enough to keep her body and inquisitive mind occupied.

CHAPTER THREE

On Saturday, Captain Fletcher sent Fergus word he was taking coffee at the Waverley Hotel and would be pleased to receive him. Fergus arrived to find the captain, an amber-tinted meerschaum pipe clenched between teeth that were of a similar hue, sitting at a corner table. He was a short, muscular man, with the typical tea-clipper captain's wind-whipped complexion.

He greeted Fergus affably. 'Tis a pity your *Ketton* got caught by that swell. I didn't witness the collision, but I've seen many another like it. Not needing coal, we always set anchor in the bay and disembark by tender. It's fortunate we're able to do that.'

'I understand it was a westerly wind that caused it,' said Fergus, thinking he sounded much more relaxed about the incident than he felt.

'Aye, a rogue westerly for the time of year. Usually they're only a danger in winter, but the weather's been less predictable this year at the Cape. There's a lot of mithering in the inns and alehouses concerning it.'

'Did you see the *Ketton*? Bill writes she's repairable.'

'Aye, with her still being on the slipway I saw her close to, and there was nasty damage. She was awaiting a lumber delivery when we pulled away. It'll depend on what they find when they begin work – but then you know that.' The captain opened his tobacco tin, put his pipe on the lid and began filling the bowl, dropping flakes on the table as he did so.

Fergus was disappointed. He'd hoped Captain Fletcher would have more encouraging up-to-date information for him. 'And Bill? How was he?'

'In as fine fettle as any captain could be under the circumstances. Angry, needlessly blaming himself, but when he'd listened to others' tales of earlier woes, he accepted it was nature's fury, not error on his part. Mind you, he wasn't idle. I can well vouch for that. He, your engineer, and that Norwegian first mate of his—'

'Sven Nielsen,' proffered Fergus.

'Aye, Mr Nielsen. All three were out and about questioning the local merchants and anyone who'd been east.'

The captain lit his pipe with a long match, blowing through the stem several times until the tobacco glowed red and he was able to draw deeply.

'What do you mean by questioning?' asked Fergus.

Fletcher took another long draw on the pipe and closed the tin. 'Quizzing all and sundry about available goods, prices, that sort of thing. He's got a natural business head on his shoulders, that Captain McRae of yours. My expertise on the price of tea wasn't of much interest, but

I was able to tell him a bit about Chinese porcelain and silks, knowing Shanghai as I do.'

'I understand he's hoping to load up on cotton.'

A server put a plate of pork pie pieces on the table and they both helped themselves.

'I can't say I'm surprised,' said Fletcher. 'I and several others were strongly recommending he buy cotton, and now I'm back I can see the wisdom of that advice. Who'd have thought the American Civil War would prevent supplies getting to our factories and warehouses here?'

'So, you think it's a sound purchase for Bill to be making?'

'I most certainly do. With none coming in from America, and Indian stocks available to purchase, how can such an investment fail?'

'I've pondered his decision, since neither he nor I know much about cotton, except that it's useful for stabilising goods in the hold. However, I don't want him filling up space when there are more profitable items to buy. You're sure it's a good investment?'

'I'm sure of it under the current situation and most certainly would not have advised him to purchase it had I not been.'

'I must thank you for that wisdom and advice to him, sir.'

Fergus would have preferred a hold filled to the brim with the exotic goods, but Captain Fletcher was right; the ports were blockaded in America, and supplies of cotton weren't reaching England.

'I have to say I was surprised when Captain McRae

told me he was heading for Mauritius and not India. I'm sure you'll be delighted with the goods he brings back. I expect you're already making room in your warehouse and taking orders.' The captain paused to refill his pipe.

'We're contracted to make a specific delivery.' Fergus was reluctant to offer more, interpreting Fletcher's comments as fishing for information. There was little on the seas that remained a secret for long, but he remained mindful of not giving too much away to a competitor. 'We carried sugar-refining machine parts.'

'So I was told. What we call a one and only voyage?'

'Possibly,' said Fergus, wondering what Bill had told him, and how much the crew had blathered in the dockside inns and whorehouses, and whether it mattered or not.

Fletcher shifted in his chair. 'I sense your reluctance to clarify further. Don't worry, Brocklebanks has too good a business further east to consider diverting to Mauritius. We're in for the longer haul to China. There's room for us all in the maritime business. More than enough sea and an abundance of merchandise.'

Fergus thought that true enough. After they'd exchanged thoughts about business practices in Liverpool and the continuing growth of steamships, and grizzled about how the rapid rise of the railways was depriving them of cargoes, Fergus thanked the captain again for conveying their post and wished him well on future voyages, before taking his leave to return to the office.

With Fletcher's comments ringing in his ears about making space in their warehouse and securing a market for the returning goods, Fergus was spurred on to confirm some of the earlier arrangements he'd made for the *Ketton's* return. This had always seemed a long way off, but it was now a rapidly advancing event. It was as if he was standing on a quay, and a vessel he had previously heard, but been unable to see because it was shrouded in thick mist, was fast revealing itself as a solid mass. He'd known for some time it was there and that it was making its way to him, but now it had shape and would soon be upon him. And the nearer the ship, the closer the time when his debts would be called in.

But even worse than the thought of losing the family home was the thought of losing Becky. He still hadn't been able to bring himself to tell her that he'd staked their house in Chapel Street on his latest venture. The news of the repairs in Cape Town were a stark reminder of how risky his gamble had been.

A gentleman in an oversized jacket let out a string of oaths and waved a rolled umbrella in his direction when Fergus bumped into him, but, lost in his own thoughts, he took no notice. Once in the office, he began writing a list of preparations to be checked or seen to and, because he was distracted, he was unnecessarily short with Dicken over an empty inkwell and immediately regretted it.

As soon as she saw Fergus's face, Becky knew something was troubling him.

'A busy day?' she asked.

He embraced and kissed her and, she thought, held her a little longer and tighter than he usually did on his return from a normal day at the warehouse.

'I met with Captain Fletcher from Brocklebanks. Do you realise the *Ketton* could be on her way back even now and here by Christmas?'

'What is there to do?'

'I need to firm up arrangements in writing with the wholesalers and with fancy-goods merchants like Padraig Conran in Dublin. The warehouse needs clearing up and tidying to create more storage. There's lots to check up on and there are other things that require money – drawing up newspaper advertisements for the exotic goods, and renting extra storage space. Fletcher has jolted me into realising the time has come to act.'

'Is it money we don't have?'

'We've a few bad debts I can chase up.'

'You haven't answered my question.'

'It could be a squeeze, but if we don't have it, I'll borrow it.'

There had been the tiniest hesitation before Fergus answered. Becky was about to ask him if he was sure their finances would hold, but he went on quickly, 'It's time I had a trip to Dublin on the *Eleanor Bell* and connected with Padraig Conran. He's expecting me. I told him I'd call before the year is out. He's the canniest agent for miles.'

'Call on him, take him to dinner at a respectable hotel. He'll love that and I'm sure he'll have words of wisdom for you.'

Fergus held out his arms. 'Come here, my love.' He kissed her. 'Our *Eleanor Bell* is expected on Monday and will be leaving for Dublin again on Thursday. I'll catch a ride with her. In the meantime, I'll make a start on the warehouse storage arrangements and follow up outstanding orders and collections to bring in funds.'

'You can set our Rory on the job in the warehouse. He'll be back with the *Eleanor Bell* and I can help too.'

He tilted her chin and kissed the tip of her nose. 'Having you amongst all that dust and those cobwebs? I can't ask that of you. Besides, you'll be busy making Rory's favourite pies and puddings.'

Becky didn't mind what she called 'clean dirt', which is how she regarded natural dust and cobwebs, as opposed to human or animal detritus, which was most definitely 'dirty dirt'.

Perhaps sensing her disappointment, Fergus added, 'Why don't you come with me to Dublin? You can see the latest fashions while I'm with Conran then we can visit the bookshop together.'

Becky was tempted but shook her head. She'd be a distraction for him. 'No, this is business. You go and pick Conran's brains. We'll visit Dublin together another time.'

CHAPTER FOUR

It was Monday and at the Indian King pub, Dolly, a pile of sticks and rolled-up newspaper by her side, was down on her hands and knees, tending the grate.

'What are you doing that for?' Becky asked her ma.

'The new girl left.'

'Walked out?'

'Aye. It's no great loss, I was about to sack her anyway. A right dreamer, but I've engaged another. She starts tomorrow.'

'That was lucky you found someone so quick.'

'There's no shortage of labour right now. Whole families from the Lancashire mills, coming up from Liverpool. They've been told there's work and they're flocking here.'

'There's no more work here than anywhere else, surely?'

'Exactly. Anyways, they're here. I'd no sooner engaged a replacement when another lovely lass came in, but I can't create jobs. This one used to be a weaver. I took her name and address, in case the first girl doesn't stay.'

'Well, whoever you've got, I'm glad they're starting

tomorrow. It's not good for you to be laying the fire at your age.'

'My age? You think I should be slowing down at forty-one? Thank you very much.' Dolly put a match to the fire, then made to stand. As she raised herself her knees cracked, and she laughed.

'Aye, well, 'appen I should give up lighting the fire. Now,' she said, studying Becky's face. 'What's brought your visit?'

'I'm a bit worried about Fergus,' Becky said.

'What's caused this?'

'He seems preoccupied. Lost in his own thoughts.'

'Well, he's always been a bit of a romantic, all that book-reading and poetry he likes.'

'No, this is different. He's having more of his headaches and is restless at night. Sometimes I think he's having nightmares.'

'Do you wake him?'

'I used to, but I found he couldn't remember what he was dreaming about, and my waking him upset him more than leaving him alone.'

'It's probably worry over the business. He's responsible for three ships in his own right, and one of them is thousands of miles from home. It's understandable if he's anxious.'

'Perhaps you're right, but...'

'I'd adopt a wait-and-see stance. I've spoken to him recently and he seemed the same.'

'You think I'm imagining a problem?

'No, not at all. Rather that I think it'll pass when he's more information about the *Ketton*, that's all.'

The pub door opened, admitting Sergeant Adams in his

army greatcoat, along with his one-eyed dog Molly and a blast of cold air. The old soldier sat in his reserved space.

'I'll get the sergeant his ale,' Becky said, 'and then I must be off. I've a pile of laundry to see to.' After serving the sergeant and giving Molly a biscuit, Becky was on her way to the door when her mother called her back.

'Listen, love, I know you said you didn't want a maid, but...'

Becky scrunched up her lips. 'Ma, I don't need—'

Dolly raised a hand, palm turned outwards. 'Hear me out. I've been pondering. That young lass that called – I liked her, she'd an honest face and was doing her best to find a job. Not sitting about moaning about not having one. Why don't you take her on? You've said yourself you've a pile of laundry.'

'You know I don't need a maid.'

'If it makes you feel better then yes, I will admit that's true, that it's a social nicety, that people think it odd that a Shackleton wife does her own washing. But – and it's an important "but" – you'd be giving that girl a job.'

'What makes *her* so special, Ma?'

'If you must know she reminds me a lot of you, and I'd hate to think of you in her position. Having to go from place to place, begging for a job.'

To her surprise, Becky saw tears in her mother's eyes, and she hardly ever cried.

'Give her a chance,' Dolly said. 'Please, for me and her, if not for yourself.'

'If it means that much to you, then I suppose I could engage her until she finds something better.'

Dolly held out a piece of paper. Becky took it and saw, written in neat, unassuming writing, 'Lois Brook. Weaver, 6 Shepherd's Court.'

'Shepherd's Court?' asked Becky. 'Where's that?'

'Top of Scotch Street.'

'Nay,' said Sergeant Adams. 'You mean Charles Street. It's at the bottom. Left-hand side, close up to where it meets George Street. I'd a marra dossed there.'

'My mistake. Look, we've a Scotch Street delivery on Wednesday. I'll send a note saying you'd like to see her. You don't have to do anything except be at home. I'll suggest Thursday. How about it? At least speak with her.'

Becky knew when she'd been outmanoeuvred. 'All right, Ma, you win, and it'll please Elizabeth. I know she finds it embarrassing I don't have help.'

'That's a good decision. You'll not regret it.'

'But let's not rush into this. I can't see her this week. I've Rory coming home this afternoon, and Fergus is going to Dublin on Thursday. I can't engage her without his approval.'

Her ma should be pleased she'd at least agreed to meet the girl.

The *Eleanor Bell* returned from the Dublin coal run carrying Rory, accompanied by his ever-faithful canine companion Charlie. Rory had been home only two hours when Elizabeth Shackleton, Becky's mother-in-law, called with a well-wrapped parcel of bones.

'We've been saving these up for Charlie,' she said.

'I ordered roast beef on the bone especially for Sunday lunch and I popped in a leg of lamb mid-week as an extra treat. Cook was surprised, but when I explained you were coming home, she understood immediately.'

Rory took the parcel. 'Thanks so much, Mrs S. I'll ask Mrs Becky to boil them up.'

Becky was amused by Elizabeth's beaming face She hadn't been surprised when she'd opened the door to see her there. 'You really shouldn't have gone to this trouble.'

'I know, but he so loves Charlie and is always so thankful. You're probably thinking I could send one of our girls to buy bones from the butcher's at a much cheaper price, but why bother, when we can afford the meat that goes on them?'

It did seem odd to Becky that someone would buy expensive meat specifically to get bones for a dog, but she didn't say anything.

After confirming he would be at Queen Street that afternoon to feed his rabbit, Harry, and asking Elizabeth if Cook could put some greens out by the kitchen door for him, Rory left for the warehouse. He was too young to join the rest of the crew in their on-shore activities, so Fergus had enlisted him to help Dicken prepare for the arrival of the Mauritian merchandise.

At six o'clock, when Rory came home, Becky was inspecting the crispness of the potato topping on a shepherd's pie. Rory pulled off his cap, twisted it between his hands as if wringing out water, then threw it in the direction of a spindle-backed chair, where it tottered for a moment on the edge of the seat before dropping to the floor.

'That smells reet grand, Mrs Becky,' he said, flaring his nostrils in an exaggerated sniff. 'Aye, that it does. I'm starving.'

Becky was charmed. 'Reet grand' was one of Rory's favourite sayings.

Charlie obviously thought the supper smelled good, too. With his tail wagging wildly, he made a beeline for Becky's skirt and began running up against it. Becky shook a drying-cloth in his direction. 'Charlie, away with you. If I drop this pie there'll be no supper for anyone.' She turned to Rory. 'And that includes you.' A blast of hot air cuffed her face as she returned the pie to the oven. 'Five minutes longer, I think. I know you and Mr Fergus like a crispy browned top.' She picked up Rory's cap from the floor and put it on the chair. 'And how was your day, Rory?'

'It didn't go well. It were a bad 'un.'

Becky was disappointed. With the daily stress of his bad leg, Rory wasn't getting his fair share of good days. Fergus was anxious to give him a grounding in all aspects of the Louisa Line. He wouldn't condone the lad sitting at home twiddling his thumbs or disappearing to Castle Meadow throwing sticks for Charlie to chase. Rory's protestations that the walk was good for his gammy leg, as well as for Charlie, fell on deaf ears. Fergus was having none of it.

'Why was it a bad one?' Becky asked.

'You know Dicken doesn't like Charlie?'

'Aye, you've mentioned it.'

'Well, today he said he wanted to tie him up. He brought out some marine twine from one of his drawers and tried to catch him. Of course, Charlie was far too quick for him and anyways, I think Dicken's a wee bit 'fraid of him.'

'So what happened?'

'He asked me to catch him and tie him to an iron ring in the wall.'

Becky grimaced and made a mental note to herself to have words with their bookkeeper the first chance she got. 'What did you say?'

'I said I wouldn't, but then I was saved.'

'Saved?'

'Aye, Miss Evangelina arrived. All done up like a dog's dinner, she was. Fancy bonnet, white gloves, giggling fit to burst.'

Evangelina Croxall worked in her parents' bookshop on Lowther Street. Becky had long suspected a blossoming romance between her and Dicken, and her discomfort over the lad's day eased a little. She was intrigued. 'Go on.'

'She turfed up carrying a brown paper parcel tied up with string. "I've got Mr Shackleton's monthly book order", she says, putting her head on one side, acting all silly like girls do sometimes.' Rory put on a display, rolling his eyes and fluttering his lashes.

Becky, matching his tone, giggled.

'So, Dicken takes the parcel and she has a good look round the office and she sees Charlie. "Oh, you beautiful doggie", she says, in a bairn's voice, bending down to scratch him behind his ears. Charlie loves it. She turns to Dicken and says, "Is he yours?"'

'What did Dicken say?'

'Quick as a flash, he's all smiles, then he gets this stupid grin on his face and – I swear this is the truth – he says, "He's Mr Shackleton's dog. He's often here".'

'Oh, dear.' Becky could see by the redness of Rory's cheeks that the remark had infuriated him. Rory and his dog were devoted to each other. Even as they were talking, Charlie was interacting, his ears pricking up each time he heard his name.

'I was about to put her right that he's *my* dog, when Miss Evangelina bends down and still with that stupid voice says to Charlie, "Perhaps if we ask politely, Mr Shackleton will allow Dicken and me to take you for a walk sometimes".' I tell you, Mrs Becky, I can hardly believe my ears as I'm standing there, and it gets worse. She's talking in a bairn's voice to a dog, expecting him to understand. Talking to MY dog.'

Becky had to smother a smile. 'It gets worse?' she asked.

'Aye, lots worse, because Dicken nods his head and says he's sure Charlie'll like to go walking.'

Becky couldn't help herself. 'I'm sorry, Rory, it's you describing the voices and my imagining Miss Evangelina talking to Charlie. It's that amusing in the telling, it's making me laugh. Forgive me.' She hoped she'd not offended him, and so it was with relief that she saw him, after scratching his head and thinking, begin to laugh too.

At that moment Fergus, arriving home, put his head round the kitchen door. 'Are you two going to share the jest?'

Between fits of giggles, Becky explained.

Fergus raised an eyebrow. 'I thought Dicken didn't much like dogs?'

'He doesn't,' Rory butted in. 'Before she came in, he was trying to get me to rope Charlie up to the wall.'

'She'll have been bringing the two books I ordered last week,' said Fergus. 'I'll speak with Dicken.'

While Becky returned to her supper preparations, as an afterthought Fergus asked Rory, 'Did Miss Evangelina stay long?'

'Well over half an hour.' Rory pulled on his ear. 'Or it could have been nearer to three-quarters. I could hear their giggling and carrying on, and I was way up on the top floor. I was glad she was there so long, because by the time she left, Dicken had forgotten all about tying Charlie up.'

'That's interesting,' said Fergus, raising an eyebrow and casting a glance in Becky's direction. 'Very interesting.'

Later, when Becky told him about Dolly's weaver lass, he made exactly the remark she was expecting him to.

'Mother will be delighted.'

CHAPTER FIVE

The following Friday, after a rocky passage on the *Eleanor Bell* where even some of the crew looked green round the gills, Fergus arrived in Dublin. Feeling a bit the worse for wear, he made his way to Padraig Conran's first-floor offices, overlooking St Stephen's Green. Fergus saw immediately that improvements had been made since his last visit. A fine painting of the Customs House had been hung over the grand marble mantelpiece and there was the cleansing aroma of fresh paint. A carved dado rail was now positioned three feet from the floor. Conran's business must be doing well.

On the first floor, the noises of the street rose up from below: coachmen urging their horses on, bottles rattling against each other in boxes, casks being rolled up planks onto the backs of flat carts, people calling out in greeting, and the occasional voice raised in disagreement. The city was exactly as Fergus remembered it: a cacophony of sounds featuring the bringing together of those-who-have-plenty and those-who-have-almost-nothing.

Conran was as cheerful as ever and looked much the same, albeit with a slightly wider girth, which Fergus guessed must now necessitate the loosening of his belt a notch.

'Let's to the business right away.' Conran motioned to Fergus to sit, then opened a desk drawer and drew out a bottle of whiskey and two glasses.

After pulling the cork between thumb and first finger, with a swift, well-practised twist of his wrist, he held up the bottle. 'You'll accept an Irish whiskey from an Irishman in Ireland, will you not?'

Fergus was happy to agree. He'd always preferred a strong Irish whiskey that caught the back of his throat to the dark-coloured Guinness he was sometimes offered in Dublin. He noted it was always presented with pride, the offer carrying with it the unspoken connotation that a refusal might cause offence.

After they'd toasted each other's health, Conran leant back in his chair, his hands clasped behind his head. 'Let us to business.'

Fergus explained how he was making final preparations for the return of the *Ketton*, and that he knew there wasn't much Conran didn't know about moving on quality fancy goods.

'I'm here to firm up the distribution plans we've discussed in correspondence. Face to face is always best and, as you know, I like to check with our Dublin agent in person now and then.'

Conran drained his glass. 'Are we any nearer to learning what goods we are expecting?'

'I can't provide exact details until the *Ketton* returns, but I'm still expecting "exotic" goods. Ivory, silver, jewellery. Mother-of-pearl boxes, chess sets, carvings, fancy textiles of Indian or Chinese origin.'

'What we call "small ornamentals" in the trade. Easy to transport and with strong decorative appeal.'

Fergus took a sip of his whiskey, appreciating its smoothness on his tongue and the hit at the back of his throat.

Conran continued, 'I can move these smalls easily enough, especially the ivory, and the market is always strong for tea-caddies and boxes. If they've decorative Christian symbols, so much the better.'

He began reeling off the names of general retailers he'd been speaking with in Ireland. They spent some time discussing commission rates, transportation and other details.

'With exotics,' Conran said, 'the successful sales are those where the customer can touch the goods. Fingertips are capable of absorbing the essence of an article in the same way we mentally taste food with our eyes before we eat.'

Fergus was reminded of seeing Dr Fincham's fine ivory chess set the first time they'd met, and how he'd wanted to put his hand out and cradle one of the pieces.

Conran continued, 'With ivory, it's the intricacy of the carving, the tracery of the design. You can see people running their fingers over a piece, almost fondling it. With silver and gold, they test the weight before they buy. We must approach our clientele as ambassadors presenting gifts, which the court are privileged to have the opportunity to buy.'

'I instructed Bill that above all it is quality the investors require. He has a good eye, and I trust his judgement. As I trust yours.' Then, almost as an afterthought, Fergus added, 'Bill's been advised to buy cotton.'

'Indian cotton?'

'Yes, I think so.'

There was an awkward pause before Conran said, 'Oh, dear. You may regret that.' There was a look of surprise on his face. Or was it verging on pity?

Attempting to keep his voice light, Fergus asked, 'Why? Cotton's in short supply.'

'Good American cotton, yes, but Indian cotton, if it's from Surat, which I suspect yours may be, well, that's a different matter.'

'What's wrong with it?'

'Finding a market for it is what's wrong with it. The mills won't touch it. It's fiddly stuff, and often there are small stones in with it, and that makes extra work. I've heard tell there can even be goats' hair in it. The hand-weavers don't much like it, either, as it's slower to card and weave. If the war goes on for much longer, then maybe the mill bosses'll turn to it in desperation, but they'll not like it.'

Fergus stared out of the window. He didn't want the dismay he was feeling to be obvious. Turning back to face Conran's gaze, he tried to put on a brave face. 'Well, let's hope, if Bill does buy cotton, it's not from Surat.'

'If it is, then you may have to be inventive about how you're going to move it on, but if I were you, I wouldn't worry about it yet. Crossing bridges and all that.'

Conran took a cigar from a silver case, offering one to Fergus, who declined.

Fergus took another sip of his whiskey. 'I've been wondering if I can beg a favour from you,' he said.

Conran lit up and drew heavily, searching Fergus's face. The cigar's end glowed a bright red several times, like a signalling lighthouse.

'And what might that favour be?'

Fergus leant forward in his chair and, as he did so, the cigar's scent flowed into his nostrils, instantly transporting him to childhood memories of his long-passed-away grandfather, Norman Shackleton.

'When the *Ketton* returns, I shall need help. Someone to support sales. You have good contacts here in Dublin and in Cumberland. Does anyone come to mind?'

Conran thought for a moment. 'Here's the thing now. I have a son, Shaun, coming up twenty years of age. You'll have heard me mention him a time or two?'

Fergus couldn't remember any reference having been specifically made concerning Shaun, but he was aware Conran had a wife and four children.

He decided on, 'You always speak affectionately of your family.'

Conran inspected the glowing end of his cigar. 'He's a useful lad, good with numbers and a worker, and to my mind shows promise in business.'

Fergus was beginning to guess where the conversation was leading.

'I agree, you'll be needing help with the sale of your goods,' Conran went on. 'I've contacts, as do you, but time is passing by and you need a representative out and about right now.'

'You're suggesting Shaun?'

'God's truth, you've plucked the words from my mouth. What say you? He's young in years, but he's not wet behind the ears in any man's book; I've been training him up.'

'And what will Shaun say to leaving Dublin? To leaving his friends? His family?'

'Oh, he's an adventurous lad. I can see his eyes lighting up at the prospect straightaway. He'll keep you entertained, too. He's a tuneful whistler, with a wonderful repertoire.'

Fergus wondered if Shaun was in any sort of trouble and Conran was taking the opportunity of shipping him out of the way. He wouldn't put it past him; he had a rascally side. Then Fergus put such thoughts away. If the young man was destined to make his way in his father's business, it made sound sense for him to have as much experience as possible. And he'd heard it was always difficult to instruct one's own offspring. Especially if one saw one's own faults replicated within them.

Perhaps sensing Fergus's hesitation, Conran nudged him. 'You need help, and he needs experience. A goodly match, surely now? However, if there were to be a problem, nothing will change between us and I will take him back.'

It was true, there was an attractive reciprocity in Conran's suggestion. Shaun could lodge at the Indian King with Becky's mother. Dolly would soon lick him into shape if he turned out to be wayward, as almost all twenty-year-olds could be, and she'd be delighted with the regular income.

'Let's see how he gets on with a month's trial,' suggested Fergus.

Conran's cigar-holding hand shot out and he grasped Fergus's fingers, peppering them with warm grey ash. 'Excellent. You can wait a few days, can't you? I can send him out on Monday's post-boat. His sister is being confirmed into the church on Sunday and his godly mammy wouldn't want him to be across the water for that. You know what Irish mammies are like concerning their religious devotions and their boys.'

Fergus reckoned a smile by way of response was sufficient. He didn't want to become involved in any religious discussion. He didn't have the time – he'd Hodges Figgis to visit. He couldn't possibly visit Dublin without an hour in his favourite bookshop.

When the *Eleanor Bell* cast off from the Custom House dock later that day, Fergus stood at the rail watching Dublin's lights fade into the distance as she made her way down the River Liffey to the Irish Sea. He reflected on the father-son relationships within his own family. His father's fractiousness had made things extremely difficult between them for years, and it had taken a life-threatening health crisis for their relationship to mellow to a workable association. Fergus was too young to remember his father and grandfather's relationship, but from what he'd heard, it hadn't been an easy one, either. He was determined he would do his best with Rory and with the son he and Becky might have in the future. Could it really be that difficult to love one's own and guide them at the same time?

As they entered the Irish Sea, his thoughts turned again to the cotton. If Bill had filled the hold with goods they'd no chance of selling, it could spell disaster. Despite Conran's advice about crossing bridges, he couldn't bat away the unwelcome thoughts he kept experiencing.

CHAPTER SIX

On his return from Dublin, Fergus called in at the Indian King on the way to the warehouse. He found Dolly in the kitchen. She was baking some of her meat pies, the smell of which was wafting into the bar to entice hungry customers.

'I can tell by your face you're hungry,' Dolly said. 'Sit down and you can have one of the next batch. It's beef and potato. In the meantime, I've some lemonade freshly made.' She filled a tumbler with pale-yellow liquid and handed it to him.

Fergus didn't argue about the offer of a pie. He hadn't realised he was hungry until he'd smelt the baking. Suddenly he was ravenous and was imagining the crispness of the crust as he bit into it, and the flavour of the gravy as it flooded over his tongue – dark brown, thick and, as always, delicious.

'I've some business for you if you would want it,' he said.

Dolly turned to face him. 'Business?'

'Yes. I've taken on Conran's son, Shaun, to help with selling the Mauritian cargo He's arriving Wednesday.'

'Local lads not good enough to employ?' she asked, with a half-smile.

Fergus laughed. 'It's partly a favour for Conran, to give the boy some experience. If he's like his father, I've no doubt he can talk his way both into and out of trouble. He's a talented whistler, I've been told. If he's as good as his father says he is, you'll be able to engage him for Saturday night entertainments.'

'The Irish gift of the gab, that's what you mean?' Dolly sounded dubious. 'You've not met him?'

'No, but I've limited his engagement to one month's trial. If he's lacking, or causes trouble, we can pack him back to Dublin. Besides, we can do with an extra pair of hands. What I'm asking is, can you put him up in one of your rooms?'

Dolly pursed her lips. 'I've a vacancy, that's true enough, but I'm thinking of a commercial traveller gentleman. They're usually quite reliable concerning payment. How old is he? Can he look after himself? I've no mind to be babysitting an Irish lad.'

'He's coming up twenty.'

'There's twenty-year-olds need more coddling than some ten-year-olds.'

'I've no doubt you'll soon get him back on the right path should he stray. What do you say?'

'Aye, well, it would have to be the usual terms. Breakfast and supper. Laundry's extra and no lasses upstairs. Church on Sundays like the rest of us. Eight shillings a week.' Dolly took the pies out of the oven and put one on a plate. 'Put yourself around this,' she said, handing it to him.

'The Louisa Line's covering costs, so you'll be paid promptly,' Fergus told her. 'About church, he's a Catholic.'

'No matter, he can still come with us. Rector Longrigg's not fussy up at St James, as long as he doesn't take communion. Besides, I'm not leaving the bar unattended for a twenty-year-old to raid when I'm at church, so it's come with us or out for a walk. Rain or shine. Since I'm not going to be lumbered with him if he turns out to be a bad 'un, I'll give him a trial. Any trouble, mind, and he's out straightaway.'

'Thank you. I'll see he behaves himself.'

'I'll air the room. He'll have strong legs so won't matter if it's on the top floor. I don't suppose he'll have much baggage, being a single man.' Dolly sat down at the table with a biscuit while Fergus ate. 'I've a bit of gossip for you,' she said.

'Have you now?'

'It's about your bookkeeper, Dicken.'

Fergus put down his knife and fork. 'Go on.'

'Did you know he's walking out with Evangelina Croxall, the stationer's daughter?'

'Rory told me she'd called at the warehouse and Dicken had been all of a dither making a fool of himself. And Becky mentioned she thought they were seeing each other, but I don't take much notice.'

'Well, I saw them walking out on the meadow, and when I mean walking out, I don't mean striding out.'

'Ah, romantically you mean?'

'Exactly. He had a face on him like a playful puppy.'

'And her?'

'Head held high and smug as a weevil in a bag full of fusty flour.'

Fergus began eating again. 'It'll be a brave man decides to settle down with Evangelina Croxall.'

'I thought you'd be amused.'

'You thought correctly. Thank you for telling me.'

After Fergus had finished the pie and was making ready to leave, Dolly asked, 'Any further word from Bill and the *Ketton*?'

He shook his head. 'No word yet.'

'Well, something will come soon, we can be sure of that – good or bad.'

Fergus said nothing, despite desperately needing further word from Bill. As well as being due to report to the investors, the time was fast approaching when he would have to inform Macintosh & Warrilow, the Glaswegian sugar-machinery manufacturers, of progress. While Dr Fincham had taken the collision setback in his stride, commenting that something was bound to have gone wrong somewhere on such a long voyage, Messrs Macintosh & Warrilow might be less philosophical.

As he neared the warehouse, he thought of what Dolly had told him about Dicken and Miss Evangelina. He knew from what Rory had said that she'd obviously been flirting and that Dicken was sweet on her. It had made him laugh at the time, but he'd wondered how a girl with such head-turning beauty could possibly be interested in his fastidious, plain-looking, down-to-earth bookkeeper.

Later, Becky had suggested Evangelina was only playing with Dicken, and when Fergus thought about it, he wouldn't put it past her.

After checking all was well and attending to some post, Fergus called in at Croxall's to see if they had any new publications. His eyes lighted upon a small volume, bound in red leather, with gold embossed lettering. *The Songs and Ballads of Cumberland.*

'What is your price?' he asked Mr Croxall, pointing at the book.

'Five shillings. It's beautifully bound. See.' Mr Croxall turned the book over in his hands before handing it to Fergus.

Fergus opened it, glanced at the index, then placed it carefully on the shop counter. 'I've been away in Dublin and this will make a nice present for my wife. I'll take it.' When he arrived home that evening, he held out the small package. 'I saw this at Croxall's today and I think you'll like it.'

Becky untied the brown-paper wrapping. Turning the book to see the spine, she read out the title, then began to flick through the pages. 'Ooh, thank you. It's lovely.'

'I saw it and thought of you.'

'Some of these song titles are hilarious. "When Jockey first to Jenny spoke", and "The Peet-Seller's Lament for his Mare". I bet that's sad. Romance and death in the same volume.'

'It's given to you as a token of love, of that you can be sure.'

'I don't doubt it. Here's another good one. "Come

Here You Witches Wild and Wanton". What *have* you bought me?'

They were both laughing.

'Don't worry, there's some Wordsworth, too.' Fergus took the book from her hands and turned to the back pages. 'Look, "To the Cuckoo".'

'I know that one,' said Becky. '"O blithe new-comer, I have heard, I hear thee and rejoice…"'

Fergus joined in and together they said, '"O Cuckoo! Shall I call thee bird, Or but a wandering voice?"'

'We both know it. It's a truly wonderful gift, I love it,' said Becky. She took the book back from him, running her fingertips over the embossed spine.

'Aren't you going to thank me properly?'

'And how shall that be, kind sir?' She tilted her head on one side, looking up at him through half-closed lids, much in the manner of a coquette.

'A kiss will do, if it's not too much of a hardship.'

She stepped forward and planted a little peck on the end of his nose.

'Is that all?' he asked, grinning at her.

'You'll get a proper kiss when you've eaten all your dinner, and not before,' she replied, laughing at the absurd face he pulled. His next words removed a touch of the joy from his gift, but she managed not to change her expression.

'I know you think you haven't got enough to do, so this might help provide some purpose to your day when you're alone.'

Reading poetry and Cumbrian songs alone wasn't how

Becky had envisaged spending her days, but he'd meant well in bringing her such a gift, and it would be unkind to complain.

CHAPTER SEVEN

The next morning, Fergus woke at 6am, exhausted. He was burning up, his chest sticky with perspiration rivulets and his heart racing deep in his rib-cage. In addition, he was experiencing an appalling sense of doom. He immediately thought of the financial distress the loss of the *Ketton* would bring him and Becky. Specifically, the loss of their home. He lay listening to the gulls cawing to each other, and to distract himself imagined them swooping down, scavenging for the rogue fish scraps that fell from fishermen's baskets. He focused his mind on the sound, trying to clear his head from the after-effects of his dream. Most dreams fled the harder he tried to remember them, but the more he thought about this one, the clearer the details became. Not just the events, but the sounds as well.

He'd dreamt he was alone in a small rowing boat, way out at sea, with no oars. The waves were vicious and the boat was swaying from side to side, tipping forward and back at the same time. He could taste the salt on his lips and feel the roughness of the sharp crystals where they'd dried. They scratched his hands as he gripped the boat's sides. He was shivering from the intense cold. A piece of wood was bobbing up and down on the white caps and the boat was being torturously drawn towards it by an invisible, evil force. To his horror, he saw it was the *Ketton*'s nameboard.

There was no floating debris to confirm the ship's demise, and no bodies in the water, but he knew, without any measure of doubt, that the dream was a warning that the ship had gone down with all hands. At that point in the dream he couldn't see the crew, but he could hear the familiar sounds they made as they cast off while singing their favourite shanty. The tune and the words were as always, but their voices were distant and, worst of all, alarmingly off-key. Something was dreadfully wrong. He knew he had lost everything: the crew, the ship, the cargo and, because of his debt, their home. It was at this point that he woke, shivering, with a shocking pounding in his temples.

He put a hand out for Becky and touched her breast through her nightgown. She was warm to his touch. Still in the thrall of his dream, he rapidly withdrew his hand, in case its coldness woke her. Then he remembered; it had been a dream, and he had woken shivering, not from the cold, but from the dream's content.

'Is this a premonition?' he asked himself. 'Is our Mauritian voyage doomed?'

As Becky stirred beside him, and his heart settled down, he realised there was a mistake in the dream. He knew without doubt, despite not having seen it, that the ship that had gone down was a three-masted barque, whereas the *Ketton* was a combination steamer. A true premonition would not have made that mistake. Did it concern one of his other ships? Or perhaps a Shackleton & Company ship?

He rose and went in search of Nicholas Fincham's headache tonic. He usually took great care measuring out the dosage in an apothecary spoon, since Nicholas had told him it was a powerful linctus that should be approached with respect, but the pain behind his eyes was so bad, he downed an additional half-spoonful.

When he shared his nightmare with Becky over breakfast, omitting to mention he had taken the extra half-spoonful, she remained silent for a while before saying, 'I think this nightmare shows your inner fears. You've no control over what's happening thousands of miles away and this is causing anxiety to build over not only the ship but, quite naturally, over the crew too. During the day you can keep such fears from surfacing, because you're busy with much to think about and to see to. At night, the fears you keep under control during the day take the opportunity to come out and play with your mind.'

Fergus shrugged. 'This may be so.'

'You have a lot of nightmares. So many, I mentioned them to Ma.'

'You did what?' He knitted his brow.

'I told her I was worried about you and the nightmares you're having.'

'I don't have that many. There was no need to involve your mother.'

'But you do have many. I don't wake you up anymore. I think you're worried about something that you're not telling me.'

Fergus blanched. Not knowing how to reply – or, more truthfully, not wanting to reply – he said nothing.

'Your silence tells me I'm right. What is it? Is there something wrong with the ship that you're keeping to yourself?'

He shook his pounding head. 'Well, there's the unfortunate collision in Cape Town.'

'You've known about that for a while. There must be something else. You're often in a world of your own, with an anxious face. And what about your headaches? These are much worse. You owe it to me as your wife to confide in me. How can I help if you won't tell me what's wrong?' Becky paused. Then she asked, 'Is it me?'

Fergus had to come clean. He couldn't have Becky thinking she was at fault, when it was him. He loved her too much for that.

'I've done something foolish. I've overinvested in the *Ketton's* cargo.' He put his napkin up to his mouth, as if in an attempt to wipe away his spoken words and, with them, his foolishness.

Becky frowned. 'What exactly does overinvested mean?'

'It means I've borrowed too much money to buy cargo, and if we don't make a profit, then I won't be able to pay back the loans I've taken out – and we will lose our home.'

Becky's hand flew to her mouth. 'We could lose here?' Her eyes ran round the room then back to Fergus. 'Our home? You've gambled our home? Rory's home?'

'I haven't gambled it like putting money on a horse. I've invested it in the *Ketton's* cargo, which is quite different. If she comes back and the sales go well, then the investors, and we personally, stand to make a great deal of money.'

'You're insured against losing the ship, I know that. Why suddenly are you doubting that you'll make a good profit on the cargo?'

Fergus readjusted his collar unnecessarily. 'I'm worried there may be a problem.'

'Why?'

'Bill talked of plans to purchase a large amount of cotton.'

Becky reached for the milk jug. 'But that's good, isn't it? Cotton is in short supply.'

'If he does buy, it will more than likely be Surat cotton. Conran told me this is poor quality, and the mill owners won't take it, which means we may lose money on it. In truth, we may not be able to sell it at all, and if we can't…'

'If we can't, what?'

'Our home may need to be sold.'

Becky's face paled. 'Oh, Fergus, what have you done? Are you telling me the threat to our home is a real one? You're surely exaggerating.'

'I'm afraid it is a real threat. I've taken out a personal debt, not a Louisa Line debt.'

Becky picked up her napkin and began wiping away tears. In a shaky voice, she said, 'How could you be so foolish? What on earth possessed you? And why didn't you discuss it with me?'

'I'm sorry, truly I am,' he said, 'but I've done it with

the best of intentions. I realise I should have discussed it with you, but—'

Becky interrupted briskly, 'But you thought I'd try and stop you.'

'I won't lie, I thought things would go smoothly, but I see now there may be unanticipated difficulties we have to negotiate.'

She put the napkin to one side and pulled a handkerchief from her pocket, and began wiping her nose. 'You always appreciated there was risk to our home or you would have told me.'

Fergus said nothing. Everything she was accusing him of was true. He should have spoken with her, but he'd been foolish and headstrong, relying too much on a situation turning out in their favour – a situation over which he had little control.

'You didn't need to do this,' Becky went on. 'We're happy as we are, aren't we? Living here? We don't need riches.'

'Yes, I know we're happy and I'm truly sorry I've got us in this mess. Can you understand why I did it? I want to better things for us, and I want the *Ketton* voyage to be a great success. I mean, there's no reason to think it won't be; it's just turning out to be more on my mind than perhaps it should be. Now I've burdened you with it.'

'It's a shock. I'd no idea, but it explains how you've been.'

Fergus gave a weak smile; it was all he could manage, with the drums beating inside his head. He placed a forefinger in each of the shallow dents at the sides of his forehead and pressed hard.

'You're still in pain,' said Becky. 'And I suppose your admission to me hasn't helped. I'm upset, you can see that, but now you've told me, we can worry together.'

'Shall you tell Dolly?'

'No, there's no need to pass on the burden.'

Fergus winced at the unspoken confirmation that he had burdened *her*.

Becky suggested, as she sometimes did when he was in the throes of one of his heads, that he lie on their bed for an hour until the linctus took hold.

'You may want to consult Nicholas again,' she said, as he left the room. 'He may have something to help you sleep. A stronger linctus, perhaps.'

As he climbed the stairs, Fergus expected to hear the sounds of the breakfast dishes being cleared away, but there was silence.

✼ ✼ ✼

The following day, the last day of the month, Becky was at Coates Lane preparing to meet her new cleaner, still reeling from the previous day's upsetting news. At ten past three there was a knocking on the door. She opened it to find a young woman clutching a piece of paper. The woman was shorter than Becky, perhaps slightly over five feet tall. There was something interesting about her face, which was oval in shape, although what it was exactly Becky found interesting, she wasn't sure. She'd a youthful mouth, wider than most, and generous lips. Her eyes were deep-set above high cheekbones, and she had a pleasant smile, although a sadness radiated from her. Becky saw immediately she was undernourished. She could be a bonny lass with a bit more weight on her.

'Mrs Shackleton?' the woman asked, giving a little bob.

'You must be Miss Brook.'

'Aye, I'm Lois Brook. I called at the Indian King a while back, as you know, and then I got this note earlier this week from the lady there to come here today. I understand you're looking for a maid?'

'Well, "cleaner" is a better description. Come in.' She led the way into the sitting room. 'Will you have some refreshment? A glass of lemonade?'

There was a slight pause before Lois said, 'Thank you, ma'am. A lemonade, please.' She was looking round the room.

Becky gestured to a chair. 'Please, sit.'

Laying the tray in the kitchen, Becky added four biscuits alongside the drinks. She thought the girl looked hungry. When she returned to the sitting room, she saw Lois's eyes move straight to the biscuits.

'Help yourself. They're ginger. I made them myself yesterday.'

'Thank you, ma'am.' Lois took a biscuit and in two bites it was gone.

'There's no need to call me ma'am. We're not grand in this house. Mrs Shackleton will do. Tell me a bit about yourself, Lois. Where are you from?'

'Blackburn, in Lancashire.'

'You're a long way from home. Are you on your own?'

'There's me, Mam, Da and the little 'uns. I've four sisters and two brothers. I'm eldest.'

Becky pushed the biscuit plate closer. 'How old are you?'

'I'm eighteen.'

Becky was shocked. The girl appeared to be in her early twenties. 'So, what brought you from Blackburn to here?'

'We're weavers. When the cotton stopped coming in because of the war in America we got laid off from the factories. We thought it would only be for a little while, but then it went on.' Lois took a sip of tea. 'And can you ken it? Even the maintenance men, the fettlers, got sent home. We did as best we could, but with no brass coming in at all, eventually we had to go on the soup.'

'A soup kitchen?' Becky had seen a sign down by the Rose and Thistle on the quay, with people queueing outside.

'Aye, soup for the needy. We got relief payments, as well. Not a great deal, but just enough. Then Mam heard there was transportation to Liverpool. I mean, that's a big city. We were sure we'd find work there, so we sold our furniture and the piano to pay for the journey. Mam was really sad about the piano, but when we arrived, we couldn't find nothing.'

'So, you only had what you were carrying?'

'Aye. Then one night in a pub down by the docks, our Da heard there were work up 'ere and he met a fella would bring us up on his boat. For a high price, mind.'

'How did you pay him if you had no money?' Becky had been curious from the start how whole families, arriving in Liverpool with no funds, could then move up coast to Whitehaven.

'Several of us, different families, pooled our relief money at the beginning of the week, which left us with nothing in hand, but we were so sure from what we'd been told that we'd find work straightaway, we thought it wouldn't matter. "Loads of work", they'd said. "They'll be plucking you off the streets", they'd said.'

'How long have you been here?'

'Two months.'

'Have you found any work?'

'Not me. We've had some parish relief and there's a soup kitchen we can go to. Da's got a sweeping-up job at the ropery for two days this week. He's hoping it'll turn up more days. His health's not that good now, He's quite deaf from the machinery noise. With the mill ceilings so low, the noise bounced off them and the walls, making it really bad.'

Becky thought it all sounded dreadful.

'The mill was always really choky, so Da coughs a lot. In Blackburn, they set him on bricklaying for a shilling a day, but it were hard work in all weathers, and with no proper dinners it's weakened him. Mam's always saying she'll take in mending, but no one seems to want any doing. I thought, well, people always need cleaners.'

'That's true,' said Becky, refilling Lois's glass.

'You'd think so. I mean, a place even after you've cleaned it spotless gets dirty again. Specially for those living near the foundry. I went round there, but I could see straightaway them folk are not the sort to be having cleaners. And then on the way back I saw the Indian King and called in. On the off-chance, you understand.'

Becky could tell by her clothing the girl had fallen on hard times. Her skirt was of good quality, as would befit a weaver, who would save up to buy best rather than settle for cheap, but it was worn and spotted. The sleeve cuffs of her blouse were frayed. Everything looked as if it needed a good wash, and it was a long time since an iron had run over any of it.

Becky indicated the room. 'I've been keeping house myself. That was my ma you spoke with at the Indian King. I used to work there before I was wed, so I know about keeping things clean. I'm not looking for a polisher or a duster, more someone to do the heavy work. The laundry, beating the rugs, that sort of thing.' She glanced at Lois's hands.

Lois turned her palms upwards, spreading her fingers. 'They may look soft, but I can see to all kinds of jobs. I'll work hard.'

Becky remembered what Dolly had said about seeing Lois and thinking of herself. She imagined how she would feel in the girl's place. Unemployed through events happening thousands of miles away. Desperate for work, but unable to find it. She wondered how many more there were like her in Whitehaven.

'When can you start?' she asked.

Lois's face lit up. 'Right now, if you want me.'

Becky knew she ought to wait and discuss it with Fergus, but she'd made her mind up to engage her within ten minutes. She liked the lass and, if she was truthful, she felt sorry for her. Dolly was right – she deserved a helping hand. From the few comments he'd made, she knew Fergus would be happy with her choice, if just to satisfy his mother.

'We'll say November the 4th, which is a Monday, laundry day. I'll provide you with two aprons, one to wear and one for spare. Your wage will be six shillings a week and the hours will be eight until noon to begin with, five days a week. Except Mondays when you'll need to be here until three o'clock. We're a small household; there's myself, my husband and, when the *Eleanor Bell*, one of my husband's ships, is in port, there'll be our ward Rory, too. He's coming up twelve and he has a small dog, Charlie. Rory has a bad leg as a result of a street accident. That's how he met my husband.'

'I can cook, if you like. With Mam having so many babies, being the eldest of seven I've been doing all that.'

'Seven is a handful.'

'Oh no, she's had way more than that, I forget how many. We've had sickness and tragedy along the way. Seems as if she's always expecting, but we don't always get to keep the babies that go with it.'

'Is she expecting now?'

'I don't think so. She's forty and probably could, but she's definitely not as strong as she used to be, and she's hard of hearing, but not as deaf as Da.'

Becky suddenly felt embarrassed listening to the account of another woman's private childbearing history. She changed the subject. 'You'll need to tell the relief board that you're working, as it may affect your household income.'

'I'd rather be working than living off the relief. Mam

and Da'll still get an allowance for the bairns, I'm sure on that. Thank you so much, Mrs Shackleton, you've no idea what this means to me and my family.'

Becky thought she could see tears in the girl's eyes. She didn't want to encourage a display of emotion, as it would make them both uncomfortable, so she went into the kitchen, gathered up the rest of the biscuits and, putting them in a paper bag, handed them to Lois.

'Take these, as a present for the little ones.'

CHAPTER EIGHT

While Becky was interviewing Lois, Fergus was on his way to meet Shaun from the Dublin post-boat. Despite it being mid-afternoon there was a wicked chill to the air, and a typically broody Whitehaven sky threatened rain. A skinny black-and-white cat was stretched out on the harbour wall cleaning itself, casting occasional forlorn glances up at the rapidly greying sky. There were no gulls for it to chase; perhaps sensing the approach of foul weather, they appeared to have taken shelter.

As the passengers streamed off the boat and began making their way to their homes and offices, there were several contenders who Fergus thought might be Shaun. The only guidance Conran had given him was, 'he looks a lot like me, but he's an inch or two taller.'

Fergus was regretting he'd not asked for further distinctive features or, at the very least, for the colour of his coat. He was on the point of accosting one youth when, out of the corner of his eye, he saw a tall young man who not only resembled Conran, but was the image of him. There was no mistaking he was Padraig Conran's son. He had his father's jaunty walk, the full lips and dark curly hair and, as he came nearer, Fergus could see he'd inherited his father's eyes. It wasn't the shape of them or the colour, it was their inquisitiveness. Eyes that missed nothing and were continually on the alert for opportunity. The effect was of a wise old fox in a young head, thought Fergus.

He held out his hand. 'Welcome to Whitehaven. I'm Fergus Shackleton. You must be Shaun.'

'Sure I am, and I'm well pleased to be meeting you, Mr Shackleton, sir.' He accepted Fergus's hand and matched his grip.

Fergus was surprised by the low timbre of Shaun's voice. 'Your father was right. You're much like him. You even share his walk.'

'I've a deeper voice though, I'm told.' He gave a loud laugh, revealing a set of almost perfect white teeth, very different from his father's cigar-stained ones. 'Folk say we've a keen likeness in manner and looks, although Da's taken on a few airs and graces dealing with some of his grander customers.'

'How was your crossing?'

'It's been a blowy trip. The ship was fair tipping at one point, with not a speck o' land in sight. I'll not deny, I'm relieved to arrive safely.'

'We'll visit your lodgings and deposit your bag. You can wash up, and then to our Chapel Street warehouse.'

Walking briskly to beat the expected rain, and pleased so far with Shaun's manner and friendliness, Fergus explained his own company was the Louisa Line, and that Shaun would be working solely for it.

'You'll hear talk of Shackleton & Company,' he told him. 'That's owned by my family, but separate from us, although I've a hand in overseeing it and am part shareholder.'

'Da told me all about it. He said he had a big falling out with your da. Hector, isn't it?'

Fergus had forgotten about that. 'A lot of tides have come and gone since then, and it was well before my time, but it's true, they had a bad disagreement.'

'He told me there was trouble here last year, too.'

'Oh, did he?' said Fergus, surprised.

'With the excise men. You'd contraband whiskey you didn't know about.'

'I think there's one thing we all learned from that, and you'll be wise to learn it too.'

'What's that?'

'Always make sure what you have in the hold is what's on the ship's manifest and show respect to the harbour officers.'

'My grandda used to say harbour masters was "eejits".'

'In his day, I'll grant you, some of them were not clever, or they'd turn a blind eye, but not now. Either way, we do things correctly. We've a good business and there's too much at stake to be bending the rules or disregarding them.'

At the Indian King, Fergus could see by the way she spoke to him that Dolly liked the look of her new lodger. He also noted that, like his father, Shaun had an eye for the ladies, no matter their age, and he guessed, with his good looks, cheery manner and obvious charm, they might be partial to him too.

✻ ✻ ✻

Fergus had planned to spend time showing Shaun the warehouse, but there was post on his desk when they arrived at his office, and a communication from Bill amongst it. He introduced Shaun to Dicken and bade Dicken take over, then sat down to open Bill's letter.

'Cape Town, October 2nd, 1861

Dear Fergus, my good sir,

The required repairs have been undertaken and we plan to continue our journey on the early tide tomorrow. We have had great difficulty obtaining the required timber, which has delayed us further. We anticipate arriving in Port Louis at the end of this month. Assuming no continuing difficulties, and a stay there of approximately three weeks, I anticipate our return to Whitehaven to be the end of December or early January of next year.

I am enclosing the papers associated with the repairs and a list of the supplies we took on board. All accounts will be settled with funds from the ship's chest before we leave tomorrow. I have to report we incurred greater expense than we expected. To save money, most meals remained taken on board, with some of the crew, as anticipated, complaining about "too much rice".

I have not wasted our sojourn here. There has been much to learn from laid-over mariners such as ourselves, and old sea hands, concerning the rest of our journey. All most helpful. A further result of our delay has been that it's permitted me to quiz the merchants and dealers, not only about availability of goods, but also pricing. I append a short list of what I am reliably informed is currently available in Mauritius for profitable purchase. You will see this tallies with expectations, as advised by Dr Fincham. On others' advice, including Captain Fletcher from Brocklebanks, I have added cotton to the list.

We expect to be back in Cape Town early November, when I will be able to send you a completed hold manifest via a Brocklebanks' clipper. It will be quicker to do that than try to send from Port Louis. I will also be able to collect any further instructions you have forwarded to us there, before we begin the long haul back. I am enclosing further correspondence from the crew for their families.

As a personal aside, the South African wine is particularly palatable and if there is adequate hold space, I intend to return with some. Hopefully we will be able to use it to toast a successful voyage.

Yours truly, and wishing you good health and spirits, Sir,

Bill.

Fergus went immediately to the potential purchase list and there it was, right at the top: 'Cotton', but no mention of its source. He rummaged amongst the various bits of paper accompanying Bill's letter until he found the repair invoice. He grimaced, but it was a sunk cost and had to be accepted. With the added expense of the repairs, Fergus contemplated the omission of the cotton's source with a heavy heart. Perhaps he could write to Bill. He checked the office wall-calendar and realised immediately he could not contact him in time to caution him.

He turned his attention to the ship's log and perused it, before sorting the crew's mail into neat piles. All the while he was wondering how much space the cotton might take up. If it turned out to be sub-standard, they would have to make sure they sold the other items at excellent prices to make up for it. They would need all the extra help Shaun could provide.

When Dicken and Shaun returned from the warehouse tour, Fergus handed the list to his latest employee. As well as the cotton, it included ivory, rum, textiles, Chinese items, and spices.

'Tell me, Shaun, how would you set about merchandising these products in England?'

Shaun scanned the list, then whistled. 'I'd rent a grand hall somewhere like Manchester or Leeds, or maybe Glasgow, and put advertisements in all the local papers. I can see it.' He took a few steps back, spread his arms and began speaking in the manner of a town crier. '"The Louisa Line begs to inform the good citizens of Manchester that the…"' He turned to Dicken. 'What's the ship called again?'

'The *SS Ketton*.'

'"That the *SS Ketton* has recently returned from Mauritius with wondrous exotic items". Then we put a list of the stock – in bold print, mind you – and below that "Great bargains to be had. All goods priced. Wholesale buyers welcome". What do you think?'

Fergus didn't know what to think. Shaun was either going to be a magnificent ambassador for their goods or he was going to bankrupt them.

'I like your grand style,' he managed to say. 'It's perhaps a little ambitious at this stage, but I can see you have ideas and imagination.'

'We could do the same in Carlisle. Or Edinburgh, even.'

Fergus didn't think it was the right time to dampen his enthusiasm and go over the cost of transporting goods, hiring a venue and all that an exhibition far from Whitehaven would involve, but he had to admit, the young man was keen. He had the sensation of a whirlwind joining the company, and it was going to need careful management. He glanced at Dicken, who was standing speechless, mouth open, eyes wide.

'Dicken, call a meeting of the investors for Monday at ten o'clock at the Waverley, and later I'll write to Macintosh & Warrilow in Glasgow.' He turned to Shaun. 'Macintosh & Warrilow are the sugar-machinery manufacturers we carried the spare parts to Mauritius for. Sit with Dicken and learn from him.'

'Shall you be replying to Captain McRae?' asked Dicken.

'I'd like to, but there's not enough time to reach him. He'll have long left Cape Town by the time we're able to transport ship's papers.'

'Can you write direct to Mauritius?'

'It will still be too late; he'll be settling negotiations as we speak.'

Fergus left the office later with clear thoughts in his

mind as to how his evening was going to pan out. *I'm going to pour myself a generous brandy, enjoy my supper admiring my beautiful wife, then I'm going to lead her to our bedroom, undress her extremely slowly, make love to her – perhaps twice – and after that I shall fall into a dreamless sleep to awake refreshed. No need to bother Nicholas Fincham about a sleeping draught.*

Yet, despite the pleasant evening he went on to enjoy, he woke in the night worrying about the cotton and the money he had borrowed.

❅ ❅ ❅

On Saturday morning, at his parents' home in Queen Street, Fergus and Rory entered via the side-carriage entrance and went straight to his rabbit's hutch, bypassing the butler, Samuel. They let Harry out for a quick hop around, then begged some leftover cabbage leaves and fresh basil for him from the cook. After putting the rabbit back in his hutch, they wiped their feet carefully on the stiff brown mat inside the kitchen door and went upstairs to the drawing room.

Elizabeth leapt up when they entered. 'I'm so pleased to see you before you leave tomorrow, Rory. I forgot to give you your birthday present yesterday.'

Rory's eyes lit up. 'A present for me? That's reet grand. You must have forgiven me for beating you at whist yesterday.'

Elizabeth said, 'I'll practise while you're away, so you'll not beat me so easily next time.'

Fergus knew full well his mother let Rory win every

time. He had tried to stop her doing it, but she said seeing his face when he won was so uplifting, it made her day.

'Yes, a birthday,' said Hector, with a severe face. 'You'll be twelve, and that means you're almost a man, so we'll expect good behaviour at all times from now on. Even when you're asleep.'

Rory seemed to take his words seriously, until Hector burst out laughing, followed by Elizabeth and Fergus.

'Oh, you're teasing me,' he said.

Elizabeth put her arms around him. 'Come, see what I have in this box over here.'

It was a large box, covered in paper decorated with different types of dogs. Rory pulled off the big red ribbon on the top and opened the lid.

'Ooh, Mrs S. Thank you, thank you.'

'What is it?' asked Fergus.

'A new set of paints.' He lifted them out.

Elizabeth beamed at her gift's reception. Fergus was pleased to see his mother so happy.

"There's more,' said Rory, taking out a second box.'

'Those are pastel chalks,' said Elizabeth. 'We thought you could use them on paper. I'll take you down to Croxall's and you can choose a sketch book. I wasn't sure which size you would prefer.'

Rory, all smiles, went up to her, then hesitated. 'I think I'm supposed to put my hand out, but to tell the truth Mrs S., I'd much rather give you a hug and a kiss.'

Elizabeth scooped him up. 'A hug and a kiss will do well, Rory.'

After twenty minutes, during which there was a careful

examination and sharing of his birthday spoils, and many thanks professed again for the present, Rory went home, stopping in the kitchen on the way for a minted soda water and some of Cook's famous cheese straws.

Fergus settled down with his parents and a glass of Madeira. 'I've news you'll be glad to hear, Mother.'

Elizabeth, her face breaking out in a huge smile, raised her chin. 'A baby?'

Fergus realised straightaway he'd made a mistake. His mother's response was something he should have anticipated. 'No, not that. Becky has engaged a cleaner.'

'About time,' said Hector. 'That means I won't have to keep listening to how she needs one, and "why hasn't she engaged one?"' He moved in his chair and turned to Elizabeth, who was pursing her lips at him.

'Hush, Hector,' she said. 'This is first-rate news. Who has she employed?'

'A weaver from Blackburn, I understand.'

'A weaver? From Blackburn?' Hector asked. 'What's she doing here? You want to be careful. Honest people tend to stay where they're from. It's the dishonest who kick their heels and move from place to place like tinkers. You can't check on references when they're from another part of the country. Count your silver spoons when she's gone home.'

'Oh, dear.' Elizabeth pressed her thumbnail against her lips.

'Father, you know full well the Lancashire mills are going through an appallingly depressive time, with no raw cotton for the looms. People are being laid off. They come here to find work.'

'That's as may be, but I still say honest people stay where they're from. For one thing, there's relatives can help out.'

'Not if they're all in the same trade, as is often the way.'

'Have you met this weaver?' Elizabeth asked.

'Not yet.'

'Asking for trouble,' said Hector, tapping his upturned pipe bowl against a brass ashtray.

Fergus felt affronted. 'I trust Becky and Dolly's judgement completely on this kind of matter. Don't you trust their opinion? We thought you'd be pleased.'

Elizabeth engaged Hector with her eyes, as if for support. 'I'll feel more content when I've seen her. When is she starting?'

'Monday.'

She picked up her diary from a small table and made an entry. 'I shall visit to make her acquaintance. Until then, I've no comment to make.'

❖ ❖ ❖

On Monday, Fergus considered inviting Shaun to join him at the investors' meeting to take the minutes, then decided against it. Better to wait until his new employee had proved himself and the investors were more familiar with his involvement in the business.

Mr Nubley was the last to arrive at the Waverley, coming in as coffee was being served, and mumbling about 'trouble at t'foundry'. Fergus, glancing out of the window a couple of minutes earlier, had seen him dashing across the short distance between the road and the hotel. He arrived out of breath and quite red in the face.

When they were all seated in the small reception room, Fergus placed his papers on the table. The three businessmen, Messrs Nubley, Heslop and Dickinson, together with Dr Fincham and their own Captain Jessop, master of the Louisa Line's *Sophie Alice,* were all looking at him expectantly.

Dr Fincham seemed different, and it took Fergus a moment to realise he was wearing gold-rimmed spectacles, the lenses of which were a perfect circle. This was a new adornment.

'I know what you're thinking,' said Dr Fincham. 'Who the devil is this? It's age catching up with me, I'm afraid. I'm now forced, under sufferance, to wear these damned appendages on my nose.'

'They're most becoming,' said Captain Jessop, with a grin.

Dr Fincham put his head down and peered over his spectacles. 'I would rather you said "distinguished", but I'll take any compliment I can get these days.'

Fergus made a note of those present and opened the meeting. He gave a short speech about the *Ketton's* progress, feeling duty bound to make a brief mention about the ship being held up at Cape Town, whilst underplaying the damage. Then he read out the list of items she'd be bringing back. At the mention of cotton, Mr Heslop's head shot up.

'We'll have no trouble moving that,' he said. 'There's nothing coming into Liverpool these days. I've spinners and weavers knocking at my door all hours wanting cotton.' He paused. 'Unless it's Surat cotton from India.'

Fergus cringed. He'd hoped he could get by just mentioning cotton until he was sure of its origin.

'What's wrong with Surat cotton?' asked Captain Jessop.

Mr Heslop, leaning back in his chair, assumed a knowledgeable air. 'I may be a flax-spinner, but I know a thing or two about cotton. The factories need to increase humidity or else it breaks, which is expensive and eats into profits. I'm not saying you can't shift Surat cotton at a decent price these days – the cotton-mill owners are desperate for cotton – but I'd not bank on it. Let's hope it isn't Surat.'

Mr Dickinson gave a quick nod. 'Aye, we only use American cotton for our sails. But not knowing how long this civil war's going to last makes it difficult.'

They spent the rest of the meeting discussing Fergus's plans for selling the exotic goods and considering the advice he'd gleaned from Conran in Dublin about costings and distribution. All the while, Fergus was feeling more and more wretched about the cotton. He was beginning to think it was impinging on his every waking moment.

He was on the cusp of drawing the meeting to a close when there was a sharp knocking sound and the door began to open. The men, as one, looked up and, to Fergus's surprise, his father, Hector, strode into the room.

'Good morning, gentlemen. Forgive the intrusion, but I called at Chapel Street and was informed Fergus was here at an investors' meeting. I didn't think you'd mind if I joined you for some light refreshment. I get so little gentlemen's company these days, apart from at the club, and that can be a bit stuffy and rarefied.'

Fergus's mind turned over. What to do? He couldn't

throw his father out, despite his having no right to be involved in Louisa Line business, so he stood up and brought a chair forward, placing it next to his own. The others moved sideways to even out the spacing.

'This is indeed a surprise, Father,' Fergus began. He didn't want the investors to think he'd invited Hector to join them, although he'd no doubt his face had relayed his shock at seeing his father enter the room.

'A pleasant surprise, I hope,' said Hector, his face all aglow. He looked round the table, acknowledging each man in turn. When he suggested they forgo more coffee and have brandies all round, Fergus realised he needn't worry – the investors seemed delighted to have the interloper join them. Conversation was relaxed, and Hector was soon telling some of his old stories and basking in their reception.

Although he was happy to see his father so animated, Fergus would have to point out later that it was a Louisa Line meeting, not a social occasion, and it had nothing to do with Shackleton & Company. His father had stepped out of line, no matter how enjoyable the experience had been for him.

There was, however, a jarring moment as the meeting ended, when Mr Heslop said, 'I'm sure I speak for us all, Fergus, when I say that we have no worries regarding our exotic cargo, knowing you personally are so heavily invested.'

Hector's head shot up. He opened his mouth as if about to speak, then closed it again. Fergus, while maintaining an unruffled appearance, was cringing inside. He hadn't divulged to his father the extent of his personal debt and had no desire for him to learn of it.

When Mr Nubley suggested he, Mr Dickinson, Fergus and Hector adjourn to the Gentlemen's Club for further refreshment, Fergus held back. As the men left the room, his father gave him a look which indicated the reference to his son's debt had not passed unnoticed by him. It wouldn't be long before he would want to unpick not only the extent of his debt, but every last detail concerning it. Fergus's heart sank.

Sure enough, mid-afternoon Hector appeared at the warehouse.

'We must have words, Fergus.' Then, looking fixedly at Dicken, he added, 'In private.'

Fergus spoke to Dicken. 'I'm sure you can find something useful to do upstairs, helping Shaun. I know he's here, I can hear him whistling.'

Dicken disappeared and Fergus began the speech he'd been rehearsing, about not bursting into meetings, in an attempt to pre-empt any discussion about his personal debt, but his father interrupted him.

'Never mind all that. I thought your *Ketton*'s profits from the Mauritius trip would come from transporting the sugar machinery for that firm in Glasgow, and that the investors I met today were putting up all the capital for the so called "exotic goods", for which you would charge them carriage.'

'That is mainly correct.'

'By mainly correct, should I take it that you've personally

invested in the cargo and are therefore also an investor in these exotic goods?'

'That is correct.'

'Not by too much, I hope?'

'That is personal to me,' said Fergus. He wasn't going to give his father any ammunition by letting him extract exactly how much he was indebted.

Hector stroked his whiskers and sighed. 'You know, son, I've told you many a time it's a risky business investing in a ship's cargo on a long overseas voyage. So much can go wrong with the change of a wind. I've always stayed clear of too much risk by looking only to carriage and storage fees for non-speculative profit on longer voyages. Speculation and risk is so much more easily managed close to home.' He paused and held Fergus's gaze. 'As long as it hasn't put your business or personal property in peril.'

'Don't worry, Father, everything is well in hand.' Fergus could see by the slight twitch at the corner of his father's mouth that he was undecided as to whether to believe him or not.

'I'll leave you to it, then,' he said eventually. 'Your mother's playing whist with Rory at Coates Lane this afternoon, so I can retire to my study when I get home. I may be able to sneak an extra cigar in if I'm lucky, before she comes back.'

After Hector had gone, Fergus opened his middle desk drawer and took out a bottle of Dr Fincham's linctus and a spoon. He pulled out the cork and was about to dose himself when he paused. Did thinking he was about to get a headache justify taking his medicine when he didn't have one? He put the bottle back. No, it didn't. He would wait.

CHAPTER NINE

Becky had hoped Elizabeth would give her and Lois a few weeks' grace before calling to cast her eye over the new help, but that was not to be. It being Monday, and therefore laundry day, an unholy mess of wet washing was spread over the kitchen when Elizabeth arrived at exactly eleven o'clock. Becky calculated Lois had been in her employ for only one week.

Elizabeth handed over a brown paper bag. 'I thought I'd call and bring you some fresh onions. Fergus is partial to onion soup, but I'm sure you know that.'

Becky didn't – he'd always told her leek and potato was his favourite – but no matter.

Elizabeth went into the parlour and sat down. 'I'll just take tea this morning, thank you. You can instruct your new maid.'

'Lois is my cleaner and helper, not my maid.'

'Oh, no, dear, always refer to her as your maid. It sounds so much better.'

And grander. 'She's busy, up to her elbows in suds. I'll make the tea.'

Elizabeth took off her gloves and laid them neatly on top of one another on a side table. 'I wouldn't advise that. She probably needs to be trained up, and I am a most suitable person for her to practise on.'

She's determined to meet Lois.

In the kitchen, Lois was folding clothes and hanging them on the ceiling airer.

'My mother-in-law, Mrs Elizabeth Shackleton, is here. She's requested tea. I'll put the kettle on, lay the tray and put the leaves in the pot. Never mind warming it this time. When it's boiled, pour the water on and bring it through. You'd better put your clean apron back on, too.'

Returning to the parlour, Becky saw a small parcel had joined the gloves on the side table. Elizabeth picked it up and handed it to her.

'It's a little something to put by.'

Becky knew before she opened it that it would be a baby's crocheted shawl, or bonnet, or something of that ilk. A 'little something' was being produced every couple of weeks and the same ritual followed. After thanking Elizabeth there would be a pause, while her mother-in-law waited expectantly. A minute would pass and, when Becky failed to fill the pause, Elizabeth's face would take on a fixed smile. Becky would then change the subject, usually to something innocuous such as the ships in the harbour, Rory's rabbit Harry, or once the price of bread.

If I open it now, Lois will see it when she brings in the tea and she'll think I'm expecting.

'Aren't you going to open it?' asked Elizabeth.

Becky put the parcel beside her on the chair. 'I'll wait until we have tea.'

To Becky's relief, Lois entered with the tray looking as if she'd done it a hundred times before. If she had to fault her it was that a strand of hair had worked loose and was hanging in front of her face.

Lois gave a little bob and put the tray down. When she'd gone, Elizabeth inspected the tray then leaned forward and, in a confidential tone, said, 'You need to teach her how to lay a tray properly. There's no cloth.'

Becky was unsure what to say. Should she point out Lois was being criticised for her mistress's shortcomings, since it was she, in haste, who had forgotten all about the tray-cloth? She thought of making an excuse, but knew it would be to no avail. The fact would remain that there was no tray-cloth. *Any minute she'll be reminding me to count the spoons when Lois has gone home.*

'She's young,' said Elizabeth, 'but she'll learn quickly. She doesn't look like a weaver.'

'What does a weaver look like?'

'Oh, I don't know. It's that she's not as I imagined her.'

'You mean she doesn't look like the thieving devil Mr Shackleton senior is expecting. Fergus told me what he thinks. No horns?'

'I'm sure he exaggerates. I wouldn't say she looks ill, but she's terribly thin.'

Becky opened the parcel and took out a small cream matinee jacket with ribbon ties and ivory silk binding-tape on the cuffs. She had to admit it was lovely.

After the usual pause, accompanied by the fixed smile, Becky went on to give Elizabeth some of Lois's background and how she'd come to engage her.

When the carriage clock on the mantelpiece struck noon, Elizabeth stood up. 'I must take my leave. Hector is expecting me back.'

After she'd left, Becky gave a sigh of relief. The introductory visit seemed to have gone quite well, despite the forgotten tray-cloth.

❖ ❖ ❖

The next day, arriving at the Chapel Street warehouse, Fergus was met by voices coming from the office. He opened the door to find Miss Evangelina Croxall and Dicken in close conversation. They jumped apart when they saw him. Dicken turned to his desk and made a sudden grab for a pencil, which fell from his hands and rolled onto the floor.

While Dicken, pink of face, bent to retrieve it, Miss Evangelina turned and looked at Fergus. 'It's my birthday, Mr Shackleton. I called to see if I could take your wee doggie for a walk as a special treat, but I hear he's gone with the lad to Dublin.'

'With Rory. He's gone with Rory. Charlie is *his* dog, Miss Croxall, not mine.'

Miss Evangelina pouted at Dicken. 'You didn't tell me it was Rory's dog.'

Dicken, looking sheepish, said, 'Oh, dear, didn't I?'

'Well, no matter. I'll have to promenade on my own then.' She put her head on one side. 'Unless you'd like to escort me?'

Dicken checked the office wall-clock. 'In half an hour I can accompany you.'

Fergus was both amused and shocked by the forwardness of the young girl. 'How old are you, Miss Evangelina?' he asked.

'I'm eighteen today. Mama and Papa are having a social gathering for me later when our shop's closed. A birthday tea.'

By the light in his eyes, Fergus could see Dicken was anxious to escort Miss Croxall and, since it was her birthday, he said, 'I've some business with Shaun. If you can find him and bring him here, then you have leave to escort Miss Croxall. I expect he's on the top floor.'

Dicken reached for his cap and disappeared. Fergus began examining some papers on his desk, while Miss Evangelina stood looking at the room. When Dicken returned, she jumped into life and began twirling one of her curls. Shaun's eyes went straight to her.

'Oh, yes,' she said, addressing Fergus. 'Father says to tell you he has some manuscripts you might like. It was him who sent me and I almost forgot.' She gave a silly little giggle and glanced across at Shaun while Dicken had his back turned and was putting on his coat.

Shaun held the office door open for them as they left and his eyes followed Miss Evangelina out.

'Who is that young girl?' he asked, when the outer door had closed.

'That's Evangelina Croxall. She's walking out with Dicken.'

Shaun raised his eyebrows. 'Is she now? Well, there's something child-like about her. Wide enquiring eyes and blonde curls. I bet she turns a pretty ankle.'

'Enough,' said Fergus, laughing. 'Don't be deceived. She's a pretty little thing, I'll grant you that, and she knows it, but when she walks, she swings her arms like a soldier on parade.'

When Dicken returned later, flushed and all smiles, and was busy lining up and sharpening his pencils, Fergus drew his attention to a pile of papers that needed filing. He then walked up to Lowther Street to collect a painting of St James's Church, where he and Becky were married. He'd seen it in William King, the cabinet maker's, window two weeks earlier and had gone straight in to buy it as a Christmas gift for her. He knew she'd love the painting and see it for the romantic gesture it was meant to be.

CHAPTER TEN

Two weeks having passed since she'd taken Lois on, Becky felt able to leave her in sole care of their laundry. She had a fitting at the dressmaker's and would be gone about two hours. She bought eggs and cheese from a farmer's wife with a stall in the marketplace, chatted to some people she met from church and placed an order for a leg of lamb with the butcher. They were expecting Rory back from Glasgow on the *Sophie Alice* at the end of the week and she knew he would appreciate his favourite Sunday dinner.

As she approached the dressmaker's, she saw the shop door blind was drawn. A note had been fastened to the glass.

'We regret we are closed due to unexpected bereavement. Please accept our apologies. We shall be open for business again on Wednesday November 27th.

(Deliveries to be deposited with Messrs Foxton next door.)'

Becky wasn't surprised. The last time she'd seen the dressmaker, she'd given a detailed account of the failings of her mother's health and how it was a miracle she'd lasted so long. She wondered about calling in at Chapel Street to see how things were progressing at the warehouse. Then she remembered Fergus had gone to Maryport to firm up arrangements with Frisby's chandlers. They'd asked for first refusal on the spices expected with the *Ketton*. She decided to call first at her home in Coates Lane to drop off the cheese and eggs, then at the Indian King to see her ma.

At Coates Lane, the smell of soap and the sound of the linen being swished in the dolly-tub made it obvious it was wash-day. Taking her purchases into the kitchen to put them away, Becky had to step over a small pile of clothing. She put the eggs down and was about to tell Lois she would be gone again for about an hour, when it struck her there was something unfamiliar about the clothes on the floor. She examined them more closely. It was a small pile of undergarments, stockings and what looked like two blouses, but she didn't recognise any of the items. Children's trousers, shirts and vests were high up on the ceiling drying-rack.

Lois had stopped turning the dolly to agitate the clothes and was looking at Becky with fearful eyes.

Becky pointed at the pile of clothes, then at the drying-rack. 'Whose are these?'

'They're a few items from home. I didn't think you'd mind, but I can see you do. I'm sorry, I'll gather them up.' She wiped her hands on her apron in a half-hearted attempt to dry them and started picking up the clothes.

Becky's first thoughts were that Lois had taken advantage of her being out of the house and that she would have to let her go. This led to a selfish regret that she'd have to do the washing herself again. That thought was replaced, almost immediately, with the practical notion that she could easily find someone to replace the girl. Then she wondered what on earth had possessed Lois to take such a foolish course of action when she'd been so desperate for work. She must have known if she was found out she would be dismissed.

While all these thoughts passed through Becky's mind, she made no further comment and stood watching Lois gather up the clothing. Lois stood in front of her, clutching the pile to her chest. A single black stocking had freed itself from the untidy bundle, a straggler running down the front of Lois's skirt. It occurred to Becky that from a distance it would resemble a swaying snake.

'Why have you brought your washing here?' she asked. 'Can't you do it at home?'

Lois, who seemed to be struck dumb, shook her head.

'Why not?' Then, as an afterthought, she asked, 'Well, if you can't do it at home, what about one of the public wash-houses?'

Lois, still seemingly unable to utter a word, had paled and her eyes were moist. It was as if the girl was in another place. Becky quickly interpreted her appearance as one of shock, and she was afraid the lass was going to faint.

She pointed to a chair. 'Sit down and tip your head forward.'

The act of sitting down seemed to bring Lois back into her surroundings. Becky fetched her a glass of soda water.

'Drink this. Have you eaten today?'

Lois found her voice. 'No, I haven't.'

Becky cut a generous slice from a round cob, buttered it and handed it to Lois on a plate. 'Eat this. It'll make you feel better.'

They sat in silence while Lois ate and drank, Becky wondering how things should proceed.

When Lois had nearly finished and was looking a little better, Becky said, 'I have to ask you again why you can't wash your clothes elsewhere. I could tell by the guilt on your face that you knew you shouldn't be washing your family's clothes here. The fact that you brought them with you indicates this was planned. You knew I had an appointment today and would be out long enough for you to do your own washing. You could have asked me.' Even as she said the words, Becky knew that no home help would ever ask or expect to wash their clothes at their place of work. It was too intimate an act.

'I'm sorry. We've no hot water at home and we can't afford fuel to heat enough for washing and we can't afford to go to the wash-house. It's wrong o' me, I know that, it's...' She paused.

Becky told Fergus later that an aura of inoffensive helplessness had radiated from her.

'It's what?' she asked, picking up a dolly peg and twiddling it in her fingers for something to do.

'It's that we're so poor now, we can't afford to live anywhere decent. We've enough trouble keeping our bodies clean. Some days we don't have any water at all. Last week, seeing everything come out so crisp and clean,

I thought I might bring a few things. I know it was wrong and, like I say, I'm sorry.'

Becky was well aware that some people lived in wretched poverty. She thought of when she used to visit Rory and his ma, Amy, up at New Houses, before Amy grew sick and died. They were poor and didn't have any luxuries, but they'd always had access to water and fuel enough to wash themselves and their clothes.

Lois cut into her thoughts. 'You'll be wanting to let me go, but would you like me to finish the washing before I leave?'

'I haven't said anything about letting you go. I have to think about this. Finish the washing. I've to see Ma at the Indian King and I'll be back shortly. When you've finished ours then you can do yours, but make sure you keep things separate. I don't think what you did was wicked or sinful, but it was foolish.'

✳ ✳ ✳

Business being slack, Dolly and Becky were enjoying a coffee at one of the smaller tables near the fire. Becky usually referred to this table as 'the Shackleton Table', being the one Fergus had occupied the first time they met. A new server was working behind the counter.

Dolly was wearing her sad face. She shook her head. 'I feel for them. I've heard the weavers have an especially bad time of it. They're packed into those stone courts, one family to a room, is what I've heard from listening to folk talk at the bar.' She pointed to Becky's empty cup. 'More coffee?' She motioned to the server to bring another pot.

'It used to be the Irish was despised in the courts,' she went on, 'but now it's the cotton-weavers. Folks say they think they should've stayed where they were, claiming off their own town relief, not ours.'

'Fergus told me that's what Hector thinks. That they should stay where they are. What do *you* think?'

'I think they're desperate. They're not proper itinerants, they're folk who've worked hard all their lives and been thrown out of work through no fault of their own.'

'It's such a shame. They're good people.'

Dolly added some coals to the fire and gave it a poke, then she sighed and said, 'I didn't realise the water situation was so bad. I mean, the girl's clothes looked as if they needed a good brushing down, but that she is reasonably clean and tidy is a great feat under her circumstances. What are you going to do?'

'They can't afford the wash-house. She said so.'

'You need to decide if you want to keep her. Then if you do, there's what you're going to do about the washing. You can't let her see to her family's washing at Coates Lane on a regular basis. It's not proper.'

The server came over with the fresh coffee and Dolly sent him back for biscuits.

'I want to keep her. She's a good worker. I can overlook one act of foolishness.'

'What about her ma? Doesn't she do anything?'

'From what I gather she's gone to pieces, and Lois has to see to the family.'

There was a pause while they stirred their coffee and tasted it.

'It's a pity they don't have any maritime connections,' said Dolly.

'Why?'

'You could've asked the warden at the Seamen's Haven.'

Becky felt a spark light up inside her. 'She *does* have maritime connections – she works for me – Mrs Shackleton of the Louisa Line, whose husband is a trustee.' The server came back with the biscuits and she helped herself.

Dolly sucked air in through her teeth, making a whistling sound. 'I don't know as you'd rightly get away with that.'

'I'll ask Fergus when he gets back tonight. I'm sure we can sort something out.' Becky was feeling energised. 'I knew you and I'd think of something.'

'What'll you tell her when you go back?'

'I'll tell her she's still got a position and that I'm making enquiries about washing facilities.'

Buoyed by their conversation, Becky stayed longer than she intended at the Indian King. When she returned home, to her surprise and disappointment she found the two aprons she'd given Lois neatly folded. Resting upon them was a note.

'Dear Mrs Shackleton,

I'm sorry for what happened. I should have known better. As you said, I've been foolish.

Yours respectfully,

Lois Brook.'

Becky went straight back to the Indian King.

'She's gone and left this note,' she said, handing it to her ma.

'Has she finished the laundry?'

'It's all airing. She's taken hers, even though it must still have been wet.'

'Wet, but clean. There's nothing in this note to say she's not coming back to you.'

'She didn't have to. She's left the two aprons I gave her folded up on the table.'

Dolly wrinkled her nose. 'What's so significant about that?'

'She's got her own peg and she always hangs them on it.'

'In that case, it looks like you've lost her. Too embarrassed to stay, I suggest. Some folks'd say she's stolen from you.'

Becky shook her head. 'I don't think she's a thief.'

'A year back, sitting at a loom, all in work, she'd never've foreseen what fate was about to throw at her family. I'd say it's her situation that's driven her to it. An honest lass in desperate circumstances.'

'I owe her money.'

'You can take it round and drop it off at Shepherd's Court. Number 6, wasn't it? If she's there you can ask her to come back.'

❄ ❄ ❄

Fergus didn't show immediate enthusiasm for Becky's plan concerning Lois and the Seamen's Haven.

'You say she's not a thief, but it's a strange thing for a maid to bring in her own washing. Perhaps Father was right – these weavers are more trouble than they're worth.'

'But if you met her, you'd think differently.'

'I have met her; I've seen her several times.'

'You've passed her coming in and going out on occasion, but you've never talked to her.'

'It's not my place to talk to the servant.'

'You're sounding like your mother, talking about "my place" and "servant".'

Fergus looked at Becky with an impatient eye. 'I'm thinking it would be easier all round if we gave the girl the money we owe her and engaged someone else, that's all.'

Becky was silent for a moment. Then she said, 'I've never really asked you for anything, have I?'

'You mean something important? Life and death?'

'Yes, I suppose I do.'

'No, I don't think you have.'

'Well, it's not exactly life and death, but this is important to me.' Becky toyed with her wedding band. 'So I'm asking you now. I'd like to help her.'

'She may turn up tomorrow as if nothing has happened.'

'She won't. It took a lot of courage for her to smuggle those clothes in. The courage of desperation.'

He gave a little laugh. 'Not the same as leading men into battle though, is it?'

Becky felt her neck redden. She was perilously close to losing her temper. 'Are you trying to undermine me?' she asked.

'No, I'm not. I'm saying it's not your role in life to save the poor. On occasion we donate appropriately for the good of all, such as when there's a missionary collection for widows of drowned sailors, for the workhouse or for orphans.' He dusted some invisible dirt from his trousers. 'It's best to keep this sort of thing at arm's length and not get involved with individuals.'

Becky's jaw dropped. When she spoke, it was with emotion. 'How you can stand there and say such a thing is indefensible. "Don't get involved with individuals". This from a man who plucked a pit lad off the streets, took him into his care, gave him an occupation, made him his ward and now has him living under the same roof.'

Becky gained no satisfaction from seeing her husband's face and neck flush a deep red. She would later describe his expression to Dolly as 'the greatest representation of awkwardness I have ever seen'.

After a short pause he coughed and patted his chest with a closed fist. 'You're right, and I'm not ashamed to admit it. It would appear this is a day when people do and say foolish things. A day for apologising. I'm sorry. What is this important thing you want to ask me?'

Becky held up two fingers. 'There are two things. First, please do not tell your mother what has happened. It will serve no useful purpose.'

'Agreed. And second?'

'I know you're not really in favour, but will you approach the Seamen's Haven about allowing Lois to use their scullery? I'm sure she'd be happy to pay back in kind in some way.' Becky had already decided, if Fergus wouldn't, she would approach the warden herself.

'As you wish,' he said. 'I will speak with the warden tomorrow morning. The only objection I can see is he will not want to commence operating as a wash-house. It will most likely have to be an individual arrangement.'

'Behind the scenes, you mean?'

'Yes. There will have to be limits she's to keep to, and I'll stress that to him.'

'Is the warden married?' Becky was nursing another idea.

'I don't think so.'

'Who does his washing, then?'

'How should I know? I expect he sends it out, as many bachelors do. Or he has his own housekeeper.'

'I've a thought,' said Becky. 'He could make a saving on laundry invoices if Lois takes it on.'

Fergus gave a slow, thoughtful nod. 'I'll speak with him on your behalf.'

'If he agrees to our plan, I'll call and see Lois and take her wages.'

CHAPTER ELEVEN

The next morning, Fergus arrived earlier than usual at Chapel Street and was pleased to see Shaun already hard at work. His shirtsleeves were rolled up and he'd made himself a jute apron, which he'd secured round his middle with thick twine. When he saw Fergus, he took off his cap and undid the kerchief from round his neck, using it to wipe the sweat from his brow.

'We had two companies collect their goods while you were in Maryport yesterday, which has cleared up a goodly amount of space for the exotic goods. There's a couple of trunks to move and then the whole of the top floor is ready.'

Fergus could see there had been a definite improvement, providing them with more shelf space. It was surprising how helpful an efficient tidying-up could be when managing storage. The barrels had been moved closer together and the sacks stacked four high instead of three.

'Good work, Shaun. And the second storey?'

'Still in some disarray. We need to get rid of those sails

we've been storing. They've been lying here for months while the seller and purchaser settle their dispute. They're paying for the space, but the sails take up so much room, being such an awkward shape, even when they're rolled up.'

'They're still arguing over payment? Can I give that to you to follow up?'

'Sure. That you can.' Shaun bent down and picked up a short length of rope that had fallen on the floor. 'Best get that before someone gets their ankle wrapped round it.' He rolled up the rope and stuffed it into a narrow gap between two barrels. 'How did you get on at that chandlers?'

'Frisby's?'

'Aye, that one.'

'They're particularly interested in cinnamon, cardamom, cloves and peppers. We've agreed first refusal, and rice, if we have any. We must hold back some spices for medicinal sales.'

Shaun pointed to a cleared area of shelving. 'I've set aside room here. It's nice and dry, and I'm thinking the spices will be in and out quickly. No use taking them to the top only to bring them down a couple of days later.'

I've been lucky with Shaun, Fergus thought. *He's got a mature head on his young shoulders.*

'Good planning, Shaun,' he said. 'It's time we visited the local apothecaries and firmed up orders.'

'How local? As far north as Carlisle?' Shaun looked at Fergus expectantly. It seemed a trip to Carlisle would suit him nicely.

'Maybe. Hopefully we'll sell the spices quickly and

competitively to bring in fast revenue.' Fergus didn't say it, but he was keen not only to bring in money, but to be seen to be bringing it in. This would look good to his creditors and the other investors. 'The exotics,' he went on, 'the ivory, oriental, silver, we can put a premium on these and they need different handling.'

'I agree,' said Shaun, folding his necktie to put back on.

'Are you ready to do some commercial travelling?' Even though he phrased his comment as a question, Fergus was relying on Shaun to be the Louisa Line's traveller. He was conscious he was putting a lot of financial weight on a young man's shoulders, and that he should probably be out and about more himself, but Shaun seemed confident enough. His face lit up at Fergus's suggestion.

'I'd love to. It'll be like spying. I can go in, enquire about prices and say I'll think about it. But I'll need a business card if I'm going to be taken seriously.'

'What were you thinking of putting on the card?'

He scratched his head. 'Hmm. "Shaun Conran" in decorative letters. Then underneath that "Fancy Goods Commercial Traveller, Whitehaven". Or I could put "Dublin". That way I can be a buyer or seller.'

Fergus took out his watch. 'Put both; it's not a lie. I've to attend to some business. We'll leave Dicken in charge. You can walk with me as far as Lowther Street, then carry on to Croxall's stationer's to order your cards. Don't get the most expensive ones or the cheapest. This afternoon we'll draw up a map and we can plan your routes.'

After they'd parted Fergus paused to watch Shaun striding eastwards. He wondered if the young man would find Miss Evangelina on duty behind the counter. He'd seen the way Shaun had smiled when he'd spoken about her turning a pretty ankle. *That's all I need*, he thought, *Shaun stealing Miss Evangelina from Dicken*. And what made it worse was it seemed to him not beyond the bounds of possibility.

* * *

That evening, Fergus reported to Becky that the warden at the Seamen's' Haven had shown great interest in allowing Lois to use the scullery.

'It is his misfortune but our good fortune that his aunt, who did for him, has recently moved to Newcastle.'

'And he agreed?'

'Leapt at it is a better description. If Lois will do his laundry and a bit of "fancy cooking", as he put it, then she can use the laundry facility for some family washing.'

'"Fancy cooking"?'

'I think he means cakes, biscuits, jellies, that sort of thing. I understand the fare at the Seamen's Haven is somewhat institutional. Wholesome, but plain. You'd better go and seek Lois out.'

'As a fellow trustee, will your father agree?'

'I see no need to draw his attention to the arrangement at present.'

* * *

When she arrived where she thought Shepherd's Court should be, Becky couldn't find it. She'd expected it to be opposite the Baptist chapel, but there was only open ground. She thought of going into the Ducal Court Inn and asking, but it didn't look inviting to an unaccompanied lady – even one who'd woken each morning to the clanging of the beer barrels her father needed for the day's business.

She turned right along Peter's Street, taking herself past St James's Ragged School. It being dinner time, the children were running amok in the playground, laughing and shouting. She stopped to watch them. There wasn't a uniform as such – more a similarity in dress, in that all the boys' jackets had holes and were ill-fitting. Trousers were too short and shirt cuffs straggly. The girls' dresses were similarly ill-fitting, being either ridiculously baggy and hitched up round the waist with a twisted sash, or too small, with sleeves stopping well before the wrist. They weren't dressed in rags, as the name Ragged School suggested, but they were close to it. To Becky's surprise, she saw they were all well shod in locally made clogs. Perhaps a patron or town benefactor had seen to that.

She cut down Michael Street past the Methodist Chapel and came out on George Street, where she was still all at sea. She'd have to ask someone. The first two women shook their heads. A third waved her hand, saying, 'It's in there somewhere. I never go in, they're bad places.'

It occurred to Becky that perhaps a young lad might take her to the place, since they liked to roam. She was right.

'I know where that is, missus,' said a lad with an uneven fringe that had been cut far too short.

'Can you take me?'

''Appen I can. For payment, mind.'

Relieved to have found a guide Becky took a ha'penny from her pocket and held it up to him. 'When we get there.'

The lad seemed satisfied and set off at a pace. After a few minutes, they were standing in front of a covered passage, like a tunnel, about four feet wide and seven feet high. It was long, dark and not somewhere Becky wanted to venture.

'Are you sure?' she asked.

'Sure, I'm sure. It's where my marra lives.' He pointed a finger. 'Can I have my ha'penny?'

Becky was apprehensive and she hesitated. Was the lad deceiving her? She couldn't see any light at the end of the passage.

'Want me t'tek you down there?'

'Aye,' said Becky. 'So I don't lose my way.'

The lad sighed as if to signal impatience 'There's nowhere t'get lost.'

He set off again, a little slower than before, and Becky followed.

On reaching the end of the covered passage they came to a stone wall and, being forced to turn right, Becky then found herself in a small square, off which were several run-down stone dwellings. They appeared to have been hurriedly built on what seemed to have been the back yards of some of the big houses that still towered over the court. Becky had heard tell of landlords aiming to get as much rent from a property as they could by making every foot financially productive. She didn't doubt it now.

Although it was a sunny day there was no warmth in the court. The big houses were too high to allow the sun's rays to penetrate, so it was always in shadow. However, it wasn't the gloominess that worried Becky, it was the smell. They'd had rats scrabbling under the floorboards in the Indian King some years back and she recognised the distinctive odour immediately – a sickly, cloying, sweet smell that was unlike anything else. They'd put poison down so the rats carried it back to their nests. After two weeks, the rat man had pulled up some floorboards to check there were no corpses rotting underneath. He'd said it was a precaution, as they usually ate each other, which was a good thing because it meant the poison spread through the group. After that, Dolly had got a man in to check for holes and fill them in, and they'd had no trouble.

Becky gave the lad his ha'penny and thanked him, and he scurried off. Several women were looking at her with curiosity in their eyes. They all had the same world-weary expression associated with poor nourishment. Becky felt self-conscious, knowing she was well dressed and healthy. She searched for number 6, but couldn't see it.

One of the women approached her. 'Looks like you're lost.' It wasn't unkindly said, but the group's caution hovered in the woman's eyes.

'I'm looking for Lois Brook.'

Another woman, with sore eyes, stepped forward. 'I'm her mam. Who are you?'

'Becky Shackleton.'

'She's stepped out. She'll not be long. You'd best come in.' The woman pointed to an open door.

Becky stepped inside. It was one room. A lad and two lasses were sitting on a stamped earth floor playing a game with small stones rounded like marbles. They were all miserably clad and stared at Becky when she entered. The youngest lass, about four years old said, 'You're a pretty lady.'

Becky replied with, 'And you're a bonny lass.'

Mrs Brook pulled a stool out from under a table and directed Becky to it. 'It's best you look at me straight when you speak,' she said. 'My hearing's failing, but I can lip-read well enough.'

It was as Lois had told her. 'I'll do my best to speak clearly,' said Becky.

There was a pile of straw in one corner, which Becky thought was their sleeping area, since some material was folded upon it. She imagined the damp from the floor rising during the night and how chilly it would be in the early hours. There was a large chamber pot beside the straw, which she guessed would be emptied into a communal ash-pit or collected by the scavenger's cart. There was no obvious source of water other than two rusted buckets by the door. The room was the picture of misery, yet there was an order to the place. The few possessions she could see – some clothes, a small brush, pans, scissors, a bible, spoons and plates – were all neatly stowed. The floor appeared to have been recently swept and there was a sense of tidiness.

'My husband has work today. Brickmaking. He were a spinner.'

'And you were a weaver?'

'Aye, we had a different life than we have now.'

'When you lived in Blackburn?'

'Aye, we'd a good life then. We even had a piano.'

'Can you play?'

Mrs Brook shook her head. 'Nay, but I wanted the lasses to learn.' She studied their earth floor. 'That won't happen now we're living like this. Well, not 'til those Amerikeys sort themselves out. You know, we'd paid for that piano, it weren't on tick, but in them days we'd three pound ten a week coming in with us all on piecework and the littl'uns bringing in a bit extra here and there, picking up broken threads and rubbish under the machines. That were a year ago.'

Becky was wondering if she dare ask how much they were living on in Whitehaven, when Mrs Brook volunteered the information.

'These days, including the relief, it's six shillings if it's a good week. I'm hoping that since you're here it means you're not going to give our Lois the sack.'

'She's a good worker.'

'She should be here by now.' Mrs Brook rubbed one of her sore eyes with an earth-stained forefinger.

Becky was ashamed that all she wanted to do was get out of the place. Its stifling poverty was overwhelming. She knew people lived in want, but to be in its midst, and see and smell it, was a real eye-opener.

Mrs Brook picked up the conversation. 'It's the babes suffer most. It's so hard to keep 'em clothed when they grow so quickly.'

Becky couldn't stand it any longer and stood up abruptly.

'I have to go. There's work for Lois if she wants it, and I've found somewhere she can see to your washing, if she's prepared to do a bit of extra laundry and some baking in return.'

Mrs Brook clasped her hands together as if to pray, in what Becky guessed was a show of relief. 'I know she's sorry about what happened.'

'Tell her there's no embarrassment and I hope to see her tomorrow. Here's her wages for yesterday.' She put two sixpences on the table.

Mrs Brook bit her lip.

'Is there a problem?' asked Becky.

'We pawned her work dress yesterday, you see? She's nothing fit to wear to a lady's house and I can't get it back until Mr Brook's been paid.'

'When will that be?'

'Day after the morrow I expect.'

'I've something she can have if she'll wear it.'

Tears came into Mrs Brook's eyes. 'That's kind of you, Mrs Shackleton. Trying to look respectable and keep ourselves and the little ones clothed is almost impossible. I worry over it all the time.'

'I'll send a dress over this evening. You can return it straightaway if she decides she's not coming back.'

Back at Coates Lane, the first thing Becky did was wash her hands and brush her dress down. Then she picked out a brown tartan dress she'd had for some time, and a shawl that had seen better days. The dress was the plainest one she had, and while Fergus often told her she looked pretty, he had never made that comment when she was wearing it. She packed it with the shawl in brown paper and called at the Indian King for one of their delivery lads to drop it off at Shepherd's Court. They all knew every nook and cranny of the town.

By nine o'clock that evening, when the parcel had not been returned, Becky was confident Lois would appear on her doorstep the following morning.

CHAPTER TWELVE

It was the last Sunday in November, with Rory safely returned home by the *Sophie Alice*. Dr Fincham was a welcome guest at their Coates Lane table, and Fergus was saying grace. Becky surveyed the leg of lamb dotted with rosemary, the crisp potatoes surrounding it and the variety of vegetables in warmed serving bowls. It was a normal Sunday dinner, the type they enjoyed most Sundays following church, and which Fergus always called lunch. Yet all she could think of was the wretchedness of Shepherd's Court. Knowing her own home was under threat and in the lap of the gods, she felt she could understand a little more how the weavers must have felt having to leave their homes. The situations were hardly comparable, but even so, she felt closer to them now she had seen the court.

The previous Friday, Lois had appeared in the brown tartan dress. It had hung off her, but with the shawl draped over it this shortcoming was well concealed. Arrangements were agreed upon for her to go to the Seamen's Haven on a Thursday after finishing her tasks at Coates Lane.

With the meal underway, Rory was in high spirits.

'We've found a baker in Dublin that makes special breadcakes. They're reet grand. I've asked Cook if we can make them in the galley, but he says you've to be Irish to make a real one.'

Dr Fincham, obviously amused, said, 'I'm sure it helps, but I doubt it's essential.'

'You'll have to stick to your duff pudding, then,' said Fergus.

'Aye, although I makes a tasty soup, too.'

'What do you put in it?' asked the doctor.

'Anything and everything. Cook says we don't have leftovers, we've "fuel for the pot". That's apart from the scraps we keep to one side for Charlie and the cats.'

'Why don't you show Dr Fincham what the second mate gave you for your birthday?' said Becky.

Rory put his hand in his pocket and presented the contents to Dr Fincham, saying, 'It's a whale's tooth.'

The doctor turned it over in his hand. 'So it is, and interestingly carved.'

'Do you think so?'

'I do. It's called scrimshaw. I saw a lot of sailors fashioning these when I was at sea. They would buy the teeth from the Newfoundland whalers, then carve a picture and fill the scratches in with soot, to outline the design. There are a lot about that are poorly done, but this one is exceptional.' He held it up admiringly and turned it round in his fingers. 'Look, it's divided into two halves, so you can see the barque sailing through the water and whales swimming beneath her.'

'I like to hold it,' said Rory. 'It feels nice and smooth in my hands. It's one of my favourite things.'

Fergus held out his hand to take the tooth from the doctor. 'That's interesting. When I was in Dublin, Padraig Conran said people liked to hold ivory in their hands.'

'Are you still painting your slates, Rory?' asked Dr Fincham.

'Aye, but they're heavy to carry. I'd like to have a go at this scrim stuff.'

'That will make you a scrimshander,' said Fergus.

Becky, who was gathering up the plates, said, 'First you'll need a whale's tooth and they don't sell those at the chandlers round here.'

Rory chuckled, 'Nor the confectioners or the butchers. And a needle. I'll want one of those. A strong one, like they use for stitching sails. I've watched them carving.'

'You'd have to be careful if the ship's pitching. You could stab yourself.' Fergus handed the tooth back to Rory. 'You'll have to ask the second mate to teach you.'

'I think he might. When he gave it to me, he said I'd an eye for drawing. He's seen it in my painted ship slates. Anyways, I like to always have it in my pocket.'

After a pudding of thick, creamy rice, into which a generous dollop of raspberry jam had been dropped, Rory took Charlie out for a walk, and the adults retired to the parlour.

Dr Fincham settled himself by the fire. 'If I may say so, Becky, you seem rather quiet today.'

'I'm not unwell, but I do have something on my mind.'

'She's been up to Shepherd's Court,' said Fergus. 'Do you know it? Near the Baptist chapel.'

'I know the chapel and I've been in some of those courts, but I'm not sure of Shepherd's Court.' He turned to Becky. 'What were you doing up there?'

Becky explained about Lois. 'The conditions they live in are heart-breaking and it's not their fault. It's politics and war that have led to them ending up here. These are hard-working folk and I'd like to do some good and—'

Fergus butted in. 'There's not much you can do. They get poor-rate relief from the guardians who visit them.'

'I know that, but this is about self-respect.' Becky told them about the piano and the wages the Brooks had been used to in Blackburn, stressing that the weavers and spinners were not the idle poor. She cast a glance at Fergus when she mentioned they'd been forced to leave their homes, but she was uncertain whether he'd noticed.

Dr Fincham took off his spectacles and wiped them with his napkin. 'I agree with you. Since whole families– and I mean extended families of cousins, in-laws and the like – were all employed in the same industry, they can't support each other when times are hard. They all go under at the same time.'

'It's not just those employed in the cotton industry,' said Becky, warming to her theme. 'If you've a grocer's shop and you let a few people buy on tick, and then a few more, and if none can settle up at the end of the month, then *your* business goes down too. The relief and the meagre wages some of the luckier ones get provides food, but nothing else. I keep hearing Mrs Brook's parting words to me – "Trying to look respectable is impossible".'

'There's sense in what you say,' Dr Fincham said. 'As well as the financial relief, there's the medical care, which they can access for free from the infirmary, but clothing is a different matter.'

'Don't local charities help with that?' asked Fergus.

'They do, but there must be some way we can help. Some way *I* can help.'

Fergus took Becky's hand. 'I realise I haven't expressed much sympathy for Lois, but if you think of something, you will have support from us both, I'm sure of that.'

'Indeed,' said Dr Fincham.

Fergus topped up the doctor's glass and the conversation gravitated to the next race meeting up on Harras Moor.

❋ ❋ ❋

On the following Tuesday, Fergus and Shaun were in conversation with Captain Jessop on the quay, watching the loading of the *Sophie Alice*. It was unusually busy, with two French brigs having docked almost at the same time. Their crews were calling out to each other and the harbour was alive with '*Bonjour, mes amis*' and phrases Fergus didn't understand, apart from '*cognac*' and '*vin*'.

'No further news from the *Ketton* yet?' asked the captain.

Ever conscious that Captain Jessop was an investor in the Mauritian cargo, Fergus shook his head. 'We're getting on with the sale preparations for her return. Shaun's been generating interest along the coast.'

'What level of interest?' asked the captain.

Shaun came to life, obviously delighted to be able to report on his travels. 'As always, it's all about profit and price. I'm forging strong links, and that's the main thing.' He brought out one of his business cards and handed it to the captain. 'These have opened many a door.' He glanced at Fergus. 'We did right having these printed.'

Fergus nodded. 'I went with Shaun to Workington to start him off,' he explained. 'But he's his father's son. The perfect salesman – charms the ladies, and congenial with the gentlemen. Firstly, he has the looks and secondly, he has the talk.'

'You exaggerate, but I do seem to have a way with the ladies. The next few weeks I'm further afield – Carlisle, then south to Lancaster and some of the Yorkshire mill towns.'

'Times are hard there,' said the captain in a solemn voice.

'There's still brass in the wool and manufacturing cities like Leeds.'

'We'll make money, I can feel it in my bones,' said Shaun.

'Your enthusiasm is infectious,' said the captain. 'I'm sure the traders and shopkeepers enjoy dealing with you.'

'I am generally known for being cheery; t'is the Irish in me.' He began whistling.

'Enough, thank you, Shaun, we get the idea,' said Fergus. He was smiling, but he wondered how much was simply Shaun's gift of the gab and how much he really could rely on him to sell their exotic goods.

Shaun stopped mid-phrase, with what he always

referred to as a 'twiddly-bit', and put his hand on the captain's arm. 'You'll carry a parcel to Dublin for my mammy and sisters, won't you, captain, sir?'

'I'll need to know what's in it.'

'Confectionery. Sugared almonds, liquorice, boiled sweets.'

'Can't they get those in Dublin?' asked Fergus.

'They can, but Da always used to bring them back for us from across the water and I want to carry on the tradition. You see, I've a strong sense of family, Captain Jessop.'

CHAPTER THIRTEEN

Two days passed and Elizabeth called at Coates Lane for tea and to drop off a jacket for Rory.

'Now the winter's really upon us, I hate to think of him being cold.'

'I feel the same way about all the weavers' children,' said Becky, thinking back to the lads and lasses she'd seen at the school and their ill-fitting clothes. 'I need to find a way of giving help without being offensive, and of getting Lois and her family's plight across to others.'

'Has Mary McRae met her?' asked Elizabeth, picking some biscuit crumbs from her skirt and putting them on her plate.

'No, but I do wonder if I could invite her, and the rector's wife Ianthe Longrigg, and maybe Dilys Croxall, too, to meet her. Lois could talk to us about her weaving, and perhaps between the four of us we could come up with something practical to help.'

'That's a good idea. Four heads are better than one.

Perhaps I could join you?' She helped herself to a second fig roll.

Becky was pleasantly surprised. To have Elizabeth's support could only be a good thing, surely?

'Neither of us have suffered poverty,' she said. 'Or from being so poor we didn't know where the next meal was coming from and nothing under our feet but stamped earth.' She rubbed the carpet with the toe of her shoe.

'"Dirt poor" I think it's called,' said Elizabeth. 'When people have a stamped earth floor.'

'Exactly. We've both always had sound floorboards to walk on, even if mine did occasionally creak a bit and yours were carpeted.'

'Yes, it's perhaps useful to think how we might feel in the same situation.'

'I do know what true poverty looks and smells like. Rory's ma, Amy, had nothing, and she took in mending. Knowing her, and how hard she tried to create a home, I understand the need for respect. Since my visit to Shepherd's Court, I've an even greater appreciation of the tragedy of working families falling into poverty through no fault of their own.'

❊ ❊ ❊

The proposed meeting between Mary, Dilys, Elizabeth, Ianthe, and Becky took place at Mary's, while her son William slept.

Ianthe spoke in a grave tone. 'I've been in some of the courts as part of my husband's parish work and felt really hemmed in. He's sometimes called to administer The Sacrament to the Dying.'

'I'm interested in Lois's story,' Dilys said. 'Do you think she'd be happy talking to us?'

'We can but ask,' said Elizabeth.

'Can I suggest that we limit our direct questions to her work in the mills and to how Blackburn's been affected by the cotton famine?' Becky said. 'That way we'll not embarrass her. Our interest'll be more general, rather than directed specifically at her and her family. If she chooses to divulge private details, that will be her choice.'

'I agree,' said Mary. 'She won't want to feel like she's on parade for a freak show.'

'Shall I do that, then?' Becky asked. 'Shall I invite her to talk to us next week at Coates Lane? Thursday?'

With the date agreed upon, Becky felt she had made a positive step towards publicising Lois's family's plight, and perhaps something good would come of it.

Lois took no persuading to talk about her life as a weaver, and a week later after finishing her work she was sitting with Becky, Elizabeth, Mary, Dilys Croxall and Ianthe Longrigg in the parlour at Coates Lane. She was wearing the brown tartan dress Becky had sent her three weeks earlier and her hair was pulled back in a tight bun. She obviously had a sense of occasion, even though Becky had done her best to convince her it was to be an informal gathering.

After being introduced, Lois hesitated a little, then began speaking.

'I learned to weave as a young lass at my aunt's home,

because she'd her own loom. Then, because the pay were better, I moved into Baxter's Mill. As well as weaving, I used to set the new lasses on and oversee.' She looked round at the ladies. 'Is this what you want to hear?'

Following nodding and smiling, she went on, 'The first we knew about there being no cotton were when they said we'd to work part-time. It wouldn't be for long, they said. A month at the most. Then it became two months, and our days were cut from three to two. Things weren't so bad because we'd savings and preserves put by from our allotment produce. It were when they announced they were putting the mill into repair that we began to worry.'

Dilys leaned forward. 'Doesn't India produce cotton? Can't the mill owners import it from there?'

'You're talking about Surat cotton, but we weavers don't like it much, and neither do the tacklers, 'cos of the stones in it.'

Becky's thoughts went straight to the SS *Ketton's* cotton. She made a mental note to ask Lois more about Surat cotton later.

'Who are these tacklers?' asked Elizabeth.

'They fettle the looms. Fix them when they're out of order. It's not only us weavers and spinners who've lost their jobs.'

'What was it like in the town?' asked Dilys.

'Everywhere were affected. Lodgers couldn't pay their landlords and so the baillies was sent in.'

'The baillies?' asked Elizabeth, looking at the others, as if to see whether she was the only one who didn't understand.

'I mean the bailiffs. It weren't the mill owners – they well appreciated the problem and didn't demand payment. It were the other townsfolk. They'd no give at all.'

'What about the relief?'

'There was a fund. It were enough to feed us to start with, but we couldn't replace anything.'

'Like what?' asked Mary.

'Shoes, coats. The shops began to empty, with no stock to sell. No one had any money to buy anything or settle their "on tick" bills, so they went under. Their windows were empty except for dusty advertising signs.'

Becky was imagining how desolate it must have been.

Elizabeth asked, 'Wasn't there any work at all?'

'Only for the men. There were brick-making and corporation road-mending, but soon there were others out of work, too. The relief meant folk weren't starving, but there was no hope. That's when folk began to leave and we left for Liverpool.'

'Were there beggars in the streets?' asked Dilys Croxall.

'You'd think so, but no. What's the point of begging when no one's got any brass?'

When Lois finished speaking, it was clear all four of Becky's guests were sympathetic. Becky wondered what would happen to the Croxall's bookshop were a similar situation to come about in Whitehaven. She couldn't imagine Dilys's daughter Evangelina applying for a position as a cleaner to contribute to the family income.

Lois departed amongst much goodwill. It was her wash-day at the Seamen's Haven and she was anxious not to be late. Becky slipped a florin into her hands at the door, and one of Dolly's fruitcakes, wrapped in a paper bag. When she returned to the parlour and her guests, she could almost touch the gloom in the air.

'How would we fare under similar circumstances?' she asked them.

Ianthe shook her head. 'Going, within months, from being financially secure to having to rely on corporation relief, and sell the contents of our homes?'

'There must be a way we can help them,' Becky went on. 'But I can't think how.'

Later that day, after Becky's guests had left, Dolly called round from the Indian King. It was the late afternoon lull, when she could sometimes take a break before the evening rush. It was a time she and Becky both appreciated away from the bustling pub.

'How are you getting on with Shaun?' asked Becky.

'He's out and about a lot these days, up country as a commercial traveller. I've to confess I've quite a soft spot for him now, and he appreciates my suppers.'

'Ah, he's caught you in his spell, has he?'

With a twinkle in her eye Dolly said, "Were I twenty years younger you might say that, but these days it'll take more than white teeth, the gift of the gab and a handsome face to make *my* heart flutter.'

CHAPTER FOURTEEN

On Tuesday December 18th, the *Sophie Alice* returned from a Dublin coal run without incident, and the next day Rory was upstairs with Shaun in the warehouse. Dicken had just returned from running errands. The afternoon was progressing in a normal manner, until they received a message there was post to collect from Brocklebanks' office.

Fergus leapt up. 'It'll be from Bill.' He was out the door in a flash and soon broke into a sprint. At Brocklebanks he was handed a large buff-coloured envelope, which he opened immediately. There was a thick letter for himself and the usual bundle of crew letters. He was back at Chapel Street within fifteen minutes of rushing out, the post spread across his desk, with Dicken, Shaun and Rory looking on.

He picked Bill's letter from the pile first, conscious everyone was holding their breath. Other than the rustling of the paper, the only sound was some soft sniffling from

Charlie, who'd stretched himself out in front of the office stove to toast his paws.

The letter was dated November 18th. Fergus began reading to himself. He wanted to make sure all was well before he made the contents public.

After a while, he said, 'We can expect them at the end of the month.'

'The end of this month?' asked Dicken.

Shaun tutted. 'Yes, she's not coming from China.'

'I was making clear,' said Dicken, giving Shaun a look. They never outwardly argued, but Fergus was aware they were hewn from different stone and sometimes grated on each other.

He ignored the two men and turned his attention to Bill's letter.

> 'I am enclosing the necessary invoices and bills of sale regarding funds received from Macintosh & Warrilow's agent "upon safe delivery". I expect they will have heard from their agent. Details of all invoices and purchases are also recorded in the log book.'

Fergus searched the papers on his desk until he found a long thin envelope inscribed INVOICES AND BILLS. A pile of papers of varying sizes and shades dropped out.

'Dicken, you take charge of these for now,' he said, pushing them to one side. 'I'll examine them in detail later. Shaun, we're full steam ahead in all senses. We'll go over the purchases, allocate storage and purchase advertising space later.'

'What about me?' asked Rory, peering through his fringe.

'You're going to need your notepad and paper to check off all the items when they arrive.'

'I might be on the *Sophie Alice* or the *Eleanor Bell*. Captain Jessop thinks I should have some trips with them.'

'I think it will be valuable retailing experience for you to be here. I'll speak to Captain Jessop about keeping you in Whitehaven.' Fergus didn't say anything, but he was thinking Becky would never forgive him if Rory wasn't at home for their first Christmas as a family in Coates Lane.

'The anchorage at Port Louis was better than I expected and the workforce set to with enthusiasm. It's not often they have to unload such cumbersome, weighty items, and they appeared to enjoy the challenge. I confess I found it anxious to oversee, but all fastenings remained secure and sound and everything was off-loaded with no damage to the parts. All did not go according to plan, though, as one of the apprentices, Clendining, got caught in the line of a rogue rope that lashed his back. He was treated by the physicians at the fort and, although badly scarred, is of good cheer.

I extended our stay in Port Louis by a few days, awaiting a Surat cotton delivery from India. I am assured it is of quality and that we will make a good profit on it.'

Fergus stopped reading, his eyes transfixed by "Surat" and its implications. Then with great effort, he pulled himself together and carried on, all the while conscious of a growing feeling of catastrophe.

'*Dr Fincham is remembered with much affection, and you will see there are several letters enclosed for him. As a result, those of us in authority were regally entertained at some of the grand plantation houses, but I will save those stories for over a brandy and cigar at the Gentlemen's Club. However, the main result of our association with him was that his letters of introduction enabled us to purchase sugar and rum direct from two sellers who have given us excellent prices. We have succeeded in circumventing the wholesale middlemen and I am particularly pleased with the Surat cotton price.*'

There it was again – 'Surat'. The word seemed to dance on the page in front of his eyes. He ran his finger over it, as if in an effort to erase it. He realised his face must be registering his distress, for Shaun asked if he was all right. He nodded and turned his attention back to the letter, the word 'Surat' moving from side to side in his brain with the regularity of a clock's tick-tock.

'*It seems over the years the doctor's medical skills have saved many lives. Should he return, I have no doubt he will be warmly welcomed, since he has left behind a great store of warmth and gratitude.*

The chief engineer has proved capable, and regarding our voyage so far, I can truthfully say we have made the correct decision investing in steam.

The weather here in Cape Town is hot and windy. We're all restless to be heading for home. The place is swarming with soldiers on parade and policemen. I understand the well-to-do spend a lot of time enjoying picnics and walking in the Botanical Gardens. It's very much an outdoor place. Fleets of fishermen come in each afternoon and the strangest looking fish go straight to market. I doubt you will not be surprised to learn that I have found stowage for some of the fine wine available here.

Yours truly, and wishing you good health and spirits, sir,

Bill.'

Fergus set Rory and Shaun to sort the post, then asked Dicken to sit with him. Soon, a steady stream of crewmen's families arrived with smiling faces to collect long-awaited letters. Word spread quickly in the town that the *Ketton* was expected at the end of the month, which gave birth to much speculation that she might be back in time for Christmas. Fergus tried to poor cold water on such comments in order to limit expectations that were most likely to be dashed, but to little avail.

Dicken was despatched to catch the post-boat to Glasgow with a note for Macintosh & Warrilow and Rory was sent to Queen Street to feed his rabbit and call on Elizabeth. After they'd gone, despite the pit in his stomach which was making even the thought of his evening meal objectionable, Fergus picked up the purchase list.

'Knowing exactly what we're getting, we can plan our action,' he said.

Shaun opened a small notebook with marbled edging and took a pencil from his top pocket. 'I bought this at Croxall's especially for recording the *Ketton's* stock. I'm after allocating one page to each item.'

'Give the receipt to Dicken and he'll reimburse you for it.'

'I already did, but he said it was an "extraneous expense" and handed it back to me.'

Fergus shook his head. 'How much was it? I'll see to it personally.'

'I got a strong one seeing as how it's an important job. It was thruppence.'

Fergus opened a desk drawer and took out a sixpence. 'Go back to Croxall's and buy another. You'll need it.'

Shaun pocketed the coin. 'When shall we plan for the advertisements and the like?'

Fergus turned round his desk calendar for Shaun to see. 'Playing safe, let's say the *Ketton's* docked by Friday January 3rd. Then we've Customs and Excise to satisfy. Add another week to appraise our stock, store it and prepare for sale. I suggest we advertise locally in the *Whitehaven News* on Thursday January 2nd and take it from there.'

Shaun made a note on the inside page of his notebook and Fergus began to read through Bill's list. He spoke slowly, giving Shaun time to head each lined page.

'Ivory. I'd allocate several pages for this. We can go into the specific details later, but this includes tea-caddies, small chests of drawers, screens, bedheads and mirrors.'

He paused. 'Goodness, there are three ivory footstools embedded with precious stones and Bill's added a note saying "As exhibited at The Great Exhibition in London. 1851".'

Shaun whistled. 'That'll be a grand selling point. What else is there?'

'Mirrors, combs, chess sets, carved-tusk ships on stands, and a lot more.'

'That's plenty to be going on with.'

'Here's the spice list. Besides cardamom, there are twenty-four sacks of cinnamon, and thirty bags of ground Indian ginger, along with five barrel of cloves that Bill's marked as medicinal.'

'We'll sell those to the apothecaries, no problem, as long as the price is competitive.'

'We'll make it so.' He returned to the list. 'Chinese: silk bolts, lacquer items and so on. Indian gold: bangles, bracelets, beads and necklaces.'

'What's the difference between bangles and bracelets?' asked Shaun.

'I've no idea. Textiles: carpets, rugs, chintzes, bunches of yarn...' Fergus broke off. He was looking at '400 bales of Indian Surat cotton'.

His throat went dry. Four hundred bales, while no doubt a small amount to a mill owner, was a huge amount for them to sell in an unstable market. With a sinking heart, he realised that selling it was vital and would almost certainly be the difference between the making of a handsome profit, and him and Becky losing their home, while the investors blamed him for financial loss.

He sent Shaun to buy a *Liverpool Gazette* and *Myer's Weekly Advertiser*, then went through the papers scattering his desk, looking for the cotton receipts. He couldn't blame Bill for purchasing the Surat cotton. He would have done the same. It was only by chance he'd discovered it wasn't suitable for intensive weaving. Like Bill, he would have thought he was purchasing a sure sale.

When Shaun returned with the newspapers, Fergus clamped all the purchase papers together with a metal clip, keeping back those for the cotton. He handed the bundle to Shaun. 'I think I'd better give you these to itemise. Dicken and I can cost everything when I've married up the invoices to this list. I'll look at the *Glasgow Gazette* at the club.'

Registering Shaun's bright eyes and obvious engagement with the cargo list, he went on, 'How are you feeling, Shaun?'

'Sure, it's exciting and I'm glad we've jobs to be getting on with. As the Lord's my witness, when word gets out what we're expecting, they'll be knocking the warehouse doors down to get their share. We'll be able to serve drinks and cakes to the queue outside and make an extra few shillings.'

Despite his depressed mood, Fergus chuckled. 'If only. We'll need to engage more help, and I'll have to sign up for that extra warehouse space we were offered. I understand it's still available.' As he was speaking, he scolded himself for dwelling only on potential adversity. The Louisa Line had two ships working profitable contracts and a third coming home with a full hold, with the potential to make a lot of money to see off his personal debts. He'd firmed arrangements with several companies to charter out the *Ketton* in the coming months. On paper, all could be potentially profitable. But try as he might, the words '400 bales of Surat cotton' kept spinning round his head.

✳ ✳ ✳

At the end of the day, Fergus strode purposefully home, to be greeted at the door by a smiling wife and a tail-wagging Charlie. Becky took his coat.

'I hear the *Ketton*'s on her way home laden with treasure.'

'I thought Rory might be home before me with the news.'

'And the cotton?'

'Four hundred bales.' He adopted what he hoped was an unconcerned voices.

'Four hundred, did you say?' Becky was sifting some flour into a mixing bowl.

'Yes. What will be will be. I've decided there's no point worrying. She's expected at the end of the month.' He picked Becky up by the waist. 'We must celebrate our cargo.'

'If you think we have something to celebrate, but I'm doing some baking right now. I'm making Christmas cakes for the folk in Shepherd's Court.'

'Not just Lois's family?'

'If I did that, I think others might be jealous, or Lois's ma might feel they have to share it out. There's five dwellings with five or more in each, so I thought I'd make five cakes.'

He bent to kiss the top of her head. 'My darling, you are so kind and thoughtful.' She was so happy, he decided not to go on to mention that the cotton was from Surat. In any case, she hadn't asked.

He took her in his arms and buried his nose deep into her hair.

'Have I told you in the last day or two how much I love you?'

'You whispered the very same in my ear this morning.'

'Ah, yes, this morning when I was late for the warehouse and Rory had left.'

'Hardly my fault.'

'Oh, but it was, a great deal so.' He grinned mischievously at her.

Becky picked up a glass-drying cloth and flicked it at him. 'Well, it won't be the last time you're late, that's one thing I've no doubts over.'

CHAPTER FIFTEEN

Two days later, at the Indian King, Dolly thought it 'grand' when Becky told her Elizabeth was taking her and Rory to the theatre the next day.

'What a surprise. Tomorrow? Fergus not going with you?' Dolly asked.

She shook her head. 'She wants it to be a special treat – just her, me and Rory. She's so good with him and he adores her. Who'd've thought they'd become so close? The pit lad and the town's *grande dame*. True, there's not many she'd let call her Mrs S.'

Dolly put a hand to her chest. 'Aye, it warms my heart to see it. She may have strange standards of refinement, and sometimes a rather dour manner, but she's a soft heart inside. Since you've wed, she's accepted you.'

'She's had to.'

'Well, there's accepting and putting up with, and they're not one and the same. Nay, she accepts you as one of the Shackleton family, and Rory too, being family as her son's ward, if not by blood.'

'She spends a lot of time with him when he's at Queen Street, feeding greens to Harry. Do you know why he's called Harry?'

Dolly shook her head.

'He came from Harras Moor, and so Rory decided Harry was an appropriate name. It was Elizabeth who bought him. She spoke to Lord Lowther's gamekeeper.'

'He's a rabbit with a pedigree, then. There you are. She wouldn't do that for just anybody. He's her stand-in grandson and when real ones come along, she'll open her heart and make more love to enclose them. As will I.'

❃ ❃ ❃

It was five o'clock, and Becky and Rory were due to meet Elizabeth at the theatre entrance at half past.

'I can't believe you've grown so much so quickly,' said Becky, pulling Rory's waistcoat together in a vain attempt to try to lessen the gap between the shiny pearl-shaped buttons and their intended holes.

'I can't help it,' he said. 'I've grown.'

'Indeed, you have. It fitted you perfectly a month ago.' Becky was cross with herself for not trying the waistcoat on earlier, when there would have been time to move the buttons.

Rory looked down at the noticeable gap 'twixt button and hole. 'What are we going to do? This is my best.'

'You'll have to keep your jacket fastened.'

'Even if I'm too hot?'

'Aye, even if you're too hot.'

Rory turned to Fergus. 'What do you think?'

'I think you'll be eating us out of house and home if you keep growing at the same rate.'

They all laughed.

'Seriously?' he asked.

'My mother used to be extremely particular about dress, but I have to admit, with you she is less so. I suggest if you get too hot you ask her politely if she'll let you take your jacket off. Don't do it without asking.'

Becky was thinking this was true. Whereas Elizabeth generally had high, rigid standards of behaviour, she was often surprisingly lenient with Rory. It was almost as if he could do no wrong. She was beginning to wonder if he was in danger of being spoiled by her. However, she quickly dismissed the thought, since his days at sea would drum out anything precious Elizabeth might manage to instil in him.

At the theatre, all comers having braved a strong westerly wind coming in off the sea and needing their winter coats, Elizabeth was greeting friends and acquaintances. When she saw Becky and Rory, she waved and beckoned them over.

'My, you do look smart, Rory, in your coat. I hope you won't be too warm.'

Rory gave Becky the quickest of winks.

Elizabeth strode over to hand their tickets to an usher, who was wearing a white curly wig and was dressed in red livery with shiny gold epaulettes. He greeted her by name and studied their tickets.

'You're not in your usual box this evening?'

Elizabeth shook her head. 'This is a special treat for

Rory here and I think he will enjoy the evening more in the throng. Especially being close to the animal entertainers.'

'If you're sure? It can get lively by the stage. We've a vacant box if you'd prefer?'

'Quite sure, thank you.' Elizabeth turned to Becky and said, *sotto voce*, 'At these Children's Opera Company events they throw wrapped confectionery into the audience. We'd be too high up in a box for him to have a chance of catching any.'

The usher led them to the second row of seats. Rory reached for Elizabeth's hand. 'It's magical, Mrs S, absolutely magical. Look at those red curtains.'

'They're what we call "plush",' said Elizabeth, beaming from ear to ear.

'Wait until they go up,' said Becky, unwrapping a barley sugar and handing it to him. 'It'll be even more magical.'

At that moment the Master of Ceremonies, in a ridiculously oversized top hat, chequered waistcoat and gaudy tartan trousers, marched onto the stage and began waving a baton at the audience. Immediately, the band at the front struck up with the National Anthem. Everyone stood and, with the Master of Ceremonies' encouragement, began singing. As they drew to the end of the last verse, the curtains opened to reveal the stage. A loud exaggerated 'ooh' rose from the audience.

Becky thought how for a small theatre it was an impressive stage – well over twenty feet in depth and thirty or more in width. It was lit by a plethora of gas lights. Voluminous side curtains billowed out, while the rear stage scenery was painted onto boards. The effect was of a wooded glade with a small lake in the distance.

Rory drew in a breath. 'It's marvellous. Absolutely marvellous.'

Becky had to agree. The whole stage glistened, and although it was not her first visit to the Theatre Royal it was proving, with Rory's obvious captivation, to be her most enjoyable.

The first act was the 'artiste singer' Madame Firenze, a portly lady with a large bosom, whose stock-in-trade was well-known operatic arias. This was followed by 'Mr Wizard Jacobs from The Strand Theatre, London', a magician who pulled a rabbit from a top hat, causing Rory to squeal with delight and half stand up from his chair. As they were so close to the front, the magician could see him quite clearly over the footlights. He bowed and took off his hat, saying, 'Thank you, young sir, for your enthusiastic appreciation.'

Becky could see Rory was thrilled at being singled out and her eyes met Elizabeth's. She was smiling broadly.

'Look at the wonder in his eyes,' she said.

'He loves it,' said Becky. 'Thank you so much for inviting us.'

Rory appeared less inspired by a tableau from Charles Dickens' *Oliver Twist*, starring Oliver and a particularly obese Mr Bumble, the workhouse beadle. Becky thought it rather slow, and the pathos it was supposed to present failed to come across to the audience, who began talking amongst themselves before it had finished.

The Master of Ceremonies, aided by a middle-aged

lady introduced as 'the celebrated comic singer Madame Celeste', led three lively songs with easy-to-remember choruses involving a great degree of audience participation and enjoyment. But the highlight for most turned out to be Mr Greenworthy's Performing Canines. Each dog wore a pointed Pierrot hat with a coloured pom-pom at the top and matching collar ruff. They began by performing a series of little tricks, jumping through hoops and standing on upturned buckets. Muffled, embarrassed giggles ran through the audience when one of the dogs, a little smaller than the rest, kept going wrong. Then, when it became obvious that he'd been trained to do everything wrong, the giggles turned into delighted guffawing and clapping of thighs. If the other dogs turned to the left, he went to the right. If they filed past in a straight line, he walked in circles, chasing his tail, causing Mr Greenworthy to bang his silver-headed stick on the ground. He and the other dogs would have to wait until the wayward performer, tail between his legs, made his way back into line.

Rory, having thrown off his coat forgetting to ask Elizabeth for permission to do so, was laughing and punching the air with his arms. Becky's ribs ached with the amusement of it all, and Elizabeth began patting at tears of laughter with a lace-edged handkerchief.

After the Master of Ceremonies' final rousing song-and-dance number, the confectionery was thrown into the auditorium. A sweet passed over Rory's head and, turning round to catch it, he glanced up.

He nudged Becky. 'Look, it's our Shaun and Miss Evangelina. Their heads are really close.' All Becky could see was a sea of faces. Rory persisted, pointing with an outstretched finger. 'Look, up there.'

Becky followed his pointing to the boxes and saw Shaun with Miss Evangelina, her hair gloriously ringleted. He was whispering in her ear and she was smiling. *Oh dear, poor Dicken*, she thought. *His heart's going to be broken.*

'Are they courting?' asked Rory.

'I don't know, but best not to mention it to Dicken. Let's keep it a secret. They're probably just friends.' Despite her words, Becky couldn't help noticing the couple were in the box alone without a chaperone. Also, that it was not one of the cheap boxes, but an expensive upper one. She knew Shaun was not without funds, receiving an allowance from his father as well as his Louisa Line wages, but she was still surprised. If Shaun was able to entertain Miss Evangelina so royally, Dicken didn't stand a chance. Although Becky thought Dicken's set ways rather waspish and somewhat peculiar, she'd no desire to see him hurt. In her heart, Becky had always thought Miss Evangelina was toying with Dicken. To her, he was a diversion, and when someone better, more worldly, showed an interest, she would soon have her head turned. When that happened, how would she feel if the boot was on the other foot?

CHAPTER SIXTEEN

Over the Christmas holiday, Fergus joined in wholeheartedly with the festivities and maintained a positive outlook, but the potential problem of the Surat cotton continued to gnaw at him. He tried not to torture himself brooding on disastrous thoughts, instead dwelling on the pleasure it had given him to see Becky's face when she unwrapped the painting of St James. It had been a great success and was now adorning the parlour wall.

After Boxing Day lunch held at Queen Street, Elizabeth and Hector announced they would retire to rest, and Rory disappeared to the Indian King to play chess with Sergeant Adams. Since it was dry, and there was an hour before the light began fading, Fergus suggested he and Becky take a stroll in Castle Meadow. Other townsfolk had had a similar idea and, as they walked, they acknowledged people they knew as they passed by.

Becky took Fergus's arm. 'You seem a little tense,' she said. 'Is it something I've done?'

He stopped walking and turned to face her. 'No, not at

all. You make me more than happy. You are the one true happiness in my life.'

She touched his cheek. 'As you are mine. Not forgetting Rory.'

'Yes, Rory too. Talking of happiness, remember his face when he opened Dr Fincham's present?'

'His whole face lit up.'

Seeing Rory's delight in the doctor's present, a whale's tooth and a scrimshaw needle, had brought Fergus much pleasure, too. 'He's already making some sketches for a design.'

They resumed their walk. Becky said, 'I suppose I should expect you to be tense on occasion until the *Ketton* returns.'

'There's a lot to see to. I'll sleep more soundly when she's back and the cargo sold.'

'Next week, do you think?'

'I'll begin scanning the horizon after we've let the New Year in. January will bring not just a fresh start, but also a returning ship.'

Up at St James's, on Christmas Sunday, after Rector Longrigg had preached an optimistic sermon about the New Year providing an opportunity for spiritual redemption, Becky and Rory began walking home with Dolly for an Indian King pork dinner. Fergus had declined her invitation to join them, saying he'd be busy at the warehouse all day and would eat a light supper in the evening at home.

Dolly told Rory to pull his cap further down to protect his ears from the cold, then said, 'Shaun's back from his Christmas visit. He arrived on the early post-boat. I encouraged him to come and pray with us, but he said he needed to catch up on his sleep after the rough crossing, and besides, accompanying his mammy and sister to church over Christmas in Dublin, he'd done more than enough praying to see the year out. So, I made an exception to my rule and let him stay in, reminding him not to help himself from the bar.'

'I've heard Mrs Conran is the boss in the family. Although I can't imagine Padraig bowing to anyone in business.'

'Me neither, but there's many a tiger in the office who's a pet lamb in the home. We get them in the Indian King. All hot air and male bluster until a message arrives their wife's looking for them. Then, quick as a flash, it's ale down their throats, tankard on the counter and a quick sprint home. Not all, mind you. Only those that's feared of their wives.'

'It's not like Fergus to miss Matins and be at the warehouse on a Sunday. He's getting impatient for news.'

'I'll send Shaun down after we've eaten.'

'Mrs S's cook's promised me some tasty greens for Harry,' Rory said. 'So I'm just going to Queen Street to feed him.'

'Don't be too long. Sergeant Adams would like a game of chess.'

'I'll be there, unless the *Ketton*'s back and then I'll be busy.' He pointed out to sea. 'Look, there's two coming in. Maybe it's one of 'em.'

They all turned to look into the distance. The ships were too far off to be able to identify. *The still before the storm*, thought Becky.

❊ ❊ ❊

The two ships docked safely, to be followed by several others. That day passed and the next was well into its afternoon before the cry went up. At first, Fergus didn't believe it when one of the harbour master's messenger lads burst into the warehouse. Touching his cap in greeting, he said, 'She's back. Your *Ketton*'s coming in.'

Fergus felt wrong-footed. He'd expected her in the New Year, even though Bill had suggested the end of December. He felt the nervous knot he'd been experiencing tighten in his stomach. His eyes raced round the office registering nothing; his brain had taken charge and was crowding his senses with information, while delight and terror were fighting for supremacy.

Today, December 30th, 1861, is to be my day of reckoning.

The messenger lad was waiting, fidgeting with his necktie.

'Are you sure it's her?' Fergus asked.

The lad sighed. 'Mister, if I were you, I'd get down there reet quick and see for tha'sen.'

Fergus gave the lad tuppence, which he knew was overgenerous, and picked up his hat. Then, opening the office door and shouting for Shaun and Rory to come down, he began issuing instructions.

'Rory, I want you to go home and tell Mrs Becky I'll see her on the quay. Dicken, after you've locked up call on Mary McRae and tell her Captain McRae's back. Shaun, you come with me.'

A little later standing on the quay watching the *Ketton* draw ever nearer, seeing figures on deck preparing the ship for arrival, with Becky, Rory and Shaun by his side, Fergus was overcome by the excitement of it all. To his surprise, he felt tears prick his eyes and, looking down at Becky, he saw she was crying and laughing at the same time. Tears of relief from them both.

Mary arrived with a drowsy William perched on her hip and stood by them, her face a picture of joy.

The original meagre welcoming group soon became a lively crowd, with the townsfolk shouting, whistling and waving. As she neared, folk were able to identify individual men on the boat and names were shouted out.

Sven, the *Ketton*'s first mate, was issuing orders, concentrating on the crew and seemingly unaware of the growing pandemonium on the quay. Bill, ever the calm captain of his ship, was standing to attention, arms folded, lips tight shut, overseeing operations. However Fergus, on two occasions, saw him seek out his wife and son, then Fergus himself. On both occasions Bill gave a half-smile and slight nod. It was not Bill's way to wave wildly and display emotion in front of his crew.

With the ship made fast and the gangway lowered, the excitement on land increased.

Rory tugged Fergus's sleeve. 'When can we board her?'

'After the Customs House and other regulations have been dealt with. You know the drill. The clearing manifest, crew list and remaining sea-stores. We don't want to pay duty on the ship's stores.'

'Will that take a long time? I want to see every single thing they've brought back.'

'Possibly until early evening.'

'But all these folk are waiting.'

'Barring the first and second mates, most of the crew will disembark soon and disperse, because we're engaging local unloaders. Then Shaun and I will board.'

'Can't I come?'

Fergus conferred with Becky. 'The day's closing in. It'll be dark soon. What do you think?' he asked.

'Take him with you to see Bill and Sven. He can go below tomorrow. I'll wait here for him.'

'Why can't I go below now?'

'Because I've harbour-master business to see to with Captain McRae. It's been a long voyage and will take a long time to report. Not to mention that I need you at your best tomorrow, both here and at the warehouse. Finally, with the holds open overnight, the air in them will be a lot sweeter smelling in the morning. You've never been on a long voyage. Believe me, a visit tomorrow will be a more pleasant experience. You can go down with the second mate.'

'Not Sven?'

'Mr Nielsen to you when you're on board, remember? No, the first mate always stands at the gangway to keep account by checking the unloading. You know that. He's in charge when the ship's in port. The captain, or master, is in charge when she's at sea.'

'I thought it might be different when there's a lot to unload. But I can board today?'

'Briefly, but just to welcome her back. Then it's home.'

Rory was dissatisfied with his answer, but Fergus knew he would get over it.

He took Becky's hand in his and, leaning forward, said, 'I don't know when I'll be home.'

'I'll expect you when I see you, then.'

He planted a brief kiss on her cheek and made his way to the customs officials waiting to board.

CHAPTER SEVENTEEN

The day following the *Ketton*'s return, expecting to wake excitedly ready to start the day watching the unloading, Fergus knew before he opened his eyes that such an expectation was not going to be fulfilled. He'd had a nightmare and he recognised the early throb of one of his headaches. *Not today, please not today. I have so much to see to.*

When he sat down to breakfast, he found Dr Fincham's medicine and a spoon had been placed on his side plate.

'I can tell by your eyes,' said Becky.

'So can I,' said Rory. 'You've got one of your heads.'

'Is it that obvious?'

'Aye, and today you need to be alert.' Becky pointed to the medicine. 'The sooner you get some of that inside you, the better. I know it makes you groggy, but it works.'

Fergus poured himself a generous dose of the thick brown liquid and swallowed it. He wiped his mouth with his napkin and sighed. 'Today of all days.'

'When things have settled down, I think you should get further advice. Will you do that for me?'

'I'll do it for myself.'

'Perhaps see a specialist?'

'Perhaps.' He glanced down at his plate of coddled eggs and fat bacon and felt his stomach turn over. He pushed the plate away.

'I'll have that,' said Rory, putting his hand out for it.

Becky put the plate next to Rory and sat down. 'Fergus, you're not fit enough to oversee the unloading. If you push yourself, you'll be queasy all day. Lie down, let the medicine take hold and start the day later. They'll have to manage without you.'

Fergus knew she was right. He needed the restorative sleep the medicine brought, but he'd waited so long for this cargo, and to be deprived of watching their treasure in the light of an English day seemed a punishment too far.

Becky spoke to Rory. 'When you've finished eating, you and I'll go down and instruct Sven.'

'Can we take Charlie with us?'

Becky shook her head. 'It'll be too busy down there to keep a proper eye on him, and unfair to keep him on his lead when there's so much going on.'

'Leave Charlie with me,' said Fergus. 'Lois will be here soon and she can entertain him. Thank you, Becky. Bill can sign off any papers for the harbour master.' As he reached the door he said, in a dejected voice, 'I guess you're right. They don't really need me. I'm only the boss.'

* * *

When Becky and Rory arrived at the *Ketton*, the quayside surrounding the ship was bustling with activity. They had no difficulty spotting Sven; he was again standing right by the gangway, directing operations. Shaun was recording the goods coming off the ship in his notebook. A gang of broad-shouldered, bare-armed men were sweating, puffing and swearing, unloading sacks in a hand-to-hand chain into one of a line of waiting carts. The man at the end of the chain, wearing heavy boots, appeared to be the overseer, for he was chivvying them along, trying to speed things up.

There were tea-chests and what Becky took to be sacks of spices piled high on deck. Some twenty barrels with RUM stamped on the side had already been stacked, ready to be loaded onto a heavy farmyard-type cart. As they made their way over to Sven, Becky saw a cotton bale being loaded onto a cart. The word SURAT was stamped on the sacking in ugly, thick black lettering. She stood and stared at it in disbelief. Her first thought was to wonder whether Fergus had known all long it was going to be Surat cotton, and if so, why hadn't he told her? Was there more he was keeping from her? In her dismay, she missed her footing and tripped, and Rory had to put out an arm to steady her.

They found Sven and told him Fergus was laid low and would be down later. Becky was disappointed to find Bill wasn't there to ask about the cotton.

'He's at the customs house, signing off,' said Sven.

'Any trouble?' she asked.

'Not yet, but customs always complain about something.

It's the nature of their job.' He pointed to an official-looking man standing by in a dark blue uniform. 'See that fella there? Any minute he's going to wander over and instruct us to stop operations and open a barrel, or a tea-chest, and that'll slow us up. Wait until the Indian furniture crates and the curios start coming off. He'll want to see those because they're different.'

Shaun called Rory over and set him on counting spice sacks, and Becky made her way back to Coates Lane, where she found Fergus in his medically induced sleep and Lois ironing their bed linen. She had wanted to speak with Fergus about the cotton, but instead she poured herself and Lois a glass of ginger beer and set out four almond biscuits on a plate.

'Sit with me, Lois, for a few minutes. I'd like to ask you something.'

Lois put the iron on the range to heat up, and sat down and helped herself to a biscuit

'What do you know about Surat cotton?' Becky asked.

'It's from India. Before I went into the mill, I worked a small handloom. It's what I learned on at my aunt's. We used Surat to make small fancy pieces.'

'What's all the fuss about it being of poor quality?'

'It's how long it takes to be carded. It usually has stones and twigs in it, so no one wants to work it. Especially if they're paid on piecework, because it's more effort for less money. It's not as strong, either, which is why we made fancy pieces.'

'Fancy pieces?'

'Decorative cloths for dressing tables, antimacassars for chair- and sofa-backs. That sort of thing.'

'Handkerchiefs?'

'Sometimes. Things that can be woven on a narrow-width loom.'

'What about the mills? Can they use it?'

'The stones are a problem with the carding-machines and the threads are too short and weak to be of practical use on the mechanical looms; they keep breaking.'

'Are the stones put in to weigh down the bales?'

'I don't think so. They're caught up in the fibres. I think it's more the way it's harvested.'

'So, it can be worked?'

'It's been a while since I worked with it, but yes, it can. May I ask why you're asking?'

'I saw some Surat sacks down on the quay.'

CHAPTER EIGHTEEN

When Fergus woke, Lois told him Becky had gone to the Indian King to speak with her ma. He arrived at the *Ketton's* unloading at half past one. Things seemed to be in order. Intending to board and speak with Bill, he heard his name called.

'Wait, hold on.'

He recognised the gruff voice instantly as his father's and paused mid-stride. He turned round, waiting for his father to catch up. He was leaning on his stick, wearing a Russian-style fur hat with flaps pulled down over his ears, and his thick overcoat was tightly buttoned. He was wearing his what's-going-on-here face.

Fergus held out his hand. 'Good afternoon, Father.'

'Where've you been? I thought you'd be here earlier watching over such an important unloading.'

'I've been taking care of things at the warehouse.' Fergus wasn't going to tell his father he'd suffered another of his headaches. The last time he'd done so he'd received little sympathy. Besides, it wasn't a lie; he had called in briefly at Chapel Street on his way down to the quay.

'I don't know what you're going to do with all that.' Hector waved his stick at one of the larger carts loaded with well-packed furniture. 'I mean, it looks so foreign.'

'That's its appeal, Father. It's different. Exotic.'

'Well, I can't see folk round here queuing up to buy that sort of over-decorated stuff.'

'Thank you for your support, Father,' said Fergus, through gritted teeth. 'We'll be having a sale in Carlisle. There'll be an advertisement in the papers this week. We're starting the New Year with a splash.'

'That'll be expensive, not least transporting it all to Carlisle.'

'We've planned and costed. The smaller items will be on sale here at the Chapel Street warehouse, and spices and spirits dispersed through prior arrangements with local chandlers, alehouses and the like. We're also having a grand sale at the Freemasons' Hall for some of the ivory and smaller pieces.'

'As I've said many times, it seems a lot of work to me. I would have bought the ship and chartered her out straightaway, then sat back and watched the brass roll in.'

When Fergus spoke, it was with a clenched jaw. 'The difference is that you're fifty-three, whilst I am in my early twenties.'

'You're saying I'm too old?'

'I'm saying you're not of an age to take risks. I have health and the enthusiasm of youth, as Grandfather Norman did setting up Shackletons and taking on the first post-boat contracts.'

'I may lack some of the verve I had in earlier years, but I'm still *compos mentis*. If your shareholders don't receive their expected return on investment, including yourself, you might have to sell everything and come back to work on the floor at Shackletons. You know there'll always be a place for you there. I expect you thought of that when you set up this Mauritian venture.'

The last thing Fergus wanted to do was lose his own business and return to working full time at Shackletons with his tail between his legs. He would never do that. In a somewhat sharp voice, he said, 'Your safety net suggestion wasn't at the forefront of my mind, but it's good of you to remind me I have this option. Thank you, and now I've business to see to.'

Hector turned his coat collar up. 'Blustery out today and it's got much worse in the last ten minutes. I think I'll find a fireside chat with your mother an amiable way to spend the rest of the afternoon. I'll leave you to stand in this wind watching the crew and gangers. Then I'd advise you to take yourself off to your office out of this wind, or you'll get one of those headaches.'

Fergus climbed the gangway to find Bill waiting for him on deck.

'We've had a good morning,' Bill said. 'The gangers have done well.'

As fate would have it, he'd only just spoken when there was a loud shout of, 'Look out!' Fergus turned to see a tea-chest fall off the back of a cart. It hit the ground and broke open, scattering tea all over the quay.

'I spoke too soon,' said Bill. 'That's the trouble with crates, they split. Several of the cotton bales fell off the back of one of the carts, but they just bounced.'

'Where is the cotton?' asked Fergus. This was his main reason for coming down. He wanted to see it. He'd dreamt about it so often, it had almost taken on a demonic personality of its own.

'It's already stored in the Carter Lane warehouse. It's a good job you rented that extra space. The bales take up a lot of room, but I'm really pleased I got it. I'm sure we'll make a lot of money on it, with the cotton famine still going strong.'

Oh, no. All that warehouse space taken up, thought Fergus. He would have to tell Bill that Surat cotton was poor quality, but this wasn't the time.

After watching operations on the quayside for a while, he made his way to the Carter Lane warehouse, where he'd put Shaun in charge – partly because he needed someone he could trust and partly to separate him from Dicken.

A cart was parked up outside and Shaun was helping unload some wooden boxes. He was always ready to roll up his sleeves and put his shoulder to a job, unlike Dicken, who was more cerebral and very much a desk man. Fergus wondered how long he would be able to keep Shaun in Whitehaven. He knew when the call to return to Dublin came, Shaun would be off.

'Mr Shackleton, sir, it's good to be seeing you,' Shaun said, in his Irish lilt. 'We've treasures galore. Step this way.' He bent forward and, with a great flourish gave an exaggerated bow, gesturing for Fergus to enter the building.

Fergus chuckled, despite his low mood. Shaun was always good company. 'It's the cotton I most want to see.'

'There's plenty of it,' Shaun told him. 'It's on the first and second floors. You can't miss it.'

Fergus began climbing the stairs with dread in his heart. As far as the eye could see, there were bales of cotton. He'd come prepared and took out a knife. After testing the blade with his thumb, he slit open the top of the first bale. Immediately his nostrils were filled with the botanical odour of raw cotton. Had he had his eyes shut, he would have known its origin was plant, for there was an earthiness to its tang. He drew the smell in and found he could taste it – or was he imagining it? So far it looked and smelt like raw cotton and his mood lifted a little.

He put his hand in the bale and drew out some strands. He found softness, which was a relief. Then he dug his arm in as far as his elbow, his fingers scrabbling a way through the tightly packed material. He felt something and latched on to it, drawing out a spherical pebble. He dug in again and pulled out a small twig. He swore out loud, although there was no one to hear him. The bales had been filled with a better grade on the top than underneath – that or else during the voyage the rubbish in the bales had dropped down. Sure enough, it was Surat cotton, and even Fergus, in his ignorance of the different grades, could see they had two floors of a warehouse stuffed with sub-standard material. So much for making a profit. They were probably going to be lucky to give it away.

Later, at Coates Lane, Fergus dropped a handful of pebbles onto the kitchen table. Becky, who was sitting at the table reading, raised her head at the hollow, empty clattering sound of stone meeting wood.

'I can tell by your face, Fergus, without those pebbles, that you know it's Surat cotton.'

'Yes, and so do you. It was stamped on the bales on the quay.'

'And you knew it was going to be Surat cotton, didn't you? How long have you known?'

'From Bill's last letter.' Fergus bit his bottom lip. 'As there was nothing I could do, I decided not to upset you.' He ran his hands over the stones, spreading them out. 'I pulled these out of the cotton bales.'

'They were in the cotton?' Becky picked up one of the stones and rolled it between her fingers.

'Lots of them. Bits of twig, too, and some animal hairs.'

'This is what they meant by sub-standard?'

'That's right. It'll have to be hand-carded and all the impurities picked out.'

'So why did Bill buy it?'

'It seems he was caught up in a wave of enthusiasm for buying cotton. Everyone was buying it. I expect the dealers were only too happy to sell it to him, and he didn't know the right questions to ask. No mill will touch it.'

'No mill, but perhaps a handloomer? Lois told me she learnt to weave with it. What will you do?'

'Someone will take it, but they'll beat me down to less than we paid for it.'

'A big loss?' She picked up another stone and examined it.

'If we can't sell it, yes.'

Becky put her hand across the table and stroked Fergus's. 'I'm so sorry. Is it serious enough to lose our house?'

'I won't lie, it could be.'

Becky had every right to be angry with Fergus and he was thankful she wasn't. She seemed almost sympathetic and he didn't deserve it. *I must make the best of this bad turn of events for Becky's sake.*

'What about the Louisa Line?' she asked. 'Can't you sell a ship?'

'Not without threatening the liquidity of the business, both financially and reputationally.'

Becky gathered up the stones, dropped them into a saucer and put them to one side. Fergus could not help but admire her stoicism and, as if reading his thoughts, she said, 'None of this may yet come to pass and perhaps we'll be able to look back and think "Why did we worry so much?"'

CHAPTER NINETEEN

Fergus stood at the front of the Freemasons' Hall, the *Whitehaven Paquet* newspaper in his hand, listening to Shaun instructing the female casual workers they'd engaged for the two days of the sale.

'If someone shows an interest in an item then decides not to buy, particularly if it's an expensive one, be sure to take their name and address. Do you understand? That way we can follow them up.'

The workers bobbed their heads up and down and some said 'aye'.

'Hold out your hands.' Shaun checked each woman's hands and fingernails. 'If someone is looking at something, pick it up and hand it to them. You don't want to be doing that with dirty hands. There's a sense of ownership letting folk feel something in their hands, it helps them decide to buy. Remember to smile at all times, even if the customer is being difficult. If anyone asks for discount, call for me or Mr Shackleton.'

Fergus opened the *Paquet* and re-read the advertisement

he and Shaun had decided on during the first week in December.

'EXOTIC GOODS SALE,
FREEMASON'S HALL.
WHITEHAVEN
Friday January 10th, Noon until 9pm
Saturday January 11th, 10am until 9pm
THE RETURN OF THE S.S. KETTON FROM
MAURITIUS
Ivory combs, boxes, paper knives, carved elephant tusks, chess sets, Indian shawls, lengths of silk, fans, rugs, ribbons, footstools, mother-of-pearl inlaid boxes, mirrors,

ALL MANNER OF EXCITING ITEMS
AVAILABLE TO THE GENERAL PUBLIC
ON GENEROUS TERMS.'

They'd decided to group items on six large tables. The small items, such as jewellery, combs and decorated card-cases, were laid out formally, each table having a centrepiece of either a carved ivory boat, a mother-of-pearl inlaid box or a piece of Chinese red lacquer. Colourful shawls were stacked inside sandalwood chests, with some artistically arranged to flow over the sides, showing the way they could be draped. There were baskets of Indian ribbon lengths placed strategically on tall stools alongside the shawls. Shaun had come up with the idea of engaging one of the town's dressmakers to help with the display. She'd brought stands with her and was arranging calico and Chinese silk.

Fergus beckoned Shaun to come over. 'Do you think the display matches the advertisement?'

'Sure, I do. I'm expecting an explosion of people through the door.'

Fergus pulled out his watch. 'Half an hour.'

'We've had dealers trying to get in early.'

'I hope you sent them away.'

'We're not stupid enough to let them have first pickings, although it's a good job I was here, as Dicken might have let them in. He was crotchety with me.'

'Dicken is always calculating. I'll wager he'll have seen your action as turning money away, and for a bookkeeper that's a shocking crime. Did the dealers offer you money to let them in?'

'Aye, one tried, with the words "Everyone has their price".'

'What did he think yours was?'

'Ten shillings.'

'Foolish man, far too cheap. Was that the best offer you received?'

'No, but I'd no intention of letting anyone in before noon, and they soon got the message.'

'They'll be first in. Keep to our agreement – discount for quantity, no automatic dealers' discount for single items.'

'I'd like to make one exception. The dressmaker who's helped us with the display. She's expressed interest in some shawls and silk. She's been most helpful.'

'She can be our first sale. Offer her ten percent off the sale price.'

'We've two of her shop girls on loan as well, but they're waged separately. We've a total of ten – three recommended by Mr Nubley, the investor, from his foundry office, and the rest temporarily poached from other town businesses. There's a lot of goodwill in the town for you. With Dicken, myself, Captain McRae and you on hand, we should be able to manage.'

'Good. My wife is coming with her mother later.'

When they opened the doors at noon, Fergus could see at once they need not have worried about drawing a crowd. The room filled up quickly, with the townsfolk anxious to view the goods. They'd got off to an encouraging start, but were folk going to spend money? And would they pay the prices Fergus needed?

As master of the ship, Bill was much in demand, providing fascinating provenances for the goods and talking about the voyage and Mauritius.

Shaun was no less engaging. Fergus heard him say to one prosperous lady of the town, 'The ship bringing the shawls to Mauritius from India was caught in a terrible storm, so bad they thought the mast would break away and come down. The whole crew fell on their knees and prayed for deliverance, and guess what?'

He paused while the woman shook her head, her eyes glued to his.

'Almost at that exact moment, the wind stopped howling and all was calm. God's will, I tell you. We were meant to have these shawls. I'd say there's luck sewn into them.'

'Really?'

'As God's my witness,' he said. 'How can it not be thus?' He spread his arms over the shawl box. 'All these were on the point of being lost in that storm and here they are, safe in Whitehaven, looking for happy homes.'

'I'll take three for myself and my daughters,' said the lady. 'Kindly make out the bill of sale.'

'Was the ivory on the same ship?' asked a woman in a wide-brimmed bonnet, looking at the chess set. She was vaguely familiar to Fergus, but he couldn't place her.

'Aye, indeed it was.' Shaun picked up one of the kings and handed it to her. 'Turn this over in your hands. Can't you just feel the luck coming out of it?'

Fergus remembered what Conran had told him in Dublin, about how fingertips were capable of absorbing the essence of an article. Looking at the way the woman took the ivory chess piece, rolled it in her hand, then removed her gloves and almost caressed it, he could see it was true. She enquired about the price and, when one of the girls told her, Fergus saw a moment of hesitation. Shaun must have seen it too, for he said, 'We can't put a price on luck. I'd say for sure this chess set is a blessed item to have in your home. Feel the smoothness of this.' He handed her one of the bishops. 'You can sense the good fortune in your hands, as well as appreciating it with your eyes, can't you?'

The sale was sealed with an enthusiastic nod. Fergus was called over to be introduced and delivery arranged.

'I know your mother from church meetings,' the lady said. 'Please remember me to her and say you've been speaking with Mrs Riley. The last time I saw her, she was telling me about your young ward.'

'That will be Rory,' said Fergus.

'She told me he plays chess.'

'He does, but not with her. She can't play.'

'Well, perhaps we can change that, if I teach her.'

His mother was such an active woman, Fergus didn't think she was the sort to enjoy playing chess, but perhaps she would play short games for fun with Rory.

Mrs Riley peered over Fergus's shoulder and began waving. 'Here comes your father.'

Fergus turned to see Hector advancing towards them. He greeted Mrs Riley by name and she began telling him about her plans to teach Elizabeth to play chess. 'You should buy her one of the lucky ivory chess sets.'

Hector frowned. 'We've a perfectly good wooden one at home that we've had for years.'

Mrs Riley appeared momentarily startled at the rebuff. She turned back to Fergus. 'So many lovely things, I'm sure you'll do well today.'

After she'd gone, Fergus asked Hector what he thought of the display.

'Lots of over-decorated trinkets, if you ask me. I still say you'd have been much better putting the *Ketton* out to charter from the start, then you wouldn't have to oversee all this fuss and commotion. Still, looks as if you're bringing plenty of brass in.'

Fergus held his tongue, thanking the gods his father hadn't expressed his opinion in a loud voice. He was glad, though, to have received a grudging acknowledgement from him of the likely financial rewards. The exotic goods would bring in excellent prices, but he was thankful his father had no idea of the amount of sub-standard cotton they had in the warehouse.

❋ ❋ ❋

Becky and Dolly followed Dilys Croxall and her daughter Miss Evangelina into the hall. They all looked relieved to see the room was busy.

'Look at these combs, Ma,' said Becky. 'They're so beautifully carved.'

'They are lovely, no doubt about it.'

'Would you like one?' she asked. 'For your birthday?'

'What would I do with it?' Dolly said.

'Well, you could use it,' suggested Becky.

'They're too beautiful to use.'

'In that case you could put it on your dressing-table and admire it every time you sit there.'

'That seems rather self-centred.'

'You like them though, don't you?' Becky asked.

'Oh yes, very much.'

'That's settled then. Choose one and I'll buy it for you.'

'I'm not sure, Becky. It seems extravagant for something I'm not going to use.'

Becky leant forward and whispered in Dolly's ear. 'I won't be paying full price for it. I'm the boss's wife. Pick one up, go on.'

Dolly lifted one and ran her fingers along its tines. 'It's much stronger than it looks.'

'I think they're quite tough, so if you do want to use it, you can. Which one would you like?'

'This one.' Dolly pointed to a comb that was divided

into three panels. The two outer panels each had a carved peacock facing outwards; the central, much larger panel, was decorated with a mass of scrolling leaves and bounteous flowers in open bloom. There were tines top and bottom of the panels, making it double-edged.

Becky asked the shopgirl to put it on one side. 'I'm Mr Shackleton's wife,' she said. 'We'll settle up later.'

The group continued looking round. Miss Evangelina began sorting through the shawls, her mother beside her. Within two seconds, Dicken had appeared.

'These are so beautiful,' Miss Evangelina said. She held one up to Dicken. 'Which colour do you think suits me best?

'Blue?'

'Do you really think so?'

'Well, red then?'

Becky would have suggested a pale pink and light blue combination, had she been asked.

Miss Evangelina put her head on one side. 'I just can't make up my mind. Papa has generously said I may purchase something today. Isn't that right, Mama?'

Dilys Croxall began blinking rapidly. She hadn't appeared pleased to see Dicken and had quietly shifted away from him. Not a great distance, but enough for Becky to note the movement.

Dicken bent down, picked up a green shawl and held it out. 'What about this one? It matches your eyes.'

'I have blue eyes,' said Miss Evangelina sounding a little peeved.

At that moment Shaun approached, and Mrs Croxall smiled sweetly at him.

'There's one I think will particularly suit you, Miss Evangelina,' Shaun said, delving into the box of shawls and forcing Dicken to move to one side.

Dicken's back stiffened and the colour drained from his face. He became so white, Becky wondered if he were having some sort of medical attack. Or was he angry? She caught her mother's eye and was about to ask him if he was feeling all right, when Shaun produced a stunning, green-fringed shawl, into which were woven large orange and blue swirls, outlined with gold thread. There was no denying it was beautiful and, Becky thought, would suit Miss Evangelina perfectly.

'Ooh,' said Miss Evangelina, 'but it's glorious.'

'The best in the box, I think,' said Shaun, handing it to her.

Miss Evangelina immediately draped it round her shoulders. She turned to Becky and Dolly. 'How do I look?'

Dolly was the first to speak. 'It suits you very well.'

Dicken, looking as if he was chewing on glass, and still holding the shawl he had picked out, said, 'I prefer this one.'

'Your choice is much cheaper,' said Shaun. 'Quality is always expensive.'

Becky could imagine Dicken wincing inside. She felt she was witnessing a mediaeval stand-off: two knights, lances at the ready, battling for the fair lady's colours. Admittedly, they only had verbal lances at their disposal, but that the two men were engaged in battle was obvious. She wondered how it was going to end, although whatever the outcome, she was certain Dicken wasn't going to come out of it a happy man.

From the pouting of her lips and the shine in her eyes, it was obvious Miss Evangelina was enjoying and delighting in the confrontation.

With the shawl still draped around her shoulders she turned to her mama. 'Can Papa afford this one, do you think?'

Before Mrs Croxall could answer, Shaun said, 'Allow me to purchase it for you as a gift for your friendship to a newcomer in this town.'

Ah, thought Becky. *This is how Shaun is going to play his cards – a display of wealth*. She could think of nothing Dicken could do to win the battle after such an opening shot, and if she couldn't think of anything, then Dicken wouldn't be able to either, since of the two of them she was far cannier than he was. Becky began to feel sorry for him, then remembered how he'd upset Rory over wanting to tie up Charlie, and the feeling evaporated.

Miss Evangelina ran her hand lightly down her mother's arm.

Dilys Croxall bit her lower lip. 'That's not necessary, Mr Conran,' she said. 'Miss Evangelina's father will be more than happy to purchase this.'

Shaun was not going to be outdone. He took Mrs Croxall's gloved hand. Becky thought he was going to raise it to his lips, in an overly ostentatious gesture, but he stopped short to look into her eyes. 'Do allow me, Mrs Croxall. The shawl is so perfect and, after all, it was I who chose it.'

Mrs Croxall blushed, completely flummoxed. It seemed she could be won over by Shaun's flattery as much as her daughter. After a short pause, she managed to say, 'Well, as you're so insistent, perhaps on this occasion we can accept your offer.'

Becky didn't want to look at Dicken for fear of what his face would tell her, but she had to. He had pursed his lips and was staring at Shaun with hate in his eyes. Not once had Shaun deigned to acknowledge or even look at him. It was as if, for Shaun, Dicken did not exist. He had swatted him as if he were a fly resting on a windowsill.

Becky felt Dolly tugging on her sleeve. 'Time we were moving on,' she said.

When they were out of earshot, Dolly said, 'Do you think Dicken realises he has no future with the Croxall girl?'

'I've no idea. He keeps his feelings to himself. I've only his expression to go by. However, I fear when he does realise, he's going to take it badly. Fergus is going to be annoyed. I've been warning him it was all going to come to a head, but he's done nothing.'

'Well, what would you have advised him to do?' asked Dolly.

'Perhaps have a quiet word with Dicken, in a fatherly way, about romance and broken hearts?'

'He wouldn't have listened. It's obvious Dicken's much taken with the girl. If you ask me, he's had a narrow escape. She'll need a strong man to marry her. She'd only make Dicken unhappy.' Then, before Becky had time to respond, she added, 'And likely bankrupt him in the process.'

'Do you think Shaun's in love with her?' asked Becky.

Dolly chuckled. 'Oh, great heavens! Not for one minute. He's enjoying the chase, and now he's vanquished Dicken and won the fair maid, I expect the thrill will fade away. Our Shaun's a ladies' man, but he'll not settle down with the likes of Miss Evangelina. Regarding family, his Irish roots'll come to the fore, I've no doubts on that. When it comes to a wife, he'll be looking for someone who's going to be a good mother and a kind, loving Christian, with long, dark, luxurious locks, like his mammy.'

'How do you know his ma's got long, dark, luxurious locks?'

'He told me.'

* * *

When Becky described the shawl incident to Fergus he sighed. 'That explains a lot,' he said. 'Dicken has been impossible all day.'

'What will you do?'

'I ought to speak to them individually and threaten Shaun with shipping him back to Dublin, and Dicken with terminating his employment.'

'But you need them both.'

'That's what makes it difficult, and why I won't do it. Hearing about them has ruined my evening. We've been busy with the small commodities, and with word getting round the inns and alehouses, I'm sure we'll have another grand turnout tomorrow. Trouble's coming with those two, but the last thing I need tomorrow is feuding employees.'

Overnight, Fergus decided that of the two men, it was Shaun with his showman selling-skills that he needed at the sale; he would ask Dicken to remain at the warehouse and enter the paid invoices from the previous day.

Mr Dickinson, the sail-maker investor from George Street, arrived mid-morning the next day.

'You've enough folk here, and from where I'm standing, they seem to be spending money.'

'We've done well on the small ornamentals, especially since January's always a time when money is tight for people. Some dealers have called in from Keswick and asked to see round the warehouse. I was able to make some big sales on large items of furniture today. I'm sure I'll be able to present a robust report to you and our fellow investors next Wednesday.'

'Are we looking to an interim payment?'

'When I have the closing figures from today, we can discuss it next week.'

'You're not dismissing the possibility, then?'

'No, but I'm not making any promise either.'

Mr Dickinson was walking away, when he turned back. 'I've heard no mention of the cotton. I understand it's in store at the rental warehouse?'

Fergus felt his stomach churn. He batted the query away with, 'I'll be discussing that at the investors' meeting, too.'

'Nothing to report on that score yet, then?'

Fergus shook his head.

'I hear there's two floors of it. I expect we'll make a killing.' Mr Dickinson grinned at Fergus conspiratorially.

Since he'd faced up to the scope of the Surat problem,

Fergus had taken to calming his unease by telling himself the situation was going to work itself out and that something was going to come along. So far, though, he'd drawn a blank, despite it seeming as though most of his waking hours were focused on trying to find a solution. The discreet enquiries he and Shaun had been making had been met with headshakes and apologies. He must brace himself for passing on bad news at the investors' meeting – although that would be nothing to losing the house.

After the sale had closed, Fergus and Dicken drew up the sale accounts and a list of products sold.

'There was a good turnout,' said Dicken, with a big grin. 'I'll wager you're delighted.'

'Highly delighted,' lied Fergus, who had expected much more. As he told Becky later, 'Really, we only sold what you could call trinkets. The larger items and the cotton have yet to bring in funds. Perhaps Father was right – the great and the good in Whitehaven are not as interested as we thought they would be.'

CHAPTER TWENTY

Fergus, feeling nervous and in need of support, decided to take Dicken and Shaun with him to report to the investors at the Waverley – Dicken to take the minutes and Shaun to report on the Freemasons' Hall sale and future events. In the private room, they found Bill adding more chairs round the table. Apart from their short discussion on the quay when the cotton had arrived, Fergus and Bill had not discussed it at any great length. Fergus had not had the heart, after all Bill's excellent work in all other respects, to tell him the cotton appeared to be unsaleable until he knew for certain it wasn't.

Mr Nubley was the first non-company investor to arrive, indicating there having been no 'trouble at t'foundry' to delay him, as at the last meeting.

When the remaining investors, Messrs Dickinson, Heslop and Dr Fincham were served with coffee, Fergus cleared his throat.

'Good morning, gentlemen,' he began. 'We have received apologies from Captain Jessop, who is currently en route to Cardiff with the *Sophie Alice*.' He paused while Dicken made a note. 'You'll see from the information I am about to give you that the first sale enjoyed a most successful two days.' He signalled to Dicken who, exhibiting a rare serious expression, handed each man a single sheet of paper with 'SALE REPORT' written in fancy lettering at the top.

'We've also delivered the pre-voyage spice orders and the other perishable goods to local chandlers, but mostly to Frisby's in Maryport. In particular, I understand our ground Indian ginger has been markedly well received. 'He turned to Shaun. 'Is that correct, Mr Conran?'

'Sure t'is. The ginger and cardamom have been much in demand. Our pricing has been competitive. We purchased the cardamom for thirteen pence a hundredweight and sold at two shillings, and the cinnamon for nine pence, selling at one and six. Both free of duty. We've operated on the principle of 'a bird in the hand' and not held out for excessive profits. As a result, we've put some of our competitors' backs up for what they see as undercutting them, but business is business.'

How positive Shaun sounds, thought Fergus. He wondered if his fellow investors would recognise they hadn't realised the sale proceeds they were hoping for, despite the liveliness of the day and the number of buying visitors.

Shaun having paused a moment, Fergus took over the reins. 'The Bransty dye-works have purchased 200 of the 320 bunches of yarn, and the two casks of Calcutta indigo—'

Shaun interrupted, 'We've good quality dyes as well as spices.'

'The flax has been reserved for me,' Mr Heslop said. 'We need to negotiate on price. Perhaps we can do this today, so the purchase is seen to be above board by my fellow investors?'

There were murmurs of assent.

'In addition to these preliminary sales,' Fergus went on, 'we were fortunate enough to be visited by the Johnson brothers from Keswick last Saturday, and I am expecting a banker's draft for seventy pounds tomorrow.'

'Seventy pounds! Their warehouse will be full to the gunnels,' commented Mr Dickinson. 'What did they buy?'

'They made some astute purchases of our larger items.'

'Skimming the cream off our stock?' Mr Dickinson frowned.

'No, a varied inventory, all top quality.'

'Ah, expensive, then.' His frown became a satisfied smile.

'Top quality always is,' said Shaun. 'But sold to them in the right way, folk can be persuaded to open their purses.'

Fergus was anxious to get on with the business in hand and get it over with. 'Thank you, Mr Conran. At this point, I would like to invite you to report on last week's two-day sale.'

Shaun stood up. Fergus noticed he was wearing a new patterned waistcoat. It suited him. He thought of Dicken in the sad brown waistcoats he wore, and how in a way they suited the bookkeeper's personality – steady and a bit dull.

'Gentlemen,' Shaun said. 'I think we should have advertised our recent sale as "a two-day Ladies' Sale", for it is the good ladies of Whitehaven we must thank for most of our profits. Cast your eyes on the sold product list. You will see the Indian and Chinese silk textiles sold splendidly. Shawls, Indian ribbons, and jewellery were flying out the door—'

Mr Dickinson interrupted. 'All at good prices?'

'In most cases double or even triple what we paid.' He went on to provide some examples. Mr Dickinson attempted to ask more questions, but on the third occasion Fergus halted him.

'Mr Dickinson, sir,' he said, waving the sale report. 'All in good time. Let us allow Mr Conran to finish.'

Shaun picked up where he had left off. 'The point I was making about a Ladies' Sale was that it was the womenfolk of the town, accompanied by their husbands, who were bought "treats". The atmosphere was of a social event. Folk meeting other folk, greeting them warmly.'

'So,' began Mr Nubley, 'I understand you to be saying we still have the main profits to come?'

Before Shaun or Fergus could respond Mr Dickinson butted in, his lips tight. 'Never mind all this reporting. What I want to know is whether we're getting an interim dividend today. Well, are we?'

The sail-maker appeared so fixed on profits and returns, Fergus wondered if he was experiencing financial difficulties now the bigger ships had moved to Liverpool. He quickly dismissed the thought. Mr Dickinson was likely just a solid businessman behaving as one.

He cast a nervous glance around the room. He would deliver the good news before broaching the subject of the Surat cotton. 'If we reach agreement today, I would suggest an interim payment of £36 per investor. This, you will all appreciate, is approximately the average master mariner's yearly salary.'

There was an awkward pause.

Mr Dickinson frowned. 'Is that all? We made our investments in June and it's now January. That's nigh on eight months. I take it I have everyone's support on this?'

Dr Fincham, who so far had remained silent, peered over his spectacles and said, 'We all knew, when we invested, that Mauritius was a long way away. The voyage alone was going to take months.'

Mr Nubley scratched his side-whiskers. 'Aye, this investment wasn't the same as putting it in the Lowther Street Savings Bank with set interest payment dates.'

Mr Dickinson shrugged. 'Aye, well, I suppose things are moving along, but it seems to me it's at a snail's pace. Even so, I want it minuted that I'm disappointed.'

'We've a load of mid-sized goods leaving for Dublin later this week,' Fergus continued. 'Small cabinets, tea-tables, that sort of thing.' He pointed to Shaun. 'Mr Conran senior is acting as our agent for these goods. He's confident he can raise higher prices than in England, as such goods are harder to find in Ireland. We're looking to Carlisle for the big profits and, if necessary, perhaps Manchester or Leeds.'

'Then there's the cotton to come,' said Mr Dickinson. 'That will see us good no doubt, with the current famine.'

Out of the corner of his eye, Fergus saw Dicken and Shaun looking at him. The moment was upon them – or, more specifically, upon Fergus. He picked up his sales report, folded it in half and put it in his waistcoat pocket.

'It is a truth we have 400 bales of raw cotton,' he said.

'That's not to be sneezed at,' said Mr Heslop.

Fergus put his hand on his chest. 'Mr Nubley. You may remember at the last meeting that you made the comment you hoped it would not be Surat cotton.' He paused. All eyes in the room were on him – some friendly, some curious and Mr Dickinson's, as always, confrontational. 'I have to report that the cotton we have is indeed Surat cotton.'

Mr Dickinson, who had leaned back in his chair, sat up straight. 'What? Surat? But we can still sell it at a profit, can't we?'

Fergus sighed. 'Perhaps.'

Mr Dickinson turned on Bill. 'What on earth possessed you to buy second-rate cotton?'

Bill blanched. 'I think it's obvious. I was advised it was a prudent purchase. I should add I was not the only English captain purchasing cotton with a view to making excellent profits.'

'It's not his fault,' said Fergus, raising his voice slightly. He wasn't going to let any of the investors blame Bill. 'Captain McRae's done a wonderful job under difficult circumstances, far from home. As he says, he was encouraged to purchase cotton because reports in Cape Town, direct from the American southern states, were that the civil war would continue for some time, and so it is proving.'

Mr Dickinson went into full flow. 'I'd say it was folk wanting to get rid of bad stock as said that.'

'Mr Dickinson, sir, I accept, with hindsight, that in my ignorance I made an error of judgement. I apologise, without reservation, to you all with the proviso that my intention was to increase our profits. I remind you that I too am an investor. Might I however suggest that we are where we are, and this going over how and why I obtained the cotton is not getting us anywhere.'

Mr Heslop shouted out, "Hear, hear. We need to look to the future not the past. To my mind the war will be over by spring and good cotton will flood in. We need to get rid of the 400 bales quickly.'

Mr Nubley spoke up. 'When I suggested Surat was sub-standard, I meant in comparison to the top quality. You may be able to sell it in these desperate times, it's a question of price. What did you pay for it?'

'We paid the equivalent of one shilling and eightpence. The price yesterday on the Liverpool exchange was one shilling and ninepence.'

'Bah, that's not good,' Dickinson said. 'There's nowt but a tickle of profit in it, and none when you factor in transportation. Perhaps we should hold on to it and watch the price rise even further, before there's an influx at the end of the war in the spring.'

Mr Nubley tapped the table with the flat of his hand. 'Gentlemen, if you will allow me. I've recently been in Liverpool and dined with a member of the Liverpool Cotton Brokers' Association. I have up-to-date information.'

'Please continue,' said Fergus. He could think of

nothing hopeful emanating from the association while the war was in full cry.

'There is unlikely to be a sudden influx when the war ends because the fine-grade cotton already harvested is decaying, or perhaps one should say rotting, in the New Orleans heat, in poorly constructed and ill-ventilated warehouses. As a result, should the war cease tomorrow, stocks will have suffered serious deterioration and be sub-standard upon reaching these shores. In fact, the current stockpiles will likely need to be taken out of the warehouse and destroyed *in situ* in New Orleans. The same will apply if we hold back our cotton. It too will deteriorate.'

'Don't you have a similar problem storing flax and hemp for your sails Mr Nubley?' asked Bill.

'We've never had a problem with storage of any of our raw materials because we don't bulk purchase,' said Mr Nubley. 'We're cautious for these particular reasons.'

'Didn't you say at the last meeting you used cotton for some sails?' asked Dr Fincham.

'Yes. American highest-grade when needed.'

'What about the ropery yon side of the meadows?' asked Mr Dickinson. 'Don't they use cotton?'

Mr Heslop smoothed his hair. 'They might for domestic rope, but cotton has a high shrinkage-rate, making it unsuitable for marine ropes, and that's their main line of business.'

Mr Dickinson cut in again. 'This is all most unsatisfactory. Tell me, Captain McRae, who did you speak with in Cape Town? Who gave you this advice on purchasing 400 bales of cotton?'

'Does it matter?' asked Fergus, irritated.

'Indeed it does. Come now, Captain McRae, kindly answer my question.'

'I spoke with several people from America and other traders. The only one you may have heard of is Captain Fletcher from Brocklebanks, who carried our post for us.'

Mr Dickinson pounced. 'Well, that tells me all I need to know. He *would* recommend you stock up with Surat cotton. Brocklebanks are a major competitor. His aim must have been for us to lose money on our investment.'

'I hardly think…' began Bill.

Fergus stood up. 'Mr Dickinson, for you to suggest such an underhand motive on Captain Fletcher's part is an abomination. I have known him for many years as an honourable, competent master. Brocklebanks do not worry about the likes of us as competitors. We are far too small. I think you should withdraw your accusation.'

Mr Dickinson rose. 'I've been in business for a long time and I know when someone's trying to swindle me.'

Dr Fincham shook his head. 'You're surely not suggesting your fellow investors are swindling you, are you?'

'No, I most certainly am not. I am suggesting that Captain Fletcher and others deliberately recommended Captain McRae purchase the cotton to reduce our profits.'

Fergus banged his fist on the table. 'Gentlemen, I have spoken with Captain Fletcher and I cannot accept this interpretation of events. He sought me out to meet with me face to face, to bring news of my crew and ship. He would hardly have done this had he tried to swindle my captain. We seem to find ourselves in unfortunate discord. I think we must move on and accept we cannot keep the cotton and we must find a buyer as soon as possible.'

'I agree,' said Mr Heslop. 'Finding a buyer is the simplest answer to our problem. Although Surat cotton is not the finest, there should be a place for it, as long as the American cotton ports continue to be blockaded. The mills will have to adapt to survive.'

Dr Fincham spoke. 'What are you suggesting we do?'

'There may be a market of some kind. It should not yet be assumed that we are forced to sell off cheaply. I would recommend we make further enquiries.'

Fergus, after Mr Dickinson's unnecessary outburst, felt a wave of relief that Mr Heslop could see a potentially positive side to their predicament. However, this was followed by a stab of doubt. He'd felt the pebbles lodged in the bales with his own fingers and pulled out the twigs.

After coming to a satisfactory price for Mr Heslop's flax, the meeting was formally closed. On the walk back to Chapel Street, Dicken, not having been free to make his Wednesday pilgrimage to balance the books at the Seamen's Haven, said he would attend on Friday instead. Then, in a voice Fergus guessed calculated to reach Shaun, who was walking in front of him, he said, 'I can't go Saturday afternoon. Miss Evangelina and I are walking out.'

If Dicken had expected a reaction from Shaun, he must have been disappointed. The Irishman continued walking and whistling under his breath as if he'd heard nothing, despite the fact he must have done.

As for Fergus, after the meeting finished he spent a short time mulling over Mr Dickinson's behaviour and his poorly judged accusations. He regretted asking him to come in with them on the cargo investment. He'd been disruptive from the start. However, he found himself dwelling more and more on the urgent need to find a buyer before the cotton began to deteriorate.

CHAPTER TWENTY-ONE

Becky spent the morning wondering how Fergus was getting on at the meeting. She knew it was a crucial one for them. Mid-morning, searching for a pair of warm gloves, she was humming one of her father's favourite, rather forlorn, folk songs when Lois tapped lightly on the door.

'I'm tidying up in the parlour, Mrs Shackleton, and there's this saucer with stones in it. Are you keeping them or shall I throw them out?'

'Oh, yes, get rid of them please, Lois,' said Becky. 'Mr Shackleton came across them in some of our cotton bales. I put them in that saucer to stop them rolling about. I'd forgotten about them.'

'I thought that's what they were. I recognised them from when I worked with Surat.'

Lois was almost out the door when Becky said, 'Wait. Can you remember how to use a handloom?'

'Definitely.'

'And the processes involved?'

'I know how to process cotton. It's something you never forget. Why?'

'If I found you a handloom, could you make something?'

'Certainly, but I don't have the time.'

She looked at Becky as if waiting for her to volunteer more information, but Becky didn't want to share the idea forming in her head, so she said, 'That's what I thought. It's a skill you keep forever.'

Later, when Fergus was home, and after he'd told her about the meeting and moaned about Mr Dickinson, he said, 'I had a quiet word with Nicholas Fincham in his rooms straight after the meeting.'

Thank goodness, Becky thought. *I won't have to nag him into making an appointment*. 'What did he say?'

'He began by asking if I had a headache today, because the investors' meeting did not end well.'

'And did you have one?'

'You would think so, but funnily enough I didn't. Anyway, I told him his linctus wasn't helping me as much as it had been and that I wanted and needed something stronger.'

'What did he say?'

'That he could increase the strength,' Fergus went on, 'but he really didn't want to. He gave me a long lecture about becoming too dependent on the medicine and that he'd prefer to take a different approach.'

'No, I can understand that, but he's right.'

'I didn't tell him I'd increased the dosage a couple of times already. The good thing is, he wants to get to the bottom of why I suffer from them. He asked me about what I ate, whether I had blurred vision, how long they lasted, all that kind of questioning. We've gone over the same ground before, but he was more probing than he has been. One thing he did ask which seemed to be important, was whether I ate three meals a day at regular intervals.'

'You do, don't you?'

'My immediate answer was yes, but when I thought about it, I quite often miss lunch.'

'You said you went to the club or that coffee-house near the warehouse. And you sometimes don't have breakfast. I can see straightaway that that's a bad thing. What did Nicholas say?'

'That I must eat three meals a day, especially breakfast. He's recommended a hearty bowl of porridge to start my days.'

'That's no problem, I'll do anything not to have to see the pained expression in your eyes when you've one of your heads. I can pack something for lunch if you don't want to waste time leaving the warehouse at midday.'

'I'll try anything. Oh, yes, he asked me about bright lights and said I should avoid them. I've to keep a record of my headaches and we've to review things in four months' time. In the end, he relented and gave me a chit for what he called "slightly stronger" linctus to collect tomorrow morning.' He took a note from his pocket and showed Becky. 'Although goodness knows when I'll have time to visit the apothecary. Perhaps you could go for me?'

Becky put her hand out. 'I can get Lois to collect it and drop it off at the warehouse tomorrow. Did Nicholas say anything else? Did he reach any conclusions?'

Fergus held back and Becky knew he was deciding whether to tell her something or keep it to himself. 'Go on,' she said. 'Tell me.'

'He said that if after the four months things are no better, I should go to London or Edinburgh and see a specialist.'

Becky's heart began thumping deep in her chest. 'You mean he thinks there's something badly wrong?'

'I didn't get that impression. Rather that there are doctors in these places who specialise in headaches and he was minded to refer me. Don't mention anything to Mother, will you? She'll enjoy thinking the worst.'

Becky shook her head. 'Of course not. Nor to my ma.' It wouldn't stop Becky thinking about it, though. She could tell by his face that Fergus wanted to change the subject and was relieved when he asked, 'And how has *your* day been?'

'I've been thinking about the cotton.'

He picked up the copy of the *Whitehaven News* lying on the table next to his chair and opened it. 'We haven't given up hope yet of selling it.'

'Why don't we ask Lois to go down to the warehouse and look at it? I think she's quite an expert, and you haven't really had anyone give a professional opinion, have you? She could take a look at it when she delivers your linctus tomorrow.'

Fergus shrugged. 'I suppose there's no harm in it.'

❊ ❊ ❊

When Lois arrived at the warehouse the next day with Fergus's 'slightly stronger' linctus, he took the package and thanked her.

'My wife tells me you've worked with Surat cotton.'

'Aye. A while ago, but I know a lot about it. I wasn't a registered cotton-grader, but I can judge it for you.'

Fergus called Shaun and the three of them walked down to the Carter Lane warehouse. Fergus could smell the botanical nature of the cotton immediately on stepping inside. Remembering the comments about American cotton deteriorating in the southern warehouses, he thrust back the stiff bolts of the main doors to the warehouse to let in the crisp outside air.

Lois took in a deep breath. 'Goodness, it's like being back in the mill. It's a while since I saw so much cotton in one place.' She looked up at Fergus as if awaiting instruction.

He pressed his hand into one of the bales. 'I've tested one of these. I drew out the stones you saw in the saucer and twigs. I won't deny that this is really not my forte.'

'Forte?' asked Lois.

'My speciality. I've no idea of the state of the rest of the bales. Do you think they are deteriorating? Can you tell?'

'From what I've learned over the years, smell is one of the most important things. As important as texture.'

'Yes, but how do we know if it's in good order?' asked Shaun.

'The best thing is for you to let me look at it properly.'

Fergus walked along one of the shelves. 'Here's the one I opened,' he said.

Lois pulled out a fistful of raw cotton. She raised it to her nose, teased it out and breathed it in, then rolled it into a small ball.

'Well?' asked Fergus.

'Since this bale has already been opened and aerated, I'd like to try some others, if you've a mind to open them.'

'We can do that.' He took his knife from where he'd hung it by a string on a nail sticking out of one of the building's beams.

'Won't they all be the same?' asked Shaun.

'That's what I want to know,' answered Lois. 'It's about…What's the word? When things are all the same?' She put the cotton ball in her pocket.

'Uniformity?' asked Fergus.

'Aye. If they're from pickings where the weather conditions were different, then the features of the cotton'll vary, too.'

'That makes sense,' said Fergus. 'I'm learning a lot about cotton from you today, Lois.' He looked at her as if for the first time. Suddenly she was no longer their maid, but someone who might be able to help them.

'Cotton's been my life for a long time. This knowledge doesn't do me much good, though, these days.'

'You're helping us,' said Shaun.

'And I'll see you're rewarded for your knowledge,' added Fergus.

'There's no need,' said Lois. 'I owe Mrs Shackleton a great deal already. I'm happy to help.'

The three of them climbed up to the second storey.

'Choose whichever bale you want and Shaun will open it for you.'

Lois walked along the rows of bales, taking deep breaths as she went. She stopped two-thirds along the central aisle and, pointing, said, 'That one.'

'May I ask why?' enquired Shaun.

'Because it's in different-coloured sacking.'

She went through the same procedure as previously, but this time she put the ball in a different pocket.

They opened two more bales before returning to the ground floor, where Lois placed the four balls she'd now made in a row on a small table by the door. She'd given nothing away whilst gathering her samples.

'I've laid them out in the order I chose them.' She pointed to the first ball. 'This is from the bale opened earlier. It has a slightly different smell to the others. I'd say that's because the air has entered and the oil on the cotton has had time to disperse.'

'Oil?' Fergus asked. Why should there be oil in with the cotton?' Had they been swindled after all.

'There's no need to be alarmed. It's the natural cotton-seed oil. When the cotton is harvested, small parts of the seed from which it springs are gathered up as well. It's normal.'

They'd been in the warehouse coming on half an hour and Fergus still had no idea whether the cotton was of any use. 'This is all most interesting,' he said. 'But what can you tell us about the quality and possible usage?'

'I'm sorry, I've gone too deeply into things. What you've got appears to be from the same place, despite the different sacking. The smell is correct for raw cotton. I don't sense any deterioration as yet, but I can't speak for every bale. Certainly, there's no mustiness or damp. They all have a uniform texture and colour. My sense is that the cotton is useable for a small loom. Certainly, no mill will take it, because the yarn will not be strong enough for the machinery.'

'So it's no good, then?'

'I didn't say that. What I'm saying is it's usable for fine handloom-weaving.'

'But –' began Fergus.

'Does there have to be a but?' asked Shaun.

'I'm afraid there does. The problem comes with the carding. It will all have to be done by hand, because of the muck in with it, and the fragility of the yarn.'

'Won't washing clean it up?' asked Shaun.

'That'll take off the oil and the bigger stones, but when I was turning the balls over in my fingers there was the stickiness that comes with the waste. You can get rid of it by careful washing and experienced carding to separate the fibres. Your cotton is usable, but in simple words, preparing the cotton for spinning will involve many people working so many hours, there'll be little profit in the finished goods for a wholesaler.'

'That's working in a mill?'

'Aye.'

'And on a handloom?'

'Much more likely, but you'd need a lot of them to shift all this.' Lois looked round at the neatly stacked bales. 'Now, if you'll pardon me, I've to be at the Seamen's Haven.'

CHAPTER TWENTY-TWO

Becky didn't see Lois again until the next day, and by then Fergus had reported back about the cotton. With Fergus at the warehouse, she walked the short distance to the Indian King, where she found her mother clearing up after the lodgers' breakfasts.

'You're here early, lass,' said Dolly, giving her a hug. 'Anything up?'

'I've an idea I want to ask you about.' Becky picked up a glass-cloth and began drying.

The kitchen clock struck half past nine and Dolly made to bustle out. 'There's a delivery due in fifteen minutes, but I'll get the barman to see to it.' She disappeared while Becky finished drying the last few pots and put them away.

'I've sorted that,' Dolly said, returning. 'Now, lass, tell me what's up.'

'There's nothing up, but I've a wild idea.'

'Go on.'

'You know all that cotton Bill brought back?'

Dolly nodded.

'Lois went to look at it yesterday and she told Fergus it's not unworkable.'

'Let me guess, you've thought of a way to use it?'

'You know me so well.'

'It's a truth. I know my lass.'

'Well, she told Fergus it could be used on a handloom.'

'So, it can be sold?'

'Yes, and no.'

Dolly raised an eyebrow. 'What do you mean?'

Becky explained about the extra work in carding.

'But it can be spun?'

'Aye. To make small fancy delicate items that could be sold.'

'Would there be profit in those?'

'Not for a commercial business, no, but I'm thinking if run as a charity, with no middleman creaming off the profits, then the cotton could have a useful purpose.'

'Who would buy it and set up such a business?'

'I would.'

Dolly's eyes widened. 'You? But you can't weave?'

'No, but I know someone who can.'

Dolly was silent for a while. Then, when she did speak, everything came out in a rush. 'I'm not sure, lass. It'd be a lot of work, and where would you get the looms, and who would work them? Who would do all this carding and, perhaps more importantly, where would they do it? Doesn't the cotton have to be washed?'

'I've thought about all that. The only real problem I can see is getting the looms. There's enough out-of-work Blackburn weavers who'll jump at the chance to rework their hard-learned skills.'

'Slow down. Let's think this through. First of all, you need the cotton. I'm assuming you can't just take it out of the warehouse.'

'No, it belongs to the investors. But I could buy it from them.'

'With what? You've no money of your own and even if you had, what's yours is Fergus's by law.'

'I thought perhaps charitable donations.'

'And then there's the washing. It's not like you can wash it in a basin.'

'No, but you could wash it in a tin bath. We'd only be dealing with small amounts at a time.'

'I think the idea is admirable, but to be honest with you, love, I can't see it getting off the ground. There's too much to organise.'

'I can try, Ma, and talking it through with you helps me sort it in my mind.'

'What does Fergus say?'

'I haven't said anything to him yet.'

'And what about the time involved? I'm assuming you'd be running operations. I appreciate you're looking for something to do, but this could take over your whole life. Think on it, lass, before you commit yourself.'

'I am doing, and—'

Dolly cut in, 'And what if you start a family? That's bound to come soon. Maybe two or three bairns, once you get started.'

Dolly's words cut Becky to the quick. She thought once again about the likelihood of her being barren. Almost nine months wed and no bairn.

'Well, there's no sign of that yet,' she said, in a scratchy voice which had the desired effect of making Dolly change the subject.

'I've to oversee the barrel changes.' She looked at the clock again. 'And Sergeant Adams'll be here soon.'

'Thanks for listening, Ma. It's early days.'

'I'll think on it too, lass. You may be onto something, but how you'd do it, I'm not sure.'

There was so much buzzing going on in her head, Becky decided a walk down to King Street to window-shop would do her good. Then, if the weather held, she'd spend a while looking at the ships in the harbour. That was always entertaining.

On the way she met Dicken.

'Good morning, Mrs Shackleton,' he said, raising his hat. 'Going somewhere nice?'

'Just for a walk. And you?'

'I'm off to the Seamen's Haven. I usually go on a Wednesday, but we had the investors' meeting. I like to keep the books straight, and missing a week will never do.'

Dicken was always so particular in his ways. The incident with Shaun and the shawl had been unfortunate, but life could be cruel. Especially to people who were a bit different, and Dicken certainly slotted into that category.

✤ ✤ ✤

'I'm thinking of appropriating your cotton,' Becky said.

Fergus, his mouth full of sausage pie, spluttered, and he had to quickly put his napkin to his mouth. Becky knew she ought to have thought more about her idea and prepared with appropriate answers to his questions, but she hadn't been able to hold back.

When he was able to speak, he said, 'Did I hear you correctly?'

'Probably,' she said, 'judging by your reaction.'

He repeated her words slowly, annunciating them as one would when explaining something to a child.

'That's right. I think it'll help everyone. The weavers get work and your cotton gets a fair price.'

'There's no denying we need a buyer for the cotton, but what exactly have you in mind and, perhaps more importantly, how will you pay the investors for it?'

'I want to set up a stock of small handlooms and use the Surat cotton to make small fancy pieces. This will give the weavers employment, and any profit can go into a charitable fund to lift their community out of poverty.'

'And paying for it?'

'I've thought about it. I'll need handlooms, baths, carding-combs, spinning-wheels and I can fund it through charitable donations. I realise that the law dictates that as a married woman I can only do this with your approval. That I can't set up a business on my own as I'm not a widow or a spinster. What's mine is yours in the eyes of the law and all that. Not that I personally have anything of value.'

'Yes, my name would have to be on any documentation. Funding via charity may not be easy. That type of funding is unreliable and you'd need trustees. And why would people want to support your scheme?'

'For charitable reasons. What do they call those

businessfolk who do good works? They get their names engraved on plaques, like those up at the infirmary.'

'Philanthropists.'

'Aye, that's it.'

'I think you've a wonderful idea that shows your concern for the weavers' plight, but you need a financial plan.'

'Is it true we don't have any spare money at all?'

Fergus felt a stab of guilt. 'At the moment, for such a venture, I'm afraid it's no.'

'Then I'm going to draw up a list of people I think will donate. Dr Fincham, for one.'

The *Ketton* had picked up a three-voyage contract to Madeira. Shaun marked off the dates on the office calendar and, while they were discussing her future tendering schedule, Dicken arrived.

Still in his overcoat and cap, and looking pointedly at Shaun, he said, 'I would like to speak to you in private, Mr Shackleton.'

'I've things to check at Carter Lane,' said Shaun, grabbing his coat and hat and making a speedy exit.

'Are you staying?' Fergus asked Dicken. 'Are you going to take your coat off?'

He waited while Dicken hung his coat on its peg and settled himself at Fergus's desk, in the seat opposite.

'Well?' Fergus asked.

'I've something bad to report. There's been pilfering at the Seamen's Haven.'

Fergus had been preparing himself for some petty grievance against Shaun. This was so different to what he'd been expecting, he didn't answer immediately.

'I'm talking about thieving,' Dicken said.

'Are you sure? What makes you say that?'

'I was there yesterday instead of Wednesday, so my routine was changed. I knew immediately that the cash-box was not where I left it.'

'Is that unusual? Doesn't the warden need petty cash? Couldn't he have moved it?'

'He always puts it back in the same place, on the right-hand side of the cupboard. It was on the left-hand side, and ten pounds is missing.'

'Ten pounds? That much? Are you sure?'

'Yes, I'm sure. There was a receipt inside for eight pounds for a donation that had been received on Thursday from the Mothers' Bible-Reading Union at Trinity Church. The eight pounds were missing, and the two pounds we keep for emergency payments for needy sailors were missing, too. All that's left is a few half-crowns and other coins.'

'And what does the warden say?'

'I haven't mentioned it to him yet. I thought I'd report to you first.'

'Why on earth did you think that? Surely the warden should have been your first port of call?'

'Well, what if it's the warden that's taken the money?'

Fergus could not stop himself from pulling a face. Then, sighing, he thought, *Dicken can be too naïve for his own good sometimes.* 'I hardly think that can be the case, Dicken. Think about it. Would the warden have gone to all the trouble to write out a receipt and then pocket the money? Apart from that, I have no doubt he would never stoop so low. He is a fine Christian man who has been in his position for many years. It may well be that he's removed the money for some purpose – an unexpected invoice, or something like that.'

'He'd have left a record. He always does.'

Fergus was cross; he didn't have the time for this sort of thing. He was sure there was a logical explanation, but to find it, he was going to have to go down to the Seamen's Haven with Dicken, and there were more pressing claims on his time.

'As soon as Shaun returns, we'll go and sort this out,' he said.

CHAPTER TWENTY-THREE

At the Seamen's Haven, the warden was escorting some visitors round. He asked Fergus and Dicken to wait in the day-room, where groups of sailors were talking amongst themselves, while a few were reading chapbooks and newspapers. Fergus thought how delighted his Aunt Louisa, who had died before he and Becky married, would have been to know the legacy she'd left was alive and thriving, and that these men of the sea were well fed and cared for.

It was ten minutes before the warden was free to usher them into his office.

'Gentlemen, you have serious faces,' he said. 'What can I do for you?'

'You judge us well, sir,' said Fergus. 'We have a serious matter to discuss that I'm hoping will turn out to be nothing.'

The warden straightened his back and assumed a sober expression. 'And what is this serious matter?'

'Dicken has reported to me that ten pounds has gone astray from the petty cash box.'

The warden's eyes grew big. 'Are you sure?'

'You can check,' said Dicken.

The warden opened his desk drawer and took out a set of keys. Then, opening the door of a small wall-cupboard, he took out a rectangular black tin box with gold-coloured stripes painted on its sides and placed it on the desk.

'Let us see,' he said.

As the box lid fell back, all three men peered inside. The warden's face drained of colour and Fergus knew immediately by his distressed expression that he was completely flummoxed. His physical reaction was such that it could not possibly have been feigned.

'Oh no,' he said. 'Where are the notes?'

Fergus drummed his fingers on the desk. 'As a trustee, I have to ask why you did not bank the money soon after you received it on Thursday.'

The warden fixed his eyes on his desk. 'It was sleeting so hard, and I thought the pavement might be icy. Then... then on Friday, I'm afraid I forgot about it.'

'You forgot about it?'

'Yes, I'm sorry, but I did.'

At least the man's honest. Fergus remembered how, after opening with a clear blue sky, Thursday had turned into a shocking day. He could understand why a trip to the bank had not seemed inviting. So much easier to wait until Friday, and then forget.

'To take the money, someone had to have access to my keys.'

'Who could that have been?'

'I suppose anyone when I'm not in my office, but who would know where the key is?'

'Someone rummaging through your desk could come across it?'

'Yes, I suppose so.'

'That means anyone in the building, then,' said Dicken.

'I suppose it does.'

'One of the sailors?' asked Fergus.

'Or the Blackburn girl?' said Dicken.

Fergus stared at him. 'You mean Lois?'

'Yes,' said Dicken. 'She comes in on a Thursday, doesn't she? She could have taken it.'

'She does laundry and cooking, but I suppose she could have access to my office,' said the warden. 'I hope not. She's a nice girl and bright with it.'

'Bright enough to steal, then?' Dicken said.

Fergus didn't like the way the conversation was going. He found it difficult to think of Lois stealing. *But Dicken's right, she could be desperate enough, and there was the laundry episode that some folks would see as stealing.*

'Did you leave your desk unattended when Lois was here?' he asked.

'I did, but it doesn't mean it was she who stole the key.'

'Shall I report it to the constable?' Dicken asked. 'He can question her.'

Fergus hesitated. He didn't think the Mothers' Bible-Reading Union members would be happy knowing their generous donation had been stolen, and it certainly didn't bathe the Haven in a good light.

'No,' he said. 'Leave it with me, and let's keep this between ourselves.'

'Will you question Lois?' Dicken persisted.

'Shall I?' The warden looked down at the box, as if hoping the missing money had suddenly reappeared.

Fergus turned to go. 'I'll speak with her, but with no evidence there's not much we can do. Besides, there are others who could have stolen the money.'

'Maybe,' said Dicken, 'but those weavers are desperate, and they're not local. The Seamen's Haven would mean nothing special to her.'

'It's not something she'd do,' Becky said, when Fergus broke the news.

'I agree,' said Fergus, 'which is why I stopped Dicken going to the constable. But then again, how well do we really know people?'

'I accept there was a time when she was desperate, but things are much improved for her. She's an intelligent young lass. She wouldn't jeopardise everything by stealing. No, I won't entertain the thought.'

'One of us still needs to speak with her. She may have seen something that can lead us to the thief.'

'I'll ask her on Monday, but in no way will I let her think she's suspected. It's far more likely to be a seaman or a delivery lad. They get all sorts of rum folk in there.'

'Any seaman who's stolen ten pounds will have up and skipped the Haven straightaway. I asked the warden if anyone had left in a hurry, but he said no.'

'What will we do? Will you tell your father?'

'As he's also a trustee, I suppose I have to. He's in Carlisle at the theatre with Mother, and there until Wednesday. I'll tell him when he gets back. We'll have to replace the money from somewhere.'

'A donation from Shackleton & Company?'

'Something like that. It's an annoyance I could do without, with the Carlisle show coming up in under two weeks.'

'Is everything going well for it?' Fergus hadn't mentioned the Carlisle sale a great deal and Becky was curious.

'Shaun's in charge. He's more than competent. He's found sale-rooms at the Lancaster & Caledonian Hotel and negotiated free accommodation for us. The goods are going up on Wednesday 29th, with the sale over the Friday and Saturday. Advertisements are in the papers now.'

'Have you had any enquiries?'

'There is interest, but the cotton famine is being felt there, too.'

'As bad as Blackburn?'

'No. Carlisle is a much bigger place and not everyone is dependent on cotton. We're aiming at the well-heeled merchants and professional people, not the working folk.'

'Has Shaun made any enquiries about selling the cotton?'

'Yes, discreetly, and no joy there I'm afraid. It's the same story – no profit in it.'

To her shame, Becky was secretly pleased. She already thought of the cotton as being hers. She could hardly wait for Monday, when she could quiz Lois about her plans.

❊ ❊ ❊

Becky waited until the laundry copper was boiling away, then said, 'Come, Lois, sit with me a while. I've something I want to discuss with you. I'll pour us some lemonade and I've some fig biscuits from a different baker we can try. You can take some home for the little ones, too.'

When they were settled with their drinks, she took a deep breath and began.

'How would you feel about helping me set up a small group of weavers using the Surat cotton? I appreciate it's not the best, but I understand it is usable for small, delicate pieces.'

'Me?' she said, in a soft, disbelieving voice.

'Aye, I'm hoping you can help me with what we'll need.'

Lois hesitated. 'I'm not sure what you mean. Do you want to set up a mill? Here in Whitehaven, at this time?'

'Not a mill, more a cottage industry. Small handlooms worked by yourself and others.'

'I'm not sure, Mrs Shackleton.'

'You don't think it can be done?'

'It can be done, but you'll need to see to the whole process. Carding, washing, spinning, then weaving. For a start, no one has a handloom. We were all working in the mills, and the few who did have them left them behind.'

'If I could get you the looms and the premises, could we do it?'

Becky waited patiently while Lois worked through the plan in her head.

'There are plenty'll leap at the chance for some work,'

she said. 'But not all can work a handloom. Many of my friends went straight into the mills.'

'But couldn't those friends be engaged to prepare the cotton? Carding it, that sort of thing?'

'I suppose they could. I've never thought about it.'

'You don't seem enthusiastic?' Becky was disappointed. She'd expected Lois to leap at the chance to be a part of her plan.

'Oh, no, Mrs Shackleton, I think it's a wonderful idea. It's whether you can do it.'

'I can't do it on my own, I'm aware of that, but I'm sure we can do it together. Will you help me? You'll be paid, and I'm certain you can find someone else to help me here at Coates Lane.'

'That bit'll be easy.'

'Let's shake hands on it then.'

Lois took Becky's hand, saying, 'There's your friends, the ones I gave my talk to.'

'Aye, Mary, Dilys and Ianthe. I'll ask them to help, and Mrs Shackleton senior, too. Now we've shaken on our joint venture, we need to make plans. I'll get a pencil and paper.'

Lois pulled an anxious face.

'What's wrong?'

'I think you've forgotten I've the laundry to see to today. It's Monday, Mrs Shackleton.'

'Oh, aye, but we can talk at the same time, can't we?'

'We can. I mean I have to get up and see to it.'

'Right, but before we do, I need to ask you something about the Seamen's Haven.'

'Aye?'

'When you were there on Thursday, how did you get on?'

'As I always do. I did the laundry, baked a few pies, left a jelly to set and went home. The warden didn't seem to have a problem with me. Was there something wrong with the pies?'

'No, nothing that concerns you. I'm only asking how you're getting on.'

'It's a nice job. I enjoy it, and we're all a lot cleaner.'

CHAPTER TWENTY-FOUR

Fergus set Rory on helping Shaun prepare for Carlisle. Most of the sale items were in Chapel Street, so Fergus went upstairs to see how they were getting on. He was met by an agitated Charlie at the top of the stairs.

'He can smell rats, Mr Fergus,' said Rory. 'He gets like this on board ship. He makes this special noise. Listen.'

There was an eerie chattering-teeth sound and suddenly Charlie was off, scrabbling down the side of a barrel.

'Go get it!' shouted Rory.

'We've had four already this morning,' said Shaun, pointing to a sack on the floor with four bumps in it.

'There'll be a nest somewhere.' Fergus peered into the dark space between two barrels. 'We need a cat for when Charlie's not here.'

'He'll clean you out in a day or too, make no mistake.'

'You should put Charlie on the payroll,' said Shaun.

'When you've finished here, take him up to the Carter Lane warehouse and let him loose. We don't want any vermin nesting in the cotton.'

'Have you decided what to do with it yet?' asked Shaun.

'There may be an answer.' Fergus pondered whether he should ask Shaun about Becky's plan. He waited until Rory had moved out of earshot and decided he might as well. 'In confidence, Becky's thinking of setting up some handlooms. She's drawn up a plan.'

Shaun opened his eyes in surprise. 'Has she? Well, there's a grand thing. If she can pull it off, that'll be a feather in her cap. She's quite the businesswoman, I'm thinking.'

'She was brought up in the Indian King, so she's a sound business background.'

'It's more than that. I sense Mrs Shackleton has a feel for trading. But if she sets up her looms, won't she need somewhere to do it?'

'It's early days on that score. It may only be talk, but I have to admire her for helping people.'

'If she needs a wholesaler for whatever the looms turn out, I'm sure my da would like to be her Dublin agent.'

'Hold on, Shaun, we're not even in the run-up to the starting blocks yet.'

'Like I said, happy I'd be to help out.'

Shaun was never going to be a half-measures man. It would always be all or nothing, as far as he was concerned. Fergus wished he could keep him, but he knew Conran would want him back in Dublin for his own business before too long.

❊ ❊ ❊

On Thursday morning, Fergus walked up to Queen Street to see his father.

'How was the journey from Carlisle?' he asked.

'The journey was wretched. Those trains make so much noise.'

'And the hotel?'

'Your mother liked it because the room had expensive velvet curtains and thick red carpet going up the stairs. I wasn't impressed. They frowned on smoking in the dining room, which as you can imagine I did not agree with, but they served a tasty cod in oyster sauce supper.'

'You enjoyed the theatre? *Hamlet*, wasn't it?'

Hector sighed. 'Yes, I suppose it was all right, but Shakespeare is so dreary, and that skull in the graveyard business – far too melodramatic, in my opinion. It didn't help that the theatre seats were narrow and too close, which gave me restless legs. Your mother kept nudging me to sit still. Anyway, you didn't come down here to ask about the theatre. What's happened? Becky all right? Rory?'

'There's been a bit of bother at the Seamen's Haven.'

'Rowdy incomers?'

'No, nothing like that. Some money's gone missing.'

Hector's bottom lip went out. 'What?'

Fergus related what had happened. Having some sympathy with the warden, he didn't think there was any need to mention him not taking the money to the bank.

'Who stole it?' Hector asked.

'We've no idea. Dicken reported it on Saturday. I've spoken with the warden and he's no idea, either. There was nothing untoward all day. It could have been anyone in the building.' He watched his father's face redden and his knuckles tighten as the loss sank in and their responsibility for it.

'Doesn't that weaver girl go in?'

'Yes, on a Thursday, to do the warden's laundry and cook.'

'I thought so. Your mother seems to think she's a good sort, but you know how I feel about them coming to our town and taking advantage of our relief. Why don't you put the constable on her?'

'Father, there is nothing to implicate Lois.'

'Don't you be too sure.'

Fergus tried hard not to show his irritation. 'Why are you so quick to condemn her when you've never met her?'

'I've heard tell of her sort.'

Two years ago, Fergus would have argued with his father and tried to make him see reason, but his growing maturity had given him the patience to accept Hector had some out-of-date ideas that no one was going to change.

'I've not involved the constable,' he told him. 'We don't want bad publicity, since it could affect further fundraising. If you agree, I think it best we make up the difference ourselves. I've given Dicken a marked pound note to place in the box. If it goes missing, then we'll have a chance to track it down before it leaves the premises.'

'You mean look through people's pockets and belongings?'

'If necessary. The warden will check the cash-box every day and Dicken will write the books up, as usual, on a Thursday. Petty thieves always come back for more.'

'Hmm. That's a good idea. I think the only way we're

going to reveal our thief is by catching her, or him, red-handed. It's strange this should happen exactly when there was so much money in there.'

'I've thought that, too,' said Fergus.

'Who would know?'

'I understand there was a presentation tea, so anyone in the building could have known.'

'I agree we'll have to replace the donation and take a loss on the two pounds' float money. Five pounds from Shackletons and five from your Louisa Line?'

Fergus had hoped Shackleton & Company would carry the complete loss, but he agreed and made a mental note that the Seamen's Haven must purchase a proper safe.

'You'll need to sell more of those absurd elephants, won't you?'

The remark irritated Fergus.

'We've the Carlisle sale next Friday and Saturday, if you remember.'

'I saw your advertisement in the paper when I was up there.'

* * *

While Fergus was at Queen Street talking to Hector, Elizabeth called at Coates Lane. Rory was painting a three-masted barque on one of his slates. He'd set himself up in the kitchen with his paints and an old jam jar filled with water and was telling Lois about being at sea, and the problem of feeding a hungry crew in a storm with the stove doused.

Seeing Charlie curled up in front of the range, fast

asleep in his basket, Elizabeth said, 'It's not like Charlie to be sound asleep during the day.'

'He's exhausted, Mrs S,' Rory explained. 'He got six big rats today and some babies, which shows we've got the nest. Shaun says Mr Fergus should employ him.'

'I think giving him a happy home and feeding him is payment enough,' said Becky.

Settled in the parlour with their tea, Elizabeth asked, 'What is it you want to discuss with me?'

Becky told her all about her idea for the handlooms, stressing it was a charitable venture. She braced herself for a negative or dismissive reaction, but as none immediately forthcoming, other than a look of confusion, she began laying out her plans in more detail.

'There are three things I need,' she explained. 'The first I already have.'

'What's that?'

'Weavers and spinners.'

'They'll need a wage.'

'Aye.'

'And the second thing you need?'

'Handlooms and other weaving equipment. I've asked Lois about these and she's sure we can pick them up cheaply somewhere like Carlisle, if not here. Especially the way things are.'

'Do you know what can be made on the handlooms?'

'Small items, like collars and cuffs and napkins, but I need to do further research on that side of things.' Becky poured them both a second cup of tea, taking care no drips from the strainer fell on the tray-cloth. 'Then there's premises,' she went on. 'Even if people work in their own homes, we'll need storage. I'm hoping Fergus will let me use some of the Carter Lane warehouse, where the cotton's stored at present. It would make things much easier.'

'Yes, I agree, it would be much better if everything was under one roof.'

'I just need donations.'

Elizabeth glanced at the parlour clock and stood up. 'Forgive me, I must leave, I've some errands to see to.' She picked up her gloves and began to pull them on. 'Would you like me to ask Hector?'

'That's most kind, but he thinks the weavers are a drain on the town's paupers' money. I don't think he'll donate.'

'I wasn't thinking of a donation so much as advice about how to proceed. Let me speak with him. I may be able to point out that weavers in work support themselves and the town.'

After Elizabeth had left, Becky wondered whether she had meant it when she offered to speak to Hector. Either way, she was right about the need for more research.

She went through to the kitchen and said to Lois, 'Put your coat on. I think you and I should go and look in some of the haberdashers' windows. I'll make sure we've finished before you need to be at the Seamen's Haven.' She tousled Rory's hair. 'You'll be all right on your own for half an hour, won't you, Rory?'

'I'll be fine, but I'll be better if I've a plate of biscuits at my elbow.'

She took down the biscuit tin from its shelf, taking out three shortbreads, which she put on a plate. 'Two for you and one for Charlie when he wakes up.'

'He's a good negotiator,' said Lois.

'I put it down to Shaun's influence and tuition.'

There were three haberdashers on Lowther Street, all with large window displays. At the first, Lois pointed out the articles she thought she could make and commented on the quality of the pieces. They discussed the antimacassars, place mats, dressing-table cottons and smaller items, like handkerchiefs and napkins.

'I think I should buy some of these items to use as samples, to show people what we want to weave.'

'That's a good plan, but let's look in the other shop windows first.'

At the second establishment they could both see that the cottons were lacking the quality and design of the first shop and were consequently cheaper.

'We don't want this sort of thing,' said Lois, her nose pressed up against the shop window to block out the sun's reflection on the glass. 'Look at those wavy selvages.'

'Buyers will turn their noses up at this sort of merchandise,' Becky said.

'The designs are uninspiring, too.'

They reached the third shop and, having decided the pieces on display were of a high enough standard, they agreed to go inside and buy.

The two men behind the counter greeted them like long-lost acquaintances. The taller of the two, who sported a bushy beard, introduced himself as Mr Herbert. His colleague, smaller and plumper of face, with closely shaven, rosy cheeks, was Mr Edris. A young lad ushered them to two chairs at the counter so they could shop in comfort.

'What can we interest you in today?' said Mr Herbert. Since he spoke first, Becky judged him the superior of the two assistants. 'We've new ribbons and lace,' he went on, pointing to a counter display on Becky's right.

'And don't forget those wonderful Italian decorative trimmings recently arrived,' said Mr Edris, indicating the window display.

'Perhaps you would like some refreshment?' asked Mr Herbert,

Mr Edris raised a questioning eyebrow. 'Tea with milk? Or perhaps lemonade?'

Becky had to suppress a laugh. They were speaking in turn like a theatrical double-act. She dared not look at Lois, who she was sure was also appreciating the humour. She managed to say, 'I'd prefer a lemonade,' before coughing to disguise a splutter.

'I'll have the same,' said Lois.

Mr Herbert clicked his fingers and the lad reappeared from behind a curtain. He must have been standing to attention, waiting and listening, so quick was his reappearance.

'Two lemonades for these good ladies, and quick with it.'

'As we were saying,' said Mr Edris, 'how may we help you today?'

'We're interested in small decorative cotton pieces.'

Mr Herbert struggled to hide his disappointment. Becky had no doubt he'd been hoping they would ask for the latest expensive fabrics and lace from London, or perhaps some enamel buttons from Paris – not what he surely regarded as 'trifles'. In a way she couldn't blame him.

Mr Edris brought out an array of antimacassars and other small pieces, while Mr Herbert explained as they went along.

Becky removed her gloves and picked up a handkerchief. 'This has a lovely soft feel to it.'

'It's French, which is why it's more expensive than some of the others. We're having to look abroad now for some of our more select stock.'

'Why is that?' asked Becky. She thought she knew, but she wanted it confirmed.

'It's because of the cotton famine.'

'Ah, and you can't source locally?'

'There's plenty of what I call ordinary cotton goods – sheets, lower-grade pieces in the warehouses. But stocks are dwindling, and for anything of good quality we're having to purchase from foreign dealers' stock. I expect that will run out, too, soon.'

'I suppose they've put up their prices.'

'Indeed. That's canny of you, Mrs…?'

'Shackleton,' said Becky.

'The young shipper's wife from Shackleton & Company?' asked Mr Edris.

'And the Louisa Line.'

'I beg your pardon. I forgot your husband set up on his own.'

'So what you're saying is, supplies locally have dried up?'

'That's the truth of it,' said Mr Edris.

'I expect it will be a relief when you can obtain quality nearer to home.'

'I'll make more profit, I can tell you that.'

Becky glanced at Lois, who she guessed was thinking what she was thinking. A gap in the market they could fill.

'Will you be taking anything today, Mrs Shackleton?'

Becky examined the pieces laid out on the counter and separated eight items. 'What do you think, Miss Brook?'

Lois added two maids' collars. 'I think these will be suitable, too.'

Mr Herbert took up an invoice pad, removed a pencil from behind his ear, licked it, and wrote, 'Mr Shackleton, Louisa Line.'

'No, that's not right. It's Mrs Shackleton.'

'I can't put that.'

'Why not? Our purchases have nothing to do with the Louisa Line. Please put "Mrs Shackleton, Coates Lane".'

'We can only make out invoices for unmarried ladies and widows.'

'Why is that?' asked Lois. 'I've never come across this before.'

'Because gentlemen settle the invoices, even though their wives make the purchases.'

Becky rolled her eyes at Lois.

The two women watched as Mr Herbert completed the invoice.

As they were leaving, Mr Edris made a valiant effort to increase sales.

'I expect you are fine needlewomen,' he said. 'Certainly you both have the eye of one. May I present the latest sewing machine?' He pointed to three shiny Singer treadle-machines on decorative wrought-iron bases, lined up against a wall like cannon prepared for battle.

Becky put out a hand and touched one. 'Tempting, I have to say. Don't you think so, Miss Brook?'

Lois turned the handle and watched the needle rise and fall. 'I'd love one,' she said wistfully.

'Not today, Mr Herbert, I'm afraid,' said Becky. 'Perhaps another time.'

'I understand, but you know where the machines are if you change your mind. Our Mr Edris here will be more than happy to give you a demonstration.'

I'll wager he will, thought Becky.

After they'd left the shop with their samples, Lois said, 'I thought they were going to ask us why we were buying single pieces.'

'So did I, but thinking about it, they probably didn't want to lose the sale by being too inquisitive.'

'I'd love one of those machines,' said Lois.

'So would I.'

Watching Lois walk away towards the Seamen's Haven, Becky had the feeling she was fortunate to have met her. Their association had the promise of genuine friendship.

CHAPTER TWENTY-FIVE

With Shaun and the exotic goods despatched to Carlisle, leaving the Chapel Street warehouse with almost empty shelves, Fergus had an attack of nerves. This felt stronger than butterflies in his stomach. It was as if something had grabbed hold of his gut. It was the same feeling he got whenever he thought of how, if he couldn't meet his debts, he would have to tell Becky they had lost their home.

Shaun and he had talked of sales in Leeds, or even Manchester, but in his heart – and, more importantly, in his head – Fergus knew the costs of renting rooms and transporting goods after a poor Carlisle sale were not an option.

Dicken wasn't much help, fussing over the dust and dirt that had made its way into the office when the bigger items had been moved out. He had a point and Fergus instructed him to get some professional cleaners in to do the job while they were in Carlisle. He would ask Becky to oversee them.

He was not looking forward to travelling to Carlisle on the train with Dicken and wondered what they would talk about. And he didn't share the sense of romance others felt about steam trains. All that bustle and cramming in of bags and boxes, people with their children in tow, and sharing a carriage with offensive things like dead rabbits and foul-smelling braces of pheasants on their way to market, or bought as gifts for relatives from the countryside to the city. What irked Fergus most, though, was that steam trains represented an onslaught on his business – stealing trade that historically belonged to the coastal shippers. They were smoky and exceedingly noisy, but he had to concede they were convenient for passenger travel.

After a few minutes looking at the coastline, he drew out his copy of *The Man in the Iron Mask* and began reading – partly because he needed something to calm his nerves and partly to stop Dicken striking up conversation. The book was a pretence, because the noise of people chattering and the many thoughts in his head kept him from any useful reading. His eyes skimmed the page and he had to re-read paragraphs. A child took up wailing and he frowned, then felt bad; in due course, it could be a child of his own. He hoped so.

As the train pulled in at Carlisle Station, Fergus could see by the well-wrapped-up people waiting to greet the arrivals that it was much colder than the Whitehaven they had left. Steam came from their mouths as they spoke. Folk were rushing past in thick coats, with scarves, and hats pulled well down over their ears. Fergus did up the buttons of his coat, pulled on his gloves and braced himself.

They were met in Carlisle by an excited Shaun and taken straight to the Lancaster & Caledonian Hotel.

'Have our goods arrived safely?' Fergus asked.

'Sure, everything's arrived. I kept a good eye out for us. Why don't you go straight to your rooms? You'll be wanting a freshen-up. I'll call for you in fifteen minutes and take you down to the sale room. We're in the ballroom. I think you'll be pleased.'

Shaun waited only ten minutes before knocking on Fergus's door. When they called on Dicken to collect him, he told them he felt a bit queasy with the walk from the station to the hotel. He said the cold air had frozen his lungs.

Fergus caught Shaun's eye, gave a small shrug, then turned away saying Dicken could join them downstairs when he felt better. He wondered if his intention was to irritate Shaun, who was so obviously keen to show what he'd been doing.

Shaun had reason to be proud. With the aid of the hired workers the hotel had provided, and the outside staff they'd employed especially, the stock looked magnificent. The Indian cabinets with ivory inlay gleamed under the wall lights. The red-lacquered Chinese cabinets were at their best. The walls were decorated with screens; boats carved from ivory sat on display stands; carpets, rugs and bolts of raw silk were piled high, along with chintz bedcovers, sheets and curtains. The smaller items were inside glass cabinets that Shaun had rented especially, saying they were important for display and security.

Within them were small circular mirrors with gold frames, paperknives, card-cases, gold bracelets and necklaces, chess sets and mother-of-pearl games counters.

It was better than they could have dreamed of and Fergus wished the investors were there to see the display.

'It's going to be all right, Mr Shackleton,' said Shaun. 'We're going to make a lot of money over the next two days.'

I hope he's right. If we can't sell the cotton, this sale and the Dublin stock is all we have.

'Thank you, Shaun. You've more than proved your worth and earned your wages.'

'It's truly a feast for the eyes. And when word gets out, we'll have them queuing up as far back as the station, wanting to furnish their homes with all this.' He spread his arms. 'Look at it all.'

Fergus felt an enormous sense of satisfaction that he, and the others who had worked alongside him and invested their savings with him, were responsible for such a wonderful display. He regretted not insisting Becky attend. He'd asked her, but only half-heartedly, so when she said she was seeking out handlooms and had other things to see to, he'd not pressed her.

He thought of the pictures in Macintosh & Warrilow's reception room in Glasgow and he turned to Shaun. 'We must have a photograph for the Louisa Line office. I wish I'd thought to arrange it.'

'Sweet Mary,' said Shaun. 'I should have thought of that. We can't let this opportunity slip by. There's still time.'

Before Fergus could say anything else he dashed off in the direction of the hotel reception, almost knocking over Dicken, who was on his way in.

Dicken's eyes widened. 'I thought our Whitehaven sale was impressive enough, but this is... I can't think of the right word.'

'A miracle,' suggested Fergus. A miracle that had begun with Dr Fincham suggesting he think about Mauritius as a business venture. Dicken was right – it was an impressive sight indeed. But an impressive sight was one thing, and a queue of wealthy buyers was quite another.

'What are you thinking?' asked Dicken. 'You've got a faraway look in your eye.'

'Nothing of any great importance. I'm reflecting on how far we've come in a year.'

Shaun reappeared. 'There's a photographer's studio on English Street. They close at seven.'

Fergus pulled out his pocket watch. 'It's three o'clock. Is English Street close by?'

'Just past the gaol, they say.' Shaun held out a piece of paper. 'The address is on here.'

Dicken was despatched to engage the photographer to come post-haste. After half an hour, a rotund, jolly man with a wobbly chin arrived unattended, saying Dicken had said he was suddenly not feeling well again and had stopped for a reviving lemonade at a coffee-house. He would be along when he felt better. It was the sort of strange thing Dicken would do, Fergus thought. He didn't cope well with minor illnesses. He'd once taken to his bed with what he'd described as a lung disease, only for the doctor to diagnose a sniffle.

The photographer, from his cheery manner and non-stop chattering, seemed delighted to be called out with little notice for what he called 'a special job'. Fergus had no doubt the 'special job' would result in a 'special invoice'; the man was not a fool and could see Fergus needed his services.

As it was, things turned out well with Dicken being away, since the photographer, having considered several angles from which to take the photograph, eventually insisted it would be enhanced by Fergus and Shaun being represented within it. Had Dicken been there it would have been awkward to exclude him. After an hour, the photographer left happy with his work and Fergus unhappy with the invoice. Shaun was insistent it was money well spent, but on his return, with rosy cheeks and a somewhat jaunty air, Dicken, ever the bookkeeper, thought it a wild extravagance.

With the ballroom doors locked and there being nothing further to be attended to, the three men ate a smoked bacon and egg supper, with ale to wash it down. Well fed and mellow, they adjourned to the taproom, where Shaun entertained everyone within with Irish folk lore. Dicken, having regained his health, announced he was going to retire early.

'You can't go until we've toasted ourselves for good luck for the morrow,' said Shaun, holding up his tankard. 'That's right, Mr Shackleton, isn't it?'

Fergus picked up his glass. 'I'm happy to raise a glass tonight to toast good luck over the next two days, but I'll be much happier toasting our success tomorrow.'

'To good luck, and let's hope the good Lord's looking down on us,' said Shaun.

'To good luck,' said Fergus and Dicken.

CHAPTER TWENTY-SIX

Aided by a single-malt whiskey in his room before retiring, Fergus fell asleep quickly, but woke early. His mouth was dry and he could tell he'd had one drink too many the previous evening. Although it was still quite dark outside, a brisk walk might help clear his head before the Friday sale. His pocket watch showed six o'clock. It was too early to ring for hot water, so he dipped the edge of a towel in the cold water that was left in the jug and gave his face a quick wipe, then poured some into the companion bowl and washed his hands. The cold made him shiver, but his plan to sharpen himself up was working, and he was beginning to shake off the fuzziness from the night before.

The hotel porter unlocked the main door to let him out into the street. The wintry air hit the back of his throat, making him cough.

'It's nippy out there, sir,' called the porter to Fergus's retreating back. 'Mind you don't slip. You've a big day ahead of you.'

'Indeed I do,' said Fergus under his breath.

Although it was early, the city's workers were awake and out of their homes. Shutters were being taken down, delivery boys with tired eyes were rushing past transporting goods in wicker baskets, young women were on their way to factory work, and carriers were jostling for parking spaces.

An enticing aroma drew Fergus to a nearby coffee shop. It wasn't grand enough to be called a coffee house, of the sort patronised by the professional classes to discuss the political and social events of the day. Being open at such an early hour indicated its clientele came from the working classes of the town, who would call simply for liquid refreshment.

'What can I do for you, sir?' asked the man behind the counter.

'A pot of coffee, thank you.'

'You visiting? Ain't seen you round 'ere afore.'

'I'm here on business.'

'Well, you're up early, I'll give you that. Must be something important t'get a gentleman like you up at this hour.'

'We're having a sale in the Lancaster & Caledonian.'

'A sale, sir? Of what?'

'Imported goods. Furniture, rugs, items from India and China.'

'An auction? They get a lot of 'em in there.'

'Not an auction, all our goods are priced.'

The proprietor brought out a large pot of coffee. Though he placed it gingerly on the table, a stream of thick black liquid jumped out of its spout to land with a loud splat.

'Overfilled this a bit, sir, begging your pardon.' He frowned. 'I'll fetch a cloth.'

'Is this your business?' Fergus asked.

'It is. I'm the boss and, while I'm not one to boast, I've built it up from scratch. I make enough to feed my family and feed 'em well. Meat thrice a week, not all cabbage and tatties. I've lots of reg'lars and I've worked hard every single day and made a success of it.'

As he disappeared, Fergus remembered something his solicitor, Edgar Needham, had once told him. 'Because people work hard does not mean they will be successful.'

The proprietor returned with a cloth and wiped up the mess.

'You're looking miserable all of a sudden,' he said, laughing. 'Has there been a death in the family while I've been gone away?'

Fergus matched his laugh. 'I was thinking about the day ahead. It's important to me and others.'

'I always says if you're "Two P's", things are likely to go well. That means "Properly Prepared". Are you?'

Fergus thought of all the effort he and his team had put into this day. 'I'd like to think so.'

'Then you'll have a successful sale. Come back and let me know how you get on. I'm interested. You've an honest face, not like some I get in 'ere.'

Another customer came in and the proprietor returned to his tasks.

Walking back to the hotel, Fergus pondered his

encounter. It was strange, but the coffee shop's proprietor had given him confidence. They were "Properly Prepared" for this sale, having learned a lot at the Freemasons' Hall sale, he hoped he could prove Mr Needham wrong and their hard work would bring success. They had top-quality saleable goods. The day ought to go well.

✻ ✻ ✻

Fergus was aware of the tension in the room as Shaun, Dicken and the helpers provided by the hotel waited until exactly ten o'clock for him to give the order to open the door. Nervously checking his watch, despite a church clock being heard to strike the hour loudly and clearly, Fergus nodded and Shaun opened the door.

Three people entered. Shaun glanced at Fergus and bit his bottom lip.

Fergus stepped forward and greeted the arrivals, inviting them to view the goods on display, while Shaun disappeared through the doors.

An elderly lady, well wrapped up against the cold, took off her hat and overcoat, placed them on a chair, then made a beeline for Fergus.

'You must be Fergus Shackleton?'

He greeted her with a broad smile. 'I am.'

The lady extended a kid-gloved hand. 'How do you do? I am Isabella Cadogan. My solicitor, Mr Trenchard, said I should come.'

Fergus took her hand in his. 'Welcome, Mrs Cadogan. I am well, thank you. Yes, I am acquainted with Mr Trenchard. We had business earlier in the year.'

'He's been telling me about your ship going to Mauritius and all the treasures you expected it to bring back.'

Well done, Mr Trenchard, thought Fergus, for recommending such an obviously wealthy lady to view his sale. He had the feeling she was bound to buy.

'We certainly have many treasures,' he told her. 'What are you particularly interested in? We have some lovely items in our showcase cabinets. Allow me to walk you over to them.'

'Thank you.'

Mrs Cadogan showed a great deal of interest. However, every item Fergus pointed out, she either already owned or she had a relative with a similar piece.

'Such a lovely comb. I inherited one from my aunt very much like it. What is the price?'

Fergus told her and thought she almost smirked with what appeared to be satisfaction. He moved on to some mother-of-pearl counters.

'I found a sandalwood box full of those in one of my father's desk drawers when he died. I'll wager they're expensive. How much are they?'

Fergus told her.

'We never went in Father's desk before he sadly passed away. You would have been so surprised at what we found there. Invoices for his cigars dating back to the 1820s, up to the week before he died. Can you imagine it? I don't think he ever cleared his desk out once. How he loved his cigars.'

It was becoming painfully obvious to Fergus that Mrs Cadogan's visit was, to her, an outing on a par with visiting a museum, and that she was pricing up her family heirlooms. His thoughts were compounded when after half an hour she said,

'Mr Shackleton, I am so enjoying looking at my family's history. My father spent some time in India and many of these things are so familiar to me. You know you don't have to go as far as Mauritius to buy this sort of thing. I have a mansion house full of similar items that I might be persuaded to sell to a buyer I liked, such as you, and with whom I've established a rapport.'

Fergus's heart sank to the lowest depths. Not only did she not want to buy anything, she wanted to sell her inherited chattels to him. His only use to her had been to advise her of the sort of prices she could expect. He hesitated before responding; it would do him no favours to release the irritation he was feeling.

'And, Mr Shackleton,' she went on, 'my treasured possessions are antiques, whereas these are all new.'

Fergus gave a curt nod, thanked her for coming and began excusing himself, stating he had other people to speak to.

Mrs Cadogan looked round at the almost empty room. 'Really?'

'Yes, really.'

She handed him an embossed card. 'If you are minded to, I will be happy to show you my own treasures, although Mr Trenchard did warn me that you may not be interested.'

Two hours passed and only a trickle of people passed through the door – mostly, it turned out, coming for a 'look-see'. The few that did buy chose small items at little cost. The confidence Fergus had tried to conjure up and carry with him from the coffee shop evaporated. It seemed the good people of the city of Carlisle had better things to do than come and view his goods – never mind to buy them.

Shaun did his best to keep spirits high, but there was no denying the room, despite its wonderful furniture, trinkets, and cabinet items, lacked atmosphere. The goods for sale needed people 'oohing' and 'aahing', as they'd done in Whitehaven. People greeting each other, chatting amongst themselves, showing off their purchases.

He expressed his thoughts to Shaun, who replied, 'T'is true, a hubbub in the room always works wonders. I've no idea why no one is coming.'

'We've not even seen the town's dealers looking for a bargain,' Fergus said. 'I expect they'll come at the last minute, when they think we have to lower the prices to rock bottom to avoid paying carriage transporting everything back. They'll not be wrong, either, because that's what we'll have to do.'

'Don't despair, Mr Shackleton,' said Shaun. 'This has happened to Da in places where he's unknown.'

'What does he do?'

'He gets a man to walk in the streets, ringing a bell.'

'I don't think that will do much good here in Carlisle.'

'If I may say so, not with you or Dicken, but let me go. I'll call in at the retailers to remind them what we've got. I can't understand it. There was a lot of interest when I called on them before.'

'I guess it's worth a try, but we haven't got a bell.'

'You're wrong there. I brought one in case of need.'

'In case of need?'

'When I told him we were doing this sale in Carlisle, Da told me he never does a sale without his bell. Comes in handy, he said. I'll get it and go out straightaway.'

Fergus had prayed that if he was going to get a headache, it would not be over the two days of the Carlisle sale. However, with things going so badly, he thought he'd better take a good dose of Dr Fincham's new linctus. He was about to leave the room when a young man arrived.

'I'm from the *Carlisle Express and Examiner*,' he said. 'Is Shaun Conran here?'

Fergus shook his head. 'He's out on business. Can I help?' Fergus introduced himself as the owner of the Louisa Line, saying, 'Mr Conran is in my employ.'

'He placed an advertisement with us which came out last Friday. We've a spare space if you're interested for this Friday's edition. We're going to press in a couple of hours.'

Fergus wasn't in the mood for extending any further financial outlay. 'I can't say any of our advertisements in the Carlisle newspapers have borne fruit,' he said. 'Why would I want to throw good money after bad?'

'I didn't expect you to be busy today, with it being Friday. The town's market is in full swing, and people do their business in Carlisle on a Friday. The professional people are writing wills, bookkeeping and so on, and the doctors are seeing their patients, because it's the day most people come into the city. They'll be far too busy to drop by here today.'

'I only have your word for that. No one may come tomorrow.'

'They will. Trust me.'

Fergus was not in the habit of trusting newspapermen and certainly not when they were touting for business. He decided not to beat around the bush. 'You can see we're not exactly overrun with customers and that we're hoping to sell goods today, not make purchases. However, if you can guarantee me an interview – a description of our goods extolling their virtues and the fairness of our pricing – then perhaps we can talk figures.'

The newspaper man chewed his lip. 'I hear what you're saying, but as far as I'm aware, we've no free editorial space today. You'll appreciate I'm on a tight timetable. The presses are being set while I'm here talking to you.'

'In my experience people look through the newspaper on the first day for the interesting articles. They then put it aside and reserve the advertisements for later in the week. Isn't that so?'

'There may be some truth in that.'

'So you see, an advertisement with no editorial attached is of no real value to us at this late stage.' Fergus knew he was verging on being aggressive, but his mood and the atmosphere in the room were not helping. 'Are you sure we can't come to some mutual agreement here? After all, we *have* placed a previous advertisement at considerable cost to ourselves. I'm thinking a quarter-price advertisement alongside ten lines of editorial.'

'You drive a hard bargain, sir.'

'Look,' said Fergus, opening his arms wide. 'I'm sure

you can write ten lines of glowing editorial that will tempt people to come and view this display. Payment will be after publication. We'll want to see we've bought what we agreed upon.'

'Agreed. You'll get your editorial. I'll take something else out to make space.'

Fergus sought out Dicken and raised his voice to gain his attention. 'Can you remember how much the *Carlisle Express* charged us for their advertisement?'

Without even pausing to think, Dicken shouted the price back.

The newspaperman agreed. 'He's got a good memory. I'll write up my copy and then I've got to run. It'll go out at five o'clock this evening and I'll call for payment tomorrow.'

'If there's an advertisement with no editorial, don't bother coming for any money.'

'I'll get it done unless I get run over by a cart on the way back.'

Ten minutes later the newspaperman passed Shaun on the way out. He stopped only to wave his notes at him, saying, 'Can't stop, the presses are ready to roll. Everything's taken care of.'

Shaun's nose was red with the cold, and he didn't look his usual cheerful self. It was with misgiving that Fergus asked him how he got on.

'It was difficult getting people to stop. Some of the few I spoke to said they'd come tomorrow.'

'Do you think they will?'

'They're all looking me straight in the eye when they say so.'

'How was the bell?'

'People gawped my way when I rang it, but it being so bitterly cold, they kept rushing past.'

Between half past twelve and two o'clock, a few more people trickled in, and they did further business on the smaller items and a few textiles. This was followed by a lull, which Dicken spent rearranging the showcase pieces.

The only potentially positive moment before they closed for the day might have been the *Carlisle Gazette and Examiner* advertisement and editorial. Dicken, who had gone out to collect a copy, read the editorial aloud.

'*IMPORTANT NOTICE FOR THE GOOD PEOPLE OF CARLISLE.*

Tomorrow, Saturday, available to view at the Lancaster & Caledonian Hotel – recently arrived from the tropical island of Mauritius – Asian and Oriental goods.'

'So far, so good,' said Shaun. 'Go on.'

'That's it.'

'What?'

'I'm afraid that's all it says.'

Fergus took the newspaper and swore softly under his breath. 'I said ten lines of editorial. "Available to view". He's made it sound like we've set up a museum. "Available to purchase" it should say, at the very least, with a much better description of the goods.'

'He's swindled us,' said Dicken. 'We should go up there and complain.'

Shaun shook his head. 'It's your decision, Mr Shackleton,

but to go up there and listen to measly excuses about lack of space, last-minute printing… I don't think it's a good idea, and a waste of our valuable time. When he comes looking for his money, we'll send him packing.'

'I agree,' said Fergus. 'Let's lock up and have some supper.'

Fergus had planned to spend the evening with a celebratory meal, but with everyone's spirits so low he ordered boiled beef with onions and vegetables in gravy. They sat in the commercial dining room alongside the business travellers. Even the hotel staff were commiserating, saying they were sure things would be better on the morrow. Fergus wasn't so sure.

No one suggested they raise any toasts, and conversation throughout the meal was stilted. When they'd finished, Shaun said he was going to wrap up warm and walk to the cathedral and back. He didn't invite Dicken to accompany him. Fergus checked everything was still in order in the ballroom and that the room was secure, then retired to his room.

There was a note from Becky waiting for him. It had been placed on the bedside table.

'*My Dearest Fergus,*

I so hope all is going well for us in Carlisle. You know how I hate it when you are away. The house feels so empty, especially at night. I've been keeping myself busy, and Lois and I have been vising haberdashers.

Lois has suggested there may be handlooms

available in Carlisle from an equipment manufacturer since the cotton industry is so important there. I appreciate you're going to be busy, but if the opportunity arises might you make enquiries? We think we can accommodate eight looms to begin with.

I am wearing the pearl you bought me in Edinburgh.

Much love,

Becky.'

Despite his worries, Fergus was proud. When Becky got an idea in her head, she ran with it. He remembered how she'd organised the beef-pie sales for Dolly at the races. There was no denying she'd a business head. He would enquire about the looms, that was the least he could do. He dosed himself up with Dr Fincham's linctus as a preventative measure and was soon asleep.

CHAPTER TWENTY-SEVEN

A fine breakfast plate had been laid before Fergus, but with nerves having stolen his appetite, he pushed it to one side. Scottish kippers were his favourite way to begin the day, and he'd ordered them the previous evening, thinking it at least a good start to what might turn out to be another trying day.

A waiter came over with toast in a silver rack. 'What time do you open today, sir?' he asked.

'Ten o'clock. Why?' Fergus pulled out his watch and checked the time. An hour to go.

'You might want to open a bit earlier,' said the waiter. 'There's a queue outside.'

'A queue?'

'Aye, reckon about nine or ten folk waiting to come in.'

Fergus felt a surge of excitement – but what to do? 'Are they here for our sale?'

'So they say.'

His brain went blank and he shook his head to clear it. He'd no plans for servicing a queue; Shaun and Dicken were both still halfway through their breakfasts. *The earliest we can open is quarter to the hour, when the helpers arrive. But what if people lose interest and leave? An hour's far too long to wait in a queue in late January.*

'Do you have any of your cards?' he asked Shaun. 'The ones with your name on?'

'They're in the ballroom. Do you want them?'

'Yes, straightaway. I'll meet you at the hotel entrance.'

With the cards in his hand, Fergus went outside, chivvying Shaun and Dicken to finish their breakfasts quickly. He walked the short distance to the coffee shop he'd found the previous day and spoke with the proprietor, then returned, telling the nine people in the queue, 'Please take one of these cards and adjourn to the coffee shop across the way for a hot drink at our expense.'

'We'll lose our place,' said one man, his cap pulled down over his ears.

'Come back at a quarter to ten, show these cards, and we'll let you in early.'

'Can't we come in now?'

'Regrettably, no, we need staff to arrive before we can open.'

Fergus and the hotel doorman watched as the crowd adjourned.

'What if more come?' asked the doorman.

Fergus handed him three cards and a florin. 'Give these out and say the first twelve have won a special early entry prize.'

'The coffee shop proprietor will be pleased with all the extra business.'

That was true. The man's face had lit up when Fergus put a gold sovereign on his counter and told him he'd settle up with him later.

Fergus collected Dicken and Shaun, picking up a piece of toast from his table on the way, and went to open up.

'What do you think's done it?' asked Shaun. 'My bell or the advertisement?'

'I don't care,' Fergus said. 'But I'm minded to ask people if they saw the advertisement.'

'I'll do that,' said Dicken.

At exactly a quarter to ten, the people holding the cards returned and were escorted by the doorman past three others who had arrived too late to obtain a card. One of the three thought the situation unethical and left, but the other two stayed when Fergus told them he would be happy to escort them round personally once inside.

The buzz that had been lacking the previous day was present that morning in abundance. By eleven o'clock they had sold more items than at the Freemasons'. The major excitement was the sale of a set of intricately carved Indian bedroom furniture with an enormous wardrobe, which was destined for a country house in the Scottish Borders. Fergus worked out the profit they had made. It was true, people would pay for things that were foreign and different. *One-upmanship*, he thought.

He set Shaun to work at the showcases, where he was in his element, charming the ladies and their escorts, while he took charge of the larger items. They had to find Dicken a wider table to cope with all the invoices the sales were generating. They had no time for lunch, and the afternoon was as busy.

At half past two Fergus heard a familiar voice. He turned and saw the solicitor, Mr Trenchard, approaching with a lady.

'Good afternoon,' Fergus said. 'Thank you so much for coming.'

'May I introduce my good lady wife, Charlotte?'

Fergus bowed his head. 'Delighted to meet you, Mrs Trenchard.'

'And I you.'

Mr Trenchard gestured to the room. 'A healthy attendance.'

His wife added, 'We saw your advertisement in the *Gazette*, but we were coming anyway.'

Fergus lowered his voice. 'In confidence, Mr and Mrs Trenchard, I have to say it is a complete mystery to me why attendance was so low yesterday. Yet today, and I am not complaining, today we are busier than I could have hoped.'

'Ah, I'm not at all surprised. Friday is a day for seeing to things in Carlisle, and the professional people are working.' He scanned the room. 'You have mostly professional people here today.' He pointed out a thin man with frizzy hair and a bulbous nose. 'That is the Carlisle and Cumberland Bank manager and, over there, the bald man with the elegant wife is one of the town's biggest mill owners, Mr Franklin, and his wife, Frances.'

Fergus thought Frances Franklin a rather unfortunate pairing, but her parents were not to know she was destined for so inappropriate a surname upon marriage.

He remembered Becky's note about the handlooms. 'How is he faring with the cotton famine?'

'It has affected the city badly, but he has several mills, and two of them are woollen, so I expect they are supporting the cotton ones.'

'Would you introduce me?'

'Certainly.'

Introductions were made and the ladies disappeared to inspect the showcases. Fergus heard Mrs Franklin say there was a nice young Irish gentleman who had shown her an ivory fan, and would Mrs Trenchard give an opinion on it?

'You're from Whitehaven, Mr Shackleton,' said Mr Franklin. 'I had an aunt lived there once. She's with the departed, but we used to visit her when I was a lad. A nice church in the centre.'

'St Nicholas's. I was christened there.'

'So, what brings you to Carlisle with your wares?'

'It's our county town and, as a businessman yourself, you'll appreciate we thought there was a market for our exotic goods here. Professional, discerning people with an eye for excellence willing to purchase.'

'Times are hard for some of us in the textile business.'

'I understand you have both cotton and woollen mills.'

'I do. All highly mechanised, but the cotton we have to buy now, from India, is no good, so I've closed two mills down.'

No good offering him our Surat cotton, then. 'Are there any hand-weavers in Carlisle?'

'Aye, a few, but piece-rates are no good. Why do you ask?'

'My wife is thinking of setting up a charitable business

243

using handlooms. We've a lot of out-of-work weavers who were erroneously directed to Whitehaven from Liverpool. She thinks she might set them on for good purpose, but she needs some looms, since none were able to bring theirs with them.'

Mr Frances tipped his head to one side. 'Charitable, you say?'

'Yes, giving them self-respect and a sense of purpose.'

'I take my hat off to her. It will prove an enjoyable hobby for her and them. I hope she's not thinking of any monetary reward, as it's unlikely she'll see any. As for handlooms, there's a craft-equipment manufacturer I could put you in touch with, but what yarn will they use?'

Fergus was too embarrassed to say they'd bought Surat cotton, so he said, 'I don't think it's decided yet. I've been so busy with the return of the *Ketton* and my other ships, I haven't paid that much notice. I'd be obliged if you'll be so good as to supply me with the manufacturer's details.'

'That I can do, if you've paper for me to write on.'

Fergus picked up a bill of sale and handed it to him. Mr Franklin leaned on a table to write the address, almost tripping over a young girl clutching a small elephant with chubby fingers.

Fergus heard her ask a question he had asked himself since the *Ketton's* return: 'But don't the elephants need their tusks?'

'He's called Stanley,' Mr Franklin said. 'And the business is the Carlisle Craft Emporium.' He patted Fergus on the arm. 'Stanley used to be one of our fettlers. He came into a bit of brass – enough to set up his own business. Judging by his premises, he's done quite well for himself. He'll be delighted to see you; the handloom business has taken a downturn along with the rest of us.'

At this point, Mrs Franklin returned, clasping the ivory fan. 'I've seen the most adorable chest of drawers and Mrs Trenchard likes several of the boxes. Have you gentlemen finished gossiping?'

Her husband smiled at her affectionately. 'Ladies gossip, my dear. Men discuss.'

'Well, we need you to come and see.'

When it was all over Fergus, Shaun and Dicken sat down to the celebratory meal he had rejected the previous evening. This time they were in the main dining room, tucking into hare soup, followed by roast pork in the German style, marinated in sage and juniper berry vinegar.

'I can't believe the two days have been so different,' began Dicken.

'But when all's said and done, we return home victorious,' said Shaun.

Dicken put his head on one side. 'A victor usually returns with his spoils, doesn't he?'

'Our earnings are our spoils,' said Fergus. He was relieved to see Shaun and Dicken in reasonable spirits with each other for once, since it didn't take much for one to be short with the other. He was thinking their successful day had paved the way clear for Becky to approach their investors, since they would now most definitely be receiving a decent interim dividend.

They discussed the various characters who had attended their sale and the items they'd bought.

'You could tell most were city folk by the way they were dressed,' said Dicken.

'When the first folk arrived today, I knew we were in luck. The men all had well-heeled boots.'

'Why does that matter?' asked Dicken, chasing a slippery buttered carrot round his plate.

'It means they can either afford to have their shoes repaired or buy new ones when they become worn. Then I saw the ladies and almost all of them were wearing fur, on their capes, and their hats. Some of the gentlemen's gloves were edged with it, too.'

'It's true,' said Fergus. 'The people who came today were wealthy and bought the bigger items. How many of those cabinets did we sell?'

For the next twenty minutes they turned their mind back to the business side of things, going over what had sold well.

When it came to dessert Fergus chose an oatmeal pudding while the other two, after extensive deliberation, decided on rhubarb tart.

With the hotel manager passing on congratulatory words on the sale's attendance and their success, Fergus made his way up to his room and, when he fell asleep, it was with a smile on his face.

CHAPTER TWENTY-EIGHT

Becky spent Sunday in a state of agitation. Twice she sent Rory round to Chapel Street to see if Shaun and Dicken had returned and gone straight there, but there was no news. The suspense was almost too much for her. When Fergus came through their front door late afternoon, with his portmanteau and a leather bag over his shoulder, she ran to greet him.

He held her to him and kissed the top of her head, before their lips met.

'Tell me all,' said Becky. 'How did it go?'

'Let me take my coat off and change first. Travelling these days is quick but so dusty.'

She took a step back, trying to read his face. 'Oh, do tell me. Did you do well?'

'All in good time.'

'Oh, Fergus, you're grinning. That means you're teasing me.'

He put his coat on its peg then made to go to the stairs. At the last moment, he turned back. 'All right, I've had my fun. We did well. Very well indeed. You are in a much stronger position to appeal for donations. Also to present your project to the investors on Friday, because we will be paying another interim dividend. This will put them in good spirits. Although how you're going to pay for the cotton if you don't get enough donations, I'm not sure. It's a question they are bound to ask.'

He appeared to forget the dust on his clothes and sat down. It was such a relief, Becky felt giddy.

Over the next half hour, Fergus relayed what had happened at the sale and told her about meeting the Franklins.

'And the handlooms?'

'I was able to call this morning before we left, since Mr Stanley, the proprietor of the Craft Emporium, lives on his premises.' He opened his bag and took out some leaflets and information Mr Stanley had given him. 'He has plenty of looms, but we both agreed it would be better if you and one of the weavers went up there. There are specifications that need discussing.'

'Lois and I can go. I'm sure she'll come with me.' She leaned forward and reached for the leaflets.

'I think it a good idea you write and make an appointment with some details of what you are looking for.'

'I'll do that as soon as we've decided on the day.' She opened one of the leaflets.

'Before you read those, wait. I've something else to show you.' He took out the photograph they'd had taken on the eve of the sale and passed it over to her. It had been mounted on thick card and in the bottom right-hand corner, in swirly copperplate lettering, were the photographer's details.

'This is wonderful,' Becky said. 'It all looks so impressive and you and Shaun look so…so competent.'

'I thought we might frame it and put it in the office in Chapel Street. What do you think?'

'That's the only place for it. The first of many showing the success of the Louisa Line. I'll see to getting it framed for you. With the right frame, we can make it even bigger and grander.'

'Perhaps one day we can put a plaque underneath saying "Shackleton & Son" or even "& Sons".' He bent and kissed the top of her head.

Perhaps indeed, thought Becky.

Three days later, Becky went to the office to collect the keys for the Carter Lane warehouse. With Shaun en route to Dublin with goods for Padraig Conran, and Rory and Charlie having gone with him, the warehouse was quiet. She wanted to take some measurements. Her meeting with the investors had been called for the next day and she needed to be prepared, leaving nothing to chance. She had no idea what they would ask her, but Carter Lane was bound to come up in some way and she wanted to show she was familiar with the premises.

After she left Chapel Street, she went up to Croxall's with the photograph. She wanted a larger mount to make it grander, but not one that obscured the photographer's details.

Miss Evangelina stepped forward to serve her. 'Good morning, Mrs Shackleton.'

To Becky's surprise, never having thought Miss Evangelina that bright a button, the young girl was quick to find the right colour mounting-card and to take the measurements.

'If you'll leave the photograph, I'll ask Papa to cut the mount for you.' As she put her hand out, a gold-coloured bracelet slipped from under her sleeve.

'That's pretty,' said Becky, wondering if it was real gold.

'Isn't it?' said Miss Evangelina, with a satisfied smile. She pulled it down so it was clearly visible. It had a cursive, almost Celtic design engraved on it.

'A suitor gave it to me, but I'm not allowed to say. That's why I keep it up my sleeve. It's real gold. It's stamped.'

'Ah, Mr Shaun,' said Becky.

Miss Evangelina shook her head. Then, leaning forward, although there was no one else in the shop to hear, she whispered, 'The other one.'

'Dicken?' Becky was unable to keep the surprise from her voice.

Miss Evangelina gave a slight nod in agreement, then put her finger to her lips. 'It's a secret. *And* he's taking me to the theatre on Friday. In a box. Did you know the upper boxes cost 1/6?'

Becky did. She also knew seats in the gallery cost only sixpence, a third of the price. 'Enjoy yourself,' she said.

Out on Lowther Street, Becky walked along wondering how Dicken could afford such a bracelet. Perhaps Fergus had let him have it at a huge discount. And a box at the Theatre Royal? Dicken was obviously trying to compete with Shaun. She was passing the Carter Lane warehouse when it occurred to her that the bracelet was nothing like the ones the *Ketton* had brought back. It was the wrong style. Miss Evangelina's was Scottish in design. Something wasn't quite right.

But as puzzling as it was, Becky had no time to ponder it. After Croxall's, she had an important appointment to keep.

✷ ✷ ✷

Becky had been surprised to receive an invitation from Hector to meet her at the Regency Tearoom on King Street. The note specified he 'wished to speak with her'.

She was five minutes late and flustered when she arrived.

'I'm so sorry. A tinker's cart ran into the back of a fancy carriage and they've closed the road and pavement off, so I had to take the long way round.'

She expected Hector to make a caustic comment about her timekeeping, but to her relief, he said 'They should separate the trade carts from private transportation. Some of those carters should be taken off the road. Sit yourself down. I've ordered some tea and a scone. And you'll have something to eat?'

'Shortbread, thank you. You wanted to speak with me?'

'It's about your weaving project. Elizabeth's been telling me all about it.'

'Ah.' She remembered Elizabeth had said she would speak with him.

Becky had thought at the time her mother-in-law was merely being polite, and hadn't expected anything to come of it. Now she regarded Hector warily. *He's going to tell me off about it. He's heard I've a meeting with the investors and he's going to try and dissuade me.*

'You're aware of my thoughts on these weavers and their families coming here and being supported by the town, but when Elizabeth explained to me that your aim is to make them self-supporting and free of town relief, I thought to myself there's logic in that, from several sides.'

Becky was so astonished, her napkin slipped from her grasp, and she had to bend down to retrieve it from the floor.

'I certainly think there's logic in my idea,' she said, hiding her surprise. 'The weavers produce something worthwhile; they get a wage, self-respect and we might make a charitable profit.' She went on to explain her plans in more detail and to outline the support she was receiving from her friends by way of small donations and their time.

'The donations are to set up your project and buy the cotton, I understand?'

'That's right. I'll have to rely on donations, as no one will give me a loan as a married woman. The law won't allow it.'

Hector nodded then motioned to the waitress to pour their tea. 'Yes, I expect in due course married women will have their own rights over their property rather than their husbands taking control upon marriage. With Fergus having, I understand, been rather rash with his personal investment in these exotic goods, he'll not be able to get a loan, either.'

Becky wasn't surprised Hector knew they were stretched; he had a good head for business.

'I've a meeting with the investors tomorrow,' she said.

'This is why I've asked for this meeting. I've been meaning to have a chat, but not got round to it, and I'm afraid this is rather last-minute, but hear me out. Having been in business a long time, and being used to dealing with investors, I have a suggestion that may help you.'

Becky wondered if he was going to donate money personally, but he could have done that without inviting her out for tea.

'In order to pay for the cotton, I've thought of a possible solution. You must present your case to the investors in the manner I am about to suggest.' He reached for a scone. 'I'm often peckish mid-afternoon.'

Becky waited in anticipation as he cut it in half and spread one side with butter. She helped herself to a piece of shortbread.

'You must state clearly to the investors what you want to do and why,' he went on. 'Point out the benefits for everyone, and then ask them to give you a particular form of credit. It's called an extended loan.'

'An extended loan? What's that?'

'You say to them you will buy the cotton, but you can't pay until you've sold some goods. They're not giving you money, they're just not asking for payment before you take possession of it.'

Becky paused to think through Hector's words. 'I understand. Do you think the investors will agree to such a plan?'

'I think it highly likely they'll jump at it. I would, in their position, and if Fergus can announce a better interim dividend at the meeting tomorrow that will be a great help to your cause. Things won't be so desperate. And you'll be taking some of the pressure off Fergus. You can take some personal credit for that.'

'I hadn't thought about buying the cotton specifically helping Fergus and his debt. My aim is to help the weavers.'

'I realise that, but you're not doing him any harm.'

'At the moment, everyone is agreed that the cotton is proving impossible to sell.'

'This is good news for you, as you have no competitors for your purchase. What you will be doing is promising the investors a probably modest profit, in due course, and perhaps not even for three or six months, but you are offering them a return.'

'What if it all goes wrong?'

'Becky, my dear, you can't start a business wondering what you will do if it goes wrong. If you don't have the confidence that you can make it work then you shouldn't be embarking on it. I have faith in you. Have faith in yourself.'

'I'm sure I can set it up. I'm just anxious about the end product, because it's out of my control. What if we can't sell the fancy pieces?'

'I can't help you a great deal with that, it's not my line of business, but a top-quality practical product, at an acceptable price, always sells well.'

Becky began to thank Hector, but he brushed her words away. 'Please don't thank me. I want to see you do well. I'll see if I can drum up some donations. I've done my bit for others in my time. Some people in this town owe me a favour.'

'Thank you, I really—'

'No more thanks. Suffice it to say I'll be watching your progress with interest.'

Later, when Becky told Fergus of Hector's advice, he listened intently, then with a brief smile said, 'I should have thought of that.'

Becky knew him well enough to see he was put out, but she ignored it. 'Do you think they'll agree to an extended loan?' she asked.

'I don't see why not and it puts you in a much stronger position than having to find enough donations to fund total purchase.'

'It's a good idea. We'll see how it's received in the morning.'

CHAPTER TWENTY-NINE

At the Waverley Hotel, as she waited outside the meeting room to be summoned, Becky could hear the men's voices, but couldn't make out their conversation. There was a round of applause, and she assumed Fergus had delivered the news they were to receive a better second interim dividend. Shortly afterwards, Dicken came out to invite her to join them.

Although she was well known to the investors, Fergus went through the formality of introducing her, and Dicken duly recorded her attendance in the minute-book.

Becky removed her coat and gloves and placed her papers on the table. When she was settled, she raised her head and acknowledged the men. They were all looking at her.

'Gentlemen, I must begin by thanking you for allowing me to speak to you today on this matter. What I plan to do, with your help, is to set up some handlooms in the Carter Lane warehouse to give some of the out-of-work weavers a chance to earn a wage and some self-respect.

These folk own nothing, having sold all their possessions and arrived from Blackburn under the false promise of employment in our town.'

Mr Dickinson butted in, 'It'll be money you're after, whatever it is, I'll wager on that.'

'In a way, yes. What I'm looking for is credit with delayed payment. In simple terms I would like to utilise your Surat cotton and pay later.'

Becky filled the short silence that followed her words by pouring herself a glass of water.

Mr Nubley rubbed his hands together. 'How will you be able to pay us?' he asked, not unkindly. 'If *we* can't sell it, then how can you?'

'By selling the products the women will make from it on their handlooms. Small, intricate, decorative pieces such as antimacassar chair backs that will fetch a good price. We then use the profits to make quarterly interim payments to you.'

'I think we should take any offer we can get for the cotton, even if we have to wait a while,' said Mr Heslop. 'I know how quickly flax can go off in storage. I expect cotton's much the same.'

Mr Dickinson leaned forward and tapped Mr Heslop on the arm, as he was wont to do. 'Sir, pray tell me, as a textile manufacturer yourself, how would you dispose of our cotton should it begin to show signs of deterioration?'

'I would pay someone to take it away and burn it before the odour became too overpowering.'

Bill spoke up. 'As a fellow investor, and the purchaser of the cotton, I suggest we discuss Mrs Shackleton's offer.'

'Yes,' agreed Mr Nubley, 'better that rather than wait and have to watch our investment go up in smoke.' He turned to Becky. 'Please, tell us more.'

Becky obliged by producing the handloom leaflets and detailing what she thought would be the approximate cost of the looms. Then she moved on to how the Carter Lane warehouse could be arranged to facilitate the necessary equipment, the approximate cost of producing the yarn, the manufacture of their goods and the wholesale prices she and Lois thought they could expect. She stressed Shaun's offer to act as their Irish agent in Dublin through his father, and finished by saying, 'I began by announcing I had a proposition to put to you, and I hope you will agree that this is a project that has the potential to be profitable for both sides. You will sell your cotton in due course and the weavers and spinners will earn a wage.'

'Tell me again about the profits upon the sale of these cotton pieces. Who gets those?' asked Mr Dickinson.

'The aim is that the profits will cover the production costs, which includes payments, by instalments, for the cotton to your good selves. I'm confident we can be profitable. But if there should be a shortfall, then I shall appeal to the great and the good to support this venture and it will remain a charitable rather than a self-supporting business. The weavers are good women, anxious to work hard. Their reward, as well as a steady wage during this cotton famine, will be a lift out of poverty with the attendant self-respect this will bring alongside the production of useful, saleable goods.'

Mr Nubley raised his hand. 'What happens when you run out of cotton?'

'I will be perfectly frank with you, Mr Nubley, I have no idea. Our great hope is that the American war will finish soon and the mills reopen. It may be that this business does so well, I shall be returning later this year to ask you all to invest in new premises for the expansion of the Shackleton Cotton-Weaving Company.' The men joined with her amusement at what she guessed they regarded as a far-fetched suggestion.

'How will you finance the purchase of the looms?' asked Mr Nubley.

'Ideally, I would take out a personal loan, but that road is not available to me. Through donation and –'

Fergus interrupted her. 'I shall, as you will all realise, have to be the signatory on any paperwork and would like to take this opportunity to confirm my support for my wife's charitable venture. There will also need to be a board of trustees to be decided upon, but, essentially to all intents and purposes, this will be my wife's project.'

Bill spoke up as soon as Fergus had finished speaking, almost cutting him off. 'We all appreciate how determined you are to set up this venture, Mrs Shackleton.'

Mr Nubley said, 'I'm sure the others share the view that no doubt you will oversee it in the same spirited manner you have addressed us today.'

Becky wasn't quite sure if he was making fun by attributing to her a humorous spirit, but she took his words as complimentary.

Dr Fincham took off his spectacles and wiped them with his handkerchief. 'Gentlemen, it seems to me Mrs Shackleton is throwing us a lifeline. Grasping and swimming with it may not save us from drowning, but it is the only realistic offer we have received.'

There was a small ripple of approval. Fergus, in an official voice, invited any further questions. There being none, he asked Becky to retire and wait outside again while they discussed the matter.

As before, Becky could hear the discussion in the room, but not clearly. She strained her ears, but the only voice she could make out was Mr Dickinson's. Fergus had warned her he was a businessman through and through, so she was not at all surprised to hear him ask quite specific financial questions about profit and loss. At one point she heard him say, 'She didn't talk about the rent for the Carter Lane warehouse.'

Fergus answered and she assumed he was telling them the Louisa Line was covering that, as they were paying for it anyway. With the *Ketton* out for charter there was more need for it. Fergus had even mentioned to Becky how the company might one day be in a position to buy it from the owners, if he could agree a price.

Called back into the meeting, Becky settled herself again. All the men met her gaze, apart from Mr Dickinson, who was engaged in inspecting the cuticles on his left hand. She felt optimistic.

Fergus signalled to Dicken to take up his pen. 'Please minute that the SS *Ketton's* investors have agreed, in principle, to delay payment for the Surat cotton currently stored by the Louisa Line at the Carter Lane warehouse, and that we have agreed to fund Mr Needham, solicitor with Needham, Baxter & Co, to draw up an even-handed arrangement linked to the sale of the finished products.'

Becky was delighted and thanked each man in turn. She was about to take her leave when Fergus said, 'The meeting is not yet closed. There is one further point Mr Heslop has to raise and I ask him to put this forward.'

Becky held her breath, hoping it was not going to be anything that would diminish the glorious euphoria she was currently enjoying.

'I have listened carefully to all you have to say. I think that, as well as the next man, I can recognise a good proposition when I see it, and I would like to underwrite the cost of the handlooms at a much lower rate of interest than any savings bank in Whitehaven will offer you.'

All eyes were on Becky. She cast a quick glance at Fergus, saw he was smiling, and interpreted this as encouragement to accept.

'My thanks to you, Mr Heslop, sir. I'm delighted to accept this generous offer and I look forward to discussing it further.'

'I would add that you may be tempted to rent the handlooms. In my experience, rented reconditioned looms are never of the same quality as those that can be bought. It will mean a higher initial outlay, but to my mind a sensible one.'

'That's because you're lending her the money and want more interest,' said Mr Dickinson.

'It may seem that way to you, being the astute businessman that you are, but I urge Mrs Shackleton to ask amongst her weavers and see what they say on the subject. They will agree with me, I am certain.'

Becky took her leave, telling Mr Heslop she would make plans for her and Lois to visit Carlisle.

Dicken escorted her to the Waverley's front door where she turned and said, 'Miss Evangelina tells me you're attending the theatre this evening, is that right?' She put forward the information as a question, so he would be obliged to answer.

'Aye.'

'Who are you going to see?'

'Mr Snipperini's dancing monkey, a comedian and a troupe of Russian ballerinas.'

'I hope you've got good seats?'

'I expect so,' Dicken mumbled. He turned away, but not before Becky saw his face and neck had turned a vivid shade of red. *Your discomfort at my conversation has given you away*, she thought. *If I'm correct, Dicken's a more foolish man than I took him for.*

Walking home, she turned her thoughts to Miss Evangelina's bracelet and her upcoming Theatre Royal visit. She knew Shaun could easily afford such things, but Dicken had only a lowly bookkeeper's wage and lived with his widowed mother in humble surroundings. An idea was forming in her mind, one she was going to have to share with Fergus, even if purely to allay her suspicions.

CHAPTER THIRTY

'Ladies do not travel alone unless they are poor,' Fergus said. 'We need someone to chaperone you and Lois to Carlisle. I have an important business meeting, but would you be happy if Shaun accompanied you? He knows his way round Carlisle. What's more, he will certainly entertain you both with his chatter on the train. There *and* back.'

'You're right about that and his stories will be new to Lois, even if I've heard most of them already.'

'Tuesday, then. February 11th. I'll ask Dicken to make the necessary arrangements and we'll use the Queen Street carriage to take and collect you from the station. I'll speak to Samuel when I visit Mother later today. Have you remembered we said we'd go to church with them tomorrow?'

'Aye, I've remembered, but before you speak with Dicken, there's something else we need to discuss.'

Fergus raised his eyebrows. 'Do I need to sit down?

Your face has lost its smile and that tells me it could be serious.'

'It might be, but more likely disappointing.'

He shrugged and, still laughing, sat down. 'What is it?'

'It's about Dicken, who may have stolen the money from the Seamen's Haven.'

'What? Dicken?' Fergus's jaw dropped. 'You mean Dicken knows who may have stolen the money?'

'No, I mean I think it was he who stole it. I've waited until I'm absolutely sure it was him before mentioning it.'

The laughter that had previously sparkled in Fergus's eyes disappeared. 'What makes you think that?' *Surely not Dicken, of all people.*

Becky told him about the bracelet and the theatre box. 'Then there's the fact he told Miss Evangelina to keep it a secret. Apart from anything else, a flighty girl like her isn't going to keep the gift of a gold bracelet to herself. Most, if not all, of her enjoyment will be showing it off to people.'

'I certainly wouldn't trust her with any of my confidences. Are you sure it's gold? Dicken has never been generous in money matters. As well as it not being in his nature, he doesn't have the funds.'

'I'm as sure as I can be without taking it to a jeweller. It may be that imagined love has turned his head. It happens.' She told him about the decoration, making her think the bracelet likely to be Scottish.

'We've no evidence he took the money.' Fergus worked through Becky's reasoning in his mind. 'Perhaps someone left it to him in their will, or he won it at the races?'

'That's possible, I suppose,' said Becky.

'But he's not a betting man. I'll have to have it out with him.'

'Maybe the bracelet was in the family. His grandmother's or something. But then there's the theatre tickets too, and how embarrassed he was when I asked him about whether they had good seats.'

'I can't understand why he would do such a thing.'

'I can,' said Becky. 'To keep up with his love rival. Shaun took Miss Evangelina to the theatre and they sat in a box, and then there was the expensive Indian shawl. She plays them off against each other, much to Dilys's despair. She more or less told Mary and me this week that she thought Dicken "too peculiar and poor" and Shaun "too Irish", whatever that means.'

Fergus wasn't sure he had reason enough to confront Dicken, but if he didn't, then he would always wonder. 'If we don't sort this out and it *is* him, he'll do it again.'

'What will you do if it is?'

'Immediate dismissal and a report to the constable. There's no alternative.'

'Do you have to involve the constable? He'll likely be sent to Carlisle gaol and if so, no one will ever employ him.'

'We can't run the risk of serious embezzlement with the Louisa Line. As it is, I'll have to employ someone to check all the books, and that will be an unnecessary expense. If it is him who has taken the money, I'll have to let him go straightaway, even though it will cause me a lot of bother.'

'He's strange and not at all personable, but can't you talk to him? Make him see the error of his ways? Give him a stern warning over it happening again? What about deducting money from his wages to pay it back?'

'For ten pounds? That will take years. Anyway, why are you trying to defend him? Stealing is bad enough, but from a charitable establishment such as the Seamen's Haven, who are attempting to help sailors and their families in need and to support them in distress, well, that's plainly wicked. It's not pilfering, it's thieving.'

'I'm not attempting to defend him as such, I want you to think about what drove him to it.'

'Miss Evangelina?'

'Aye. It's obvious she's been toying with him, egging both him and Shaun on. It was an uneven contest, any fool can see that. Shaun is far more experienced in matters of the heart and Dicken is an innocent. Several times you and I've talked about what Miss Evangelina saw in Dicken. Would you like to know what I think?'

Fergus nodded. Although his mind was made up over Dicken's fate should he be found guilty, he was prepared to listen to his wife because he loved her and he could see she was upset.

'It's about power. Miss Evangelina can snap her fingers and Dicken will dance, and with her having no real feelings for him except as entertainment, he will never hurt her.'

'You're saying he's a plaything to her?'

'Exactly that. Now, with Shaun it's the other way round. She's *his* plaything.'

'That's not a nice thing to infer about Shaun's character.'

'I don't mean it badly, but he's a handsome man with a voice that always sounds as if he's singing, and she's a pretty girl. She's let her head be turned by his Irish lilt and his attractiveness. Dolly mentioned to me once that when Shaun takes a wife it won't be a Miss Evangelina, it will be a "nice" girl who'll make a good mother for his children.'

Fergus stood up and put his arms around her waist. She leant into him. 'You are such a caring person, a true force for good, and I understand what you're saying about matters of the heart.'

'But?'

'Yes, there is a "but". Dicken's a grown man who knows the difference between right and wrong.'

'I agree. What you're missing is, he probably sees himself as a love-tortured Romeo and she as his Juliet, and I'm sure he thinks he loves her. Part of the excitement must be that, in his right mind, he's aware she's unattainable and I'll wager that makes her more desirable.'

'So he's infatuated with her and that's driven him to steal?'

'Yes, exactly. Understanding how she's led him on, will that change your mind about going to the constable?'

'I hear what you're saying in his defence, but it will depend on what he says when I confront him. What his attitude is.'

'You'll do it right away?'

'Yes.'

'I almost wish I hadn't told you of my suspicions. Will you tell your father?'

'Only if we're sure of Dicken's guilt and then, as a fellow Seamen's Haven trustee, I will have to. Whatever the outcome I will urge Father to keep the facts to himself.'

'That'll be a tall order. He'll be furious.'

'You've done the right thing sharing your thoughts. Think how bad you'd feel if in the future he stole your weavers' profits after all their hard work and you'd kept your suspicions to yourself. Perhaps this will put the wickedness of his actions in perspective for you. If it turns out to be him.'

Becky gave a slight nod and kissed his cheek.

'I have to go and find out the truth,' he told her.

✳ ✳ ✳

At the warehouse, Dicken was at his desk entering details in their stock book. He turned round when Fergus entered.

'I'm getting everything up to date for when Shaun gets back tomorrow with all the Dublin receipts and sales information.'

Fergus asked him to finish what he was doing and bade him sit opposite him at his desk. When he was settled, Fergus rested his hands on the desk edge and interlocked his fingers.

'I understand you went to the Theatre Royal last evening,' he said. 'Did you enjoy it?'

'Aye, I did.'

'And you went with Miss Evangelina?'

'Aye, she came too.'

'And you had splendid seats. In a box, I hear.'

'Aye, we did. Not the most expensive ones. We were in the gallery boxes.'

'Yes, Mrs Shackleton told me you were going, and Miss Evangelina told her you'd reserved a box.' So far,

Fergus saw no sign of any discomfort on Dicken's part. He went on. 'All the boxes are expensive. Perhaps there was occasion for celebration?'

'No. Miss Evangelina wanted to see Mr Snipperini's dogs and I agreed to take her.'

Fergus wasn't surprised the dog show had been her choice rather than Dicken's. He had certainly never shown any affection for Charlie. Quite the reverse. 'I wonder, what price was the box?'

The left side of Dicken's mouth gave a slight twitch. To another it would have been barely perceptible, but Fergus, because he was looking at Dicken so closely, did not miss it.

'A shilling,' replied Dicken.

'That's strange. I thought the gallery boxes were one and sixpence.'

Dicken tugged the end of his nose with his thumb and forefinger. *He's lying*, thought Fergus.

'Well, they are usually, but I only paid a shilling.'

'Why was that? You did well.'

'One of the lads who works there is a marra of mine.'

'He gave you a cheap price? On the quiet? I expect the management would be interested to learn about this lad and his cheaper seats.'

'I think it may be a perk he gets. He's one of the stage staff and does the bill-posting.'

There were the beginnings of a slight flush on Dicken's neck.

'It must have been quite an expensive evening for you. Confectionery and refreshments for the interval?'

When Dicken began to go into detail about what was

available and what they had chosen, Fergus decided the time had come to stop beating around the bush.

'Tell me, Dicken, how can you afford on your wages not only to take Miss Evangelina to the theatre in style, but also to buy her a gold bracelet?'

'Gold bracelet?' Dicken was looking more and more uncomfortable.

'Yes. Miss Evangelina told Mrs Shackleton you gave it to her. Did you?'

Dicken's head went down and he began focusing on the table, his eyes scanning its surface as if he were following a glass marble rolling around on it.

'Look at me, Dicken. I have a simple question for you.'

Dicken lifted his head slowly. The slight redness had travelled to cover his whole neck, and still he said nothing, as if he could not trust himself to speak.

'Did you give Miss Evangelina a gold bracelet?'

Dicken bit his lips. 'I think that's my business.'

'Indeed it is, but I think it may be *my* business too. Especially the source of your funds. Where did you get the money for the gold bracelet?'

'It…It's my savings.'

'And you chose to spend the money on Miss Evangelina rather than help your mother out with her coal bill or buy her a new winter coat? I find that hard to believe. Or was it that you couldn't help your mother out because she would have asked you where you got the money? As I am asking you?'

'I tell you, it's savings.' Dicken was blinking excessively and following the imaginary marble on the table top again.

'And you have a savings book to prove it, do you? Perhaps with the savings bank on Lowther Street?'

'I kept the money in the house. In a jar.'

Fergus put his head back and gave a scornful laugh. 'A trained bookkeeper who saves some money from his wages keeps it at home in a jar, rather than puts it in the bank to earn interest? I don't believe you.' He could hear the intense irritation coming out in his voice.

'It's true.'

'You're forgetting that you work for me and that I pay your wage. You come from what many would describe as a humble background and live modestly. Let me put a proposition to you. I think it was you who stole the ten pounds from the Seamen's Haven and that you have been using that money to gain favour with Miss Evangelina Croxall.'

'It wasn't me.'

There was nothing for it – Fergus was going to have to call Dicken's bluff. 'Then let me put another proposition to you. If you're so sure of your innocence, let us go together to the police constable and ask him to investigate the matter of the robbery at the Seamen's Haven.' In truth, Fergus still wanted to avoid any bad publicity for the Haven, or for that matter the Louisa Line. They had reimbursed the missing money, so as far as the warden was concerned the matter was closed. The last thing he wanted now was for it to become public knowledge. He imagined the headline.

"SERIOUS CHARGE OF THEFT AT WHITEHAVEN'S SEAMEN'S HAVEN CHARITY.
A Louisa Line employee…"

'I don't think there's any need to involve the constable.' Dicken's face was now bright red, and there was sweat on his upper lip.

'I can see you would prefer not to alert him. Were you to be found guilty, that would involve a spell in Carlisle Gaol.'

'I tell you it was my savings.'

'Then you have nothing to fear. But should there be the slightest doubt in your mind that you might be unable to prove how you came by your sudden wealth, let us pause for a moment and imagine your incarceration. Apart from the shame and your mother's undeserved distress at you being a criminal, let us imagine the noise, the dust and dirt, the caterwauling of the other inmates through the night. The label of thief forever attached to your name.'

Fergus allowed time for Dicken to imagine the position he might find himself in – a situation he was sure his bookkeeper, with his fastidious ways and habits, would find a great deal harder than many. The problem was, if Dicken did not confess there was little he could do except dismiss him on another pretext.

'If you admit you stole the ten pounds from the Seamen's Haven and we quietly ask Miss Evangelina to return the bracelet, there will be no need to invite the constable to look into the matter. You will be immediately dismissed without references, but you will not have a police record.'

After a short while, Dicken made a choking sound. His face crumpled, and tears rolled down his cheeks. He wiped them away with the back of his hand then, in a quiet, trembling voice, said, 'I was going to pay it back, honestly, Mr Shackleton. I mean, it's not like I really meant to steal it, it's not in my nature. I can pay three pounds of it back. I still have that. It's at home.'

Fergus hoped his relief at the admission of guilt was not showing too strongly. He sighed. 'I would take greater heed of your intention of paying it back had you not denied it so vehemently when challenged a few moments ago. Even so, you planned to steal, you made an opportunity to purchase the bracelet, and may I remind you, you deliberately tried to place the blame on Lois. That in particular is unforgivable.'

Dicken wiped away more tears. 'That's true enough, but I'm an honest man at heart.'

'I have always thought the same. That you were trustworthy. Let me remind you of the phrase "Straight as a die". That is how I would have described you.'

'I'm not sure what's come over me.'

'Tell me, did you not grapple with your conscience when you opened that cash-box? What were you thinking when you put your hand in and brought out money meant for charitable purposes?'

'I can't say. I knew it was wrong, but I couldn't stop myself. I wanted her to love me.'

Oh, Dicken, you poor, poor fool.

Fergus stood. 'Gather up your things and we'll go and collect the three pounds.'

'I'm sorry.'

'I'm sorry, too.' Fergus thought how Becky had pleaded Dicken's case an hour earlier. 'You understand I can't let you remain in our employ?'

Dicken, beginning to sniff, didn't answer. He pulled a handkerchief from his waistcoat pocket and blew his nose.

'We will say you left for personal family reasons. I will speak to your uncle, Mr Rudd, while at the same time asking him to find a temporary short-term replacement from Shackleton & Company's staff.'

Fergus asked where the bracelet had been purchased, thinking perhaps, under the circumstances, it could be returned.

'I bought it in Carlisle. That first day, when I sent the photographer back on his own with a message saying I wasn't feeling well, I stayed away so I could buy it.'

His explanation made sense. 'I'll speak with the Croxalls. They'll have to return it.' Miss Evangelina's parents would be only too happy to have the offending article removed from their home when they learned it was the proceeds of theft. Their daughter perhaps less so.

Dicken, still sniffing, said, 'She'll never look at me now without employment.'

Fergus wanted to say 'She was never, ever looking at you', but he held his tongue. Instead, he said, 'Money and possessions will never buy you love. It's a hard lesson you're learning, Dicken, take note.'

✳ ✳ ✳

Fergus had his work cut out persuading Hector that, for the sake of the Haven's reputation as an honest and reputable charity, his chosen course of action was the best one. As well as being horrified and furious at the turn of events, Hector was piqued Fergus had not consulted him before challenging Dicken.

'As a trustee it's my right to be involved. I accept you try and shield me from the harsher aspects of business these days, but this concerns my sister's legacy. I insist on hearing what Mr Rudd has to say about his nephew. Send for him.'

They waited twenty minutes while Shaun went to fetch Mr Rudd who, besides being Dicken's uncle, was the accountant for Shackletons. All the while Hector kept shaking his head, saying he couldn't believe it. When the accountant arrived, Fergus sent Shaun on an errand so he wouldn't overhear anything and asked Mr Rudd to sit down.

'You must have something serious to say,' said Mr Rudd, looking first at Fergus then Hector. He gave a flippant chuckle.

Hector thrust out his bottom lip. 'You're right, by God, and it's no laughing matter.'

Mr Rudd's expression changed immediately. Fergus didn't trust his father not to lose his temper and it was hardly the man's fault his nephew had proved untrustworthy. He set out the situation and Mr Rudd's hands began to shake.

'Are you sure? He's so timid. Set in his ways and extremely particular about some things. I've always thought that a good trait in a bookkeeper.'

'We have no qualms over his work for the Louisa Line, although I'll have to get the books checked. It is purely the theft at the Seamen's Haven that concerns us.'

'And you say he confessed?'

'Yes.'

'All for this Evangelina Croxall?'

'Indeed, and—'

Hector butted in. 'She's the bookseller's daughter on Lowther Street.'

'I know the Croxalls, but not her. A pleasant couple.'

'If you saw their daughter, you might understand why Dicken's head was turned,' said Fergus.

'What will my sister say? The shame of it will kill her.'

'Partly with that in mind, and with your own many years of exemplary service to Shackleton & Company, but more to protect the Seamen's Haven, we have decided not to prosecute. We will say Dicken is leaving the Louisa Line for personal family reasons.'

Mr Rudd gave a relieved sigh. 'Thank you. Thank you, gentlemen, both of you.'

'We see no reason why you, or your family, should be embroiled in this.'

'How can I repay you?' asked Mr Rudd, taking out a red-spotted handkerchief to mop his brow.

'You can loan the Louisa Line one of our bookkeepers from Shackletons, until they engage someone else,' said Hector. 'Who've we got?'

'There's Isaiah Parsons. He's reliable. Been with us for over ten years.'

'Can we manage without him?' asked Hector. 'Only for a short while, mind.'

'I can take up his reins myself and, if there is anything further that I can do to make amends, I will gladly attend to it. I include financially. I have some savings. You will forgive me, but this is a dreadful shock. I need some time to consider it. Please accept my apologies.' Then, in what appeared to be an afterthought Mr Rudd said, 'I feel I should offer my resignation. It was I who recommended him.'

'It's nothing to do with you,' Fergus said. 'I speak for us both when I say there is no need for any resignation and we don't expect the family to take any financial responsibility. You've been with us for over thirty years; we will not let this affect our business relationship. You are a valued employee.'

'Thank you, but your forbearance in not alerting the constable puts me greatly in your debt. I'm aware of that.'

They agreed Isaiah Parsons would begin the next morning with a thorough edit of all the financial books.

Fergus checked his watch. He needed to call at Croxall's before they closed. Within twenty minutes he was back at Chapel Street, with the gold bracelet safely tucked in his waistcoat pocket. Miss Evangelina had taken it extremely badly and Mrs Croxall had retreated to lie down in her bedroom with the curtains drawn.

CHAPTER THIRTY-ONE

As Fergus had predicted, Shaun kept up a steady stream of Irish tales and interesting conversation on the train to Carlisle. It wasn't long before he had the whole carriage listening in and laughing along with him. When they stopped at Wigton for some people to get on, he whistled a fanfare to welcome them aboard, and further merriment ensued. After that he calmed down a bit. In the conversation that followed, he made a brief reference to Dicken, saying they were advertising for a replacement.

When Becky asked him if he'd ever thought of taking up bookkeeping himself, he guffawed loudly and shook his head.

'Selling's my game,' he said. 'I'm not a sit-in-the-office worker. You should have seen me in Dublin these last few days. I don't want to boast, but talking with my own kind in my home town, I tell you it was a true treat. There's none can toss words back and forth like my own countrymen. Mind you, it takes a lot more chatter to get a sale in Ireland than here in England, but it's worth it for the amusement.'

'You did well, I hear,' said Becky.

'Aye, we sold most of the small items, and Da's keeping what we didn't sell.'

'Isn't he going to sell some of our cotton products for us?' asked Lois.

'He's agreed, as long as the quality is of the highest. He says anyone can produce small cotton items, but quality always sells. I said we'd send him samples as soon as we get them.'

'We'll only have quality, won't we, Mrs Shackleton?' said Lois.

'Aye. On the understanding we can buy the looms and that it will be a while before we'll be ready to work.'

'You're setting up quite a business, Mrs Shackleton, if I may say so,' said Shaun.

Lois bent down to pick up a basket from the floor. 'You've no idea, Shaun, how much difference it makes for us Blackburn folk to be earning a wage and using our skills.' She opened the basket and took out a brown paper packet. 'Ma's baked us some biscuits. Would you like one?'

The movement of the train was making Becky feel slightly nauseous and the thought of a biscuit baked in Shepherd's Court, with its earth floors and poisonous vapours, intensified this. She declined Lois's offer and said she'd have one later. She turned slightly so she could see out of the window, hoping Shaun and Lois would talk amongst themselves so she could rest. It had been an early start and the train's rhythm was making her sleepy, but the noise and the jolting kept her awake.

By the time they reached Carlisle, Becky thought it seemed everyone in the carriage was Shaun's friend. She hadn't missed the exchanges that passed between him and Lois, and she was glad she'd decided to let them sit next to each other, rather than putting herself between them.

It was as cold as Fergus had said it might be, and Becky was pleased she'd brought shawls for her and Lois to drape over their coats. It was only a short walk from the station to the Craft Emporium so they set off on foot, but the bustling streets made Becky wish they'd taken a cab. She was overcome with tiredness again. It was the sort of tiredness that made her feel she would be asleep as soon as she closed her eyes. She asked Shaun if she could take his arm and that helped her stay awake.

When they arrived at Mr Stanley's Craft Emporium he was expecting them and warm in his welcome. After the preliminary greetings, introductions and travel enquiries, he led them into a side room off the main showroom, which was full of handlooms of varying sizes.

Becky turned to Lois. 'This is where *you* come in.'

Lois explained what they needed and Mr Stanley asked various technical questions. After about ten minutes, when both had agreed on size and weight, Mr Stanley pointed out several he thought would be satisfactory. Lois walked amongst them, running her hands over the wood, then singling one out to sit at. She stood and walked round it before focusing on one of the beams.

'What have you seen?' asked Becky.

'I'm looking at these initials. "J. F. W." They've been carved really deeply. A true sign of ownership.'

'It's the previous owner's grandmother's,' said Mr Stanley. 'It came in a couple of months ago. It would be nice to tell her it's gone to a good home.'

'You know her?'

'I see her from time to time.'

Lois ran her fingers over the initials. 'Is she working?'

'She's taken a place in a fish shop. Not what she's used to, but it's work.'

'Don't tell me her full name, but what is her Christian name?'

'She's Josephine, but most folk call her Josie.'

Lois turned to Becky. 'I'd like this one for myself, if the price is acceptable.'

'Let's decide on the eight we need and then we can discuss price. Mr Conran will conduct that side of the business with you, Mr Stanley.' They had agreed this on the train. Becky knew that although she was quite capable of negotiating on price, Shaun was much better at it.

Mr Stanley wrote down the cost of each loom then added them up and wrote the total at the bottom. He handed Shaun the piece of paper.

Shaun frowned. 'This is a bit steep, sir.'

'I've a business to run.'

'Aye, but there's quantity to consider. For sure that's to be rewarded with a discount, isn't it? We're purchasing a product you've no market for. There's no rush to purchase handlooms at this present time, is there?'

'I'll admit to both your points, but these are quality

looms. The American war will not last forever and when it's over, looms will fly out the door again.'

'But we're buying today. And there's the third aspect – we're a charity. We're looking to you to offer support to disadvantaged people who, through no fault of their own, have fallen on hard times.'

'Mr Conran, I run a business. I'm almost a charity myself with this war.'

The bargaining went on for another fifteen minutes and only came to an end when Mr Stanley agreed a suitable discount and offered to meet the carriage costs to Whitehaven.

'As soon as payment is finalised, I'll send them over by the end of next week. If you've spinners ready with yarn, you'll be warped up in two or three weeks, I dare say.'

Becky thanked Mr Stanley and, as they made their way to the Lancaster & Caledonian Hotel for refreshment before making their return journey, all she could think of was that in a few weeks, or perhaps a bit more, their looms could be up and running.

After lunch, Becky asked Shaun to escort Lois for a short walk to inspect the shop windows. She would have accompanied them, but she was suddenly overcome with a great tiredness, and the comfort of the chair she was in, and the heat from the hotel's log fire, were making her sleepy. Recently she'd felt exhausted, having done little to warrant it. She didn't think, as she was sitting in a corner, that anyone would notice if she rested her eyes for a short while.

CHAPTER THIRTY-TWO

Although Becky had negotiated her looms and was awaiting delivery, and the Carter Lane warehouse was being adapted on the ground floor for the carding and washing processes, Fergus decided they would have one last big effort to see if they could sell the cotton.

He shared his reasoning with Becky. 'It doesn't put your weaving project under threat because I'll make sure enough is held back for your handloomers to work with. Enough to establish your business. Also, if we can move some it will create space for you.'

'As long as you can promise me that, then I'm happy. I'm no more than a cottage industry, and there's far too much cotton for us as things stand, but I can't call a halt now. So aye, by all means see what you can do. How will you go about it this time?'

'I'm going with Shaun to Lancaster and staying overnight. We're taking samples. Shaun's father has given us some contacts.'

'When?'

'Monday. We'll be back on Tuesday.'

'Why Lancaster?'

'It's one place we haven't tried and there's a lot going on there with the new dyeing methods. We thought we'd try our luck one more time.'

Becky thought they were going on a wild good chase, but she didn't want to hurt Fergus's feelings. She lifted her hand and, moving Fergus's dark fringe to one side, ran her fingers lightly across his high forehead. 'Whatever happens, everyone knows you and Shaun have done your best.'

Suddenly she leaned forward and began studying him closely. 'You've more silver hairs than you used to have.'

'You knew I was going grey early when you married me.'

'They're silver strands to me. I'm not complaining. In fact, quite the reverse.'

'Let's put it down to living with you.'

'You'd better see how many silver hairs I've got living with you. I'm surprised I'm not completely white-haired.'

❄ ❄ ❄

Hector had asked Becky to call and see him at Queen Street. When she told him Shaun and Fergus were in Lancaster, he shook his head.

'Can't say as I see much coming of that. How are *you* getting on?'

'I set on six carders and four spinners yesterday at Carter Lane. I've urged them to put quality at the top of their list. Never mind if it takes longer, it'll pay off in the end. We're planning four tubs installed on the ground floor for washing, and with Lois's help we've found more than enough willing workers. She's even found a replacement for herself at Coates Lane.'

Hector placed a long thin envelope on his desk. 'Here's a little something to help you along. Go on, open it.'

Becky drew out a sheaf of notes and some gold sovereigns.

'There's £30 to help you with your venture. I'm sure you and those weavers can do with it.'

'Thank you, this is so encouraging.'

'It's not all from me. I was at a meeting at the harbour offices. Mariners, townspeople and the like, and someone who shall remain nameless because you know him, began spouting off about the itinerant weavers and what a nuisance they were.'

'That's terrible.'

'So I told the gathering all about you and what you're doing.' Hector gave her arm a light pat. 'I'll admit I was proud of you. No, that's not right. I was, and am, very proud.'

Becky grinned and took his hand. She felt tears welling up behind her eyes and turned her head away so he wouldn't see them.

Hector went on, 'They were all impressed. I stressed how you were saving the town money by putting all these people in work, and then I struck.'

'You struck?'

'Yes. I said, "Since you're all so supportive, I think we should show our support in the time-honoured way by making a donation". I asked for a dish and we sent it round the room.'

'That's wonderful, thank you so much.' *Thirty pounds. I can do a lot with that.*

'There's always one tries to wriggle out of a collection, but when the meeting finished, I said I'd walk with him to his office, where he said he'd left his wallet.'

'That was naughty of you.'

When Hector paused, Becky wondered if she'd been too cheeky. Then he leaned forward conspiratorially and said, 'You're right, that was naughty of me, but you've got an extra pound because of it.'

❄ ❄ ❄

Fergus and Shaun's trip proved as expected.

'As soon as we said the word "Surat", no one showed the slightest bit of interest. Didn't even ask the price.'

'You tried, and that's the important thing. Don't think of it as a wasted journey.'

'I don't, because Shaun had a brilliant idea you'll love.'

'What was that?'

'That we go window shopping, making notes of the cotton items for sale and their prices.' He pulled a package from his coat pocket and handed it to her. 'Here you are.'

In her excitement, Becky did a twirl, her skirt billowing out as she went. Fergus put his arms out and caught her by the waist, bringing her close.

'You'll make yourself giddy.'

'Aye, giddy with love and gratitude. Thank you. That was such a good idea. I'm proud of you both, as Hector is proud of me.'

'Father proud of you? Why is that?'

Becky told him about the meeting collection and what Hector had said. 'It's not like him to express any emotion so I was shocked.'

'The older he gets, the mellower he becomes.'

❋ ❋ ❋

Dr Fincham had recently decorated his waiting room and the smell of fresh paint hung heavy in the air. After five minutes, it began to make Becky feel nauseous, and she was relieved when she was ushered in to see him.

He stepped forward to greet her. 'Welcome, my dear. Do come in.'

Becky always felt comfortable in Nicholas's presence and today was no different. His beaming face across the desk was reassuring, reinforcing her confidence in him. She'd practised several different phrases to impart her news, but when the time arrived, she came straight out with it.

'I think I'm expecting a baby.'

Nicholas grinned at her. 'I'm delighted to hear this news. I expect Fergus is pleased.'

'I haven't said anything to him yet. You're the first.'

'Well, when he does learn, he will be as delighted as I am.' He chuckled. 'What am I saying? Far more delighted than I am, since he's the father.' He asked her various questions before saying, 'I calculate you are nine weeks into your pregnancy, so we must prepare for the last week of September.'

'It seems a long time away.'

'It'll pass quickly, mark my words.'

'I'm a little afraid.'

'This is perfectly normal, my dear. However, you are young, in sound health and at a good age to have a first child. The senior Shackletons will no doubt be pleased, too.'

'I expect so, but I don't want to tell anyone yet.'

Nicholas scratched his head. 'May I enquire why?'

'Because they'll make a fuss of me. They'll tell me to rest and bring me flowers to press and arrange in albums. That sort of thing.'

'Indeed they will, but is that such a bad thing – to be fussed over? You'll tell Fergus, though?'

'No, not yet.'

'He may guess. Especially if you experience sickness in the morning.'

'I haven't so far. If Fergus and the family are told I'm expecting, they'll say I'm doing too much, that I must rest. "Think of the baby", they'll say.'

Nicholas was quiet for a while. 'They may have a point. And remember, it's their way of showing they care for you and the baby.'

'But you've said I'm healthy, and what can be more natural than having a bairn?'

'You *are* healthy, but that doesn't mean you will always feel as well as you do now. We're in early days. In a few weeks you will most likely be tired. It will be an exhausting, unrelenting tiredness and your body will force you to rest. Soon, it will be obvious to all.'

'Aye, but I don't want all the fussing.'

'Have you thought how special this time can be for you and Fergus? Enjoying the news that a new child is to be born. A time when only you and he have a special secret to share.'

'You mean he'll be cross when he finds out I kept it hidden.'

'I doubt he'll be cross. I'm thinking more of his being upset at the loss of intimacy. You had wonderful news that you did not share with him.'

'I'm not ready to tell him yet. You won't, will you?'

'No, my consulting room is like a priest's confessional. But you are putting me in a difficult position for the future, as he will realise I knew long before him and said nothing.'

'That's all right, because he will appreciate you couldn't. I'm sorry, but I have to be like this. I have my project to see through.'

'I'm not advising you to give up your weaving project, just to do less and allocate time for rest.'

Becky walked home with a bounce in her step. Although she'd been certain she was expecting, to have it confirmed by Nicholas Fincham somehow made it real. She needed enough time to set up her handloomers before her pregnancy became obvious. Of all those close to her, it was her mother she thought most likely to notice a rounder, bonnier face and a small amount of weight gain to her middle. She would have to be vigilant and not let anything slip.

After Fergus had left the next morning, Becky opened the chest in her bedroom and took out the gifts Elizabeth had brought her each time she'd visited – the lambswool matinee jacket, the crocheted shawl, the tiny nightgowns with ribbon ties. If this was what Elizabeth was buying now, what was she going to provide when there was a real bairn to prepare for? She picked up the shawl and buried her face in it. A small lavender bag fell out of the folds. *I wonder if I will always associate our child with the smell of lavender?*

CHAPTER THIRTY-THREE

Mr Stanley's time prediction proved to be over optimistic and it was almost a month, the second week in March, before the first loom was warped up and in operation. The Carter Lane warehouse took on a new lease of life. All the sounds associated with cotton production could be heard every day, except for Sunday morning to allow for church attendance. The women wanted to work. In the mornings there was the washing of the raw cotton set against the all-day background of women chatting over drop-spindles and the soft whirring of spinning-wheels. The most constant and truly rhythmical sounds came from the throwing of the shuttles and the opening and closing of the sheds in the handlooms. The most joyous sound for Becky was the women's laughter and, occasionally, their singing.

After a week of full operation, Becky invited Elizabeth to visit the women at work. Afterwards, and when Elizabeth had enthusiastically marvelled at it all, they retired to try a newly opened tea shop on King Street, where they ordered a glass of ginger beer and a fancy cake each.

'It's wonderful how you've managed it in your condition,' said Mrs Shackleton.

Becky's heart sank. 'In my condition?'

Elizabeth was looking happy. 'I think I'm right that you're expecting?'

Becky had been wrong. It wasn't her mother, who saw her all the time, who noticed the slight weight gain and rounder face – it was her mother-in-law, who noticed it because she didn't see her as often.

'You're right.'

Elizabeth's face lit up. 'Oh, my dear, this is wonderful news. When are you and Fergus going to announce it?'

'I haven't told him.'

Elizabeth's eyebrows rose in surprise. 'You haven't told him?'

Becky shook her head.

'That may be wise. I can confide in you that although I brought Fergus to term, there were two possibilities before him that ended in tears quite early on. But I mustn't put needless worry into your head. You are young and healthy. All will be well, I'm sure. When can we expect the new arrival?'

Becky had never seen her mother-in-law so animated. In a way it was heart-warming, but she knew from this point she was going to be regarded by Elizabeth in a different way – as precious.

'Dr Fincham says the end of September.'

'You will find the heat somewhat troublesome near the end.' Elizabeth put her hand into her bag and brought out a small parcel. 'I brought this for you, and at last you will have need of them. A small gift for you to put away until September.'

Becky opened the parcel and took out a pair of knitted bootees with pale yellow ribbon ties. 'Thank you. I'll put them with the other items.'

'Now, a friendly suggestion, dear, if you will allow me. I think you should tell Fergus.'

'I haven't told Ma yet.'

'You haven't told Dolly? My goodness, that does surprise me.'

'I thought I'd wait until things are more definite.' Becky wasn't going to tell her the true reason – that she'd kept the secret because, as soon as everyone knew she was expecting, they would make her rest and curb her activities.

'I see, well I think she'll be surprised, and perhaps a little disappointed, when she learns I heard this wonderful news before her. Best that you tell her quickly, for I shall find it difficult keeping it to myself.'

'Elizabeth, please don't tell folk yet. I'd like to keep it private for now.'

Elizabeth clasped her hands. 'But I have to tell Hector. Anyway, it'll not be long before people notice for themselves. I expect Lois will take over for you at the warehouse, and your other friends can help too.'

'I don't think I need worry about that yet,' said Becky, bracing herself for what she knew was about to come.

'But you can't go on working.'

'I intend to continue overseeing my charitable work.'

'That may be so, but you've the next little Shackleton to think about. What if you slip walking past one of those baths, or fall down the warehouse stairs? My dear, you are going to have to seriously rethink your activities.'

Becky didn't feel up to arguing. She picked up her ginger beer and took a sip.

'And entering those courts,' Elizabeth went on. 'That can't be good for you. I've heard not even the sunlight can penetrate those places, so tightly are the dwellings packed in.'

'There are women in those courts who are expecting and they are all right.'

'Are you sure?'

In truth, Becky wasn't sure, but she was always careful not to eat or drink anything when visiting. 'What I mean is, I'm not ill. I'm having a bairn, that's all.'

Elizabeth appeared unmoved and since Becky didn't want to fall out with her, she added, 'I'll speak with Dr Fincham and I promise I'll take his advice.'

'You'll have Dr Lennagon for the delivery, won't you?'

'I'd prefer Dr Fincham.'

'Oh, no, I wouldn't advise that, he doesn't have the experience in childbirth our dear Dr Lennagon has. I mean Dr Fincham spent all that time at sea.'

'I'll think about it, I promise,' said Becky, hoping to close the topic.

Her response seemed to bring some satisfaction to Elizabeth, for she turned the conversation to Becky's new home help, Edith, another Blackburn weaver, and asked how she was getting on.

❖ ❖ ❖

Becky was left in a quandary. Should she tell her mother or Fergus first? And then there was Rory. He'd left the day before and would not be back until the end of the month – another two weeks before she'd see him. She decided to tell Fergus first and spent the next two hours waiting impatiently for him to come home.

It was gone six when he came through the door.

He greeted her with, 'I've spent the day with some carriers from the Isle of Man. They want to charter the *Ketton*. I'm not sure about it. There may be more Mauritius work from Macintosh & Warrilow in Glasgow, and Bill and I'd be tempted to finance another run, now we have a better idea of what we're doing.'

'Mary won't be happy.'

'We might send Captain Jessop. There's a lot to ponder. Do I smell apple pie?'

'Aye, with a golden top, and there's thick cream to go with it.'

'Are we celebrating?'

'I thought we might decorate the small room next to Rory's.'

'Is that a reason to celebrate?'

'We're going to be needing it and it looks a bit dreary. I think something brighter will be more welcoming.'

She was grinning like an idiot, but Fergus's confusion was so amusing.

'Who's coming to stay?' he asked. 'Do you want Edith to live in?'

'No.' Becky couldn't contain herself any longer and burst out laughing. 'We're expecting a permanent resident.'

Still Fergus look confused.

'The clue is in the word "expecting".'

As the truth dawned, his eyes grew wide. 'A baby?'

'Yes, there's a bairn on the way.'

'Really? That's wonderful. I'm highly delighted.' There was a brightness in his eyes Becky had never seen before.

'Confirmed by Dr Fincham.'

'When?'

'The end of September.'

'But that's only six months.' He pointed to her waist. 'I thought you'd put on a little weight due to contentment. I see I was mistaken and happily so.' He pulled her towards him for a hug. 'You didn't think to tell me earlier?'

'I wanted to make sure all was well.'

'Certainly you may have your room painted. Whatever colour you like. Stripes, even. We must prepare.'

Becky stepped back reluctantly from his embrace. 'For a man who usually does everything at the last minute, I'm impressed by your forethought. There isn't much to prepare for.'

'Should I be doing something?'

'You can practise answering to "father". That'll be a good start. I'm going to tell Ma tomorrow.'

Becky realised Dr Fincham had been right and she should have told Fergus earlier. She was sad she'd not done so. She'd deprived him of the joy he was obviously experiencing. However, his next words confirmed her fears.

'If I'd known, I'd never have let you take our precious cargo to Carlisle and back.'

Is this the beginning? Becky asked herself. *Am I going to be molly-coddled and wrapped in cotton wool?* She gave a giddy laugh, hoping to convey a light-heartedness she suddenly wasn't feeling. 'I don't think I need to curb my activities. It's not as if I'm doing anything taxing.'

'Aren't you supposed to rest? You're taking on a lot with these handloomers.'

'As the time draws near I'll make sure I rest more, but right now all I'm doing is organising folk. There isn't anything I'm doing I can't keep doing.'

Fergus didn't look at all convinced, but he took her by the waist again. 'Anything?' he asked, a broad grin stretching from ear to ear.

For a few seconds Becky didn't know what he meant. Then it dawned on her. 'Fergus Shackleton, you are a wicked lad and I love you for it.'

Before they retired for the night, as Fergus was stoking the range to see it through the night, he asked. 'Do you think the baby will have mine and Aunt Louisa's grey eyes?'

'I've no idea, but there's a good chance. Put it like this, they won't resemble Sergeant Adam's from the Indian King.'

Fergus picked up a ball of wool from her open sewing-basket and threw it at her. 'They'd better not.'

Later, Becky lay listening to Fergus's regular breathing. She felt as if she was on the edge of a precipice. Everything was going so well, but what if she really did become unable to carry on? It wasn't all about helping the weavers and spinners; a lot of it was about her having a point to her life.

There was a growing fear in her heart that she could have underestimated her stamina and that she really might have to choose between motherhood and her fledgling business.

In the morning, when Fergus asked if she'd slept well, she kept the truth to herself. She suspected that if she told him of her wakefulness and her worries, he would deem it harmful for their baby.

The welcome news that he was to become a father encouraged Fergus to focus his mind on his financial affairs. He spent some time working out future expenses: what might be coming in, what they could save on and what could go wrong. He was meeting everyday expenses from his Louisa Line drawings and his Shackleton & Company dividends, but they were still not covering all the interest on the personal debts he'd taken out to finance his investment in the goods brought back by the *Ketton*. The interim payments he and the other investors had received had enabled him to settle some of the payments, but he remained personally far too indebted to the Lowther Street Bank, and the fate of their home rested on that.

Gathering the invoices and receipts from the Whitehaven and Carlisle sales, he cursed the fact he'd had to let Dicken go just when he needed a competent bookkeeper. It wasn't the first time he'd felt this way, but as always, when he went over it in his mind, he concluded he'd had no choice, for the good of the Seamen's Haven's reputation and the financial security of the Louisa Line.

After working out what they'd sold, what was remaining

and what he could hope for from Conran's continuing efforts in Dublin, it always came down to the same thing: selling the cotton was crucial. Not just because they needed profit, but because it was preventing the Louisa Line from taking in storage custom by occupying space in the warehouse. How things had changed. Were it not for Becky and her charitable enterprise, they would be planning to sell the cotton at a great loss or, at worst, paying someone to burn it. If he was honest with himself, he wasn't sure how he felt about his wife being accountable for his own financial future. It wasn't the way things were supposed to be.

'We need to sell the rest of the *Ketton*'s goods,' he told Bill, when he arrived with some Customs and Excise papers for Fergus to sign.

'I know. What's left?'

Fergus handed him a list. 'I think we need to be positive over this. There's enough here for another sale in Whitehaven, but we need buyers to come to us, or it's not going to be worth it.'

The next morning Dolly was out when Becky called at the Indian King. Sergeant Adams, his dog Molly fast asleep on his knee, beckoned her over.

'Come sit with me and Molly, lass. It'll be grand catching up with you. I've not seen you in a while.'

'Did Ma say when she'd be back?' Becky was anxious to deliver her news and get on her way. She had a backlog of errands to run.

'Said nowt to me, but I o'erheard her tell that barman she was off to the butcher's for a bit o'pork.'

'That'll be the one on King Street,' said Becky. If her ma ran into someone she knew, or if she remembered another errand, she could be some time. She scratched Molly behind her ears and sat down.

'What's this I hear about you and some of them Blackburn weavers?'

The sergeant refilled his long pipe as she told him about going to Carlisle for the looms and setting up at Carter Lane. He listened intently and gave the occasional encouraging nod as she spoke.

'You've a kind heart in you helping these folk.'

Half an hour passed. Becky was on the point of leaving when Dolly arrived carrying a brown paper parcel and a bag full of groceries, which she put on the bar.

'Hello, Becky, love.' She pointed to the parcel. 'I've a lovely bit of pork to boil up, and I picked up a chicken. All for a fair price. The bird needs plucking. I don't suppose you –?'

'Sorry, Ma, not today, I can't.'

'Always busy these days running around town.'

'I need a word.'

Dolly turned to look at her. 'Something amiss?'

Becky shook her head, picked up the parcel and inclined her head in the direction of the kitchen. 'You go ahead. I'll bring this through for you.'

With the parcel unpacked, and the kettle heating up on the range, Becky sat down on one of their least rocky kitchen chairs. She felt awkward. With neither of them having time to spare, this wasn't how she wanted to tell her mother she was expecting a bairn, but she couldn't trust Elizabeth not to say something.

'What is it, lass?' asked Dolly, sitting herself down.

Becky hesitated.

'If it's not important, can it wait?' her mother asked. 'I've jobs to see to and I was longer at the butcher's than I intended to be.'

'It *is* important.'

'Well?'

'I'm expecting a bairn.'

Dolly's jaw dropped. 'Oh, lass, I wasn't expecting that.'

'It's me that's expecting, Ma, not you.'

They both laughed.

'That's a blessing for you both. When?'

'End of September.'

'Fergus happy?'

'I only told him last night. I didn't want a fuss. Are you happy?'

'Happy? You have to ask? Of course I am.'

'You seem a bit downcast.'

'Nothing like that. I'm thrilled.'

'What is it then?'

'I wonder if you realise what expecting a bairn involves, with all you've taken on recently.'

'Let me stop you there, Ma. I've already had it all from Elizabeth, and Fergus, too. Dr Fincham says he's going to look after me when the time comes. I'll do as much as I can because I've plans and I want to see them through.'

Dolly shifted in her chair. 'You told Elizabeth before me? When?'

Becky put her hand to her mouth, realising she'd made a big mistake. 'Yesterday. I didn't tell her. She guessed and I confirmed.'

'I see,' said Dolly, tight-lipped. 'Well, I've a right to advise you and look out for my own daughter, haven't I?'

'And I've a right to make my own decisions in life, haven't I?'

With her mother informed of the good news, all Becky wanted to do was leave. The morning was not turning out as she'd thought it would.

She told a white lie. 'I'm expected elsewhere.' She gave her mother a quick hug and left.

Outside in the street she allowed tears of frustration to flow. She'd worried that once she was with child this was how it was going to be, but it was proving worse than she'd imagined. Her family advising her to rest, to step back. Well, she wasn't going to do that. She was going to rush into the fray with a banner in one hand and a sword in the other. *Let them stand aside and watch me.*

❖ ❖ ❖

Later that day, Becky called in at the Seamen's Haven. The warden, always welcoming to her, was delighted to receive the books Fergus was donating for the sailors' rest room.

'Having a tidy-up, are you?' he asked.

'Aye, I think my husband thinks if he donates books here he can always seek them out as old friends if he misses them.'

'We're always happy to receive them. Even those who

can't read like to be read to. Understandably, *Moby Dick* is a firm favourite.'

As the warden went into the excitement of whaling ships, Becky felt a tiny fluttering, like butterfly wings deep inside her. She instinctively made to put her hand on her front, but the fluttering stopped. She thought she'd imagined it, but it happened again, and then again. Outwardly she was giving the impression she was listening to the warden's every word, even nodding appropriately. But her mind was searching for a word. *What's it called? There's a name for it, I know there is.* Then it came to her. *Quickening, that's what it's called. Quickening.*

'What did you say?' asked the warden.

Becky, realising she'd spoken out loud, said, 'Oh, it's nothing.'

But it wasn't nothing. It was the most wonderful thing in the world – her and Fergus's child making its first stirrings.

CHAPTER THIRTY-FOUR

The first weeks of the quickening brought with it unexpected bouts of nausea. Becky first noticed it when she put in a leg of lamb to roast. As the odour of hot fat began to fill the kitchen, she had to open the windows and leave the room. She began losing weight, not as a result of actually being sick, but because the constant nausea stole her desire to eat. She began taking a short walk in the half hour before noon to settle herself and to try to muster an appetite. Returning from one of these, she found Elizabeth waiting for her in their parlour, having been ushered in by the new help, Edith. Becky sighed; Lois would have had the sense to send her away, advising her to call later.

Elizabeth was clutching a small brown bottle with a cork stopper. 'You'll forgive me calling without an invitation or giving you notice, but I've brought you some ginger barley syrup. I've been told it's a most useful aid for your type of sickness. Mixed with boiling water and taken three times a day, it settles the insides wonderfully.'

She brandished the bottle. 'I never had your problem with Fergus, so I shouldn't really advise you, but it may help.'

No, you wouldn't have, thought Becky, who'd been irritated recently by the way Elizabeth seemed to think she'd had a perfect pregnancy, and that Becky, with her nausea, was somehow failing in that respect.

Elizabeth removed the stopper from the bottle. 'Perhaps you'd like to try some?'

The thought of drinking anything other than pure water was abhorrent, but Becky knew Elizabeth was trying to help.

'Thank you. Perhaps a small amount.'

Elizabeth disappeared into the kitchen to return with a large cup from which steam was rising. 'Best let it cool a while,' she said, putting it down.

There was a short awkward silence. Then she said, 'I saw an unopened parcel in the kitchen. Have you had a delivery? Shall I bring it through so you can open it?

Becky shook her head. 'No, it's a plucked chicken for the weavers' families in Shepherd's Court. I was supposed to deliver it this morning. Dolly gave it to me yesterday.'

Elizabeth tut-tutted. 'I'm aware I've made my position clear about all that you undertake, but honestly, my dear, I can see you'll be a lot better off today staying here than delivering a chicken. Especially to one of those courts.'

'I agree I'm not at my best, but I'll be better later and I'll see to it then.'

Elizabeth frowned. 'Can't someone else deliver it?'

During her walk Becky had wondered if it really mattered if she put the delivery off by a day, but the chicken would go off if she left it too long.

'I could ask Mary. I mentioned it to Edith, but she has to take her ma to the infirmary when she's finished here.'

To Becky's surprise, Elizabeth said, 'Can I help?'

'That's a kind thought, but I hardly think so. Really, I'm much better in the afternoons and the weather is fine today.'

Elizabeth looked at her with questioning eyes. 'Are you sure?'

As Becky lifted the cup of ginger barley to her lips, an idea surfaced. 'Perhaps if we could get the chicken to Mary, she could deliver it for me. She knows several of the Shepherd's Court women. She won't mind, even though she's found out she's expecting, too.'

A sunny smile brightened Elizabeth's face. 'This is happy news, and a timely playmate for our own new arrival. I'll be happy to take the parcel to Mary and I can congratulate her at the same time.'

They chatted for a further half hour, during which time the ginger barley syrup did make Becky feel a little better, and she was grateful to Elizabeth for that.

✻ ✻ ✻

The next day Fergus was at the Gentlemen's Club, enjoying an end-of-the-week early evening apricot brandy with Jeremiah Todhunter, the shipping agent. They were discussing potential business opportunities for the *Eleanor Bell* when the club secretary approached.

'Forgive me for interrupting, Mr Shackleton sir, there's a gentleman says he's employed at your Louisa Line offices. He's here to speak with you.'

Fergus excused himself and was met by Isaiah Parsons, the replacement bookkeeper at the club's entrance.

'I'm sorry to bother you, Mr Fergus, but there's word from the Queen Street butler your mother's not well and would you please attend immediately.'

Fergus raked his fingers through his hair. 'Unwell? What did Samuel say, exactly?'

'That she's suffering an illness.'

'Not an accident?'

'Not as far as I'm aware.'

'And father, is he there?'

'He wasn't mentioned.'

Fergus was alarmed. If he was being summoned, his mother must be most unwell. He apologised to Mr Todhunter and within a short time was being greeted by Samuel at his parents' front door.

'What's happened?'

'The mistress woke feeling unwell. She took no breakfast and returned to bed. She's been there all day. The master and Dr Lennagon are with her.'

Fergus took the stairs two at a time and met the doctor in the corridor outside his parents' bedroom.

'How is she?'

'It grieves me greatly to say this, Fergus, but my initial diagnosis is that your mother has a severe bout of cholera.'

'Cholera? Surely not?'

'I agree, it is most unusual for someone of your mother's status in the town to have contracted it.'

'Isn't it a disease of the poor?'

'Yes, that is the usual case, but the yellow bile coming

from the gut leaves me no doubt. I'm taking the precaution of messaging Dr Fincham to call and proffer his opinion on treatment. You'll forgive the details, but I have instructed that a specimen of the bile *vomitus* be retained for his inspection. Having practised abroad, and in hot climes, he will have a much better opinion on the outcome than I can. I must leave now to report to the Board of Health.'

'Must you? Don't they make people whitewash their walls?'

'It is a legal requirement, but I don't think they will find it necessary to whitewash here, as Queen Street is most unlikely to be the source of your mother's infection.'

'And Father? Is he well?'

'He shows no signs of sickness. He's taken this all badly, so I've prescribed a restorative tonic – not strong enough to sedate him, just enough to calm him. I should add that he is unhappy with my decision to consult Dr Fincham, but I told him this was not the time for ancient squabbles and left-over feuds. I had to be quite firm with him.'

'He is devoted to my mother, so I'm certain he will be arguing for what he truly thinks is best. I will speak with him.'

'Before you enter, you should prepare yourself. Cholera is very quick to change the physical appearance of its victims.'

'Is she alert?'

'There have been moments of lucidity, but unfortunately, these moments so far have coincided with ongoing bouts of nausea. It is a vile disease. I'm afraid you can expect the bowel distress and griping pains to become worse.'

'I must send for Becky.'

'No, you must not. In her condition it is far too dangerous. I would go so far as to say it would be prudent for you to keep your distance too, and you may consider spending the night here, rather than returning home to your pregnant wife.'

Fergus thought of how he'd visited Aunt Louisa after her fall, when she was dying. He had the same helpless sick feeling in his stomach as he'd had then. He paused to say the Lord's Prayer before knocking gently and entering his parents' bedroom. His eyes went straight to his mother, who appeared to be asleep. Her arm, with bluish fingers, was outside the sheets, resting on the covers. The skin over her cheeks was stretched and her features much shrunk. Fergus knew cholera attacked its victims mercilessly, but he hadn't expected to see such a rapid decline in his mother's visage, despite Dr Lennagon's warning. There was no doubting she was seriously ill.

His father, looking as if he'd aged ten years or more in one day, was slumped in an armchair about six feet away from Elizabeth's side of the bed. Seeing Fergus, he lifted a shaking hand and placed two fingers to his lips for silence, motioning him with his other hand to come closer.

With a tremor in his voice, he said softly, 'We'll talk in my study. Dr Lennagon has given your mother a sleeping draught.'

Fergus let his father lead the way. Hector took small steps, shuffling rather than walking, and at one point he put a hand against the wall to steady himself.

In the study, he bade Fergus sit and turned his own chair away from his desk, so they were sitting face to face.

'How can this be?' asked Fergus. 'Where has she been to catch it?'

'Over dinner last evening she told me she'd visited one of those courts to deliver a chicken.'

Fergus leaned forward in his chair.

'You may well look confused,' his father said. 'You heard correctly; I *did* say "deliver a chicken" to one of the courts.'

'Why would she do that?'

'It seems Becky was unwell, the parcel needed delivering and your mother offered to take it to Mary. When she called there was no one at home, so she decided to deliver it herself.'

'Why?'

'She told me she was curious. "I thought it an opportunity to see for myself how these people are living", were her exact words.'

'How did she find the place?'

'Perhaps she asked for directions, but she obviously did find it. All through dinner she was telling me about it, and how awful the conditions are, and how she could well understand why Becky wanted to help. She seemed proud of herself for having braved it.'

'She could have brought the chicken home and asked Samuel to arrange delivery.'

'Exactly. But she didn't. Her curiosity got the better of her.'

'But surely she can only have been there a few moments?'

'That's what I thought, but Dr Lennagon asked her if she had anything to eat or drink when she was there. One of the women offered her a cup of tea as a "thank you".'

'Dear God, don't tell me she accepted it?' Even as Fergus said the words, he knew his father's answer was going to be in the affirmative.

'Regrettably, she did. You know your mother, always alert to social niceties. She told Dr Lennagon she took it "because it would have been so rude not to".'

Fergus put his hand to his brow. 'I can't believe it.'

'She's paying a heavy price for having good manners.'

Their discussion was interrupted by Samuel, who announced Dr Fincham had arrived.

After observing Elizabeth for some minutes and inspecting the *vomitus* specimen, the doctor confirmed his colleague's diagnosis of cholera, and Fergus saw his father's face pale.

'Will we lose her?' asked Hector.

'People don't always die, do they?' asked Fergus.

'The mortality rates here in Whitehaven are high, but I have seen unexpected recovery several times following the best care. I must warn you, however, it is unusual for people to survive. This is a disease that follows a regular path and its course passes through definite stages that are obvious to see. Once some of those are passed, there is no turning back.'

'What stage are we in?' asked Fergus.

'We are at the stage where a draught of chalk julep, opium and oil of peppermint should still be effective. We used this in Mauritius.'

'Do you have some with you?'

'No, it needs to be freshly dispensed.' He wrote out a prescription sheet and handed it to Hector. 'Any apothecary will do. The ones in Lowther Street are the nearest and should still be open. If necessary, knock one up.'

'I'll send Samuel straightaway.' Hector pressed a round bell-button beside the fireplace.

'In the meantime, I will bleed her by cupping and administer a teaspoon of calcined magnesium, rhubarb and ginger powders, mixed with sugar water, every few hours. I have the ingredients with me. I can mix this up myself.'

'Is there anything else we can do?'

'When she next stirs, she must be wiped down with water as warm as she can stand it, followed by flannel rubbing. It's important she fights the disease with heat. After this, we must keep her well covered with blankets, with a view to encouraging perspiration.'

'Dr Lennagon said she will ask for water.'

'Yes, it's the draining of the fluid from within the body that is the devil of this disease. We can give her water, but no more than two or three tablespoons at a time.'

'What is the next stage?' asked Hector.

'She may appear to be sinking. Her pulse will drop, her skin will become colder and her breathing more laborious. There will be a definite change. I will sit with her so that at this point I can inject two pints of warm water into her hand.'

Fergus cringed at the thought.

'When will we know if she's going to win this battle?' asked Hector.

'The third stage is the crucial one. I'll be watching for a rise in her pulse and for her natural colour to return to her features. It's at this point that all stimulants should be removed and she must be kept quiet. At this juncture, she will either recover with proper care and pass into a state of convalescence, or there will be a sudden sinking.'

'Is there anything else we can do?' asked Fergus.

'You can pray,' said the doctor.

'I'll hold family prayers and instruct all the staff to attend,' said Hector.

'Since I shall be keeping watch here and unable to attend, may I say a prayer I used in Mauritius before I begin the cupping?'

'Yes, of course,' said Fergus, thinking the more prayers said the better it must be.

Dr Fincham took a small piece of parchment from his bag, cleared his throat, and began reading.

'To Thee, oh Lord, who are the resurrection and the life, we acknowledge Your power and goodness in staying the course of this deadly pestilence. To Thee we beseech deliverance for our dear Elizabeth when the travails of man can do no more. In You and through You may she receive health and salvation, through the name of our Lord Jesus Christ.'

The three men's voices came together in unison with a robust, 'Amen.'

Before family prayers began, Fergus sent a note to Becky briefly setting out the circumstances of the situation and how it had come about. He'd never felt so helpless in his life. His mother was probably on the cusp of death and there was nothing he could do about it. At the same time, the one person he needed to turn to for comfort he was not allowed to be near. During the household prayers he negotiated silently with God that if his mother did have to die he would grant her the strength to live long enough to see the child he and Becky were bringing into the world.

CHAPTER THIRTY-FIVE

Upon receiving Fergus's note, Becky felt as helpless as he was feeling in Queen Street. The clock struck nine. Rory, two days back from Glasgow, was half-undressed, preparing for bed. Becky rushed upstairs and told him to put his clothing back on as they were going to the Indian King.

'Right this minute?'

'Aye, I need to speak with Mrs Dolly.'

'What's up?'

'Mrs S's not well.'

'A little bit sick or really poorly?'

'Sick enough for me to want to talk with my mother. I'll wager Shaun'll be there having his supper. I'm sure he'll entertain you, or you can show Sergeant Adams how you're getting on with your scrimshaw. Bring your jacks' bag in case you have to entertain yourself.'

Shaun *was* there, his feet firmly under the kitchen table and, to Becky's astonishment, Lois was sitting across from him. Becky left Rory with the two of them to seek out her ma and found her in one of the guest rooms, turning the bed down.

'I didn't expect to find Lois here sitting with Shaun,' she said, unable to keep the surprise from her voice.

'Those two have been deep in conversation for the last two hours.'

'Really?'

'Aye. She was here last night too, and the evening before that.'

'Do you think they're...?' Becky left the obvious word hanging.

'Aye, I do. Nothing untoward, mind you. All above board. In my book, there's nothing wrong with it. The little I've eavesdropped, he's been talking to her about Ireland.'

Becky would have asked more questions, but she'd not got Rory dressed and out of the house for gossip. As she told Dolly about Elizabeth, her ma's face assumed the serious expression Becky saw only on rare occasions, in response to genuine concern.

'The cholera? That's bad, really bad and it's always so quick.'

'Do you think I'm to blame, letting her take the chicken?'

'No, how could you possibly expect she'd take it into her head to take it there herself? There were lots of other ways that parcel could have been delivered. Mind you, this may not do your charitable work any good in Hector's eyes. From what you've told me his view of the weavers has softened since he first learned about them. He can be opinionated and once set it takes a lot for him to back down. I hope this won't fuel any prejudice.'

'It's hardly my weavers' fault.' Becky knew her mother had a point. 'And after he's given me so much help, too.'

'No, but thank goodness *you* didn't go.'

'I'd not have been foolish enough to accept food or drink. What can she have been thinking?'

'Heaven knows. How are you? You don't look as peaky as the last time I saw you. Have you told Rory you're expecting yet?'

'Fergus took him for a walk on the meadow the first night he was back.'

'How did he take it?'

'Fergus said he was pleased and thought it'll make us more of a family.'

'You're so fortunate with that lad's good nature.'

'He'll be distraught if we lose Elizabeth. I've only told him she's not well, but the lad's no fool.'

'The one it will affect the most is Hector. Their marriage has been a successful love match. He might be sharp and caustic with others, but he truly loves her, it's plain for all to see.'

Word had spread quickly about Elizabeth's illness and the handloomers at Carter Lane sublimated their usual chatter into respectful murmuring when Becky arrived. Shaun, with Lois at his side, greeted her.

'It's a sad day,' he said, 'and I've been praying for Mrs Shackleton, but we do have some cheerful news. We've the first fancy antimacassar samples to show you. Come and see. I'm sure they'll soon be gracing the backs of fine armchairs in grand houses.'

Shaun and Lois led the way to the back of the warehouse, where an area had been set aside for the inspecting and packaging of finished goods.

Becky picked up the top textile from a pile. It was softer to the touch than she'd imagined it would be. The pattern was of two swans, touching heads, on a pond surrounded by bulrushes. It was intricate and effective.

'It's wonderful and decidedly a quality product. Is this the first?'

'Yes.'

'How many do we have?

'Enough to send to my father in Dublin tonight, to test the market for quality and pricing.'

'Who made this one?'

'I did,' said Lois. 'I'll be quicker next time.'

They walked amongst the busy handloomers. To one side were several small jute sacks, stacked by the back entrance, as if waiting to be loaded onto a cart.

'What's in those?' asked Becky.

'It's the stones and bits of straw and dry muck we've taken out of the cotton. I've found a buyer for it,' said Shaun, looking smug.

'A buyer? Who'll buy that debris and what for?'

'Seeing it lying here, I thought to myself, sure there's got to be a use for it, and it came to me. I put the idea to Lois and she agreed. It's our surprise for you: Surat Stone.'

Becky was intrigued. 'Go on, who's the buyer?'

'All kinds of folk. It's perfect for small footways. It can be put down on earth to give a firm footing. We've been approaching folk who's got pigs and privies a short walk from their homes in their backyards. Makes all the difference in the winter if you're walking on a bedded-in path rather than trekking through squelchy mud.'

'You're selling it to make pathways?' Becky was astonished.

'That's correct. A shilling for a small sack. Folk can't get enough of it.'

'But it's small stones and twig-like rubbish,' she said.

'Aye, but it's the right size and texture for a pathway if you put enough down and stamp on it. We're paying the carter a penny a sack to deliver in town, and we get eleven pence profit. All for the cost of setting a small jute sack for the carders to fill when they're teasing the cotton.'

'Who thought of that?'

'Shaun did,' said Lois. 'You should hear him selling the sacks. You'd think he were offering them a palace carpet.'

'And when Lois isn't weaving and comes with me, she explains about the cotton and where the stones are from. She makes them sound wonderfully exotic, coming from India. That's why we call them Surat Stone. It does the job and does it well. That's the most important thing. In fact, folk are grateful for the opportunity to upgrade their walkways so cheaply. God's truth, it's all in the name. You don't mind us setting this up, do you?'

Becky was in awe. 'Not at all. Most enterprising. You two make an excellent team.' She didn't miss the exchange of looks that passed between the two of them. There was definitely more to this Anglo-Irish friendship than most other folk realised.

What will happen if he sweeps her off to Dublin? I depend on her for advice and expertise? Becky told herself someone else would step forward to take Lois's place, but she didn't want anyone else. *He can't leave us before we've made a success of everything.*

❋ ❋ ❋

While Becky was at Carter Lane talking to Shaun and Lois, Dr Fincham was presenting a progress report on Elizabeth to Fergus and Hector in the drawing room. No one in Queen Street had slept well, and some not at all. Family prayers had been a sad, sombre affair, with Samuel having to remove a distressed laundry maid, whose loud sobs began upsetting the others. At 2am, Dr Fincham gave Hector a mild sleeping draught, promising him that if there was any major change, he could be easily woken.

Hector thanked the doctor before retiring, fully dressed, to one of the small guest rooms along the landing, asking only for a blanket to cover himself with. The chaise longue from the drawing room was brought in for Dr Fincham so he could sit with Elizabeth and doze should he be able to. Fergus settled himself in the drawing room in his father's favourite chair. He rose several times and, on each occasion, found Dr Fincham awake, tending to Elizabeth. The doctor had sent for two nurses from the Fever Hospital who had taken over the nursing and practical side of things. All soiled laundry was being placed in sacks to be taken away and burned in the infirmary's incinerator.

Conversation at breakfast the next morning was muted, with both father and son deep in thought. Similarly their appetites had deserted them, with Hector managing a small portion of scrambled egg and Fergus just toast and marmalade. They went in together to see Dr Fincham.

'Gentlemen, I can report that although Elizabeth endured a painful, restless night, she has held her own. I have been able to offer her a small glass of spirits this morning and she took it well. However, we have reached the disease's third stage, where it always looks as if there is no hope. This is the point at which the disease will retreat, should we be lucky enough for the miracle we're all hoping for.'

'You're saying we're at the crisis point, and it can go either way?' asked Fergus.

'Yes. I've arranged for mustard plasters, and in half an hour shall offer her a light cinnamon cordial.'

'Can we see her?'

'Yes. You'll notice one of her thumbs is unnaturally purple from an abscess. It appears to be a specific centre of infection and I intend to lance it when I return to her. It will be helpful to me if you're there, for the pain of the lancing may break through her current inertia and it will help her to see you both there at her side. You must not come too close, though.'

'You want us to distract her?' asked Hector.

'Yes, gentlemen. If you will kindly follow me, we can attend to the business in hand.'

Fergus's eyes went straight to his mother's thumb. It was greatly enlarged and a shockingly dark purple colour.

Were she more conscious it would be extremely painful; he imagined the blood must be pulsating inside. He had once had a small boil on his cheek, and it had caused him pain, but nothing as severe as his mother's thumb appeared to be.

One of the fever nurses laid out a small basin, some muslin cloths and a scalpel on the bedside table. She picked up Elizabeth's hand in a clean towel and clasped her firmly by the wrist. Dr Fincham took up the scalpel and Fergus turned away.

After the deed was done, Elizabeth, woken by the sharpness of the lancing, focused her eyes first on Hector, then Fergus, and finally on the fever nurse, who was wiping up the blood and mucus that had been released from her thumb. Eventually she settled her gaze on Hector, who had rushed forward, only to be pushed back by Dr Fincham.

'I don't want the cere cloth,' she said, in a raspy, crackly voice.

'What?' asked Fergus 'What's she saying?'

'She doesn't want the cere cloth,' said Hector.

The nurse explained, 'All those who die from cholera must be buried within twenty-four hours, wrapped in a cere cloth. It's linen that's been saturated with pitch or coal tar. Sometimes they dip it in wax, as well.' She turned away from Elizabeth and dropped her voice to a whisper. 'They don't let hardly anyone at the graveside, either.'

'That's dreadful,' said Fergus. He spoke directly to his mother. 'We won't let that happen. Anyway, you're not going to die, we won't let you. Dr Fincham is doing all he can to help you. He's lots of experience. You won't die.' Fergus thought he must look as if he were throwing straws to a drowning woman, but he couldn't stand there and not give her any hope.

The bedroom door opened and Samuel put his head round.

'Your wife is at the door, Mr Fergus, sir.'

'Go to her,' Hector said. 'I'll sit with your mother. She may speak again.'

Dr Fincham signalled agreement. 'Keep your distance, do not touch your wife or allow your breath to reach her.'

'I'll go ahead and ask Mrs Becky to step back,' said Samuel.

✻ ✻ ✻

Becky was so shocked when she saw Fergus, she began to cry. It wasn't the obvious lack of sleep, or that his clothing was badly creased, showing he'd slept in it – it was the deep sadness in his eyes. She wanted to run and put her arms round him, to protect him by wrapping him in all the love she had for him. For one fleeting moment, she wished she wasn't having their baby. It was creating a barrier between them, for were she not pregnant, she would not be the outsider in the drama that was unfolding. A drama perhaps she had brought about.

'Oh, Fergus, this is all too, too awful. How is she?'

'We're at a crisis point. She may pull through, or...'

'Has she spoken?'

'Nothing we can understand.' Fergus wasn't going to tell her about the cere cloth. It was too dreadful.

'She's conscious, though?'

'She drifts.'

'Is she in pain?'

'It's hard to tell, unless she's awake, and then she's obviously uncomfortable.'

'When will you be home?' Becky didn't want to upset him by saying how horrible it was being on her own, knowing him so close.

'It depends...If anything happens, I'll send word by Samuel straightaway.'

She blew him a kiss. 'Be careful.'

'I am.'

The conversation dried up. Becky knew she should leave and let him get back to Elizabeth, but she couldn't. He would have to turn away first. An awkward silence followed, until Fergus said, 'I should be getting back.'

Becky watched as he stepped back inside and the door shut behind him. She stayed looking at the closed door, wondering how what was happening inside was going to affect them. She was nervous about seeing Hector and wondering whether he would blame her in some way over the parcel delivery. Even if he didn't, he was certainly going to blame the weavers for making Elizabeth ill, there was no doubt about that. But there was more – ever since Elizabeth had fallen ill, Becky had had the feeling that whether she survived or passed on, her illness was going to change things for her and Fergus. Quite how, she wasn't sure, but she knew it in her bones.

CHAPTER THIRTY-SIX

Returning to his mother's bedside, Fergus wasn't sure enough to say it out loud, but he thought perhaps her colour had returned a little. Her thumb had been bandaged, enlarging it grotesquely. She was asleep, having had one of Dr Fincham's draughts, and was swaddled in blankets. The fire was roaring in the grate. He loosened his necktie.

Dr Fincham was standing by the fireplace. 'The crisis is upon us. Her pulse has risen.'

'Is that a good or a bad thing?' asked Hector, who was perched on the edge of the chaise longue. He'd taken off his jacket and was perspiring from the heat in the room.

'It's at this point of apparent recovery that we must pray the hardest. I don't go so far as to say this is a sign she may recover, but there has been urine production after a long period with none.'

'Surely it must be hopeful?' said Fergus, following his father's example and removing his jacket.

'Some would say so, but I've been caught out before.

It's the internal workings that will provide us with a more readable prognosis of possible recovery. A healthier discharge is a good sign. The nurses are keeping me informed.'

Poor Mother, having to go through all this indignity. She has always been such a private person.

'There's something I must share with you both,' said Dr Fincham, in the most serious of voices.

'We're listening,' said Hector.

'When I say possible recovery, I don't mean a full recovery. Should we receive the answer to our prayers, and Mrs Shackleton survives, she will pass into a state of convalescence. By that I mean she will require specialist nursing, the strictest care over her diet, and the avoidance of certain animal products, such as offal and pork. She will have weakness of body and possibly, from time to time, some confusion in her mind.'

'How long will this last?' asked Fergus, thinking he would arrange for a live-in nurse.

Dr Fincham's voice wavered. 'It's not a state that will change.'

'You're saying she'll be an invalid for the rest of her days?' said Fergus.

'It sorrows me greatly to confirm this, but she will not recover completely.'

'She'll be able to walk, to go outside? Won't she?' Hector paused. 'To talk?'

'I fully expect her to be able to speak. It's more the physical side of life that will be difficult and as such, it's perhaps advisable to consider she will most likely be bedridden. You have to understand, her body is undergoing a fearful assault.'

Tears ran down Hector's cheeks, and the sight of them brought a lump to Fergus's throat and a wetness to his own eyes. He removed his handkerchief from his waistcoat pocket and handed it to his father.

'She'll still be with us, Father, and here for your grandchild. There will still be joy in your lives together.'

'Fergus is right,' said Dr Fincham. 'You'll continue to grow old together and it must surely be a comfort that you'll not face your last years alone.'

'Sweet words of consolation from you both, and I thank you for them, but this turn of events is a bitter pill to swallow.'

'You must rest, Father. If Mother comes through this, she won't want you looking weary and out of sorts.' What Fergus didn't say was that his mother wouldn't want to see how much her husband had aged so suddenly, and how frail he now seemed to be.

✻ ✻ ✻

On April 7th, Fergus, having been given permission from Dr Fincham to move back home with Becky, was arranging to engage a full-time nurse for Elizabeth. Dr Lennagon had given him several names, and he and his father were holding interviews that afternoon. Becky hadn't said anything, but she thought they might have asked her to sit in on the interviews, too. As it turned out it was just as well, for at the same time as Hector and Fergus were assessing their first applicant, much to Becky and

Shaun's surprise, Padraig Conran arrived unannounced from Dublin at the Carter Lane warehouse.

'Well, it's good to be seeing you, my son,' were his first words. Then, turning to Becky, he said, 'And it's a wonderful sight for my eyes, Mrs Shackleton, to see you looking so well and blooming.'

'You're most welcome here, Mr Conran.' Becky wondered whether his sudden arrival boded well or ill. *Has he come to collect Shaun?*

He gave her one of his engaging smiles. 'Now, who is it I'm to be dealing with? Yourself or my Shaun here?'

'In connection with what?' asked Becky.

'The fancy cotton goods.'

Shaun stepped forward. 'It's Mrs Shackleton's business, Da, but I'm her financial adviser and general manager.'

'Then it's with the both of you I'll be wanting to speak.'

They adjourned to the same tea room on King Street where Becky had met Hector, away from the noise and bustle of the warehouse.

'Having inspected the samples, I've come over to see for myself what's going on and to give you my verdict.'

'You like them?' asked Becky.

'I'm well pleased with the pieces you sent me and, if the price is acceptable, I'm after taking all you can produce.'

'All our stock?'

'To be sure.'

Becky looked at Shaun. 'Am I hearing correctly?'

'I'm thinking the same – my brain's saying my hearing's amiss.'

'Have the two of you stuffed cloth in your ears?' Conran

made a great play of inspecting Shaun's ears. 'What I'm saying is I'm wanting to buy what you've got. The quality is top class, up there with French merchandise.'

'Really?' Becky was delighted. She thought of the haberdasher she and Lois had visited for their samples and his French pieces.

'Sure, those French haberdashers' prices are as high as the Tower of Babel, so if we can negotiate an acceptable price, I can undercut them and still make a good profit. So, what are your prices?'

Becky straightened her back. 'We sent the prices with the samples.'

'And so you did, but you'll be negotiable on those?'

'Our price is our price,' said Becky, thinking she sounded quite firm.

Conran let out a loud guffaw. Several people turned and looked across at them, frowning over their teacups. Wearing a playful smirk, he placed his hand on Shaun's arm. 'You're not telling me you let this astute gentle businesswoman fix her prices with no room for negotiation, when you knew she was sending her samples to me?'

'What do you think, Da?'

Conran reached over and slapped his son's thigh. 'I knew you didn't. I trained you up. I've sent you over here, Shaun, to learn how to carry out business. Show me what you've learned and what you both can do.'

'I'll start,' said Becky, producing a written list from her pocket. She wasn't going to let Conran think she didn't know what she was doing. 'I'm not surprised you want first buy; you've always had an eye for quality. Considering costs, adding on profit – and seeing what inferior goods are selling for here in Whitehaven – we're looking at a dozen antimacassars at 10/3 for the large and 7/9 for the smaller ones. Armrests at 7/6 per dozen.'

Shaun leapt in with, 'We've a new line you're going to like in maids' cuffs. 7/2 a dozen.'

'You'll appreciate that these prices are slightly lower than the list we sent with the samples,' said Becky with a smile.

Conran checked some notes he'd been making on the back of an envelope. 'Is there room for further trimming of these prices, Mrs Shackleton?'

Becky was ready for him. 'In my dealings with haberdashers I've always thought quantity the deciding factor as far as discounts are concerned. The more you purchase, the better the deal. Isn't that right, Shaun?' She was having difficulty keeping a straight face.

'It is indeed. That's something you taught me, Father, and I remember mentioning the very same to Mrs Shackleton.'

'"Hoist by my own petard", as you English say,' said Padraig.

Becky thought she detected a touch of fatherly pride in his eyes.

Shaun took up the negotiating baton. 'While you're thinking of quantities, we can discuss delivery and dates.'

Conran folded his envelope and put it in his waistcoat pocket. 'I'll be wanting to buy by the gross, twelve dozen. Anything less than that per item, it's not worth the effort and the seasickness crossing the English Channel.'

Becky began trying to estimate what several dozen of each item would come to, but her excitement kept getting in the way and she couldn't concentrate enough to keep the figures in her head.

'When will you take delivery?' she asked. 'As you can imagine, we don't have that sort of inventory to hand.'

'I'll be leaving Liverpool the first week in July. Can you transport to the docks there?'

Becky was sure they could, but she'd thought of something else. 'Mr Conran, isn't carriage paid by the purchaser, and isn't it usual to lay down a deposit for a large order? We've other businesses we can approach who'll pay us before the end of June, and we've payments to make ourselves that need honouring.'

'I hear your words, Mrs Shackleton, but do you really want to walk away from a profitable arrangement for the sake of a few more pennies?'

'Mr Conran, you have my best price so it would be you walking away.'

Padraig proffered a big smile. 'Well, you're the one, Mrs Shackleton, indeed you are. Good negotiating points you've made. No doubt, Shaun, if this good lady hadn't beaten you to it, you'd have made the same points yourself.'

'The words were perched on the tip of my tongue, all ready to tumble out.'

Conran rubbed his palms together. 'I've to find a room for the night, but let's all sleep on the figures and the details and meet tomorrow. At your warehouse at noon?'

'You must come and stay at the Indian King with me.

I'm sure there's room. I'll introduce you after you've had a proper tour of the warehouse.'

With Conran avidly peeping into the dark corners of the warehouse, it was well over half an hour before he and Shaun departed. When they'd left, Becky took stock of the afternoon. They'd gone from no custom at all to having sold all the stock they could produce. She'd no doubt they could negotiate on price to everyone's satisfaction, otherwise Conran wouldn't have made the journey from Dublin.

Later, when she was alone, she went up to the top floor of the warehouse and surveyed the bales of cotton, neatly stacked as far as she could see. She now saw them with different eyes. They represented a lifeline, not only for the weavers, but for Fergus and herself. Importantly, if Conran was so keen to take their wares, then there must be others. As long as they were able to keep up production of the highest quality, they could pay for the cotton. The investors would make a small profit, the weavers would have wages and self-respect and, best of all, Fergus would be able to pay off his debts and they would keep their lovely home. Small it may be, but it was *their* home – the special, intimate place where they had conceived their bairn with passion and love.

Later, when she told Fergus with undiminished excitement about Conran's offer and the indication that she could have a viable business, he put his arms round her waist and, despite his worries, waltzed her round the office, humming joyfully.

'Can we stay in Coates Lane?' she asked, eyes full of hope.

'If things work out as we are being led to believe, then I am confident all will be well.'

Becky started crying. 'You say "if".'

'Only because "there's many a slip 'twixt cup and lip".'

'Don't say that. Your father said if I wasn't confident about the weaving venture, I shouldn't launch it. So, no expressing of dismal thoughts, please, Fergus.'

He took her in his arms and buried his nose in her hair. 'Have I told you, you have the most beautiful eyes and I love you very much?'

'Not recently, but I know you think that.'

CHAPTER THIRTY-SEVEN

There was a haze of cigar smoke in the study at Queen Street. Fergus and Hector's third session of interviewing applicants for a live-in nurse had not gone well. It had proved to be a dispiriting task, and with heavy rain now beating rhythmically against the windowpanes, the afternoon had become dreary outside too, adding to Fergus's gloom.

He was becoming exasperated. 'I'm sure we could engage a good nurse for Mother if you were less exacting, Father.'

They'd interviewed nine prospective nurses in total, with Hector finding them all miserably lacking. Too shy, too forward, not bright enough, too knowledgeable, too tall, too fat, scrawny-looking and likely to answer back. The weakest criticism, thrown at a middle-aged lady whom Fergus thought eminently employable, had been, 'spoke with a Scottish accent.' That was the remark that told Fergus no one was going to be suitable. Also, it seemed locally that the pot had run dry.

'Neither Dr Lennagon nor Dr Fincham, nor the Warden of Nursing, can think of anyone else to recommend, Father.'

'I'm not prepared to tolerate anyone second-rate and neither will your mother. With the fever nurses gone and our own staff so good with her, I'm beginning to think we should abandon the search.'

'They're good with her because nursing is a new experience for them and they're enthusiastic. I expect in a few months they'll tire of all the lifting and nursing, and who's to blame them? They weren't engaged as medical staff. Besides, some of the duties are personal and somewhat unwholesome.'

'I'm not suggesting we place the total responsibility on our staff. While we were interviewing this afternoon a sensible solution came upon me.'

'Which is?'

Pyramiding his hands and looking over them, Hector said, 'With no one to oversee the running of the house, the obvious answer is for you and Becky to move here. What do you say?'

To cover his surprise, Fergus paused, then said, 'You don't really mean that, do you?'

'I do. Rather than have strangers living here, if you move in, the family will be together, and you and Becky will have a lot more room. We'll engage a day nurse.'

Ah, that's it, thought Fergus. *He's made up his mind he doesn't want a stranger living in, so I'm right, no interviewee will be suitable.*

Fergus chose his next words carefully. 'That's an

interesting idea, but Becky won't want to leave Coates Lane. We've only been there coming up a year. It's our home and soon we'll be welcoming our child into it. She's busy preparing and decorating.'

'I don't doubt Becky will not be overjoyed, but it's about duty to your mother.' The word 'duty' rose high into the air and rattled around the rafters.

After taking a moment to digest his father's suggestion, Fergus said, 'I admit, on the surface it's a sound proposition, but I don't think it a solution.'

His father drew on his cigar. 'Why not?'

'It's not fair to place the running of Queen Street on Becky's shoulders.'

'I don't see why. We've a solid butler in Samuel, a decent housekeeper of sorts in our cook, Mrs Harvey, and plenty of others to do the physical chores. Damn it, she'll be living in one of the nicest houses in Whitehaven and not have to lift a finger. Won't that mean anything to her?'

'Father, there's no need to swear. Becky has no airs and graces. Yes, our home is small and we'll be cramped when the baby arrives, but Becky loves it. It's her domain and this is Mother's. Can't you see it that way?'

'And your mother? Confined to her bed or forced to lie on the chaise longue in the drawing room? What a dismal existence it will be for her. You being here would change everything – especially having Rory to entertain her. She loves him as her own, just as you do.'

Fergus tried another argument. 'What about the noise? What will it be like with the rumpus an infant brings? And then there's Rory. He can be quite an irritating bright spark when he wants to be, and it sometimes seems he can mess up a tidy room just by sitting quietly in it.'

'That was then. Everything has changed. Your mother will welcome Rory and he can play chess and read to her when he's home. He'll be close to his rabbit. I like the boy. Besides, he's often away at sea.'

'What about his dog, Charlie? They're inseparable, day and night. Charlie has always had free run of the Indian King and Coates Lane. They bed down together every night at sea. It'll be cruel to them both to banish Charlie to sleep in a kennel. And he'd soon cause mayhem with your fine carpets and his scratching. He's not trained to roam a grand house such as this. He's a mongrel, still akin with his wild ancestors roaming the great forests, and it's too late to train him. He'd never understand.'

Hector took out his handkerchief and wiped his forehead. 'I'm not saying there won't be minor problems to sort out, but we've a family crisis and we need to pull together.'

'It's a big thing to ask.'

'We'll not discuss it now, son. I realise it's a big step for you. Think it over. Talk to Becky about potential change. She loves you, she wants the best for you and, more importantly, in her heart she knows she has a duty to your happiness. And with that duty, through marriage to you, comes a secondary duty to your mother. Becky's a bright girl, anxious to please. She'll come round eventually because she wants *you* to be happy. It's an excellent platitude that "a true wife follows her husband's path in life".'

Fergus could think of nothing to say that his father would want to hear, so kept his thoughts to himself. 'I must go and see Mother before I leave.'

'She was able to tolerate a half bowl of chicken soup last night and some porridge for breakfast. Genuine signs of improvement.'

Elizabeth was awake when Fergus entered the sickroom. To his horror, there seemed even less of her, but she smiled pallidly at him and knew it was him. He had to restrain himself from rushing forward and putting his arms around her to protect her from all the evils of the world.

As if she could read his mind, she said, 'Don't come too close.' Then she added, 'Rory hasn't been to see me.'

'He's at sea, Mother. Halfway to Dublin, I expect.'

She nodded sagely. 'And Becky, how is she?' she asked, in a whisper. 'And the baby?'

'Well, both of them.' He was going to add that Becky could feel the baby moving, but it was too late. Elizabeth had closed her eyes. By the rise and fall of her chest, Fergus could see she was asleep.

He sat with her for ten minutes, during which time he thanked God for her deliverance from death and prayed He would look down on her with kindness and provide her succour to face the trials and tribulations ahead. He banked up the fire then left, treading carefully to avoid the two floorboards by the door that creaked and needed re-laying.

❋ ❋ ❋

At Coates Lane, Becky was sitting on the sofa, her legs tucked up beneath her, skimming through her book of Cumbrian ballads and songs.

'Fergus, I'm glad Elizabeth was a little better today,' she said. 'I've arranged to visit her tomorrow. Dr Fincham says there is no danger to me or our baby now.'

'She'll be pleased to see you.'

She put her book down and studied her husband. 'What's wrong? You seem elsewhere. In fact, I'd go so far as to say you seem nervous.'

'We need to go and see Dolly.' He knew it was cowardly to involve Dolly, but he was afraid Becky would become so upset, she might find her mother's company comforting.

'She'll not thank us. She'll be getting ready for the early evening rush. In half an hour the place will be full of thirsty colliers.'

'She's not on her own. She can ask one of the barmen to help out.'

Becky gave him a funny look. *Something is amiss. But what?*

At the Indian King, Dolly didn't need to be asked twice if she had a little time to spare. Becky thought she too must have detected something out of sorts in her son-in-law's demeanour.

'We'll go in the kitchen. I'll make some tea.'

'Could you and I perhaps have something a little stronger?' asked Fergus. 'A glass of Madeira? Lemonade for Becky?'

Dolly made no comment, placing the order with the barman and instructing him to deliver it to the kitchen.

While Fergus and Becky took off their coats, Dolly busied herself putting out a red chenille tablecloth. She raised her eyebrows and cast a quizzical look at Becky, who responded with a slight shrug. She'd no more idea than her mother what was going on.

The barman arrived with the glasses on a tray and was about to serve them when Dolly waved him away, saying, 'I'll see to it.'

As soon as the door closed Dolly put her hand on Fergus's arm. 'Right, Mr Shackleton, son-in-law, what's all this about?'

'My father has made a suggestion.'

'Concerning what?'

'With Mother bedridden indefinitely, he has suggested Becky, Rory and I move into Queen Street.'

'What?' said Becky.

'Permanently?' asked Dolly.

'Yes.'

'I hope you put him straight right away,' said Becky.

'I told him we'd think about it. Don't look at me so crossly, Becky. You haven't seen Mother. You might think differently if you had.'

'I told you earlier, I'm seeing her tomorrow. You really told your father we'd think about it?' *This is why he looks so uncomfortable. He's seriously considering it.* Becky rubbed her forehead as if in pain.

'It's a sensible suggestion,' said Dolly.

'Sensible it may be, but we're not going.' *No, no, no.*

'Wait a minute, love. Hear Fergus out.'

'I see you're on his side?' Becky was aware there was an out-of-character tetchiness to her voice.

'I'm not on anyone's side, lass. The suggestion is perhaps a good one on a temporary basis. I'm not saying you should take it up, just that there's some merit in it. It's for you and Fergus to decide. I'm not going to interfere.'

Becky, feeling herself burning up with frustration, said, 'Temporary will undoubtedly become permanent. I'm not falling for that.'

Fergus began fiddling nervously with his shirt cuff.

'Becky, you'll not do the bairn any good being so upset,' said Dolly. She put out her hand, but Becky snatched hers away before she could reach it.

'Father says he has a duty to Mother to care for her as best he can,' Fergus said.

'Hector is her husband and as such, he has a duty to her,' Becky said impatiently. 'But so do you have a duty to me, and I to you. Coates Lane is our home, Fergus. I'm preparing it for our child.'

'I know, and I did spend some time trying to alert Father to this, and to all the disadvantages his plan entails, but I feel there's something deeper to your antipathy.'

'There is. I'm afraid I'll become another Elizabeth, keeping the household accounts diary but in another woman's home.'

Tears of frustration began tumbling from Becky's eyes. She wiped them away with spread fingers. She felt as if her life was spiralling out of control.

'There are advantages,' Fergus continued. 'I think we need to consider them. More space for everyone, we can oversee Mother's care and—'

'Rigid meals with your father morning and night. My

mother having to ask a butler to let her into her own daughter's house. The staff knowing all our business each hour of the day. I don't want a life like that.'

Dolly stood and embraced her daughter. 'It's all right, lass. I'm sure something can be worked out. I don't think, in his heart, Fergus wants it either, do you?'

When Fergus didn't answer immediately, Becky lifted her head. 'Is this something *you* want, Fergus?'

'It's not, but we could let Coates Lane out and bring in some rent. We don't have to sell it.'

'This isn't about money, Fergus, it's about us. About our marriage. About you and me and Rory and our bairn.'

Dolly had motherly tears in her own eyes. 'I thought you were getting a nurse in to look after Elizabeth?' she asked.

Fergus explained how his father had given up the idea of employing a live-in nurse and was refusing to move on that score.

Before he'd finished, Becky butted in with, 'You haven't once mentioned the responsibilities I have to my weavers. They depend on me financially and are not yet a self-supporting group. They need me. You seem to be forgetting the rescuing role they're taking on with the Surat cotton. Without them, you and your investors would be scrabbling about, trying to get rid of it. Have my weavers and I saved our home from your debt-collectors, only for you to effectively snatch it from me?'

'That's unfair, Becky. No one's expecting you to give up your business, but I would agree there would need to be some reorganisation in management, purely because you won't have as much time.'

'I feel I'm fighting to keep my home and my business, both of which I'll lose if you bow down to your father's demand – because believe me, it's not a suggestion, it's a demand. Pray tell me, Fergus, what will you be giving up that means as much to you? You seem perfectly happy to give up our home.'

'I'm seeing this in a wider context than giving up our home. I'm seeing my mother, sick at heart, effectively bedridden, reduced to the life of an invalid. My father ageing before our eyes, distraught that the woman he loves almost died, and having to ask for every task to be done for her. If I can make things better for them by giving up our home then, yes, I'm prepared to do it.'

'I think this a good moment to pause this discussion,' Dolly said. 'There's much for both of you to think about and, in my opinion it's best slept on, otherwise you're going to be going round in circles, with neither of you getting anywhere.' She stood up. 'I've work to be doing. Go home, both of you.'

'I'm not going anywhere,' said Becky, in a tremulous voice. 'I know you've a spare room at the moment. I'd like to spend the night in it. I can do my thinking there.'

An uneasy silence fell in the kitchen. All that could be heard was some hissing and crackling from inside the range.

Fergus picked up his coat. 'If that's what you need, a night apart, then I'll not demand you come home.'

After he'd left, and Becky had shed more tears, Dolly said, 'Fergus isn't the villain here. He loves you – his face lights up when you enter the room – but he loves his mother and father, too. You have to ask yourself, wouldn't you be torn in the same situation? Wouldn't you also at least want to think things through? You didn't marry a man who would turn his back on his family when they appealed for help. As he is with them, loyal and dutiful, so will he be with you when you need him to be.'

'All this because Hector won't tolerate a live-in nurse. What would you do, Ma?'

'You've to think on it yourself. I can't decide for you.'

Can't or won't? thought Becky.

CHAPTER THIRTY-EIGHT

When Becky arrived home, having spent most of the night in fitful sleep and waking even before the gulls, she felt ready to continue her discussion with Fergus with less emotion. Finding he'd already left for Chapel Street, she was both relieved and disappointed. She'd deliberately dallied at the Indian King so she wouldn't have to face him, but when she opened the door and saw his coat missing from its peg, she wished she'd followed Dolly's advice to, 'Get home with all speed before he leaves for the warehouse.'

There was only one thing for it – she would have to seek him out. It was the responsible thing to do. She couldn't go all day without speaking with him, even if it was going to be awkward. On her way into the warehouse, she collided with the auctioneer, leaving in a hurry.

Shaun and Conran were in the office, which was a surprise as she'd only expected to find Fergus and Isaiah Parsons who was nowhere to be seen. Fergus gave a curt nod when she entered. She thought his eyes looked sad.

'I met the auctioneer coming out,' she said. 'Have you set a date for the last auction?' She directed her question at no one in particular.

'We've confirmed Wednesday, the 23rd,' said Fergus.

'Shall you come?' asked Shaun.

Becky shook her head. 'I've commitments with my weavers.'

Conran, buttoning up his coat in readiness to leave, said, 'It's a grand thing you're doing, my dear lady, it really is. Helping all these women, and we're all benefitting.' He addressed his next words to Fergus. 'You're fortunate to have such a capable wife, sir. She's a real asset to you.'

Fergus gave what Becky thought was an uncomfortable smile and handed Conran his hat. 'It's always good to see you, and thank you for letting us keep Shaun a while longer.'

'Thanks to you, too, for the experience he's getting. I'm proud of him and the way he can charm businesspeople.'

'He's *your* son,' said Fergus. 'What did you expect?'

Conran let out one of his loud laughs and turned to Shaun. 'Don't you go getting a big head on your shoulders. When you're back in Dublin I'll be in charge, and your mammy'll have you in church every Sunday come what may.'

'I'd have it no other way,' answered Shaun, laughing.

'There's no need to charm *me*. I'm your father, remember?'

Becky thought it an appropriate moment to enquire about future plans. 'Shaun, when are you planning on returning to Dublin?'

'I'm away there today,' Conran answered, 'but we've agreed Shaun'll stay for the auction then return to Dublin. We'll be back to collect the weavers' goods and set off for France at the end of June. I've a sailing booked for France the first week in July.'

'So, another five or six weeks. Then when you're back from France you'll both return to Dublin to expand your business?'

'Da's got big plans.'

'We'll miss you, won't we, Fergus?' She turned to look at him.

'You'll not see the back of me easily,' said Shaun with a big grin. 'I'll be back to visit on business, and I've friends here.'

Becky guessed he must be referring to Lois. She thought they'd make a good couple and had told Fergus so.

'You'll know when I'm back – you'll hear me whistling before you see me.'

Shaun left to escort his father to the Dublin post-boat, leaving Becky and Fergus alone in the office.

'I trust you slept well,' said Fergus.

'I did, thank you.' She wasn't going to tell him she'd tossed and turned.

'Have you had further thoughts?' he asked.

'Aye.'

'And you've talked more with Dolly?'

'A little, but she says it's not her business. Don't think she's on your side.'

'It's not about sides, it's—'

'Say no more, please, Fergus. I'm expected at Queen

Street this morning to see your mother and I don't want to upset her by being late. This afternoon I'll be at Carter Lane with the women. There's some packing needs overseeing. Let's talk this evening.'

Normally, if they were in the office alone and she was about to leave, Fergus would take her in his arms and kiss her. However, on this occasion he remained behind his desk.

'I'll be home at six,' he said, somewhat abruptly.

At the door Becky paused, wondering if she should approach him, but when she looked back, she saw he'd transferred his attention to some papers.

With a lump in her throat and a sadness in her heart, she closed the door quietly behind her and set off for Queen Street.

✲ ✲ ✲

'The mistress is asleep,' Samuel said. 'Shall I tell the master you're here? He's in his study.'

Becky shook her head. She'd no wish to speak with Hector. Certainly not before she'd had the conversation that she knew she had to have with Fergus at six o'clock. 'Perhaps I can sit with Mrs Shackleton senior a while. I won't wake her.'

'I understand, Mrs Shackleton.'

'There's no need to tell Mr Shackleton I'm here. I don't want to interrupt him. I'm sure he's many things to see to.'

'As you wish. Shall I arrange for coffee to be sent up?'

'Thank you. In due course. I'll ring for it.'

The fire was lit in Elizabeth's bedroom, always a sign of illness; there were nursing accoutrements on a side-table and the room had been stripped of unnecessary ornaments for ease of cleaning. Becky thought this a shame, for it seemed ridiculously bare and must surely be depressing for its occupant. She would never have allowed the room to be stripped in this way. It was a nursing tradition she had never thought necessary.

Elizabeth was propped up on pillows looking pale, feeble and alarmingly thin. Her thumb, resting on the sheets, was bandaged. Becky was shocked. Fergus had spoken truthfully; his mother was in a dreadful state and far worse than Becky had imagined.

Sitting quietly, listening to the muffled sounds of the daily workings within the house, Becky wondered what it would be like to be mistress of Queen Street. She surveyed the room, taking in the carpet and the curtains, all carefully and lovingly chosen by Elizabeth. It occurred to her that had Elizabeth died, then having to move and take up the reins would have perhaps seemed a natural step, but the fact her mother-in-law would be party to all Becky would be taking on was one of the reasons that made it so objectionable. She remained captured by her 'what if' thoughts for ten minutes, during which short period Elizabeth stirred several times, before becoming fully awake.

Looking at Becky with dull eyes, she said, 'Ah, Becky, my dear, I am so pleased to hear you and Fergus are going to be moving here. It will be such a comfort to me to have you both so close to hand and to have you here for Hector.'

Becky opened her mouth then shut it. *What can I say? I can't tell her we're not going to.*

'Hector tells me Rory will be thrilled that he'll be close to Harry, and there's the kennel Hector is going to have built for Charlie.'

All morning Becky had been reasonably successful in sublimating the anger she felt towards Hector, even trying to see the situation from his point of view, but he wasn't playing fair – not to her, to Fergus, nor to Elizabeth. She couldn't be angry with her mother-in-law because it wasn't her fault: she'd been misinformed. No, she was angry with Hector, and she would seek him out and tell him so.

Becky changed the conversation to the new baby, then to Rory, and nothing more was said about future plans. The more she thought about Hector's meddling, the angrier she became inside, yet the more she chatted with Elizabeth, the more she realised how desperate her mother-in-law's plight had become. As their conversation ran its course, Elizabeth began taking pauses, and the pauses became longer.

After another quarter of an hour's small talk, Becky took her leave, promising she would call again soon. She went in search of Samuel, finding him in the kitchen chatting with Mrs Harvey.

'If it's convenient, I'd like to take that coffee upstairs, Samuel, if I may. I'm going up to Mr Shackleton's study. Please inform him I shall be there shortly. I want to check on Rory's rabbit before I do. Thank you.' In truth, she was greatly in need of fresh air to pull her thoughts together and urgently required a moment on her own to calm herself before tackling Hector.

She was at the kitchen door leading outside when Mrs

Harvey called after her, 'We're looking forward very much to you being here.'

Luckily, Becky was facing the door and her involuntary grimace was hidden from both Mrs Harvey and Samuel. She bit her bottom lip to stop herself from making a comment she would regret. Just as it wasn't Elizabeth's fault she'd been fed misinformation, so it wasn't Mrs Harvey's, either. It was Hector manipulating events. Becky turned back, not trusting herself to speak, and gave a smile, doing her best to make it reach her eyes.

The door was open when Becky finally reached Hector's study. She was taken aback by his appearance. He'd lost a lot of weight; his cheek bones were protruding, his whiskers needed a trim, his hair was untidy and there was a sharpness to his face she'd never seen before. He looked washed out and seemed to take up a lot less space, both physically and in spirit.

Samuel appeared with a silver tray and proceeded to pour the coffee. He put Hector's cup beside him on his desk. As he did so, Becky noticed a half-drunk glass of brandy by her father-in-law's hand.

'These are dark days, Becky, but I don't need to tell you that.'

Becky felt her anger diminish, even though she tried hard to keep hold of it, for it was this anger that had driven her to instigate what she fully expected to be an unpleasant confrontation. However, suddenly she had no opponent. There was nothing honourable about berating a man so eaten up with sorrow he was forgetting to comb his hair.

'You've seen Elizabeth?' he asked.

'Aye, she was pleased to see me and I her.'

'Yes, she would be, but you realise even though she still lives, we've lost her?'

'I don't agree. She was talking well with me.'

'Superficially it's Elizabeth, but she's lost her merriment and joy. And where will she find it in her life now?'

'We talked about the new baby and she became quite animated, although for a short while only, I'll admit. It seemed to exhaust her, but I don't think we can say we've lost her. What I do want to talk about is that you've told her and the staff that Fergus and I are moving into Queen Street.'

Becky experienced a momentary glimmer of satisfaction when Hector's face flushed; it seemed he had the grace to feel embarrassment.

'But you will, won't you?'

'Nothing is decided.'

'Ah, then you are angry with me for anticipating?'

Becky would have used the word 'manipulating' rather than anticipating, but she let it pass. 'I'll not deny I'm upset. Telling Elizabeth and the household staff is a cruel trick you've played.'

'I want to make Elizabeth happy and, to me, uniting the family under one roof seems such a perfect solution to everyone's problems. Is that so wrong?'

'On this occasion, aye. You've raised Elizabeth's hopes and caused Fergus and me to be at cross-purposes.'

'Then he is with me and you are against. Am I right?'

'Fergus is undecided, torn between duty to his parents

and his own soon-to-be-expanded family. But I know if I say yes, he'll agree. However, I've found a niche for myself with the women from Blackburn and whilst initially you couldn't understand their plight, and probably have reason to resent them, since it was a weaver who made Elizabeth ill, the Carter Lane handloomers mean a great deal to me. They place purpose in my life. I'll be the first to acknowledge I'll have less time when our bairn is born, but with Queen Street added to my responsibilities, I'll have to give up my projects completely just as they're coming to fruition. It seems to me, I'm expected to take on new chores and responsibilities without having been consulted. I'm the one giving up the most and benefitting the least.'

Becky was relieved to see Hector seemed to be considering what she had to say.

'Whatever I first thought of the Blackburn incomers, I've thought well of your charitable intentions, and it's true you have made a name for yourself in the town as a force for good.'

'I wouldn't go so far as to say that, but I've done a little to ease some people's lives. Some of them are dependent upon me for their living and I carry the responsibility for that.'

'I'll not undermine the pride of both of us by begging, but I ask you to think long and hard about—'

'Please don't say duty.'

'I wasn't going to. I'm asking you to think long and hard about what will be best for your family in the two, three, perhaps more years to come. To think about growing up in this spacious home, with all the advantages it has to offer, your children surrounded by a loving extended family. Rory loves being here; your own children will too. There will be support close at hand for you at all times.'

'Fergus and I are discussing the situation this evening. No doubt he'll report to you in due course.'

'Ah, you don't want to discuss it with me. Then so be it. I await your decision.'

CHAPTER THIRTY-NINE

While Becky was sitting with Elizabeth, imagining what it would be like to live in Queen Street, Fergus was having his own thoughts. He tried to put himself in Becky's shoes. How would he feel if he had a fledgling business and was asked to step back from it? On a whim he left the Chapel Street offices and, walking up Roper Street, turned into Carter Lane. He stopped for a moment outside what he'd recently begun thinking of as 'Becky's warehouse'. Someone on the first floor was singing a folk song and the women were joining in the choruses. The overall feeling, even before he'd set foot in the door, was of a place of happiness and endeavour. He said aloud under his breath, 'My Becky created this.'

He decided not to go in, because he didn't need to. The question of how he would feel if he were Becky had been answered. He walked the length of Lowther Street, pushing his way through the Wednesday afternoon crowds. He acknowledged people he recognised but, lost in his own thoughts, he didn't really see them and narrowly avoided stepping out in front of a cart rumbling past with a squeaky wheel. On the quay, the gulls were cawing at full volume, following a fishing boat with a full hold. He stood and watched a brig depart for foreign parts. A line of schoolchildren walking crocodile-fashion marched past, and Fergus's thoughts shot ahead to a future where his and Becky's own child would be walking in such a line. Perhaps more than one child.

How can I make this right for us all?

❖ ❖ ❖

Anxious to keep busy before her six o'clock appointment with Fergus, Becky spent the afternoon in the Carter Lane packing-room with Lois and another girl.

After half an hour, when the girl had left and they were alone, Lois said, 'When Shaun gets back from France, he wants me to go to Dublin with him, Mrs Shackleton.'

'This is rather sudden,' Becky said. 'Are you saying he's proposed?'

'Not down on one knee, no, but he talks of Dublin and how much I would like it. He wants to take me to see it when he gets back from the French trip with his da.'

'Do you want to go?'

'Well, he makes it sound wonderful. It's a busy city, you know? A port like Whitehaven, but much bigger. Lots of old buildings and wide streets. There's a river runs through it and you can stand on this big bridge and see all the ships coming and going and unloading.'

'I see, and looking way into the future, for you must admit your association is recent by any standards, if he asked you to marry him and move there, would you go?'

'I can't. Well, not until the civil war's over and cotton comes back in. I'm the family breadwinner. Then there's you.'

'Me?'

'All you've done for us. I couldn't walk away at a time when you're going to need me more than ever, when the bairn arrives, and with the business expanding.'

'I was thinking quite a way ahead in the future. When you've had time to get to know each other better.'

'It wouldn't be before he comes back from France.'

Becky was relieved a Dublin visit wasn't imminent. It was true she relied on Lois a great deal for the day-to-day running of the warehouse and overseeing the women. She was reconciled to losing Shaun, but to lose Lois so soon, and at the same time, would create problems when she least needed them.

'Have you spoken with your family about his interest?'

'Oh, no. They'll be against him because he's a Catholic.'

'Your parents won't approve?'

'Mam won't. On occasion she's whispered to me of people, with a hand covering her mouth, that "they're Catholics". Recently I asked her why she said that and she said, "Because my mother said it and her mother before her". I said, "But why? What's wrong with them?" Mam wouldn't be drawn, which makes me think she doesn't know. There's a word for how she feels, but I can't think of it.'

'Prejudiced?'

'That's it.'

'Has Shaun brought the subject up? He must know you're a Protestant.'

'He's told me that in Dublin there's Catholics and Protestants live separate lives, going to different schools and working in different places, so as a rule the two sides never meet. He says I'm the first Protestant girl he's ever really got to know. I mean you can't count that empty-headed Miss Evangelina. He doesn't see her anymore; she's been sent to York to stay with some cousins.'

Although she side-stepped making a comment, Becky was thinking how different the two young women were.

'I see three obstacles for you and Shaun,' she said. 'Your role as the family's breadwinner, your religion, and the fact you don't really know each other that well. Shaun may be a very different person in Ireland. Your loyalty to me regarding Carter Lane is most honourable, and while I undoubtedly view you as irreplaceable, if I had to, I would with regret have to manage.'

'What's your advice, Mrs Shackleton? Should I mention Shaun to my family?'

'I can't advise you on such a personal matter, but I will say Mr Shackleton and I met strong opposition to our marriage from his parents, because I was the daughter of a widowed publican and they were a ship-owning family.'

'You mean your social classes were different?'

'That's the truth of it. Because of that we both had to make difficult choices and sometimes still do. All I'll say is if Shaun truly cares for you and decides, in the fullness of time, he wants you for his wife, he'll court you respectfully and not give up easily. I do believe that. My mother once said for all his casual Irish ways, when it comes to a wife he'll choose wisely.'

'I'll make someone a good wife.'

'I've no doubt you will. My husband burned his bridges with his family to be with me, but as time has passed, most of those bridges have been soundly and securely mended. It's clear, if you do decide to wed, one of you'll have to move away from their family. It's the price you'll have to pay, and only the two of you can decide whether it's worth it, and which one of you it'll be, and when.'

'It'll be easier for me if Shaun chooses to live in Whitehaven.'

'Certainly he'd have solid employment with Mr Shackleton, myself, or both.'

'My family'd still have a wage coming in and the civil war can't go on forever.'

'Then, if the time comes, you and Shaun must discuss where your best future lies. Perhaps you could persuade his father he needs an office in Whitehaven and that his mammy would love to come over from Dublin on one of our ships to visit her grandchildren.'

'I can try. There's wisdom in what you say. I'd be useful in a haberdasher's and he's wonderful at selling.'

'There you go. You've created a vision for the future.'

'Thank you. Thank you so much. I feel there's something I can do now, rather than let events happen to me.'

Lois's words resonated with Becky and she thought about her own future. Compared to Lois's, her life was ideal. A loving husband, a bairn on the way, her venture showing returns, both financially and for the well-being of the Blackburn weavers. What was it about Coates Lane that she resented leaving it so much? Was it time for her to grow up and accept the new responsibility being offered to her?

Thinking through her words to Lois, she realised she and Fergus had a decision similar to the young couple's, but theirs involved moving to neighbouring streets, not countries. She could give up Coates Lane for the happiness and security of others, but not give up her handloomers, and she would tell Fergus that.

CHAPTER FORTY

Fergus arrived home with a half-full decanter of South African wine.

'I thought we could enjoy this while we talk before dinner. Bill brought several casks back from Cape Town and Dolly has been good enough to decant some for us. It's a little on the sweet side, but surprisingly palatable. I think you will enjoy it. A small glass will be medicinal for you and the baby.'

Drinking wine before their evening meal, rather than with it, was something they never did. Becky put out two glasses.

'Let's sit in the parlour,' Fergus said.

Becky chose the sofa and Fergus the wing-backed chair he sat in to read the *Whitehaven News*. Becky, self-conscious and nervous, took a sip of her wine. If Fergus had asked if she enjoyed it, she couldn't have answered. She was aware of liquid entering her mouth and throat, but how it tasted didn't register and she was in no state to notice whether she liked or disliked it. The raising of her glass had been something for her nervous hands to occupy themselves with.

Fergus drained half his wine. 'I think it a good idea one of us sets out the benefits and disadvantages of Father's suggestion. Since you don't seem to have much to say at this juncture, shall I begin?'

He's addressing me as if we're in a business meeting. I suppose we are. 'Aye, you begin. I expect I'll have plenty to say later.'

'You may not agree, but hear me out, and then we can discuss what we might do. I'll begin with the physical side of our problem – the moving to Queen Street. My parents' house is grand, much larger than this one, requiring a great deal more management. However, there are experienced staff to oversee this. Are we agreed that the burden can be delegated?'

'Agreed, although I'll add that the staff themselves will need management and we'll need to employ a nurse. There *will* have to be changes.' Becky was thinking specifically of less formality for Rory. Some of Elizabeth's rules would have to be relaxed to accommodate his youth and background.

'The staff will expect change,' Rory said. 'The advantages of more rooms do not need setting out. The disadvantages are that we'll be living cheek by jowl with my invalid mother and my father, who can be both challenging and demanding. There'll have to be negotiation on some decisions and sometimes it will be difficult.'

'And in the long term?'

'My parents won't live forever. One day the house will be ours alone.'

'So, in summary,' Becky said. 'Your father and mother gain the peace of mind of our presence, bringing them greater security. Coates Lane is sold or let out, bringing greater financial security for us. Do you agree?'

'I do, but—'

'Please let me finish. Without sounding too selfish, what do I personally receive to compensate me? I'll lose being mistress of my own home, I'll have the continual presence and responsibility of your oft-times tetchy father and your bedridden mother, with whom I have, on occasion, had a scratchy relationship. As a consequence of these new responsibilities and our bairn, I'll inevitably be forced to step back from my handloom warehouse. I have to tell you here and now I won't desert my handloomers.'

Fergus drew in a breath to speak, but Becky, trembling inside, raised her hand, palm outwards, to stop him. 'I haven't finished. I've a proposition to make.' This was her make-or-break moment.

Fergus, looking at her quizzically, poured himself a second glass of wine. 'What's your proposition?'

'First I must ask some questions.'

He pointed to her half-empty wine glass, and she shook her head.

'Whether we sell Coates Lane or let it, we'll receive capital or rental payments, won't we?' she asked.

'Yes, there will be a pecuniary advantage for us.'

'In that case, here's my proposition. If we sell or let Coates Lane, I'd like £85 to provide financial security for my handloomers' business. I'll promote Lois to a managerial position on a full salary to take my day-to-day place and I'll move into Queen Street with good grace. That way, the loss of our home will be put to the greater good.'

Becky wondered if she'd overplayed her hand. It was not in her nature to ask for money or make demands; she'd only found the nerve to do it because she was doing it on behalf of her weavers, not her own personal gain.

'If we sell Coates Lane then, yes, we can make such an arrangement, and the idea of promoting Lois to give you more time is an obvious one that I heartily endorse.'

'The women know her, she's one of them, they'll take direction from her.' Becky stood up and went to stand by Fergus's side. 'Promise me you'll honour your word and that I'll receive the £85 upon the sale of Coates Lane, or via instalment through rent. We've a good buyer in Conran, but we're putting all our eggs in *his* basket. This money will allow us to expand and court other buyers and it provides my women with greater job security.'

'There's no need to explain. I understand the sound reasoning behind your request. I'll honour my promise.'

'Thank you,' said Becky.

'But there is another thing we must promise each other, and that is that neither of us will make our businesses the main focus of our lives. Can we agree that you, me, Rory and the baby – our own family – will always be the most important things in our lives, and that our businesses will take second place?'

'I agree,' said Becky, speaking straight from her heart.

Fergus stood up and drew her close. 'If it's any consolation, I'm sure we'll be doing the right thing in the long term, and I thank you again.'

He raised her chin and placed his lips on hers. Becky, relieved they were back on good terms, responded eagerly and leaned in, enjoying the warmth of his body against hers. She knew there would be a loving closeness between them to look forward to that night and that it would help heal the remaining wounds of their recent division.

* * *

'We did well today, Mr Shackleton,' said Shaun, accompanying Fergus on a post-auction inspection of Chapel Street's recently crowded, now depleted shelves. 'I'm pleased for two reasons. First, for the profit we've made, and second, for me leaving on a high note.'

Isaiah, still on loan from Shackleton & Company, was totting up columns of figures in the office.

'Mr Shaun and I are leaving in a few minutes,' Fergus told him. 'Have you added up the total sales yet?'

The bookkeeper handed over a piece of paper. 'This is from this morning and includes some of the afternoon sales.'

Fergus checked and rechecked the total sales figure then showed it to Shaun, who whistled the opening bars of an Irish jig he was particularly fond of, before saying, 'That's a fine sum with more to come.'

'The next dividend is going to put a smile on the investors' faces,' said Fergus, sounding relieved. 'And the auctioneer's fee?' he asked.

Isaiah rummaged amongst the papers on his desk. Fergus rolled his eyes at Shaun. There were times when he still missed Dicken's efficiency and this was one of them.

'Their fee is £8 15/6. Shall I settle the account?'

'Oh no, he'll not be expecting immediate payment,' Shaun said. 'Wait a week or two. That's right, isn't it, Mr Shackleton?'

'I think not this time. Pay him early next week. He did a splendid job.'

Isaiah held out a thick winter scarf and a pair of gloves. 'Before you leave, Mr Shackleton sir, I found these in the back of the filing cupboard.'

'They're Dicken's,' said Shaun.

'I suppose we ought to drop them off at his mother's,' said Fergus.

'It'll be a bit of a trek,' said Isaiah. 'He and his mammy have upped and gone to Maryport.'

'Who told you that?' This was news to Fergus, although he wasn't surprised.

'The post-master asked me why I was handing in the post and not Dicken. I said he'd left and a lad from behind me in the queue told us he'd gone to Maryport and his mammy had followed on.'

Fergus took the scarf and gloves. 'I'll give these to my wife to pass on to one of her weavers.'

They left for a celebratory post-auction ale. The Crown and Anchor was crowded, so they had to prop up the bar. The landlord told them there was going to be an arm-wrestling competition and asked if they were minded to lay down a wager. Shaun put a shilling on the slighter man, saying, 'Looks are often deceiving. I've learned that lesson the hard way.'

'There'll always be a job with us if you want one.'

'That's generous of you, Mr Shackleton.'

'My wife, too. She'll always have an opening for you.'

'I'm much obliged to you both, but I've my father's business in my sights. You must understand what that's like?'

'I know things don't always work out as we think they're going to. It's good to have options if you need them.'

'We'll have business to see to with Mrs Shackleton's cotton so I'll be back from time to time.'

There was a cheekiness in Shaun's eye that Fergus didn't miss and, although he wouldn't dream of asking him, he felt sure it was going to be more than the cotton that would bring Shaun Conran back to visit the Carter Lane warehouse.

THE RECEPTION

Wednesday May 8th 1862

A lthough it was only a short physical distance from Coates Lane to Queen Street, Becky was moving into another world: a world of servants, formal meals and expensive surroundings. A world where, as she'd thought about her future life over the previous month, she'd prepared herself to have to negotiate and bargain, to experience tension, appeasement and argument. It wasn't a joyful prospect, but she'd told herself it wouldn't all be taxing. She'd made the bargain and must keep to it. She would do her utmost to maintain good grace when confronted by the inconveniences she anticipated would be coming her way.

When Samuel officially opened the door to Fergus, Becky and Rory for the first time at Queen Street, to her surprise the staff were lined up in the hall, ready to greet them.

Samuel pointed to a large flower arrangement on the table. 'These flowers are from all the staff, Mrs Shackleton, to welcome you to your new home.'

Unanticipated tears pricked Becky's eyes. Surrounded by flowers and smiling faces had not been at all how she'd imagined her first moments in their new home. Her eyes filled with tears.

Mrs Harvey stepped forward. 'On behalf of all the staff may I say we are delighted to welcome you and wish you every happiness here. On a practical note, I've taken the liberty of preparing a light evening supper. Mrs Shackleton senior has requested I confer with you concerning all household matters in future.'

Becky turned to look at Fergus, who said, 'I've had to keep this a secret. Samuel came to me a few weeks ago saying the staff would like to give you the honour of a formal welcome.'

'I told you she'd cry,' said Rory to Fergus.

'Happy tears, Rory. Happy tears. Thank you, thank you. This is quite a welcome.'

Hector's voice boomed out from halfway down the stairs. 'Ah, you're here. Make your way into the dining room. Make haste, we've glasses to raise.'

The dining-room table had been set out with the best glasses, generously filled with wine. There was one for each member of staff, including the kitchen maid, who scurried about the house like an inquisitive mouse, and a lemonade for Rory.

When everyone was attended to, Hector ushered Fergus to the head of the table.

Fergus seemed caught unawares, and Becky leaned forward and whispered in his ear. 'Your father wants you to propose the toast.'

He recovered quickly and, raising his glass, said, 'To the Shackletons of Queen Street.'

Everyone responded with, 'To the Shackletons of Queen Street.'

'And all who sail in her,' added Rory.

THE END

ACKNOWLEDGEMENTS

As always, I am immensely grateful to the archivists at the Whitehaven Archive Office who look after me so well during my research visits. I am also indebted to Alan Cleaver who provided me with a transcript of "Streets of Whitehaven" he co-wrote with Lesley Park about Whitehaven's stone courts. This was fascinating and a great spur to my imagination.

Jackey Savage's online Streets of Whitehaven Through Time is always fascinating and this year I've especially enjoyed her posts about Whitehaven's courts.

Writing this novel has provided me with the opportunity to delve into an important topic of mid-19th century social history – the cotton famine – about which I knew very little. Needless to say, I know a lot more about it now than I did a year ago. Apart from reading first-hand accounts and other assessments of the period I visited the Stanley Cotton Mills near Perth and it was there I noted the low ceilings and understood more fully the price of deafness that the cotton workers paid in return for their employment. Gerald Schofield's "Hard Times – a short history of the famine" focusing on the Blackburn weavers was a mine of primary source material not only on the human situation, but, in particular covering the various relief services offered – from soup kitchens and men's brick-making to women's sewing groups.

Thanks once again to my trusty beta readers, Carrie Armitage, Mike Bird, Pat Langridge, Carol Meads, and Dr Christopher Roberts. Their eagle-eyed reading, as well as reporting on the plot, helps me avoid foolish inconsistencies for which I am most grateful.

My editor, Helena Fairfax, my proofreader, Julia Gibbs, and my publisher, Sarah Houldcroft of Goldcrest Books make up my production team. This will be my fifth novel and they have all travelled the journey with me. Once again, my cover is designed by Dissect Designs.

I owe so much to my fellow authors in the RNA's Leicester chapter the Belmont Belles & Beaux and also to the RAG Retford Authors Group. They have all encouraged and supported me, they know who they are and I thank them here.

ABOUT THE AUTHOR

Lorna was born and brought up in the UK. Her forebears on her mother's side fled the Irish famine in the 19th century to settle in Parton, near Whitehaven in Cumberland. In the mid-1850s they emigrated to Vancouver Island, Canada, to open up the new coal mines. Coal was also important to Lorna's father's side of the family as they were involved in the coal-trading business with Coote and Warren, covering East Anglia and the north London suburbs.

After teaching the piano and raising a family, Lorna exhibited and lectured on antique Chinese textiles in the UK, New York, China and Hong Kong. Following on from that she studied and taught at the School of Oriental and African Studies (SOAS) in London gaining a doctorate in Chinese history. She now writes historical fiction full time and lives in Stamford in a very old house with stone walls and lots of beams. Just the place for a historian. She is very fond of rabbits.

Contact Lorna

www.lornahunting.com

X: @lornahunting

Facebook: @huntinglorna

Instagram: lornahunting

Threads: @lornahunting

Blue Sky: @lornahunting

If you've read and enjoyed this book, please leave a review on Amazon or Goodreads.

ALSO BY LORNA HUNTING

All books available from Amazon

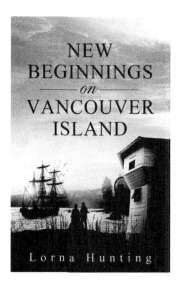

The year is 1854 and Stag Liddell, a young collier from Liverpool, signs up to work in Vancouver Island's new coal mines. Whilst waiting for his ship to Canada, he meets ambitious school teacher Kate McAvoy who is also making the trip.

As the ship nears its destination, Stag and Kate's relationship begins to blossom, but damning information comes to light and a pact made years before comes into play.

Will their budding romance survive these devastating revelations? And will they both achieve their dreams in this new land?

5* Reviews for *New Beginnings on Vancouver Island*

'This is not merely a fascinating "good read" it is also a wonderful learning experience of 19th Century life and culture in Cumbria of the time; the hazardous sea-faring travelling to the "New World" with its dangers round the Cape, it's harsh on board traditions and class divisions; culminating in the uncertain life expectations for new people joining earlier settlers on Vancouver Island, all hoping to extend their often tenuous hold on life itself. Altogether an excellent and well researched historical novel which leaves us wanting more!'

'A great debut novel. In depth characters to hold one's imagination and visualise how tough travel would have been. Obviously much research has gone into this with very readable results. Look forward to the next one.'

'This book... is a cross between a history book and a novel. It is particularly well-written and the author clearly has a love for the subject matter. With an explosive start, the reader is drawn on. I enjoyed the relationships within the story, although these almost played a supporting role to the historical facts. I look forward to the next book by this author.'

'This is a well-researched story with a compelling plot which above all is a good read. Some parts are predictable, but others are not, and the trauma of such a long voyage round Cape Horn is thought provoking in its detail. This was real travel, and not for the faint hearted. Most enjoyable.'

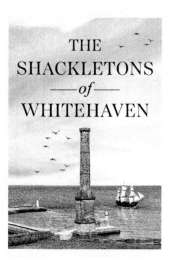

THE
SHACKLETONS
——*of*——
WHITEHAVEN

L O R N A   H U N T I N G

Will book-loving Fergus Shackleton find success in business and love despite his overbearing father, Hector?

By forging his own path is Fergus going to turn into his father, the very person he is trying to escape?

Is chasing success going to change Fergus so much that his girlfriend, Becky, is forced to doubt their future together?

Will the price of success be a broken heart?

5* Review for *The Shackletons of Whitehaven*

'The characters were relatable, the setting vivid, and the plot highly engaging. The book is beautifully written and as I was drawn into the story I found I couldn't put it down. I highly recommend this book and can't wait to read more by this author! Five stars!

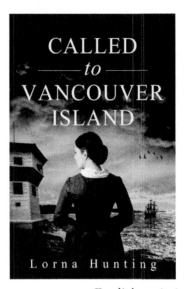

CALLED
to
VANCOUVER
ISLAND

Lorna Hunting

Grace Williams, a young English missionary, arrives in Colville, Vancouver, in 1857 to find the community neither wants nor seems to need her. When her superior, Reverend Palmer, disappears into the snowy woods, on a foolhardy mission to seek converts amongst the Salish First Nations people, Grace is left behind to oversee their mission. There are no half-measures in this place where they do things differently, and she is forced to find self-confidence and rise to the challenge.

Grace is grateful to Sam Gray, a widower, and Long Ben Sloane, the sawmill manager, who befriend and aid her in her mission to improve people's lives and find acceptance. In this wild outpost, the two men become an invaluable support, but only one will win her heart...

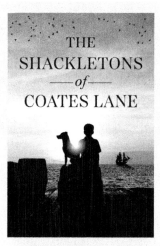

THE
SHACKLETONS
——*of*——
COATES LANE

LORNA HUNTING

It's 1861 in Whitehaven, and Fergus Shackleton is about to marry his sweetheart, Becky. With a new house to maintain, and a wife and ward to look after, money has never been so important, but Fergus's shipping line is rapidly losing business to the railways. The days of sail are numbered. For the sake of his family, Fergus is forced to risk everything on one throw of the dice.

Helping her ma behind the bar of the family pub is no longer suitable for the young wife of a Shackleton, and Becky soon finds herself with time on her hands. That is, until a stranger arrives who could change everything for their beloved ward.

In an era of rapid change, there is much at stake for the newlyweds – and no guarantee they won't lose everything...

Printed in Great Britain
by Amazon

58755991R00219